THERE GOES
THE NEIGHBORHOOD . . .

"You were saying," Rinpoche hinted, "that not all the members of your family were in favor of buying that solar system, no matter how reasonable the price."

"I wasn't involved, of course . . ." Nixy said. "Well, it didn't take long to find out why the Klosh were selling cheap. I mean a supernova gives off plenty of warning signs, and it was only two systems away. But this salesbeing gets in touch with Gramps and points out that all you'd have to do is timeslow the explosion . . ."

Rinpoche achieved a grunt; speech would have risked spraying pseudoslaw dressing all over the table.

"Having a slow supernova in your night sky must be kind of spectacular," Kardek suggested. "It'd be a great tourist attraction . . ."

By John Brunner
Published by Ballantine Books:

BEDLAM PLANET

THE BEST OF JOHN BRUNNER

CATCH A FALLING STAR

CHILDREN OF THE THUNDER

THE CRUCIBLE OF TIME

THE DRAMATURGES OF YAN

THE INFINITIVE OF GO

THE LONG RESULT

A MAZE OF STARS

MUDDLE EARTH

PLAYERS AT THE GAME OF PEOPLE

THE SHEEP LOOK UP

THE SHOCKWAVE RIDER

STAND ON ZANZIBAR

THE TIDES OF TIME

TIMES WITHOUT NUMBER

MUDDLE EARTH

John Brunner

A Del Rey Book

BALLANTINE BOOKS • NEW YORK

A Del Rey Book
Published by Ballantine Books

Library of Congress Catalog Card Number: 93-90182

ISBN 0-345-37851-2

Manufactured in the United States of America

First Edition: September 1993

I dedicate this book

To LiYi

because before her
it had been long and long
since last I felt like laughing

Author's note

If some of the jokes herein seem
funnier than average, that's probably thanks to
Dave Wood

Contents

Discontents

Malcontents

. . . oh, the hell with it

SOME OF WHAT RINPOCHE GIBBS WOULD HAVE LEARNED IF HE HAD TAKEN HIS ORIENTATION LECTURE—SERIOUSLY

AMONG THE SELLING POINTS THAT SECURED THE Earth contract for the Yelignese was their undertaking to revive the cryonuts* of California. By the time the fad for freezing petered out—partly because no one had yet been thawed without terminal damage, partly because most people who could still have afforded it had left for deep space and the chance to live two or three centuries anyway, and partly because the state was under several centimeters of snow—the tombs of the undead occupied ten percent of the land and the cost of liquid nitrogen had become the single largest item in the continental budget. As everyone agreed, this was ridiculous. In the upshot, therefore, generations passed without any attempt being made actually to pay for the stuff. It was taken for granted that some Californians manufactured it, others hauled sleds across the tundra to deliver it on site, others still poured it into the vaults, and then the same thing happened again the following week. Meantime each of the parties concerned handed credit vouchers to the others certifying the job had been done, and against these frayed, grimy scraps of paper they obtained food, drink, and lodging. There was no obvious reason why such

---

*Some insist that the original spelling was "cryonauts." If so, the "a" must have been dropped very early.

a system should not continue indefinitely, except that (a) the vouchers were dissolving into shreds, (b) the sea was beginning to freeze, and (c) the whole setup had proved offensive to an influential group of mystical economists. These latter held that something had to be *done* to underpin a currency, and passing bits of paper from hand to hand didn't count. The fact that the galactic economy had survived for aeons on nothing more substantial than an occasional exchange of nudged neutrettos signally failed to impress them.

Also there were grumbles among the hungry to the effect that an awful lot of protein was going to waste. Which was true enough, but raised the hackles of relatives and descendants of the frozen. Therefore the Yelignese offer was accepted, and their rivals—most of whom had proposed superior and in some cases cheaper schemes for the rehabilitation of the planet—retired to nurse their grudge among the stars.

Leaving the Yelignese to nurse theirs on Earth.

However, despite having declined from their glory days they were not a totally inefficient species. They automated cryonut recovery from the start, and the operation went smoothly enough for the climate of California to revert more or less to what it had been in the twentieth century, and to provide a sizable labor pool for the Los Angeles Reenactment Zone. Indeed, after initial problems due to excessive reliance on what proved to be fictional rather than historical data—thereby wasting rather a lot of time on projects designed to ensure that adequate supplies of fresh blood would be available for the resurrectees, tradition indicating this would be their sole sustenance—raising the dead became such a routine matter that when one of the inevitable glitches did occur it was sometimes overlooked for quite a while . . .

"The computers suggest that we do WHAT?"

ONE

CONCERNING THE DISTILLATION OF RESURRECTION BITTERS

"However sympathetic I may or may not be," said the Chief Bureaucrat, *"toward your plan to reclaim the Earth from humans and allow the dinosaurs a second chance, my hands are tied."*

He displayed them. They were. In a granny knot, naturally, so they could easily be pulled apart again.

At that focus of the Ground of Being that is the consciousness engendered by a human brain:

A sparkle, brilliant as a diamond. A point of infinitesimal smallness became a nucleus, an expanding shell, a—

Well, no. Not a Big Bang. A bang as tiny as it is possible for any bang to be. Not even a tremor in the fabric of spacetime. A hint of a shiver of a flash.

To be succeeded by a gleam, reflective as anthracite is reflective when cleft correctly down the perfect plane.

Replaced in turn by a dull sheen like graphite, smeared as it were on the brown paper of a parcel intended for a different address.

And ultimately by another concept also fundamentally carbonaceous, though a lot less organized than even the lead of a pencil. Figuratively speaking, that's to say. There was nothing strictly physical, though an awful lot of energy, corresponding to the concept that galvanised/infused/pervaded the minuscule, pointlike, neutrinoesque location of what would in a little while again start to think of itself as Rinpoche Gibbs: not because it wanted to, but because it couldn't be helped, and never mind how unwelcome the fact might be. Said high-in-but-not-exclusively-composed-of-carbon concept ran:

Oh, shit.

And was followed a moment later by the qualification:

Still, at least I'm not bathed in smoky red light, so it can't be the Bardo Thödol shtick. I couldn't have put up with that.

On the other hand, what was happening instead was far from pleasant. Once his lungs had begun to fill and empty, his legs started jerking back and forth, first left, then right; moments later his arms did the same, fingers curling and uncurling. A tube was forced between his teeth and, bypassing his attempts to swallow, discharged warm thick liquid into his stomach. Almost at once there ensued a resounding fit of borborygmus. He tried to protest at such cavalier treatment, but the resuscitation process had not yet extended to his vocal cords.

Then he felt his eyes open, though for the first few seconds he could not focus properly. He felt his ears pop. He felt saliva ooze into his mouth, which had been as dry as the cardboard tube inside a toilet roll. He felt an electric tingling pass clear through his body from scalp to soles. After that he saw, but did not clearly understand, what was reviving him: a many-faceted machine glowing with ice-blue radiance, floating ten centimeters above the floor and currently retracting numerous and illogical appendages within its carapace. As it vanished, the last of them shed a drop of bright red blood—but only one drop, promptly wiped away.

Meantime a confusing medley of emotions flashed through his brain: delight, despair, surprise, alarm, excitement, switched on and off with such compartmented neatness that even in his befuddled state he realized they must be artificially induced. Not until anger put in its appearance did he feel that any of these emotions reflected his real state of mind. Even then the anger was muted, more like a mild and diffuse annoyance than the screaming fury he really wanted to give vent to. No doubt he was being chemically soothed. Why should that be a matter of routine? Granted, some people might resent being revived, especially if they hadn't wanted to be frozen ...

Hang on a moment. That's me!

But there was no time to pursue the matter. The machine spoke.

"Can you hear me?"

Muscles that had not been used in—how long? Centuries?—moved with surprisingly little stiffness. Rinpoche heard what emerged from his mouth as a croak, but it was indisputably a word.

"Yes."

"Can you see me?"

"Yes."

All of a sudden his eyes were focusing perfectly. He was able to see that on the front of the machine there hung a label. It read:

THEODOR
Surgeon

"Can you stand up?"

He realized he was lying on a kind of padded table rather below waist height. With barely a trace of giddiness he lowered his legs to the floor, noting from the lower edge of his vision that his unclad body appeared neither older nor younger than he remembered it, and eased himself into an upright posture. He was startled by how clearly he could see the floor; he had been used to wearing glasses before—

But why in the name of all the countless Tibetan hells had he been frozen in the first place? (The second place, this one, was amazingly uninteresting, considering that it was offering his introductory glimpse of the future: a long, vague room containing rows of anonymous cabinets with numbered tags hanging from their door handles. In the middle distance he discerned another identical machine, doubtless awaiting orders for its next resurrection.)

He tried as hard as he could to summon the full force of honest rage, but it was no use.

"Can you walk?"

Rinpoche essayed a few steps with tolerable success.

"Can you dress yourself?"

He blinked. For an instant he was poised to counter, "What in?" Then he realized that a package wrapped in clear plastic was being extruded from the side of the machine. Taking it, he saw that it held underwear, socks, slippers, slacks, a sweatshirt, and a pair of dark glasses. If this were truly a time long after his own—as he was bound to assume because he felt none of the lassitude that had accompanied his decline into leukemia, implying that he had in fact been cured—why were these garments so familiar in cut, in color, even texture?

Oh, maybe the people here were trying to make him feel at home!

He donned the clothes. They fitted fine. The machine waited until the shoes were on. Then it said, "You have been cured of all infirmities. Do you regard yourself as enjoying normal functionality?"

"Uh ... I guess so. Not that I've had much chance to find out as yet."

"That concurs with my readings. You are now required by law to confirm that you have been well and truly restored to the status of a cognizant human being responsible for all debts public and private. Details of relevant costs including supervision, maintenance, and the supply of liquid nitrogen are herewith furnished to you. Sign, please. Any recognized terrestrial script will do."

A strip of paper like the lolling tongue of a terminally anemic dog spewed out of a frontal orifice. A pen thrust itself into Rinpoche's temporarily nerveless hand. He scrawled his name as instructed because arguing felt like too much trouble. He was briefly tempted to use Tibetan writing but settled peaceably for the Roman alphabet.

The machine's appendages folded the paper, tucked it neatly into an envelope, and handed it over. "Please," it said, "present this to the emissions officer, who may be located by following the signs."

Thereupon it retreated to the wall and became motionless.

Docilely, Rinpoche looked for the promised signs. They proved to be a series of green arrows that led him along a windowless corridor—featureless, too, but for the many closed doors on either side. Eventually it debouched into a wide, low-ceilinged hall with glass doors at the far end. Through them he glimpsed grass, trees, flower beds, a skyful of scudding clouds ... Perhaps being brought back to life wouldn't be so bad after all, no matter that he had really deserved at least a thousand years of nonexistence after the ordeal he had undergone in his latest incarnation.

And then his attention fell on a personage who sat at a horseshoe desk in the middle of the hall, halfway between where he stood and the threshold of the outer world. The said individual was clad in a green surgical gown and calf-high white rubber boots. Above plump apple-red cheeks twinkled bright blue eyes. A shock of white hair surmounted his freckled forehead. For a long moment he seemed unaware of Rinpoche's approach; then teeth even whiter than his hair were exposed as he parted his lips in a broad smile of welcome.

Along the front edge of his desktop—which was bare apart from a jar of pink capsules—a luminous sign identified:

WRONG GHOULART
Emissions

"Congratulations on your successful resuscitation!" this personage exclaimed. "Welcome to your new lease of life!"

"Uh—thank you," Rinpoche muttered, unable to rid himself of the suspicion that the other had been in some way *activated* when he crossed some invisible line, or electronic beam, or whatever.

"It is my invariable custom to minimize the shock of awakening by telling a few traditional jokes. Have you heard the one about the isolated head?" He broke into two distinct voices. " 'Were you a head of state?' 'No, head of traffic control.' 'Ah, a sleeping policeman!' 'Yes, the jams were awful.' 'Really? What fruit were they made of?' Good, that's out of the way. May I have your documentation, please? *Thank* you."

He took and ripped open the envelope. Glancing rapidly down the paper within, he said, "That appears to be in order, Mr. Verdi. Now all you have to do is—Just a second!"

Rinpoche blinked at him.

"Mr. Verdi, why have you signed this document with the name of Rinpoche Gibbs?"

"Because that's who I am," was the bewildered answer.

"And by what right do you claim not to be who you actually are?" The blue eyes were no longer twinkling, but flashing ire. Rinpoche hoped for a pang of genuine alarm, a sign perhaps that the dullness of his reactions might be wearing off, but all he managed to feel was a hint of mild anxiety.

"Do you deny that this account is made out to Guido Sansepolcro Verdi?"

"Is it? I can't say I'd noticed."

"Then notice now!" Ghoulart invited sarcastically, practically spiking the paper on the end of Rinpoche's nose. But the name at the top wasn't what seized his attention. That was usurped by the bottom line.

Three hundred and sixty-five BILLION crunits?

Whatever a crunit might be, it wasn't likely to be Monopoly money—not in any society that really could revive the dead! And he'd signed the account, if not in the correct name . . . but with so large a sum at stake surely they would find a way around that minor obstacle!

Casting about desperately for a way of escape (*I never asked to be frozen in the first place, it was done completely against my will, can't you send me back to sleep until humanity evolves far enough to manage without money?*), Rinpoche suddenly saw the paper snatched by a thin pale hand on a thin pale wrist sticking out of a black sleeve. A voice said, "Don't worry, *nonno*! I've taken care of this!"

"The hell you say! He's mine!" boomed a resonant bass.

"Too late to argue! I just transferred enough credit to—"

"But I paid in advance!"

Professionally urbane once more, Ghoulart donned a tolerant smile. "That is correct," he said. "But it is a matter of the greatest possible indifference who pays Mr. Verdi's fees, or—come to that—how many times. My compliments, Mr. Verdi. You are free of all debt. And that, for someone who has spent so long in freeze, is quite remarkable."

But I'm not called Verdi . . . Rinpoche bit back the words. It did indeed seem like rather a good idea not to be in debt to the tune of several billion crunits. But who were these—these Good Samaritans, who weren't looking the least bit pleased about their charitable deed?

On his left were three persons dressed identically in black hats, jackets, trousers, shirts, socks, and shoes, the whole ensemble highlighted solely by white neckties. At first he assumed they were all men; a second glance revealed that one who hung back a trifle was in fact a woman.

Confronting them was a tall, bulky, white male human wearing an iridescent kilt and matching ankle boots, a costume scanty enough to reveal that he boasted wobbly pads of fat wherever there ought to have been muscles. But it was not this person on whom Rinpoche's eyes dwelt in horrified fascination. It was his companion.

Who had an awful lot of blue tentacles—eighteen or nineteen, at a guess—and an awful lot of mouth, fuller of teeth than any mouth had a right to be, plus an awful lot of what might possibly be a tongue but put Rinpoche more in mind of a lamprey, being tubular, with rasps.

Yes, this is the future, he concluded. He wished he could summon up at least a shiver of awe.

The black-garbed trio stepped back, reaching in unison inside their jackets, presumably for concealed weapons.

The fat man snatched from his right boot something that gleamed and sizzled as he used it to carve a luminous arc in the air. To Rinpoche it resembled nothing so much as a battery-powered butcher's knife. Meantime, his—his . . . the thing that had come with him, anyway, did nothing except look even more repulsive, if that were possible.

"Gentlebeings!" Ghoulart exclaimed, rising to his feet with both hands on the desk and a shocked expression on his face. "Such behavior is unseemly!"

"You stay out of this!" barked the leader of the three in black. "This is human business!"

"But if it weren't for us," Ghoulart countered, "there wouldn't be any wrecks for you to argue over!"

Us? Wrecks? Rinpoche blinked at the man in green and realized that he was in fact looking at a projection of a man, that up to this point had been tolerably convincing but now had started to waver. Disguised by it was—was . . .

Well, it wasn't quite as disturbing as the creature in plain sight, but it was well along the way. Rinpoche was glad when the visual camouflage restored itself.

"So let's discuss this like rational beings," Ghoulart went on in a soothing tone, "bearing in mind that chattel slavery is illegal on this planet except in certain yet-to-be-approved re-enactment zones. May that be stipulated?"

There were reluctant nods from all save the alien, who merely waved an impatient tentacle.

"Very well. Don Marco"—to the leader of those in black. "You assert a claim on the person of this resurrectee"—*oh, of course!*—"based not merely on having paid his debts in full but on a blood relationship: that's to say, you addressed him as *nonno*, which in Italian means male progenitor of one's own male or female progenitor. I hope that's right; as you know, we have no counterpart of sex."

Rinpoche struggled to digest the implications of those words, with minimal success.

"Oh, he is not merely our grandfather, but our four-times-great-grandfather!" cried the black-garbed girl.

"Yes!" affirmed Don Marco. "And don't worry, *nonno*!

Even if we have to shoot our way out, we'll convey you to a place of safety!"

"And there," said the third of them, who had sleepy low-lidded eyes and a mustache not much thicker than a pencil line, "we shall find out what became of the mazuma from the Continental Scam. We know it's not on Earth because at eight percent per annum compound it would have become the biggest fortune in the world by now, and it hasn't. So it must be in space. Where in space? Do you feel like telling us at once, or do you prefer the slow and painful way?"

"*Consigliere!*" said the girl, shocked. "Is it polite to talk so to our great-great-great-great-grandfather? Especially when he's only just woken up."

Meantime the thing with teeth had been whispering, or rather hissing softly, to the fat man. Who unexpectedly burst out laughing.

"Ah! I see! You think he's the notorious Guido Sansepolcro Verdi, don't you?"

The trio in black were visibly at a loss. Uncertainly Don Marco said, "Of course he is. That's why we paid his revival costs—"

"So how come you don't know Guido faked his death? His henchmen put in his vault someone else who had really died on the same day!"

The girl plucked at Don Marco's coat sleeve. "He doesn't look much like those old home movies, does he?" she muttered. "What do you think, *consigliere*?"

"Ah . . ." With much rubbing of his chin. "Well . . . Well, what I want to know"—a sudden flare of spirit—"is how come you two claim to be so well informed about this matter! Why should you be interested in the fate of an obscure *mafioso* and petty racketeer who died long ago and—well, not very far away, but at any rate in Nevada?"

"The hell he did! If he's dead at all, which he very well may not be since he got away with such a planetoid of loot, he was laid to rest far out in space." The bulky man stumped toward the three in black, leering. "I told you: he faked his death and cryostasis! That's how my friend and I got involved."

He gave a mocking bow, as best he could for the size of his belly. "Permit me to present ourselves: I am Horace Saketori-Shang, the greatest gourmet of the planet Dahlia and arguably of our entire species, and my friend is Leuyunk-Lun, of equal distinction among his own race. Together we have quested across the light-years for the rarest, most remarkable, most memorable foods. We form a perfect team, for our metabolisms are incompatible, yet we can mind-bind flawlessly. The upshot is that each of us can taste with amazing fidelity dishes that, were we to physically ingest them, would upset or even kill us.

"There is, however, one compliment Leuyunk-Lun paid me, years ago, which I have not so far managed to return. He enabled me to learn how the flesh of his own species tastes. To him the sacrifice of a limb is no great matter, for it will quickly regenerate. My attempts to enlighten him as to the flavor of humans, however, have met with failure. No matter how my robochef prepares tissue cultivated from my cells, there always seems to be something lacking. I have been driven to the conclusion that only a complete body, with all its interacting organs, can display that subtle, that unique, that *addictive* flavor of which the quality is attested in the memoirs of countless South Sea explorers, and indeed in the folklore of the people that they went among.

"But how to obtain a complete human being for gustatory evaluation? *Where* goes without saying; the supreme, the unmatchable flavor can *a priori* be found only on the birth world of our species. Why, here are millions of them, totally unspoiled by the freezing process, as is proved by the fact that they can be reanimated. So we instituted a search for a body wrongly labeled, or misfiled, or for some other reason of no value to itself or anyone.

"In due course, we established that the vault said to contain Guido Sansepolcro Verdi could not possibly do so, for we found proof he had survived his alleged demise. Pooling our resources, we transferred to Earth sufficient credit to

have the impostor thawed, and it was only by ill luck that
we arrived here fractionally too late to lay claim to him before his resurrection." With a scowl at Ghoulart: "But we
think it was disgraceful of you to accept a double payment
from these—these *interlopers!*"

"And I have been looking forward to my taste of human
for so long!" buzzed Leuyunk-Lun. The voice was nearly,
if not quite, the worst part of him. Or possibly it. However,
much though Rinpoche wanted to shudder, he failed. How
long was this emotional numbness going to last?

"Never mind that," snapped the *consigliere*. "As far as I
can make out, you, Ghoulart, permitted my clients to make
a nonreturnable payment in respect of the debts incurred by
Mr. Verdi despite their already having been paid by another
party!"

The sign on the front of Ghoulart's desk had altered.
Now it read:

COUNT YOUR CHANGE—NO REFUNDS

"But the debts weren't incurred by *nonno* Guido!" interrupted the woman. "It wasn't him in the vault after all!
Now what's happened to your brilliant idea about gaining
control of all those quadrillions? What you've done is
squander our entire savings—and your own!—on reviving
someone who can't possibly tell us anything about the Continental Scam!"

"What's more, a person rights to whom had already been
purchased by us!" bellowed Horace Saketori-Shang.

"Now look here!"

"No, you listen to me!"

"Oh, shut up!"

"Shut up yourself!"

"I'll sue you for every crunit you've got!"

"You should live so long! My seconds will wait on you
tomorrow!"

"Gentlebeings, please, *please!*"

No one seemed to be paying much attention to Rinpoche

at the moment, not even Ghoulart. Concluding that it made
sense to sneak away before someone decided he did owe
billions of crunits after all, he sidled across the resilient
floor of the hall toward the nearest exit door. Obligingly, it
slid open at his approach. He took to his heels.

"The computers suggest that we do WHAT?"

TWO

UNITED WE STAND, BUT NOT NECESSARILY EACH OTHER

"DAMIA I GOSPODA, *I HAVE SOME GOOD NEWS AND some bad news. The good news is that the Yelignese have finally agreed to include Moscow among the cities to be reconstructed as they used to be, along with New York, Paris, London, and the rest, so as to attract tourism.*"

After the cheering subsided, from the far end of the council table a voice called, "So what's the bad news?"

"The Moscow that they've chosen is in Idaho."

So unpleasant had Rinpoche found the prospect of being eaten, it had evoked a semblance of fear in him. Accordingly he kept on running until he was nearly out of sight of his point of departure, or, putting it another way, arrival. When he glanced back, he could no longer discern the doors through which he had made his unceremonious exit, since the bulk of the cryonut vault was concealed below a grassy hillock and the surrounding area was planted with flowering shrubs—for the most part, pink and blue hydrangeas. The only indication of the vault's location was a discreet sign pointing to The James White Resuscitation, Reanimation, and Rag Trade Facility.

Despite the hastiness of his flight, he must still be under the influence of tranquilizers. At any rate he was able to consider with remarkable detachment, rather than the gibbering terror that he felt would have been more apt, the predicament wherein he found himself: completely alone, completely friendless, an unknown period into the future, in a society that still used money (of which he had none) and might at any moment conclude that he was enormously in debt, and into the bargain ignorant of where he was and what might happen.

What in the world was he to do?

Such rational analysis as he was yet capable of informed him that there was no more sensible course than to put maximal distance between himself and that pair of cannibals ... No, that wasn't right. Only bulky Horace could be termed a cannibal, since the other creature would be eating flesh of a different species. Just a moment, though: it had eaten its own limb so that Horace whatever-his-name might vicariously enjoy the taste, therefore it had been guilty of the counterpart of cannibalism in respect of its own kind ... Or perhaps not. Did cannibalism not imply some element of noncooperation on the part of the person being eaten? Certainly in his own case it would have done—he would have had to be borne kicking and screaming to the cauldron, or oven, or whatever the chosen means of preparation might be, regardless of being tranquilized. But a person's own limb could scarcely be regarded as an unwilling party to consumption by its owner ... Speculation along those lines, however, promised to be fruitless. Rinpoche composed himself, drawing a deep breath, and took stock of his surroundings.

It was, he judged, early on a spring morning. Trees nearby were newly into leaf. (But what about those hydrangeas? He took a second look. Oh. Plastic.) Part of the sky was blue, although the sun was veiled by shreds of grayish cloud. The air was mild, but a breeze bore a smoky tang that made his eyes water. Shading them with his hand, he stared around for signs of habitation and spotted one at once, in the shape of a board reading:

WELCOME TO
SUBURBIA
POP. 128
Vacancies

Beyond it lay just such a residential street as he had seen by the thousand in his former life, lined on either side with houses all of basically the same design but ingeniously personalized with trelliswork, bolt-on conservatories, additional carports, and machicolated battlements of extruded plastic textured to resemble weathered stone.

And he was definitely right about the time of day, for men in gray suits and gray snap-brim hats, carrying briefcases, were emerging from their front doors, kissing wives in pretty print frocks, and entering cars of which one was parked in front of or alongside each house.

All bar two of them, neighbors, who paused awhile to chat and pencil notes in pocket diaries.

A twinge of puzzlement afflicted Rinpoche. Diaries? Pencils? Cars that obviously ran on gasoline, that were in fact gas-guzzlers? He saw a Packard, a Cord, a Studebaker, a Mercedes . . . How could this be the distant future? Besides, there seemed to be something wrong with the names. Mercedes Impala? Packard Stingray? Cord Fourteener?

However, here he was incontestably cured of what had ailed him—and if the creature that wanted to eat him wasn't from another planet, where could it hail from?—and debts were calculated in crunits, which he was now able to dissect as "credit" plus "unit," and his feet had borne him to a flagstoned footpath fronting the homes of the two men, by this time putting their diaries away.

"All right, all right," the taller of them muttered, settling his hat squarely on his head and turning toward his car, which described itself as a Cadillac Rabbit. "But you can't grudge us the time we need to organize our monthly wife-swapping party! It's about the only thing that makes life worth living!"

Slamming his door, he drove away in the wake of the dozen or so other cars that had set off during the past few minutes, leaving Rinpoche and the shorter man by themselves.

After a pause the latter said, "My friend mistook you for

a Yelignese authenticity inspector. But you're not one, are you?"

Unwilling to trust his voice, Rinpoche shook his head.

"I thought not," the other said, tipping back his hat with a quizzical expression. "To me you look like a regular wreck."

Rinpoche almost said, "Huh?" In the nick of time he remembered: wreck—resurreck—resurrectee. He cogitated for a moment. "I guess so," he admitted at last. "It's just I'm not used to the idea yet. They only woke me up about a half-hour ago."

"And turned you loose, just like that?" A snap of the fingers. "Man! You must have had more than just considerable foresight! What bought you out? Was it old money, or were you Mafia? Triad? *Yakuza?* You certainly don't look Arabic."

Odd! Rinpoche's attention was, if not jolted, then at least diverted out of neutral. That sounded like another person speaking, though the words had emerged from the same mouth. Now he looked more closely at his new acquaintance, he detected a difference between the left and right sides of his face. One eye was brown, the other dark blue. Also the hair on one side was mousy, on the other black.

He wasn't sure that the last question required an answer, but this person being so much out of the ordinary it seemed advisable to provide one. "No, I'm not Oriental or Arabic. And I'm not Mafia either. I met some people who seem to think I am, but they got in an argument with a fat man and a—a *creature* that both wanted him to eat me, so I decided not to stick around."

The man clicked his tongue against his palate. "Eat you, hmm? That's rough. So what do you plan to do now?"

"Mainly, I'd like to get the hell out of here."

"Okay, you can ride into the city with me. I like helping people—do it every chance I get because it fits my name so well. Now just an everlovin' moment! Two bodies in the car you lose the smog bonus! You know the rules as well as I do! What difference does one extra rider in one car make? It means we lose the smog bonus, how often do you have to repeat myself? Even if the passenger doesn't own a car? You don't, do you? I thought not. Though they're bound to issue you one because they're so short of commuters—wait a second, you said they turned you loose, so you're one of the lucky ones—all right, all right, argue the toss if you must because we're late already and if you delay us any longer, we won't get in our contribution to the smog quota at all, so why don't you run round the other side and jump in? I don't see how they can object to someone who isn't neglecting to use his own vehicle. Oh, get the hell in, will you?"

Rinpoche did so—the vehicle was a pink and yellow Oldsmobile Maverick—and moments later they were high-tailing it after the rest of the commuters from this suburb.

Or, as it turned out, more sort of from this block.

"Uh . . . Thanks very much for your help. By the way, I'm Rinpoche Gibbs. Please call me Rin if it's easier."

"Glad to meet you, Rin. I'm Sal Munday. Don't give me that! I have the right because I'm dominant today, so stop interfering. It's not Sal as in Sally, it's short for Salvador, which is a common Hispanic given name—and simply doesn't *go* with a fine old patronymic like Munday, which actually it does because the hell with it I won't have you trying to take over my day! But it isn't Monday. That wasn't even funny the first time. Why don't you shut up and give my tongue a rest? What d'you mean, *your* tongue?"

Rendered uneasy by the dialogue his companion was having with himself, all the more so since the highway they had reached was cracked and potholed and beset with fallen branches, Rinpoche tried to distract himself by surveying the environs. They were far from reassuring. He saw no more houses, only tumbledown ruins interspersed with hummocks.

Shortly the state of the road grew even worse. After crossing a bridge where concrete was falling away in great slabs from rusty reinforcing bars and the parapets were rife with ampelopsis, by which stage the air was almost unbreathably foul even though the windows were shut and a lever labeled "Air Conditioning" was pushed over to maximum, Sal swung the car down an access ramp at the end of which a stoplight was permanently set to green.

Beyond, on one side of an eight-lane freeway, a few straggling cars were striving to catch up with others in the distance. A sign on an overhead gantry warned, with many missing letters and figures, of a 50-meter snarlup 17 km ahead.

The other half of the freeway was vacant except for a Conestoga wagon with slogans painted on it, hauled by a team of mules. Their shape was more or less okay but there was something wrong about their color, which was a sort of olive green. Along the median a pack of wild dogs—well, they must be, given that they clearly mingled everything from dachshund to Great Dane—stalked them from bush to shrub to clump of grass as the best available substitute for buffalo. Aboard the wagon four or five gloomy-visaged people were taking it in turns to recite through a megaphone the same words as were written on the visible side of the canvas:

"Support our campaign to make the Donner Pass a Reenactment Zone!"

They didn't look as though they were expecting a very enthusiastic response.

"There's no need to worry about a low smog reading today," Sal said, sniffing with audible satisfaction. "Count myself lucky! I could have been given another ten years! Oh, don't be ridiculous! Ridiculous myself! And slow down! We've got to spend at least an hour in the car, remember!"

Rinpoche coughed discreetly—which, given the filthiness of the air, was quite difficult.

"You're—uh—on your way to work in the city?"

"I'm working already," was the sharp retort. "Wouldn't

expect anyone to do this without being paid, would you? But yes, when I get there I do have a job of sorts. I work for Napoleon Halfanour, the publisher. He puts out this mag here." He tapped a finger on a pile of bedsheet-sized periodicals lying between them on the bench seat. Its title, in bulging red letters, was *Raunch Romances*. The top one was stated to be the June issue, and the lead story was "I Screwed Up—and How!" by Caresse Cox and Peter Standwell.

Underneath it was the May issue. The lead story was "I Screwed Up—and How!"

Underneath again was the April issue. The lead story . . .

Rinpoche felt a transient access of giddiness. He said faintly, "Are the contents always the same?"

"Hmm? Oh, of course they are! This sort of thing only sells to explans from worlds with strict blue laws, and they never stick around long enough to worry about buying a second issue. It's strictly for comet heads, anyway: 'cerisian tips,' 'ferrous malenesses,' 'embraceful orifices'—I ask you!"

"So what exactly do you do? Are you the editor?"

"Hell, no! I'm a lawyer. One month I prosecute *Raunch Romances* because it's an obscene and worthless rag. Next month I defend it on the grounds that it stands for freedom of expression and the American Way. It's a living. And it keeps up interest among the mugs."

The giddiness returned, only worse. Closing his eyes, licking his lips, Rinpoche whispered, "I'm dreadfully sorry, but I'm finding it hard to follow you."

"What I'm saying—that's me, Salvador, who ought to be dominant today because it's my *turn*—is perfectly clear. It's what Joe says, Joe Munday, that's making things so tough for you. But that's typical of him. He simply won't accept what our name implies. You caught on at once, though, didn't you? Salvador Munday?"

As politely as possible Rinpoche said, "I'm afraid not. Is it Spanish? The only foreign language I understand is Tibetan, and not much of that."

"Oh."

As if obeying instructions from himself, Sal was letting the car roll slower and slower, although the road ahead was now almost as vacant as the side with the wagon. "Sorry about this," he added in an undertone. "But I'm right on one point: it wouldn't be authentic if I didn't spend a full hour each way in the car. At least, like I said, they've got the smog up to strength without my help."

Rinpoche had again been searching for signs that the tranquilizers or whatever were wearing off, and found little comfort save that the prospect of coping on his own in this strange epoch had induced a few butterflies in his belly. However, they were far from numerous enough to make him glad that the liquid forced into him had proved both nourishing and digestible. (How, incidentally, was he to obtain food and drink without money? But that was a fence to be jumped when he came to it.) He supposed one must assume that here in the future all drugs, not just tranquilizers, would be more efficient and longer lasting. It was still a disappointment, though, finding the unique and unrepeatable quality of this experience blurred behind a chemical haze.

His giddiness, at least, was receding. Delayed shock, perhaps.

Reduced to taking his cues from Sal for the time being, he harked back to the driver's previous remark.

"I'm afraid I still don't understand. You have to spend an hour a day in this car? Helping to generate smog?"

The reply emerged in the same bipartite fashion as before.

"No, *two* hours. One in the morning, one in the evening. How else could tourists share in the authentic experience of the twentieth-century commuter? It was the lot of so many of their ancestors in one industrialized country or another, virtually every explan visitor wants some of it to splice into his or her memory album, and the majority of them take it from LA because it's by a country kilometer the nearest to authentic. They tried it for a while in Krasnoyarsk, but people complained it didn't ring true. You probably don't realize how lightly you've got off. I wonder who it was who renounced what must have been a huge fortune, just so you could come back to life and make a nuisance of yourself! Don't take any notice of that. You're not being a nuisance, not in the least. Matter of fact it makes a welcome change after doing this run five days a week for twenty years without anybody else to talk to outside my head. *One* used to listen to the radio, back when there were human-made tapes, but all of those wore out, same as the TV programs. Now it never says anything I can understand. We've just been swamped by stuff from other planets. It's not worth their while to get it translated for a backwater world like ours, not even automatically, and in any case it's centuries old, of course. Still, you'd imagine they could send us some stuff from systems like Paprika and Gorgonzola. I'm told a lot of it is very good."

He glanced wistfully at a radio dial on the dash, which Rinpoche had not previously noticed. It was illuminated, but no sound emerged from the four speakers mounted left and right, front and rear. Diffidently he pointed at the volume control.

"That's set to low," he ventured. "May I turn it up?"

Sal shrugged. "If you like."

Rinpoche did so. At once the car was filled with a noise like chirping birds. Puzzled, he pressed in turn each of the station presets. They produced loud groans, shrill cries of agony, a series of thumps and booms, a sound like a forest fire crowning, a blast of noise as from a dentist's drill magnified beyond endurance ... Hastily he wound the volume down again.

Sadly, Sal said, "Even if the laws against unsocial working hours do make it illegal to run a radio station round the clock, the Yelignese claim they want everything to be authentic, so you'd think they'd provide at least one channel for humans. It could be recorded once or twice a week during the daytime. I wouldn't mind it being repeated. Or maybe the duty station could move around the planet following the sun, so we'd always have something to listen to—Nuts! If they really wanted everything to be authentic, you wouldn't be here!"

More baffled than ever, Rinpoche involuntarily echoed, "What do you mean? I didn't want to be here! Never asked to be frozen, never asked to be revived!"

"Nor did I," Sal sighed, slowing still further as they hovered in sight of a couple of other cars passing beneath a sign that announced a 17-km talkback 50 m ahead. "Like I said, I was a lawyer first, then I went into politics. I'm told someone tried to kill me just before an election. Most of my supporters were Hispanics like me, and owing to the lousy education they were given, they didn't know much about science—That's not why! You Spics were lazy minded and just plain ignorant! Shut up! They did their best, but they were slow putting me into freeze, so one hemisphere of my brain got frosticled."

"Frosticled?"

"Like it started to go bad before they stashed me in the vault. But there was this other guy, you see, who was also a lawyer, and the equal and opposite thing happened to him. So the Yelignese decided to salvage what they could of each rather than junk the lot. Of course, this was back when they'd just taken over and didn't really understand about human identity, so they did cut corners, they did make mistakes. But this time it wasn't just an ordinary error.

"It was the will of God made manifest!"

Rinpoche started. It was far from the first time he had heard a similar phrase. In fact he'd uttered the like a few times himself. But he didn't want to think about his past life; on the contrary, he had hoped to forget it entirely. Maybe in this modern age they had a drug for selective amnesia.

"How could anyone miss the point?" Sal demanded. "Don't meddle!"—presumably to Joe. "*Salvator mundi* means 'savior of the world!' Those that have ears to hear, let them hear!" He leaned earnestly toward Rinpoche, oblivious of the need to steer the car, and clasped his hands over his heart with a pleading, even desperate expression.

"As soon as I've paid off the cost of storing us—I make more than you do when I take over so why don't you let me speed things up?—as soon as I escape this hideous daily grind, which I will do pretty soon, provided they keep on paying the smog bonus, I'm going to live up to our joint name. What d'you mean, *you* are going to live up to *our* name? Shut up! It's my mission to save humanity from itself, whether these damned atheists want it or not! My name proves it! What d'you mean 'my' name? Half of it's mine, remember—"

Crunch.

Uncontrolled by its driver, the car collided with the last vehicle in the vaunted talkback, or tailback, or whatever, which according to its insignia was a De Soto Charger.

Actually it was more of a bump than a crash, for Sal's foot had been off the accelerator so long, most of the car's impetus was due to a gentle downgrade. However, the impact was noticeable enough for the driver in front to haul on his parking brake and pile out of his seat shouting insults, while other drivers craned their necks to see what was going on, relishing this break in the monotony.

Likewise it afforded sufficient distraction for Rinpoche to fling wide his door and dash for the median. Dazed and confused he might still be, but he had regained enough of his senses to realize that riding in a car with somebody one half of whom had decided his mission was to save the human race against both its own wishes and also those of the other half of himself was a poor harbinger of enjoyment and enlightenment in this future age.

On the other hand: here he was stranded in the middle of an eight-lane freeway (even if only four of its lanes were in use other than by a wagon), conceivably at the mercy of wild dogs, with not a cent to his name (or whatever the equivalent was of a cent nowadays, not that there was likely to be one if the cost of keeping him available for resuscitation ran into billions, ((though there was a cheering thought: might it be that in fact money had been so debased that he could pay off such a debt in a day or two? Something similar had happened in Germany and Hungary after World War I when people had to take their pay home by the wheelbarrow load, and later on in Eastern Europe and South America and many parts of Africa. But hang on! That was ruled out by the fact that (((if he had followed the implications correctly))) Sal had been commuting two hours a day for twenty years, to a job that consisted in pointlessly prosecuting and then defending a porno mag but for which he did at least get paid, yet he still hadn't wiped out his own debt))—and what was all this about explans and memory albums?), so . . .

Tired of thinking in parentheses, Rinpoche started over.

Or would have done, save that a helicopter swooped from the sky and hovered a few meters away from him. The blast of its rotors rendered the air fouler than ever, adding a khamsin's-worth of dust to the smog that at this point was close to visible, close to *chewable*. Unnerved, he broke into a run. Even as he did so he knew his behavior was irrational. Why should he try to flee from a machine that could outstrip him with ease, and what reason did he have to be afraid of it, in any case?

The goddamned thing was buzzing him, that was why! And from it something black and tubular and menacing was pointing down as though at any moment it might loose cannon shells, if not some more futuristic means of dealing death.

He ran!

And ran until he was gasping for breath, whereupon the machine roared overhead and swung back on its former course. Yelling, he, too, tried to go into reverse, but even as he made the attempt he trod on a stone that turned beneath his weight and sent him sprawling among prickly dry grass. As he rolled over, cursing, the chopper hovered above him . . . and he realized that the menacing black tube was attached to a huge old-fashioned movie camera with immense round spools on top, like Micky Mouse ears.

Huh?

Leaning out of the chopper's side door was a man wearing a safari jacket, riding breeches, and leather boots, barking through a megaphone. He had a strong but not entirely consistent German accent.

"Dot vos nodt badt! Nodt badt at all! I can use dot footitsch in *Gone vit der Birt of a Kane by Nortvest*! Hoch aye! Now ged bored! Ve god please tousand tousand tourist, *nicht wahr*?"

A rope ladder spilled and dangled. Well, it did at least offer escape from the deserted road. From this stretch the last of the straggling vehicles had long vanished. Clawing up rung by rung, Rinpoche scrambled aboard the 'copter. As he fell into a seat the leather-helmeted pilot tilted the rotor disc and they rushed toward a distant city that from this height had suddenly become visible—partially visible, that was, it being largely shrouded in yellowish vapors. Shortly they overflew two or three dozen atavistic cars, including Sal's and the one Sal's had hit, pretending to be a major jam.

It began to dawn on Rinpoche that the world he had arrived in was not merely peculiar, but weird.

He tapped the breeches-clad German on the shoulder. "Where are we going?" he shouted above the roar of the engine.

"Vare? *Vare?* You make ze Amerikanski yock, *nicht wahr*?"

He pointed. Ahead, looming through the mist on a brown hillside, were arrayed huge grimy-white letters. Rinpoche's heart sank as he read them, albeit not very far because that was disallowed. What the letters spelled was HOLYROOD.

"That," said the pilot gloomily, "is the Yelignese for you. Am I right, or am I fucking *right*?"

"The computers suggest that we do WHAT?"

THREE

YOU OUGHTA BE IN PICTURES THOUGH PERHAPS NOT THIS ONE

"OH, NO! IT CAN'T BE MY TURN AS SOCRATES AGAIN!"
"Yes it is. Check the roster."
"But that hemlock tastes so vile!"
"We all have to put up with it, don't we?"
"I know, I know. Well, at least they've promised us new chitons—Hey! What's this shiny black stuff?"
"They sent chitin."

"Who or what," Rinpoche inquired as the Holyrood sign faded again into the yellow smog, "is or are the Yelignese?"

His companion started in disbelief. The pilot turned to stare over his shoulder, revealing a face as brown as his helmet. He kept on staring for so long that Rinpoche began to feel worried, on the grounds that a crash in an aircraft, even a 'copter, must be riskier than one in a car, even Sal's. However, he reverted to his controls in time.

"You mean they didn't feed you the usual data?" the phoney German demanded. And thought to add: "Incidentally, I'm Gustav von Scheidelberg, the famous movie director."

"Ha, ha," said the pilot in a cynical tone.

Looking uncomfortable: "Well, I am for present purposes. It's a nasty job, but someone has to do it. And you can call me Gus. I'm not proud."

Rinpoche uttered his own name mechanically, and went

on, "No, I wasn't given any kind of information. I guess I quit the—uh—the vaults in kind of a hurry."

"Sounds like another case of Yelignese inefficiency," the pilot sighed. "I'm Harry, by the way, Gus being too rude to introduce us."

"Glad to meet you, Harry. But these Yelignese: who are they? Or, like I said, what?"

"The people—except of course they aren't exactly people—who won the contract for Earth when the explans put it out to tender."

Rinpoche blinked in confusion, visions of contracts on an individual rather than a planet having distracted him— prompted perhaps by his unwished-for pseudo-identity as a *mafioso*. "I don't follow," he admitted after a pause.

"Well, someone had to take on responsibility," Harry grunted. "No one can deny that it had become a pretty second-rate piece of real estate, given the mess we'd made of it, but it does retain a certain sentimental value—for which thanks be, because if it weren't for the tourist trade we'd be bankrupt. The trouble with the Yelignese, though, is that they're on the way down, and they know it, and even though it's not our fault they do tend to blame us. Oh, I grant they've done a fair job of cleaning up, especially the oceans, but they won't *listen*. That's the root of the problem. They won't let themselves be *told*. Like that sign back there. You know it's wrong, I know it's wrong, and the Yelignese know it's wrong—or at any rate they ought to by now. Even if people like Gus did let them get away with it for so long! I've complained a dozen times if I've done it once. So have hundreds of other people who can tell a neuron from a neutron. But will the Yels put it right? The hell they will!"

Rinpoche was about to inquire why Gus and Harry didn't rope in a few friends and do the job themselves, when another point distracted him.

People like Gus? Oh.

Somewhat foggily he hazarded, "Harry, you mean you're a—a wreck? Same as me?"

"Where d'you think they could find someone to fly an antiquated crate like this, nowadays? 'Course I am!"

"But Gus isn't?" Rinpoche twisted to stare at the man beside him.

"Why did I open my big mouth?" Gus said bitterly. "The moment they realize I'm not actually Gustav von Scheidelberg who directed umpteen masterpieces in the days of the silent cinema, there'll be hell to pay. Not, of course, that it makes any difference who does my work. It may be a living, but it isn't a job. It's a rôle, that's all. And boring with it—boring to the nth degree and squared!"

"Haven't they realized that if you had been directing movies in the silent days you wouldn't have lived long enough to be put in freeze?"

"Ah, the explans don't know," Harry sighed—and detecting puzzlement as he glanced at Rinpoche, elucidated, "Like expatriates, dig? But on other worlds. Far as they're concerned, the whole of Earth history happened in the same place at the same time. And the Yelignese don't care. Why should they? This isn't their planet. Want to see how bad things can get? Don't bother to ask—just look."

He brought the 'copter to a standstill in midair, adding as he did so, "You've got plenty of time. They're nothing like ready for us, and watching the arrival of the director is included in the deal, so—!"

How the pilot knew, Rinpoche had no idea, for there was no sign of a radio. Maybe he was receiving signals by telepathy. That ought to be awe inspiring. But it failed to raise the requisite shiver along his spine, so he went on staring at the ground below as he had done for minutes past. At this height the smog was perceptible only as a translucent veil.

The area of the city they had so far passed over had struck him as improbably like what he had been familiar with in his own time, though shabbier and to his surprise (muted, like his other reactions) altogether lacking in tall buildings, as though its downtown area had evaporated—or fallen down from lack of maintenance, like the houses he had seen approaching the freeway.

This section, though, was an utter contrast. Here was a large open space paved with irregular stone flags. On three sides of it had been reconstructed houses of an ancient design. Timber frames, stained black, surrounded whitewashed plaster infill and latticed windows, while over all thatched roofs loomed like beetling eyebrows. In total contrast the fourth side was closed by row upon row of wooden seating, raked sharply upward beneath an awning. At the center of the oblong area thus defined had been erected a platform on which stood a tall man with bulging muscles, naked save for a black breechclout, black boots, and a black cloth mask. From time to time he tested with his thumb the blade of an enormous ax.

Just out of sight behind a row of the fake houses there stood a gilded coach drawn by four perfectly matched black horses—

Rinpoche looked again. They were standing impossibly still.

Oh. Machines.

"Is this the set for a movie you're making?" he inquired, wondering why, if nowadays people could create such a convincing replica of a horse, anyone would bother with that sort of elderly technology—except, of course, in the interests of the "authenticity" Salvador Munday had been so exercised about.

"Yup," Gus answered. "The same damn' film as usual. Every mortal week . . . Ah, hell. I better get back in character. Vy tit I haf to pretent to be Tscherman? Vy tit I not tschuss an accent I can issily kip up, like Eye-ritsch hoots begorrah look you gorblimey?"

"The same film as usual?" Rinpoche repeated in bewilderment. Down below, under the guidance of young men and women bearing colored flags on poles, a horde of people was flooding into the square. Many wore what looked like sixteenth-century Western European dress, but others had costumes from earlier periods and a dozen different countries: burnouses, saris, even togas.

Harry muttered a curse, presumably in response to a message on the nonexistent radio.

"Are they still not ready?" Gus demanded.

"Not by a kilometer. They say we'll be catering for sixty-seven million today. We'll have to set down to save fuel."

"Oh, shit. I mean: *ach, Scheiss!*" Gus folded his arms and sat back in what could only be termed high dudgeon as the 'copter swept to a landing beside the coach. The horses were definitely machines; they twitched not a tail, not a nostril, at the dust and noise.

"I don't understand," Rinpoche said doggedly into sudden quiet as the engine died. "The same picture over and over?"

"Vot? Oh! It's the Holyrood experience, of course! What does that name call to mind?"

After a bewildered pause: "Well—nothing, to be candid."

"Vare ver you etschugadet?" Gus rasped, and interrupted himself by saying, "Christ, I know a lot of Hollywood directors really were German, but it's a beast of an accent, it really is . . . Mary Queen of Scots, of course!"

"Who?"

"Executed on the orders of Queen Elizabeth of England. A great tragic heroine. Schiller wrote a play about her, there were operas even. Holyrood was the royal palace in Edinburgh. Because of that goddamned sign, the Yelignese laid it down: all tourists who come here get the Holyrood experience! So far as they're concerned that means the chance to appear as extras in a film about Mary Queen of Scots—or take an acting or even a speaking rôle at extra charge. And I'm sick to death of it! We can't even afford enough costumes of the proper period; we have to make do with anything not too ridiculously modern, never mind how antique it would have been, or foreign. I mean, how many Pakistanis in shalwar-kameez would have been at the Scottish court in Mary's day?"

"Even that's not the worst of it," Harry said somberly. "Mary was actually beheaded indoors, in private, with just a chaplain and a handful of other witnesses, but because no one wants to miss out on the grand climax we've had to move it to the open air, like you see. We even had to take one whole side away from the reproduction city square we'd built to make room for those bleachers because each time more and more people insist on getting a clear line of sight—and, of course, on figuring recognizably in the crowd shots."

"And what's more," Gus supplemented, "though Mary did take off her dress to save it from being spoiled by the blood, she kept on her shift—her underslip."

"Whereas now they insist on her doing a full strip," Harry rasped. "Right down to her skin. Oh, it does pull the punters, I guess. Sixty-seven million this time! Where's it all going to end? That's what I want to know."

"Million? But there's barely room here for a couple of thousand—three at most." Rinpoche blinked in confusion, sure though he was that his own experience of addressing large crowds (and he didn't want to remember that!) had enabled him to judge the numbers aright.

"Oh, that's only the ones physically present. Some people just won't be satisfied with secondhand memories, even from the finest observers. Those are the hyper-rich, of course. But many of our audience represent planetary populations, or at least whole cities."

"Huh?"

"Sure! Interstellar travel isn't cheap, you know, not even with a Duckman's Dumper. So when somebody can nearly afford to visit Earth, but not quite, they often make up the difference by arranging to sell their memories when they get back. Pretty often they undertake to have some special experience that one of their sponsors would like to recall but doesn't care about enough to make the physical trip. 'Course, the more copies you take of a memory the less sharp it becomes, but techniques are improving all the time,

and several of today's spectators have contracted to service
half a million."

"Is that a whole planetary population?" Rinpoche asked
foggily.

"Of a human planet, you mean? Oh, no! Just the maximum one can cope with using present-day techniques. It's
the aliens who send along a single representative to bring
back impressions of Earth for their entire species." Harry
stretched and yawned. "Heaven knows, though, what the
folks back home make of a queen getting her head chopped
off."

"Confirms them in their view that we're uncivilized upstart barbarians," Gus suggested sourly, and muttered another unprintable comment about having to make the same
movie over, and over, and over.

"But when you filmed me trying to run away from the
helicopter," Rinpoche countered, "you said you could use
the footage in some other picture altogether."

The director brightened. "Ah, *Gone with the Birth of a
Kane by Northwest*! That's what I'm pinning all my hopes
on. Thirty years in the making, combining elements from
four of the undisputed masterpieces of the Golden Age, it
cannot fail but be the box-office smasheroo of all time. I
only wish I could figure out how to include *Casablanca* in
the title."

Anxious to be helpful, Rinpoche pondered a moment.
"How about calling it *Casablanca II* and using the rest as
a subtitle?"

"Well, I don't know about subtitles." Gus frowned.
"Having so much wordage on screen across the lower edge
of every single shot . . . Harry, what do you think?"

"I think the punters are getting restless," the pilot answered, restarting his engine. "Ready?"

"*Ja.* Ass ready ass I sall effer be! Vare's my megaphone?
Ach, dare. Hoch aye! Ve go to ze zet, *bitte schnell*!"

And, moments later, amid swirling dust and smog, the
celebrated director Gustav von Scheidelberg strode to confront his players. He seemed to have forgotten about

Rinpoche, and Harry wasn't interested; having cut his engine again, he thrust a stick of gum in his mouth, leaned back, and closed his eyes, chomping.

With a trace of faint relief—inevitably faint—Rinpoche dropped to the ground and stole away. He had been given much to think about, and since his mental processes were being rendered sluggish by, presumably, the same chemicals that kept his emotions remote, he needed somewhere quiet to ponder his discoveries at leisure. Before he could make himself scarce, however, one of the guides mustering the tourists bellowed at him, waving his flagstick.

"Hey, you! Yes, I do mean you! What are you doing in gear like that? Some people here have paid millions to appear in our movie! Do you want to ruin everything?"

"Sorry!" Rinpoche shouted back. "Lost my way!"

And darted around the nearest corner, noticing as he passed that someone had switched on the horses and they were whinnying and pawing at the ground.

A few hundred meters further on he reached a stretch of concrete sidewalk into which had been impressed footprints, palmprints, and the prints of extremities he dared not even make guesses about. Each of the ones that were recognizably human bore a name that to him meant nothing: Lazarus Long, Phoebe Zeitgeist, John Carter, Telzey Amberdon, Giles Habibula, Gilbert Gosseyn ...

By now the smog was making his eyes water to the streaming point. He needed to escape indoors. Staring around, he caught sight of a blur that suggested an illuminated sign. After blinking away his tears he was able to decipher it into SPOTCH'S SPOT, THE BAR OF THE STARS! AUTHENTIC ATMOSPHERE OF OLD HOLYROOD! TOPLESS WAITRESS! PROHIBITION RAIDS NIGHTLY! HAPPY HOUR 0800-0600!

Under which, in smaller letters:

Aliens welcome. Fluorine breathers 24 hours' notice.

Gratefully, he pushed open the door.

Within, he found a large, dark, low-ceilinged room set with tables and chairs. There was a bar at the far end, with shelves of bottles behind it. The lights were dim, the air was cool and clean. But there was no one else in sight. For a moment he wondered whether he had misread the sign. It could scarcely be later than nine A.M., so perhaps the joint was not in fact open. Uncertainly he approached the bar, noting with a fraction of his attention familiar labels on some of the bottles: Seagram's, Jack Daniels—

Just a moment. He took a squarer look. Preconception had betrayed him. Sevagram? Jack Dann's?

While he was still staring, a curtain behind the counter rustled. A long-faced girl with a mop of untidy brown curls and glistening tombstone teeth poked her head around it, fighting to control a yawn. He approached uncertainly, having suddenly remembered that he had no money. Perhaps, though, she would let him stay inside long enough for his eyes to stop stinging.

But she addressed him before he could speak.

"Would you like a long slow comfortable screw against the wall?"

His jaw dropped.

"No? Are you sure? What about between the sheets?"

His jaw dropped again, this time to its limit.

The girl emerged into clear view, her expression dispirited. She wore nothing bar a red miniskirt fractionally broader than a belt. She was thin and bony with small flat breasts, below which her ribs could easily be counted.

"I'll never make my fortune in this job," she muttered. "My fool of a professor at the Institute of Historical Imbibology swore that the double meaning of drink names like that was a surefire way of inducing red-blooded males to purchase them ... Not gay, are you?"

"Not that I know of," Rinpoche admitted.

"Thought not. I can't boast much in the way of tits, but they have the right effect on straights. I can tell by the way their eyes try to look anywhere else except directly at me. What *do* you want? How about a sidecar? A Manhattan? An old-fashioned or a dry martini or a Gibson's? A grasshopper, a brandy Alexander? A Moscow mule, a margarita?

Traffic lights? I mix all those pretty good—except you don't mix a traffic lights, of course—and it's supposed to be a big deal having a real live person fix your drink. You wouldn't think it if you worked here, though. Jer know you're the first daytime customer I've had in three months?"

Forcing his jaw to close again, Rinpoche hoisted himself on to a stool at the bar and wiped his forehead with the sleeve of his sweatshirt. He wished they'd included handkerchiefs in his outfit.

"You were offering me something to drink," he hazarded.

"Sure I was! Authentic twentieth-century cocktails! All, of course, available in indistinguishable alcohol-free versions."

He was about to admit his lack of funds and ask for water, when the unlikelihood of her last statement got through to him.

"How's that possible?" he exclaimed.

"For clients who eschew alcohol we can mix any drink with Fomalhautian crench instead. It induces identical effects." She brightened. "Would you like to try a cocktail with crench? It comes in whiskey, gin, rum, vodka, saké, grappa, kava, and tequila flavors, and also cognac and crème-de-menthe, though I'm out of those."

Rinpoche felt his cheeks growing hot.

"Well—uh—apart from it being kind of too soon after I woke up, to be perfectly honest, I don't have any money."

The girl leaned her elbows on the counter and linked her fingers, at the same time raising one foot behind her to the level of her hips.

"Just my luck," she muttered. "First daytime customer in yonks and he turns out to be a bankrupt wreck. My fault, I guess, for being a sucker. All those romantic dreams about Old Earth, cradle of the species, source of our culture and civilization . . ."

Rinpoche started. "Do I take it that you weren't born on Earth?" he whispered. The concept should have been staggering; he wanted to quake with wonderment. But once again he couldn't make it happen.

"Can't you tell from my accent? No, I'm from Trigon, and sometimes I wish I were back there!"

"Is Trigon a planet? I don't remember a planet called Trigon. I remember Mars, Venus, Mercury . . ." His words tailed away. She was staring at him in disbelief.

"Are you or are you not a wreck on the run?" she demanded.

"What? Oh! Oh, yes! At least I suppose I must be. I mean, I was woken up from freeze this morning and—"

"Weren't you given the standard data dose?"

"No! You see, I—"

"This doesn't make sense." Her voice was abruptly firm. "I just figured it out. You do have money. You must. Only you think of it the old-fashioned way, cashes or credicharts or whatever it was called—things you physically carried around with you. Let's see if I've guessed right. It'll be the first time in years . . . Hold still."

While speaking she had reached to a shelf behind her for a pencillike gadget that she now presented to Rinpoche's right eye. Before he had time to blink it emitted a flash of light so brief it barely left an afterimage, and she was saying in an angry tone, "What do you mean, no money? If I had a tenth of your credit, I'd be off this garbage-pile planet like a shot!"

"I don't understand!" Rinpoche cried.

"According to this reading, you have three hundred and sixty-six billion crunits!"

"What?"

"That's what it says!" She tossed the device back on its shelf.

"Well, all I can think is . . . Just a second." There were paper napkins on the bar; he seized a couple and mopped his face. "You said three hundred and sixty-six? Not sixty-five?"

"When you're talking in billions, how much difference does it make?" Her tone was bitter.

"It's just that I thought . . . Oh. It must be invested at a high rate of interest."

"What else would you do with that much money?"

"I don't know! I didn't know I had it! That's the honest truth!"

"But you must have known!" she flared. "Why else would they have left you to undertake your own reeducation? They only do that to people who can easily afford it!"

"*Who* only do it?"

She hesitated. Then, in a completely altered voice, she said, "You really don't know what's what, do you?"

"I do not!" Rinpoche blared.

"Hmm . . ." As though it were a matter of habit she brushed at her nipples, making them stand up like finger joints. "Well, I've told you you're rich. For that, how about buying me a drink?"

"Uh . . . Sure! Of course! But how?"

"Oh, you're listed as creditworthy by every computer on the planet—how else do you think I found out so fast? There are some things the Yelignese are really quite good at, despite what people say. Well, I'll have . . ." She licked her lips with a pink and pointed tongue. "I'll have a coffee!"

"I expected you to ask for something special."

"Isn't that special enough? . . . Oh!" Her eyes rounded enormously. "Of course! I suppose you hail from a time when people could drink coffee every day!"

"You mean nowadays they can't?"

"Grief, no! Not since the crunchiform blight! It was just as well seeds had been smuggled off-world illegally, or the Yelignese would have had to reconstruct the whole thing by analogy, and they'd've been bound to get it wrong. I mean, consider beer! Can you imagine anyone *liking* that stuff? I just can't believe it's authentic!"

There was a faint ping. From a small compartment under the bar she produced a yellowish-brown cuboid with frost forming on it. Raising it to her lips—or more exactly to her teeth—she said, "Thank you *very* much! You know, this is only the seventh time I've ever tasted coffee? It's so special I keep count . . . Well, mud in your hatch!"

She bit off a corner of the cube, rolled it around her mouth, shut her eyes, and tilted her head back in ecstasy. "Mm-*hm*!" she exclaimed. "But this isn't fair! How about you? What do you want?"

"I guess a glass of water," Rinpoche sighed.

"Here on Earth?" She looked offended. "Didn't they even warn you about that? Oh, those Yelignese!"

"Not to drink the water? On our own planet? Where we evolved?" Rinpoche searched eagerly for any sign that he might have regained his usual spectrum of emotions, but without success; for all the strength of feeling evoked by the idea that water on Earth had become undrinkable, he might as well have been talking about some remote world the other side of the galaxy.

"Not without treatment and purification like what most of us including yours truly can't afford—though you could, of course." She bit another corner off the cube and wriggled with delight as it melted on her tongue. "Ah, coffee! Coffee! The most amazing flavor, isn't it? By the way, you're Rinpoche Gibbs, right? I'm Spotch."

"That's an unusual name."

"Not on Trigon. Come to that, yours isn't exactly commonplace."

"It is in Tibet."

"Tibet? Oh. Ought I to have offered you brick tea with rancid yak butter?"

"Have I woken up after all this time to the same old stereotypes?"

"Sorry!" She blushed. He had never before seen how far a blush could extend away from the face.

"But how did you learn my name, anyway?"

"Checking your credit, how else? Though something odd happened." She frowned, searching for words. "The data feed sort of hesitated, like it had you mixed up with someone else. Ever use an alias?"

"Uh—no!"

She shrugged the matter off. "Ah, must be someone with a similar retinal pattern, I guess." The last of her "coffee" vanished between her oblong teeth. "Mm-*hm*! Thank *you* . . . Oh, come on! Don't you want anything? The boss machine will give me hell if all it finds on today's sales record is something someone bought for me."

"The boss machine?"

"I mean the Yelignese that actually owns this place."

Rinpoche drew a deep breath. "Now let me get this straight. Are the Yelignese people, or are they machines?"

Spotch bit her lower lip thoughtfully. She said, "According to what I've been told, they do the same as most intelligent races—trade their vulnerable bits for longer-lasting artificial ones and switch off their nervous systems as often as they can in order to prolong their lives . . . You know, it's awfully odd talking to someone who doesn't know basics I've been living with for ninety years."

"Ninety?" Rinpoche nearly fell off his stool.

"How old did you think I was?"

"Well, uh . . ."

She wasn't waiting for his answer. She plunged on, "Yes, I know! Same as my grandparents always say: old enough to know better! But I could never have qualified in law like my family wanted. I kept failing my sincerity probes."

"Your what?"

"Sincerity probes! Proving I honestly believed the truth of every case I had to argue. Too cynical, that's me. Besides, I did so much want to visit Earth before I settled down. 'Course, it cost an arm and a leg, but they did a great job on the replacements. I bet you can't tell which they took." She swung her bare legs to the bar top in turn and invited him to inspect them and her arms for scars.

"Yes, you're right," Rinpoche sighed, trying not to shudder at the idea of having healthy limbs cut off and finding it easy because disgust was numbed along with his other emotions. "A perfect match. But you were going to tell me about the Yelignese."

"Ahyah. Well, you see, when humans first got out to the stars—"

"When was that?"

She shrugged. "Don't ask me. I was never any good at dates."

"But how did we manage it?"

"I can't tell you how it works, either. Science is another of the things I'm not good at. All I remember is that it has something to do with rubbish."

Rinpoche snapped his fingers. "Duckman's Dumper?"

"Hey! You do know! Why pretend you don't?"

"Honestly, it's true. I just happen to have heard that name from someone I was talking to. Please go on."

"Ahyah. They thought it was going to fix the garbage problem. Only it turned out not to get rid of things, just shift them somewhere else. And there were all these other races out there who knew about us, because what with radio and TV broadcasts Earth was the noisiest planet in this entire volume, but they hadn't got in touch because they expected our species to go extinct pretty soon. Of course, once we discovered interstellar travel, they had to let us join the Galactic Conglomerate, especially because our method was cheaper than anyone else's so everybody wanted to license it, and before you could say Third-stage Lensman, most of the people of Earth got rich enough to emigrate. But none of the explans wanted the same kind of crisis to develop on their new planets, so they imposed population limits more or less straightaway, so a rump got stuck here, and since all the humans who were good at organizing things had left, they needed to hire somebody to sort the place out and passed the begging bowl for funds to pay for it. Not everybody was in favor. Lots of people on Trigon, for instance, thought it would be better to let Earth rot—there was this big campaign under the slogan 'Let Trigons be Trigons!' But in the end a majority voted to help, out of sentiment, I guess, and chose the Yelignese. They were the richest and most powerful species until quite recently, and people do say they dream of making a return to the top—Oh, hi, Elliot! Rin, this is Elliot Mess!"

The door of the bar had swung open again. A thin, stern face under an octagonal black cap was peering in.

"Morning, Spotch!" he called. "Morning—uh—Rin! Look, we got a new wreck on our team, take the place of Garry who paid off. Mind if I run through the moves, show him what to do tonight?"

"Sure, go ahead!"

Instantly three men and three women pushed past the stern-faced man, who was wearing a twentieth-century American police uniform, and sat down at various points around the room.

"Okay, it's nine P.M.," Elliot announced as soon as they were settled, then whipped out a gun, yelling, "Freeze! Don't anybody move!"

Four more "policemen," also armed, rushed into the room. The six "customers" who had entered first tipped over their tables, ducked behind them, and produced guns of their own. One of them shot Elliot in the face. His skull exploded in a mist of blood and brains, definitively adding the Mess to the Elliot.

"Say!" Spotch commented in an admiring tone. "They really got the effects to a fine art, don't they?"

One of the policemen fired at the killer but missed. The girl beside him threw her arms in the air and keeled over. Blood jetted from a hole in her throat. More bullets flew. Several of them smashed bottles in back of the bar. Kegs of beer concealed behind the curtain Spotch had drawn aside were punctured and began to flood the floor.

"Is this the prohibition raid I read about on your sign?" Rinpoche shouted over the roar of gunfire.

"That's right! Elliot brings in his cops every night at nine. It's always a big hit."

"Don't the customers mind? I mean, if a place I were visiting for a quiet drink got shot up like this, it would ruin my evening."

"It's just effects," Spotch reassured him. "Terrific, aren't they?"

But they were too realistic for Rinpoche's taste. While she was applauding the destruction of another row of bottles, he stole toward a sign reading MEN and to his great relief found beyond the rest room a back door giving on to a deserted alley.

Well—in actual fact to his very slight relief. He still couldn't experience a full-strength feeling, and that was becoming an undeniable drag.

"The computers suggest that we do WHAT?"

FOUR

THE EVOLUTION OF MARY QUEEN OF HEARTS, AS IT WERE

"YOU ASSURED ME HUMAN FEMALES CAN BE INDUCED TO compete for titles associated with a location, an occupation, or a product, such as Miss Irkutsk, Miss Interior Decorator, or Miss Baked Goods. Did you not?"

"Yes indeed."

"Then why has there been zero response to my latest contest? Your species has little organizational ability, but it's traditionally been the women who display it, and we can't go on doing all the work!"

"Please reflect. Who would wish to be elected Miss Management?"

Rinpoche thought he had headed away from the movie set as he left Spotch's, but emerging from the bar by its back door had clearly disoriented him, for shortly he found himself once more in sight of the oddly garbed crowd. Gus's voice, enormously amplified, was barking orders for apzolute kviet and no vun to moof.

Not wanting to be noticed, yet curious about what was going on, he glanced around. Some of the "buildings" were merely false fronts. It occurred to him that he could stand behind a window to watch; even if people did glimpse his face, that would detract less from the authenticity of the scene than people in Roman togas.

If, of course, the windows had glass he could see through, and weren't just painted.

As it turned out, the panes were indeed opaque, but some

frames could be opened, and moments later he had a very fair vantage point. He could see Gus in a sort of breeches buoy slung from a swiveling boom, megaphone to mouth as he uttered further commands that became less and less comprehensible. He could see half a dozen camera operators, on wheeled trolleys at ground level, on platforms about shoulder height, and on another boom similar to Gus's but with an extra joint. Prior to the director's call for action they were zooming in and out on groups of onlookers, no doubt so that personalized footage of the tourists could be spliced into the copies of the film they would take home.

The crowd, he noticed, contained individuals of just about all ages, from babes in arms to extremely senior citizens crowned with hair as brilliantly white as Wrong Ghoulart's, but most of them looked like twenty-first-century people in their middle thirties. Remembering his (mild) surprise on being told that Spotch was ninety, he gazed at them with a sense of (mild) awe, wondering how old they actually were. To people who could cure leukemia, it must be a trivial matter to restore at least the appearance of youth—especially since these people probably took care never to lose it in the first place. Some of them, indeed . . .

He blinked.

Some of them—and at this point he again had to wipe his forehead with his sleeve, wishing he had had the presence of mind to liberate a few paper napkins from Spotch's—were quite remarkably good-looking. Quite alarmingly good-looking. For example, that girl in gray emerging from the gilded coach in the wake of an actress wearing elaborate sixteenth-century costume, ruff, stomacher, farthingale, and all, being first greeted and then escorted by youthful dandies in cloaks of plum and green and royal blue over gaudy doublets and hose: she, playing no doubt a maid of honor or the like, was downright gorgeous!

Briefly astonished at how clearly he could see her, for she was on the far side of the square (but Theodor Surgeon had said he was cured of all infirmities, which presumably included myopia), he could not help wondering what magical blend of genes could have given rise to her golden skin, her lustrous black hair, her delicate hands, her slender form (insofar as it was visible, but it was no corsetry that made her shapely), her rich red mouth, her dazzling eyes—Oh-oh!

Suppressing a gasp, he stepped back. So mesmerized had he been by the approaching beauty, he had failed to bear in mind that she *was* approaching. She, and the actress she was accompanying, were making straight for his watch post!

Enlightenment followed. From the general blur of Gus's shouted instructions emerged a few salient data: this was, as he had guessed, meant to be Queen Elizabeth of England with her courtiers, come to watch the beheading of her deadly enemy, so the spectators ought to be either cheering or shouting execration. If they knew how to curse in a Scottish accent, so much the better.

This could not of course possibly be authentic; Harry had explained why. Rinpoche, though, was past caring. All he wanted was to feast his eyes on this amazing, this miraculous, this incredible summation of female loveliness, who was making him react as though someone had analyzed him down to the hormonal level and systematically concocted the recipe for a woman whose mere appearance—and in an almost all-concealing garb, what's more—punched every single last one of his emotional buttons ...

Why! It's a real feeling! Or at any rate, I think this is what a real feeling feels like. Isn't it?

His moment of Cartesian-Berkeleian confusion lasted long enough for the queen to reach a highback chair that had been readied against the very wall that concealed Rinpoche, where she permitted her attendants to install her with much bowing and scraping. As the girl made her mistress comfortable with cushions, Rinpoche caught his clearest glimpse so far of her heartrendingly beautiful face and noticed something he should have spotted straight away.

She wore an expression that no woman so beautiful (if there were any others) ought ever to wear. She looked half miserable and half terrified.

He wanted to burst from hiding, rush to her side, fall on his knees, and kiss her hands, pledging lifetime allegiance to the cause of making her happy, order the queen to drop dead if she tried to interfere.

Then reason returned.

Of course. She's an actress. This must be the right expression for her rôle. Maybe the queen has just insulted her or something. I imagine the old bat must be in a filthy temper. I seem to remember it was with the utmost reluctance that she ordered Mary's death ...

But his knowledge of European history was shaky at the best of times, and this wasn't one.

A hush fell. There was a renewed stir at the far side of the square. A farm cart lumbered into view, hauled by a donkey, no doubt as mechanical as the horses. (Rinpoche wondered in passing how many animals—apart from humans, of which there still seemed no lack—had survived to the present day, whenever that might be.) Guarded by soldiers with pikes, here came, presumably, Mary Queen of Scots. At any rate she wore a pearl coronet and an embroidered velvet gown. Her supporters tried to organize a disturbance among the crowd, or somebody did, at any rate; from the way Gus was parodying tearing his hair out Rinpoche suspected that some of the extras were entering rather too enthusiastically into their rôles. Shortly, however, soldiers started plying pikes while the camera operators zoomed in for close-ups of stabbing and disembowelment. Rinpoche recalled Harry's sour phrase about such scenes confirming aliens in their view of humans as backward and upstart barbarians. How many aliens were there in this crowd, recording the events of their trip for those back home? He couldn't tell; they must be in disguise or invisible.

An episode followed even less flattering to humanity.

A tall man with a bullwhip drove Mary toward the scaffold: lash, crack, lash. At each contact of the whip with her back a garment fell from her, so that when she stumbled up the steps to the platform she was already half-naked, though still retaining her coronet and shoes. She was quite pretty, with a full bust, good legs, and not excessively generous hips, but Rinpoche could not imagine anyone preferring to look at her while the girl playing the maid of honor was in view. He ached with desire to mingle with the crowd, purely so as to gaze on that fantastic face now turned away.

The headsman gave a lascivious grin, passing his tongue across his broad lips and his thumb, once more, along the blade of his ax.

A man in an ankle-length robe, clasping a book and wearing a wooden cross around his neck, followed Mary onto the platform and implored mercy of the executioner. He was rewarded with a blow from the ax handle and fell, arms upflung, back into the crowd. The whip removed yet more of Mary's clothing; now she was bare to the waist.

And revolving slowly so that everyone watching could enjoy a good view of her body. What could the aliens possibly think of that? Did they carry guidebooks explaining the psychology of humans? Or tapes, or intravenous computers, or whatever?

If so, they'd have to be extremely well contrived to clarify what followed, Rinpoche decided. For Mary began a stamping dance back and forth across the planking, indicating with gestures that she didn't care a hoot for the man with the whip—let him strip her completely!

Which he proceeded to do, and then retired to a corner of the platform while the girl turned her attention to her would-be killer. She danced up to him and snapped her fingers under his nose, infuriating him so that he snarled and raised his ax, then darted away again as he lumbered clumsily after her.

But now the pikemen ringed the stage on which the last act of the drama of Mary's life was to be played out. By degrees their weapons closed off her avenues of escape, then even of retreat, until only a few square meters remained.

And at their center was the execution block.

Rather to his surprise (though since the maid of honor still had her back to the window he was peeking through, there would have been little point in gazing at her) Rinpoche found he had actually been watching "Mary" for some while. Vulgar though it was, the quasiballetic action bore the stamp of competent direction—presumably Gus's—and as the actress spun around to find the ring of pikes complete, then bowed her head and let her shoulders slump, resigned to her inevitable fate, there was genuine pathos in her movements. Rinpoche felt his eyes sting.

Slowly she knelt before the grooved block, her nakedness making her pitiably vulnerable. The executioner kicked at her feet, forcing them into a tidier position. She winced but did not cry out.

By now the crowd, large though it was, had fallen silent. All that could be heard was their breathing.

Satisfied at last with the posture of his victim, the executioner took a fresh grip on his ax, raised it so far that its blade was behind him, about level with his waist, and *swung*.

At which point, if not all then a considerable quantity of hell broke loose.

It started with the ax head. At the peak of its arc it separated from the helve and soared upward, leaving its wielder to slam at the block something far less massive than expected—so light, indeed, as to cost him his balance. The result was that he missed Mary's neck and went staggering, having sustained a shock to both arms violent enough to make him drop the helve with a curse and rub his offended elbows, while the startled actress rolled over and sat up in bewilderment. Triggered by some concealed mechanism, a blood-smeared duplicate of her head shot across the platform and fell off the edge, ignored—for a second later her eyes, like everyone else's, even Rinpoche's, though he would far rather have been staring at the girl in gray, were drawn as by a magnet to the detached blade.

It was hovering—spinning, too, but that seemed to be of lesser relevance and was definitely of greater probability.

It was hovering, to be precise, as though figuring out how it could initiate the greatest possible amount of consequential mayhem.

Time stretched.

A decision was reached.

The blade—spinning so rapidly now that one could hear it whine—sideswiped Gus's boom and left his breeches buoy dangling by a thread. Cries of alarm rang out from his director's megaphone but were swiftly drowned by screams of terror as the blade ricocheted toward the camera boom and severed its power cables, creating a spray of brilliant electric sparks.

As though it had ingested new energy the blade whirled faster yet. Lurching sidewise, it slanted toward the bleachers. The spectators yelled and jumped to their feet. The structure swayed ominously. People ducked as the blade zigzagged so close above their heads that their hair—if thin and relatively free of grease—stood on end to follow its electric charge.

And then it plunged.

The bleachers, whether in the interests of authenticity or of economy, were held together with treenails and coarse rope. As though capable of deducing at what spot the structure was most vulnerable, the blade struck at it: a breastsummer knot. There were two, one either side. The blade opted for the one on the left. Once severed, it permitted the collapse—gentle but remorseless—of the entire stand, so that people tumbled one upon another amid a welter of planks, screaming and pissing with fright.

Concerning the latter, the stench allowed no doubt.

Of all those present, thanks to the dullness of his emotions (in all respects bar one—but he had no time to ponder that) Rinpoche was perhaps the least disturbed. The fact that he was at a safe distance from the collapse must have helped but could not account entirely for his detachment. For example, though they were at just as much of a remove, "Queen Elizabeth" was overwhelmed along with her courtiers, including the beautiful maid of honor—her above all, to the extent of clasping her hands and shouting aloud:

"Oh, no! Not here as well! *I can't stand it!*"

And tears spilled from her lustrous eyes.

Those about her scattered in panic, none offering comfort. Rinpoche cursed the wall that separated them, bethought him of the possibility that he might smash through a mere façade with his bare hands, bruised his knuckles painfully in proving that he couldn't, and finally ran around the end of the deceitful frontage.

More frightened people blocked his way. By the time he gained the spot where the girl in gray had stood, there was no sign of her.

At length, philosophically, he shrugged and went to see what he could do to help the injured.

The answer, in brief, was: precious little. It was plain from the most cursory inspection that someone had reacted with amazing promptitude, and a second or at worst a third glance revealed who.

Tall and handsome, though not otherwise noticeably alike, forty teenagers of both sexes, tossing aside Elizabethan cloaks and ruffs to reveal identical uniforms of blue tunics and purple breeches, had instantly taken charge. They themselves had been in the front row, the one least affected by the collapse; Rinpoche remembered noticing them while he was relishing the standard of good looks among the crowd—before the girl in gray arrived, of course. Clearly they had responded like a platoon of trained medics; it was only now that other assistance was arriving, but the situation was already under control.

And then a sort of gap opened in the air.

That was the only way Rinpoche could think of to describe it. It looked like—only then again it didn't, but more sort of . . .

Well, to be absolutely candid, it didn't look like anything else he had ever seen. Better to concentrate on *what* was happening instead of *how*, because until he witnessed it with his own eyes he would have declared categorically that such a thing was impossible. Could this have something to do with a Duckman's Dumper? He made a mental resolution to ask at the first opportunity—aware even as he did so that at the rate this weird and future age was bombarding him with mysteries he was more likely to forget than remember.

A portly woman dressed in black stepped from the hole in the air, adjusting a chain of office across her ample bosom. She cocked her head as though listening to a message, then cleared her throat and called out.

"Say, you youngsters! I'm the mayor of this burg! Hello!"

The ones in blue and purple turned, their expressions bashful.

"I'm told you just broke the Earthly record for spontaneous response to an emergency!"

Embarrassed, the teenagers shifted from foot to foot.

"I'm also told that you come from that most distinguished of galactic schools, Superlativo College on Bibraxia!"

Their embarrassment evaporated. They stood taller and prouder and beamed at one another as they cried out with a single voice, "Yes!"

Rinpoche had grown gradually aware that standing beside him were a man and woman, drably clad, holding hands. Until now he had thought nothing of them. Abruptly, however, he realized that they were on the verge of tears: she snuffling, he striving not to sob.

The mayor, beaming broader than the youngsters, declared, "In token of your selflessness and presence of mind we insist you be our guests at a grand civic reception! Presumably you are traveling with teachers? Yes? Then they must be honored, too! Only profound dedication and spiritual insight could induce young people like yourselves . . ."

Rinpoche lost the rest of what the mayor was saying. The man and woman at his side had fallen blindly into one another's arms and were weeping without shame.

"Can I help?" he ventured, his Samaritan impulse unassuaged. "I assume you have lost dear ones in the calamity that just eventuated. While I am myself a stranger and afraid in this world I never made—"

"We're . . ." the woman choked out, raising her head and wiping her streaming eyes. That was as far as she got. The man took over, but likewise achieved only a single word before he, too, broke down.

"Their . . ."

And the woman recovered enough to conclude the sequence.

"Teachers!"

They sobbed harder than ever, while Rinpoche stared blankly.

"I confess I don't understand," he said at length. "Why are you not proud? The mayor of this not inconsiderable conurbation, reduced though it may be from the days when I remember it—being what I gather is now termed a 'wreck,' meaning me, not the city—has decreed a civic reception to acknowledge the admirable discharge of their charitable duty that your pupils have displayed . . . if you see what I mean, which perhaps you don't. Uh . . ."

He drew a deep breath. "Why aren't you over the moon?"

They drew apart, baffled, staring first at him, then each other.

"Over the moon?" the woman echoed. "You want us to run away from our responsibilities? When we don't know what's become of the children we're supposed to be in charge of?"

"Except," her male companion supplied, "that we did deliver them to Earth. We're sure of that. We would take an oath on it in any court in the galaxy."

He produced handkerchiefs. They each wiped their eyes.

Rinpoche said foggily, "But these youngsters! The mayor just said they've done you credit!"

The woman gave a contemptuous snort.

"*Those* aren't the children committed to our care!"

"I—uh—don't understand."

"That's obvious." She glanced at her companion. "Will you explain, or do you want me to?"

The man sighed, passing his hand over a lank brown forelock.

"Okay, I'll take a zoom at it. But don't hesitate to interrupt if you think I'm misstating the case ... Well, to begin with, this is Lasky Frumple and I'm her secondary orthowife Crognis."

Rinpoche wanted to ask how a male could be an ortho- or indeed any other kind of wife, but for fear of upsetting the couple further he merely nodded and did his best to look wise.

"I don't know how much you know about Bibraxia?"

That at least Rinpoche could answer with assurance: "Nothing."

They both looked at him strangely, but Crognis resumed.

"Well, it's the galactic educational center *par excellence*. If you're worth billions per year, yet you can't get your children into a college on Bibraxia, you're a failure."

Lasky was on the verge of saying something. He cut her short.

"All right, I exaggerate, but not much—hmm?"

She subsided.

"And Superlativo is *the* college among all the other colleges. I know Lasky won't contradict that. When we were coopted to its subordinate faculty we were so elated we couldn't begin to tell you even with computer help. As for the moment when the Dean and Chapter informed us that we had been chosen to escort a group of students from the richest and most prestigious families of the galaxy on their first trip to Earth—!"

"Unfortunately," Lasky cut in, her expression grim, "it's

ours as well. And absolutely certain to be our last. You see, *those are not our pupils!*"

"What makes you think so?"

"What are spoiled teenagers from hyper-rich families like?" Crognis retorted. "Do they eagerly aid victims of an accident? Do they boast of their loyalty and gratitude to their alma mater?"

"Or," Lasky thrust in, "do they evade the boring educational component of their visit to Earth by substituting convincing simulacra programmed to go through the motions in the most impeccable manner, while they get on with other things?"

"Such as what?" Rinpoche said after a pause, having glimpsed but not grasped the scale of the teachers' problem.

"You name it!" Crognis retorted. "We've seen what they get up to back home—or rather, at college. Where would you expect to find them, Lasky? Where are the wildest whacks, the bossest bangs?"

She shrugged hopelessly. "Whoring in Montmartre in hopes of clap and crabs?"

"Rotting their minds in a Shanghai opium den?"

"Getting amusingly mutilated in a Spanish bullring?"

"The Colosseum, more like!"

"Eating long pig in Polynesia?"

"I'd say personally slaughtering the victims!"

That evoked a pang of alarm in Rinpoche. Perhaps his emotions were at last reverting to normal— No, they weren't. He found himself wondering why, if cannibalism were indeed available in Oceania, Horace and his buddy had needed to go to such lengths to obtain a newly thawed wreck, and that was far too rational and logical a frame in which to think about people being eaten. It was probably just a rumor, anyway. He said hastily, "Oh, surely—"

"Surely what?" Lasky snapped. "The more extreme the experience, the more likely they are to go for it. If you knew what we know about the already twice-jaded appetites of our 'little treasures' ...! Before long they'll be

buying planets to blow up for fun—inhabited planets!
Right, Crognis?"

Downcast, her orthowife gave a nod and shrug.

"When did you realize something was amiss?" Rinpoche
demanded.

"Not as soon as we should have," sighed Crognis. "During the trip they were their normal unbearable selves, but
the day after we reached Earth they started to behave in
such an orderly and tractable manner that it made me feel
uneasy."

"So why didn't you tell me?" Lasky snapped.

"I did! But *you* said it was because they were overawed
by the knowledge that they were treading the ground of the
planet where our species took its rise—as though anything
as abstract as a sense of history ever impressed the likes of
that lot!"

"It seems to me," Rinpoche ventured, "that there's one
consolation. Your own stay here will be much more enjoyable, won't it? As you might say: less fraught."

"That's true," Crognis conceded glumly. "On the other
hand, when we get home and have to confess what's happened, the proverbial ice-cream's chance on Hades One will
far surpass our own."

"Yes. I do see your problem."

The teachers were silent for a moment. Then they pulled
themselves together, wiping their reddened eyes one last
time.

"Well, nice to have met you, I guess," Lasky muttered.
She took her secondary orthowife's hand and together they
moped away in the direction of the patiently waiting "students" from Superlativo.

Who in repose, as Rinpoche now noticed, displayed the
same betraying stillness as the horses.

Those seated in the grandstand who had escaped with a
shaking and a bruise or two—fortunately the vast
majority—had by now recovered to the stage of contemplating lawsuits, insurance claims, and premature departure.

Abruptly the men and women with flags returned to rush hither and yon among the remnants of the crowd, deflecting complaints and threats as best they could. A shrill amplified voice, blurred by echoing off the buildings, uttered barely comprehensible statements about infinite regret, generous compensation, absence of precedent, impossibility of occurrence let alone recurrence, though it had been a unique experience, hadn't it, fulfilling the publicity claim that out of all inhabited worlds Old Earth could best be relied on to take you by surprise . . . ?

Rinpoche was trying to make sense out of that as an excuse, and likewise the idea of being compensated for something that couldn't possibly have happened, when he felt his elbow jostled. At his side he found one of the flag bearers, a harassed-looking youth (though of course he could have been a hundred). The flag he bore was yellow.

"Sir, I know you're upset after the awful thing that happened—and believe me, so are we, especially when we consider what a slice of our hoped-for profit will now have to be returned to our clients as salt in their wounds. Uh . . . I'm not sure that's quite right," he ended lamely.

"All that matters," declared another yellow flag-waver, female this time, arriving at the head of a straggle of authentically costumed tourists who had been in the square rather than the stand, but were scowling nonetheless, "is getting our head count right. Is it?"

"Yes! We arrived with forty-eight and we leave with forty-eight! Remember our slogan—we count 'em out and we count 'em back!"

"Splendid! Let's be on our way. Ladies and gentlemen, lunch is next on our schedule. You will enjoy another selection of Old Earth's finest dishes prior to San Francisco, where you can mingle with rough-and-ready prospectors from the days of the Gold Rush, unless you have previously registered a conscientious objection to (a) obscene language, (b) simulated violence, (c) the excavation and smelting of noble metals, or (d). Come along! Please!"

Rinpoche found himself hesitating. It seemed obvious

that he had been mistaken for a member of this tour group—and what a shame that it didn't include the beautiful girl in gray!—but the error was not his fault, and by now the notion of lunch was distinctly tempting, even if it did have to be on the way to visit San Francisco in the days of the Gold Rush. But what in the world had the woman meant by "(d)"? Her words had sounded like a bad edit in a tape.

So was she really a woman? The teachers from Bibraxia had claimed that their students had substituted simulacra for themselves. Were these guides imitations, too?

In the end he hesitated too long. Before he reached a decision his nostrils were assailed from nowhere with the aroma of the most delicious meal he had ever dreamed of tasting.

Well, if he needed to pay for his food, at least Spotch had assured him that he was registered as creditworthy by every computer on Earth.

Who, though, could have been lost from the head count to make room for him? For one wild moment he found himself imagining that the missing person might be the girl in gray, swept away amid the panicking crowd (and how *had* that ax head executed its path through the air? Executed? Oh, no!), who would find a way to rejoin her companions, allow him to make her acquaintance . . . He trembled at the prospect of addressing her face-to-face.

But the missing tourist had to be a man. The alternative was too ridiculous. Anyway, the scent of food was drawing him in the wake of the yellow flags along with everyone else. Resistance was out of the question. He dared not even risk explaining the mistake, for by now his mouth was watering so much he feared that opening it would spill drool down to his knees.

"The computers suggest that we do WHAT?"

FIVE

LIFE IN A PSEUDO-TEMPORAL DAGWOOD BUMSTEAD SANDWICH

"WHAT'S ALL THIS ABOUT POLLUTION IN THE BAYOUS BE-ing worse than it was before the Yelignese? I can't believe it! Louisiana is supposed to be back to its virgin state! Didn't they agree to our application to reintroduce Spanish moss, and wasn't that the finishing touch?"

"In a sense it was. Now we have to start over."

"What do you mean?"

"What they supplied was spinach mess. It comes in cans."

What happened next, Rinpoche could not be sure. Afterward he recalled following the rest of the party through a portal in the air like the one the mayor had emerged from and being surprised to find that no special sensation accompanied crossing its threshold, although it led to a place invisible from where he had been a moment before.

The odd thing, however, in retrospect . . .

Well, the oddest of several things . . .

Well, what it boiled down to was . . .

Well, afterward he remembered everything quite clearly. The only trouble was, he remembered everything simultaneously, too.

Which was logical enough. Obviously there wasn't room in so little time for so many events to follow one another, so they had to be packed in side by side. Had to.

Nonetheless, it was a trifle disconcerting.

Perhaps one got used to it?

Rinpoche didn't think, even on reflection, that he particularly wanted to get used to it.

To be candid, he would just as soon not bother.

He was sitting in a comfortable chair watching and listening to an advertisement for the Holyrood Experience. Some of the sound effects were deafening. Some of the images made no sense.

"*Your* personalised copy of the super-spectacular Holyrood movie, *The Execution of Mary Queen of Scots* featuring *yourself!* as a player /RAH RAH RAH!/ will be awaiting collection prior to your departure from Earth, or at a small extra charge can be forwarded to your usual place of residence or any other address you nominate within the Galactic Conglomerate. Yes, you will be able to share with your friends and loved ones this unique re-creation of the ancient art of 'moviemaking,' no mere copy of a past achievement but newly honed on the mental anvil of resurrectee director Gustav von Schildenstein!"

There was a minor shift in the tone of voice—slight, but perceptible.

"What is more, this version is unique. It, and it alone, incorporates the unprecedented sequence of the collapsing grandstand! Hear screaming onlookers howl in terror! See them pissing themselves with fright! Smell, if you wish, for a small extra charge, the resulting aroma! This is footage never before included in any motion picture of *The Death of Mary Queen of Hearts*!"

The voice dropped half an octave and oozed sincerity, thick as honey dripping from the comb.

"You may of course be assured that under no circumstances will *your* copy of the movie contain images of *you* in a humiliating predicament, unless you expressly wish it to, in which case advise your courier as soon as convenient. Either way, you *Nixy Anangaranga-Jones* have just added yet another to the grand collection of cherishable souvenirs you are acquiring, thanks to your wise choice of Earth as a destination!"

"Just a moment!" Rinpoche blurted.

"Yes?"

Presumably it was a machine delivering the commercial. If so, it was a highly sophisticated one. Which was of course to be expected.

"My name isn't Nixy—whatever. It isn't Nixy anything."

Which was true. A moment later, however, he found himself regretting his attack of honesty.

He was in what ought to have been a cubicle, like a changing room in a clothing store, but exhibited important differences, such as that each of its walls, and, indeed, its ceiling, too, as he realized when he glanced up, was a transparent screen displaying publicity images. He recognized the Pyramids even though they were inverted overhead, then Great Zimbabwe, Machu Picchu, and—like an old friend even though he had never been there—the Potala, though it took him a long moment to identify the fifth image: the creeper-draped remains of what could only be Cape Canaveral. Well, if they'd figured out how to travel to the stars, what use would people have for those old polluting rockets?

An intersexual voice murmured out of nowhere:

"Do you wish, in the interests of historical authenticity, to doff your clothing yourself, or would you prefer it done for you? To save embarrassment the character of this vocal message may be altered toward that of your own sex or the opposite, as you direct."

There was a pause. While Rinpoche was still trying to figure out whether he ought to undress himself or—if only for the sake of the experience—ask for it to be done (and why did he have to undress at all? Was he going to be disinfected or deloused before being allowed to enjoy the meal whose delicious aroma lingered in his nostrils? Oh, hell! Here he was thinking in parentheses again!)

He started over, but too late. The machine had drawn its own conclusions, and its next words were in a purr to match Eartha Kitt's.

"Many humans being embarrassed by nudity except in same-sex company as at baths or a gym, and since you have given no other instructions, a female voice will be employed and your garments removed for you."

Rinpoche was on the point of remonstrating when soft appendages assailed him. From his feet up, from his neck down, his shoes and clothing were caressed away. Electric tingles flowed from his toes, his fingers, his scalp, and met with an explosion like ball lightning at his solar plexus. Never had he imagined that the act of removing clothes could be so sensual.

Nor that their replacement by others could be even more so.

Especially when what he found himself enrobed with turned out to be a waspie corset, open-crotch drawers, a frilly off-the-shoulder gown of green silk trimmed with black, stockings gartered just above the knee, and high-buttoned boots with six-centimeter heels. He was so taken aback that not until a ringleted wig had been deposited on his head and topped with a jaunty bonnet did he recover the presence of mind to blare, "What the hell are you playing at?"

The Kittish voice murmured, "Nixy, I am obliged to remind you that when you signed up for your trip to Earth you consented in advance to don such garb as is appropriate for the historical—"

"Who the hell is Nixy?"

That got through.

"Why, you are! Although come to think of it . . ."

"Come to think of it, you didn't register that Nixy is supposed to be female and I'm not? You weren't struck by any sense of inconsistency even when you were putting on these . . . these . . . ?"

Words failed him. He could only haul up his skirt and jab a thumb in the direction of his genitals.

"One is obliged to admit that something does seem out of kilts."

"Out of kilts? Kilts *shmilts*! Give back my own clothes!"

"No."

"What?"

"You have undertaken, as I just reminded you, to wear clothing suitable for the occasion. Your former garments are inappropriate for San Francisco in the Gold Rush period of 1849."

"And where, during that or any other period of history, was this—this *drag* appropriate for a male?"

Rinpoche checked of a sudden. He was growing angry! Marvelous! What a relief to be able to feel strongly again! Not, of course, that he was in any sense an antifeminist, but enough was enough. Besides, this corset *hurt*.

"Uh—!"

"Gotcha," Rinpoche said grimly, and began to toss aside his ridiculous finery.

At the same time, however:

What this place had to be was obvious: a restaurant. Soft light shone on long tables draped with bright white linen, set with silver, porcelain, and crystal amid a thousand gaudy flowers in vases, garlands, and festoons. Gentle music pleased the ear. There was a sense of vast expectancy.

Then the air, that had been devoid of odor, clanged like a smitten bell to the same delicious scent Rinpoche recalled from just before his—well, his departure from Holyrood. He felt every cell in his body jump, as it were, to attention. When in his life had a meal offered such a premonitory vision (hang on, you can't have a vision of something that's assailing you via your nose ((oh, shit, here I am thinking in parentheses *again*, and I'm getting sick of it!)) such a foretaste, that would do)—okay, such a foretaste of itself?

He was surprised to find that he'd remembered the need for a question mark at the end of that sentence.

Gradually he took stock of the rest of his surroundings, which consisted of the other members of the group he had accidentally been swept up with. People, in other words. Tourists. From other planets, if he had understood aright what he'd been told since waking. This very morning? Yes, this very morning! Now he could react to some extent normally again, he was simultaneously growing worried by the fact. He didn't want to consider the implications of everything he had been told in these few short hours. If all those data hit him at once, he suspected his brain would burst like Elliot's but without a bullet.

Best not to think of things like that.

Why, though, had he not been offered the orientation lecture that the people he had so far talked to assumed all wrecks received? Even a simple briefing sheet would have been useful. Being forced to snatch like this at odds and ends of information was proving stressful, to put it mildly. Of course, Wrong Ghoulart must have been considerably distracted, what with *mafiosi* and cannibals. Even so . . .

Still, here he finally was in a position to pick up a few more data, for he was definitely sitting at table with the other tourists.

Or am I?

The question annoyed him. As though some solicitous guardian angel had detected his transient disquiet, he heard a voice without sound, without sex, but with a grave and ominous inflection:

"*So* sorry for that unpleasant sensation! We can assure you it will not recur. Was it due to sitting beside one of our nonhuman patrons? If so, please be reminded that all the participants in this tour were required to certify that they were devoid of species prejudice."

There was a meaning pause.

"However," the voice resumed in a brighter tone, "it could have been that despite our utmost precautions some waft of odor from your seat-neighbors' assigned nourishment caused an involuntary reaction—No, excuse me. The diet specified on your behalf at the outset of the tour . . . Excuse me again. There is some confusion."

Indeed there was. What had been an apparently stable restaurant was starting to waver and fade. Rinpoche, foggy though his mind still was, began to catch on. More or less.

"I was sitting next to a nonhuman?" he exclaimed.

"Wonderful! I've never had the chance to speak to a creature from another planet! Put us back together, please!"

Meantime wondering why it was that he couldn't remember being next to anyone at all.

And also why he wasn't being allowed anything to eat.

He was sitting with his knees under a long table that contrived to be at the normal height he himself was used to, close to ground level for those humans among the group who preferred to squat or kneel while eating, and at other spatial locations suitable for those who were not human at all. There was a babble of voices, although too many people were talking at once for him to make out more than the general tenor of the conversation; mainly it seemed to consist of complaints about the food, the accommodations, and the standard of entertainment up to now.

A moment later, however, all that was forgotten as a wave of excitement thrilled through his body. (He was indubitably regaining his normal emotions.) For not only had a delectable dish just appeared before him—or would materialized be a better term? Certainly he had not noticed it arriving—but in addition he had realized that the creatures either side of him belonged to the nonhuman group. He barely restrained himself from jigging up and down.

I'm in the physical presence of beings from other planets! It's wonderful! It's incredible!

Which would take precedence, filling his belly (and the food did smell marvelous!) or satisfying his curiosity? He had just decided in favor of the food when the bowl before him vanished again.

"Excuse please," said a voice that seemed to be inside his head. "Your problem will be taken care of expeditionably."

"Huh?"

His hand had been poised to pick up a spoon, since that seemed the appropriate utensil out of the many arrayed before him. But that, too, had disappeared.

There ensued the kind of pause that in his day would

have been ascribed to the passing of an angel. Into it broke a shrill soprano voice.

"No, it isn't charming, and it isn't quaint! I've told you before! It's revoltingly *primitive*! Having to put food in your mouth with your own hands—that is pukish to the enth and tenth!"

"This is Earth, remember," came the caustic baritone reply. "What else did you expect? And it was you who insisted that we come here!"

Rendered uncomfortable as he always had been in his previous existence by people making loud public complaints, Rinpoche turned to his left side seat-neighbor. Upright, the said personage would have stood about as tall as himself, but was garbed—apart from a sort of harness supporting what Rinpoche took to be cameras and recorders or their contemporary counterparts—exclusively in scaly skin, rich dark green on back and limbs, washy bluish yellow on chest and belly. The head was prognathous, to put it mildly; both jaws boasted fierce ranks of teeth, while the forelimbs terminated in knife-sharp claws that were slashing gobbets of flesh from the carcass of what looked like a rabbit (or a cat?) on a Limoges *assiette* bordered with a design of honeysuckle.

Doing his utmost to suppress any impulse that might brand him a speciesist, Rinpoche smiled winningly—then canceled the expression, having once read that the expression humans regard as ingratiating might well strike an alien as exposure of one's fangs prior to attack. He hesitated, then summoned all his courage and spoke.

"Hello!"

Baleful lidless eyes fixed on him by turns. The effect was a bit like watching a chicken watching a scuttering bug. He remembered that birds were descended from dinosaurs. No doubt this alien stemmed from a parallel branch of the evolutionary tree.

"Do excuse me! But, you see, I'm a wreck. I was only thawed out today. So I never had the chance of talking to an alien before!"

The scaly head reared on high. The jaw gaped, spilling shreds of red flesh. A thick rough tongue licked the air as though tasting it for the spoor of vengeance.

"Did you say alien?"

The voice emerged from not the mouth but a box hung near the top of the creature's harness. And there was no mistaking the anger it conveyed. Rinpoche shrank back.

"Alien?" his seat-neighbor repeated with a roar, rising to full height. Others at the table hesitated in their eating. (How come they had lunch and he didn't?) Strangers' faces turned his way. Some bore expressions of puzzlement, but most of annoyance.

"ALIEN?" the creature howled at the pitch of its lungs.

Inside Rinpoche's head a voice whimpered, "Nixy Anangaranga-Jones, you committed yourself to refrain from overt expressions of speciesism during this tour! Why did you go back on your pledged word? I am compelled to advise you that you have invalidated the insurance policy against being sued in the Deep Court of the Galactic Conglomerate, which your tour operators provided as a conditional benefit of—"

But by this time Rinpoche had been heaved clear off the ground, supported by claws in the material of the dress he was wearing—

Just a second. Dress?

Corset??

High-heeled boots???

"There appears," the same feeble voice whimpered again, "to have been some sort of mistake."

His reptilian captor uttered a snort with its mouth, while the box on its harness snapped, "Mistake? I'll say there's been a mistake! You seat me next to this pea-brained mammal, and she calls me an *alien*! On my own home planet, and never mind that I'm a reconstruct! Listen, you!"— shaking Rinpoche so hard the fabric round the claws began to rip. "My people lived on this planet seventy million years before your lot showed up! We didn't turn it into the biggest garbage dump in the galaxy! That was you! What's more, you murder your own kind and then boast about it, as was proved by that disgusting exhibition we were forced to attend this morning! On that basis alone the Chief Bureaucrat was wrong to reject my petition to dispossess you humans and—"

"Correction!"

Another voice spoke inside Rinpoche's head. This one rang with authority. At first, at any rate.

"The largest garbage dump in the galaxy is recognized to be the one created by the Hugglemunchits of *here insert galactic coordinates in form comprehensible to indigenes*, who became extinct in *here insert date in form comprehensible to indigenes*, and any rival claims should be submitted to *here insert address of Galactic Records Office in form comprehensible to indigenes.* XQQQZ EXCUSE THIS SEGMENT INCOMPLETELY EDDY-TED EDITED SO SIDREGARK SIRDEGRAK DISREGARD DISREGARD DISAGREED

He was in some kind of enormous room with indistinct walls a long way off. Soft bluish radiance made him feel as though he were inside a fluorescent light tube. A stern-faced personage was confronting him. His garb was not at all like any police uniform Rinpoche was familiar with, but his posture and expression left small room for doubt, even before he spoke.

"I am Space Detective Carstairs. Nixy Anangaranga-Jones, I arrest you on a charge of impersonating Nixy Anangaranga-Jones. You are not obliged to think anything, but whatever you do think will be mind sucked and analyzed for evidence of intent."

"Now just a second!"

Rinpoche had been about to say that. Someone had beaten him to it. A woman, by the voice.

He was in some kind of enormous room with indistinct walls a long way off. Soft bluish radiance made him feel as though he were inside a fluorescent light tube. A stern-faced personage was confronting him. Her garb was not at all like any police uniform Rinpoche was familiar with, but her posture and expression left small room for doubt, even before she spoke.

"I am Space Detective Blue. Nixy Anangaranga-Jones, I arrest you for evading the tax due on your sex-change operation. You are not obliged to think anything, but whatever you do think will be mind sucked and analyzed for evidence of intent."

"Now just a second!"

Rinpoche had been about to say that. Someone had beaten him to it. A man, by the voice.

"*So* sorree," murmured a polite but casual voice, different from any of the previous ones. "There has been a trivial episode of concertinaing and superloop. If you meet yourself as a result, it is a legal requirement that both of you run do not walk to the nearest dumper, passage via which will automatically eliminate the duplicate, or the original as the case may be. Failure to comply will render you liable to disintegration on sight or on site, whichever is the sooner. This is a complimentary service of Yelignuman Enterprises LGC."

Whereupon, in a single instant, everything became clear. Rinpoche found himself saying under his breath:

"As though it weren't bad enough to be thinking all the time in parentheses! Now here I am living in the stinking things!"

"The computers suggest that we do WHAT?"

SIX

THE EARTH MOVED BUT I DON'T THINK IT WAS FOR ME

"WHAT DO YOU MEAN WE CAN'T ADD THE GREAT CHI-cago Fire to our re-enactment? Gangsters are all very well in their way, but there's nothing like a good disaster to drag in the punters."

"Sorry. Out of the question. It'd take us over budget. In any case, where would you find a cow to kick the lamp?"

Slowly registering one another's presence, the two detectives exchanged glares. Detective Blue was the first to speak.

"What have you been told she's wanted for, John?"

"Impersonating an explan. You?"

"Tax evasion on a sex-change op."

"Ah!" Carstairs brightened. "That explains why she looks like a man. So when did this operation take place?"

"Never!" Rinpoche shouted.

They cast disdainful glances at him.

"You keep out of it, Nixy," ordered Blue. "This is police business."

"Right!" Carstairs barked. "Okay then, Sue: which of us is going to take her in—or him, I guess I should say?"

"I guess it depends on which of the offenses was committed first."

"Comet dust! It depends on which of them was more serious."

"Comet dust yourself! Priority is all. The evasion of tax—Just a moment." Sue Blue frowned, apparently listen-

ing to the air like Harry in the helicopter. In a changed
voice she said, "That's odd. I don't seem to have a date for
her operation."

"It wouldn't matter if you had," Carstairs retorted.
"Changing sex sounds to me like a clumsy attempt to es-
cape the consequences of impersonating an Anangaranga-
Jones."

Sue Blue's eyes widened.

"You mean—?"

"Yes! Those Anangaranga-Jones! Ziz!"

"Hah! No wonder you're so anxious to snatch her from
under my nose! You hope arresting her will make you famous, don't you?"

"How low can you stoop?" Carstairs cried. "That was a
blow below the belt! For that, I may just ask the Chief Bureaucrat to decide which of us is to take her in—take *him*
in, I mean."

"Neither of you!" This time Rinpoche managed a roar.
Whether or not his emotions were back to normal, he could
at least give the impression that they were. "Because I'm
not Nixy whatever, and I never have been! I don't know
who she is, I don't know where she is, and I don't damned
well care! But *you* ought to!"

Taken aback by his forcefulness, they blinked uncertainly.

"Uh . . . why?" Carstairs ventured.

"Because that's who you were sent to arrest! Now you're
wasting time on the wrong person while this—this das-
tardly criminal may for all you know be fleeing the planet!"

He was rather pleased with that touch of contemporary
color. Not bad, he thought, for a wreck who had only been
woken up this morning, especially one who hadn't yet had
lunch or even breakfast.

"Now just a second!" Carstairs took a pace forward. "If
you're not Nixy Anangaranga-Jones, who are you?"

"John, you're dropping your guard!" Sue Blue warned.
"The point is, we know she's Nixy, and we can prove it!"
From a pocket she pulled an instrument Rinpoche did not

recognize that hummed and twinkled. "We have the complete list of the tour party, and the only one unaccounted for is her, *capisc'*?"

"Right!" Carstairs exclaimed with relief. He produced a pocket device in his turn and leveled it at Rinpoche's right eye. Like the one Spotch had used, it emitted a flash so short as barely to be perceptible. "A sex-change operation doesn't alter your retinal patterns, so if you thought you were going to get away with it—"

His face fell.

"Ah, shit," Sue Blue muttered. "How have you fouled up this time?"

"Fouled up?" Carstairs echoed. "Not me! The stinking computers! Know what they just told me?"

"Out with it!"

"According to police records this is Guido Sansepolcro Verdi! Who died back in the twenty-first century! Except that this very day it's been reported that he isn't actually dead!"

There was a gloomy pause. At length Sue Blue brightened.

"Well, in that case can't we book him for impersonating a corpse?"

With a snap of his fingers: "Damn' right! Nixy Anangaranga-Jones, I arrest you—"

"No, no, *no*! You've just been told that his real name is Verdi!" Sue Blue shouldered her colleague aside. "Guido Sansepolcro Verdi—"

"I am not called Verdi!" Rinpoche howled. "Why the hell can't you just let me finish my lunch? I'm starving! And it did smell so good," he concluded under his breath.

"No!" the detectives exploded as one.

"Then I demand to see a lawyer!"

"Lawyer?" Carstairs echoed, and gave a sardonic chuckle. "Who do you think you are, one of those billionaires in the tour group? If you could afford a lawyer—"

Sue Blue, who seemed to have been consulting computers again, prodded him in the ribs and whispered something. He turned pasty pale.

"He's worth *how* much?"

And, too impatient to wait for a reply, listened to the air for a moment. Gradually his jaw sagged open.

"Does that mean he actually is an Anangaranga-Jones? One of that family so rich they bought an entire solar system?"

"Oh, you're such a void!" Sue Blue sighed. "You've just been told he's not! He's really called Verdi but chooses to be known as Gibbs. The point is, though, he can afford a lawyer, so if you want to push ahead with this deal, you better let him call one, huh? Me, I don't mess with lawyers. *I* don't want to spend the rest of my allotted wrangling over who did what and with which and to whom!"

She vanished. So, with a look of infinite regret, did Carstairs.

And there Rinpoche was back in the restaurant . . . where the tablecloths were spattered with juice and gravy and spilt wine, the flowers had wilted, the air smelled of exotic herbs and spices, and everyone else, even the *revanchiste* dinosaur, was being urged toward the exit by the man and woman waving yellow flags.

Hey! Don't go without me! And don't I get any lunch?

The words died unspoken on Rinpoche's lips. After all, he didn't belong to the tour party. And, lost and lonely though he was—

Oh, shit.

There were drawbacks about regaining his normal emotions. He had just discovered one of them. Realization of his true predicament had networked his abdomen with invisible electrodes and he badly needed—*now!*—to disappear.

Miraculously, his eye was caught by a group of signs at the far end of the room: *His—Hers—Its.*

He ran.

When he returned, the restaurant was empty—to the extent that the furniture had vanished—except for the man and woman with the yellow flags. The former was saying, "We counted them in, and there were forty-eight; I can swear to that."

On the verge of eruption: "Yes, Zoltan, but we just counted them out, and there were only forty-seven, right? And what's worst of all, the one that's missing is richissimo, and I mean richississimo—"

Zoltan tugged her arm, looking over her shoulder. "Here he comes."

"He?" she started to object, but he ignored her, striding toward Rinpoche.

"Please come this way! We are overdue for our visit to Gold Rush California, so—Oh."

Rinpoche was about to ask whether he could get lunch on arrival when the alarm on Zoltan's face penetrated. "Is something wrong?" he demanded.

"Your—uh—costume is inappropriate to the epoch."

Rinpoche had been too distracted by the detectives attempting to arrest him to register that he was, somehow, out of his silk dress and back in the clothes he had been given at the cryonut vault.

"Not another foul-up!" the woman moaned. "I never knew a tour like this! Whatever can go wrong is going wrong! The suits for compensation will last into the next universal cycle!" She clasped her head in both hands and swayed back and forth.

Zoltan, face crumpling like wet brown paper, put an arm around her shoulders to comfort her, though his next words were the reverse of heartening, for he said, "It's worse than that, Georgina dear. Things are going wrong that *can't* go wrong."

Hastily, not wanting to cause unnecessary problems, Rinpoche said, "Look, don't you have some means of—of disguising people like the dinosaur I was sitting next to? Or making them invisible? If you think I'm not appropriately dressed, I wouldn't mind if you sort of—well—concealed me, and just let me watch what's going on."

They cheered up instantly, beaming.

"You mean it?" Zoltan exclaimed. "Why, that's wonderful! You are living proof what they say about the hyper-rich cannot be true. Well, not for all of them."

"What do they say?"

Georgina replied. "That they are selfish, arrogant, inconsiderate, greedy, lazy, and jealous."

"And contemptuous," Zoltan put in. "Don't forget contemptuous. But you, though"— He turned to Rinpoche. —"you have persuaded me of what I could never previously accept: the notion that some at least of the hyper-rich are no less human than the rest of the species." His voice was quavering with emotion. "May I shake your hand?"

"Uh . . ."

It had already been seized and was being pumped up and down with vigour while Georgina looked on cynically. Rinpoche still could not make up his mind whether these two were genuinely human, or simulacra, or Yelignese in disguise like Ghoulart. But they were most convincing.

"When you've quite finished," Georgina hinted.

"Now we shall share the experience of California in 1849 at the time of the Gold Rush."

There was something amiss with the commentary, like listening to a badly tuned radio station . . . except that, disturbingly, the message was being delivered directly inside his head and included images that functioned like footnotes apart from being visual, olfactory, and even visceral. When sourdough was mentioned he felt his belly gratifyingly full but of a horrid mess he could remember choking down, even though he never had.

"You will see how gold was panned from muddy water flowing along wooden troughs called flumes. You will learn how it felt to stand knee-deep in a chilly stream with sodden leather boots on, growing more and more miserable, until suddenly your skilled manipulation of the pan separates a gold nugget from the sand and silt. The weight of the nugget will of course depend on your tour grade. Don't you feel sorry now that you opted for a Grade Two or Three tour, when you could have gone home with a nugget weighing a full hundred grams?"

Pause.

"You are reminded that you will be required to declare your nugget at Customs when departing Earth. For a small extra charge . . ."

Rinpoche, who had no slightest interest in departing Earth with or without a golden souvenir, discovered at this point that he could to a limited extent pick and choose among the data being infused into his brain. He realized he could look at slanting muddy roads, too rough to be called streets, down which (and now he could feel it, too!) trickled cold streams of rain—

Just a second. Are these streets, or are they flumes?

A calm voice said, "What you are witnessing is of course a cerebrelectrical impression cohering many aspects of the physicality that you shall encounterize very shortly. The integraliciousness of the transmissitude necessiticates concretion, as you humans would say."

Huh? Oh! I suppose that has to be a Yelignese talking! An alien!

But by this time he had absorbed the clear impression that whether or not the transmissitude had been concreted (and there was no sign of any of these roads being paved or even cobbled) this place that he took for a re-enactment zone was in fact tolerably convincing, even though the buildings—mostly stores offering provisions and mining tools, plus a few saloons and cheap lodging houses—looked as though they had been assembled elsewhere, then set down more or less randomly on their designated sites. Two of them were definitely back to front.

On the other hand . . . Where precisely gold had been found to spark the Gold Rush, he couldn't remember, but he could well believe that just the kind of bewhiskered men he could see trudging up and down these hills in slouch hats and shabby coats, their pants and boots crusted with mud, might have been lured here to defy privation in the

hope of striking it rich. The sole really conspicuous flaw
was the fact that everything was tinted sepia, as though
someone had assumed that photographs from the period
were in accurate color.

What exactly, though, was the experience that members
of a tour group like this had paid so much for? ("Interstellar
travel isn't cheap even with a Duckman's Dumper!")
Was it truly so important to stand, as the commentary indicated,
in cold, dirty water waiting to pan out a nugget
whose size and price had already been agreed? That could
hardly constitute a welcome surprise, or a surprise of any
kind.

Well, maybe it offered insight into the past . . .

The commentary seemed to end. He glanced around. He
found himself among the other tourists, none of whom appeared
to be aware of him (and that was as agreed, which
was fine, except that he still hadn't had any lunch), but all
of whom were in appropriate costume: either like the miners
he had glimpsed a few moments ago; or—less
adventurously—in high hats and frock coats and silk cravats
held in place with diamond pins, imitating bankers,
merchants, and gamblers; or, if female, in Quaker bonnets
and plain ankle-length gowns or risqué bare-shouldered
dresses over corsets like the garb he himself had so resented.

But those memories whirled and swirled into oblivion like
dreams washing down the plug hole of his morning bath.
For they had arrived in what could only be a saloon of the
Old West: planked floor, rough-hewn walls, bar inaccurately
planed (no barman would risk trying to slide a mug of beer
along that splintery surface! Full marks for once to the
Yelignese or those who had advised them), and the most
beautiful girl in the world—no, in the galaxy!—had just
marched in and was glaring at him despite his theoretical invisibility.

Oh, there was no mistaking that golden face, those luminous
eyes, that torrent of dark hair! Even though the rest of
her was clad in buckskin shirt, canvas jeans, huge fleecy

chaps that made her waddle wide astride, and embossed high-heel boots with jingling spurs.

Not to mention—or more exactly, now to mention, if a trifle late—a leather gunbelt beset with cartridges and a holster from which she had just snatched a businesslike albeit pearl-handled Colt forty-four.

"So you're the one!" she snarled in a voice like diamond dust on velvet soaked in olive oil, that made Rinpoche's skin crawl in the most delectable of ways: *yum yum more please more!* "You're the hoot owl who's been hornswoggling my visit and ruining my memories for Gramps!"

She pulled the trigger. The gun flashed. Reflexively Rinpoche winced before realizing he had felt nothing, nor was he bleeding, so he had time to wonder why this incredibly lovely—uh—*woman* (because if Spotch was anyone to go by she could be a centenarian) should want to shoot him except on general antimale principles.

And how had she pierced his promised invisibility?

Shrugging, various members of the tour group began to mutter about value for money, with special emphasis on the element of surprise. The collapse of the grandstand at Holyrood, they allowed, had been within the terms of the brochure, but this was frankly disappointing. The dinosaur emerged from a holograph that disguised him as a whiskey drummer to hold forth about the evolutionary inferiority of homo the sap, thus provoking a shouting match with some of the humans, while the remainder flinched away.

Meantime Zoltan was wringing his hands and moaning, "Oh, Miss Anangaranga-Jones! Just when one had begun to imagine that being hyper-rich did not necessarily entail being an utter cow—if you don't know what a cow was please ask—you have to go and do this!"

Rinpoche started, forgetful of the fact that she had just fired a pistol at him. She—this amazingly beautiful lady— *she* was the Nixy Anangaranga-Jones in clothes meant for whom he had been dressed by machines devised by aliens that on Ghoulart's testimony had no counterpart of sex? Seemingly: yes!

Certainly it was she who, having cast aside her gun on realizing it was useless, was striding toward him (in fact she was lumbering because of her enormous chaps, but somehow she made even that ungainly cowpoke's gait seem graceful) with the firm intention, not cancelable even by whoever or whatever was in charge of this tour group, of slapping him on both cheeks, first with her left hand, then with her right: *blap, BLAP!* Following which she stepped back, panting, her expression bitter, rubbing her palms together because she had hit Rinpoche so hard it hurt her, too.

Her eyes had the tints of lapis lazuli. He hadn't registered the fact before. Now he could relish the spectacular contrast between that jewel color and her golden skin. She was indeed extraordinarily, even amazingly beautiful.

Wow.

If only she were not bestowing such a hate-filled glare on him!

"You were at Holyrood, weren't you?" she rasped.

"Uh—yes!" he admitted, flinching under her flame-thrower gaze.

"And before that you were at Cuzco, and before that—"

"Hang on! I don't even know where Cuzco is!"

But his protest fell on ears not deaf but blocked. He could read it in her expression.

On my first day in this derangement of a future age I see, then I meet, the loveliest woman I could possibly have dreamed of. She thinks I'm responsible for—

What? Well, it would at least be worth asking. Before he could do so, however:

"Admit it was you!" Nixy shouted, and stamped her right boot.

As though the stamp had been a signal, the ground began to shudder. The tour group, not excluding Zoltan and Georgina, exchanged startled glances.

Another temblor followed, this time strong enough to shake glasses and bottles off the crude shelves behind the bar. Bewildered, Georgina whispered to Zoltan loudly enough for Rinpoche to overhear, "But the earthquake isn't due this week! This is the wrong setup!"

Zoltan shrugged. "Like I told you, things are going wrong that cannot possibly go wrong. Here's just one more case in point."

The ground shifted like a ship's deck in a rough sea. The rear wall of the saloon, bar and all, creaked outward, leaving the rafters of the upper story tilting at a dangerous angle. Above was a bedroom; one leg of a brass bedstead, complete with pink ruffled valance, was suddenly visible hanging over the edge of what had been a level floor, while a washstand with a china bowl and ewer slid past and crashed to the ground outside.

Outside . . .

The whole visible area was shivering. At first the motion was vague, like a gelatin dessert wobbling on its way to table. Next it became definite, like ground coffee being tapped down in a storage jar to cram in the entire contents of a packet. Then it became vigorous, as though the hills were bread dough and the baker was kneading them from *underneath*. At this stage people poured out of the buildings with cries of alarm, many of them in dishabille, one man madly waving a cutthroat razor hot on the heels of another with his face half covered in white lather, as though enacting a homicidal maniac and his victim.

Finally the quake turned violent, and the hills began to slide down their own lower slopes.

Most of the tourists watched in dead silence, but there were exceptions, including the woman who had complained about having to convey food to her own mouth. She said after a few seconds, "I don't think much of this! Who wants to see a bunch of shacks fall down, when they look like it would have happened anyway come the next light breeze?"

"Madam," Zoltan blurted, darting to her side, "I do assure you this is fully in keeping with our declared policy of always offering the unexpected to our esteemed clientele!"

The woman scowled, while a man standing a little apart

with the immemorial air of one hoping not to be identified as his wife's husband affected to be paying no attention.

"You certainly have done that!" she snorted. "We came here particularly to be blown up at Hiroshima. Didn't we, Geronimo?"—this to the man, who acknowledged their relationship with a resigned nod. "It was emphasised in all your ads. And what did we find when we arrived? You'd discontinued it. You'd discontinued it!"

"Well—uh—that is in fact so," Zoltan admitted miserably. "To be frank, our clients kept saying they were disappointed with the atom-bomb experience. It was over too quickly. And if we moved them from Ground Zero to the periphery, where they could experience severe burns and long-term radiation sickness, they couldn't watch the actual explosion without being blinded, which sort of spoiled the effect."

"However," Geronimo said in the soft but steely tone of one who is being driven to the limit of endurance, "they do now offer the chance to enjoy an *auto-da-fé* in Spain. I think you should try it, my dear. It involves being tied to a wooden stake, surrounded by faggots, and burned alive."

Glad to find one of the customers quoting his sales talk, Zoltan nodded vigorously.

"Yes, indeed! Many of our masochistic clients find it greatly superior to being atom-bombed!"

"What do you think I am?" the woman fumed. "Surrounded by faggots? I have nothing against the poor, confused—"

Thrru-u-u-ump.

A noise like a clumsy drumroll merged into another resembling the sound of a mass of wet laundry being tossed on a table—a *large* mass, as it might be clean bedding for a regiment of infantry or an averagely populous residential street. The floor canted, fortunately away from the wall that had collapsed. Yelling, the tour group half stumbled, half tumbled, into a confusion of bodies. The dinosaur's voice box could be heard above the general tumult:

"Isn't this just what you'd expect on a planet run by mammals? I mean, what a!"

A pause. Then the same voice said, "Regret. Last word not in vocabulary. Request synonym or alternative."

But Rinpoche had stopped listening. Vivid memories of the recent past, so improbable that it had taken him until now to realize that such events had really happened, were bringing him gradually around to acceptance of the fact that the most beautiful woman he had ever seen was clinging to his arm and muttering reluctant thanks for having saved her from slamming straight into the end wall of the saloon and very likely—for others had gone that way—through its window into the cascade of mud now slathering down the street.

Bringing his other arm up to join the first, he cleared his throat.

"I still don't know where Cuzco is."

The ground shook again, and another thousand tons of brown ooze slid past the window.

"To be perfectly honest," Nixy said after a pause, "I'm none too sure myself. I keep meaning to check with my Hypermem, but if I use it too often it gives me headaches. What does it matter, though? Gramps is going to be so mad I might as well give up right now."

Somewhere nearby, Georgina could be heard shouting at invisible authorities: "What the hell do you mean by triggering a quake while the Gold Rush layout is in place?"

"Not good to let the clientele realize the couriers are panicking," Nixy muttered. "Tourists may panic—in fact I've realized that that's what a lot of them book their tours for, to inject a bit of ersatz terror into their drab and predictable existences. But it's unseemly for the couriers . . . Excuse me."

Straightening, she pushed away Rinpoche's arms. Pity.

"Sorry I tried to shoot you," she went on, not looking at him. "Though naturally I'm insured eleven ways from x cross y, so by now you'd be none the worse. But for a moment I was sure it must be you who's sabotaging this tour just because I'm on it. I'm getting desperate! Gramps is going to be positively volcanic! If not you, though, then who? Some gang of anti-Gramps demonstrators? How could they be that well organized? And why in all of space did you pretend to be me, so that they left me behind at Holyrood and I had to make my own way here, picking up this ridiculous outfit on the way?"

"Why?" Rinpoche babbled. "Well—uh—it's a long story!"

Inside his head a sarcastic voice warned: *Don't exaggerate. It only started this morning.* This time, however, the voice was at least his own.

Providentially, Zoltan was bellowing in Georgina's support: "Whatcher mean you didn't? Gold Rush Frisco is sliding into the Bay! How are we supposed to get the suckers to the flumes and away with their gold in time for Vegas at twenty hundred local without a timeshift that will take us over budget?"

At which exact moment a mudslide engulfed the building. Rinpoche expected it to flood in through the window they stood next to, or at least the gap left by the collapse of the opposite wall, and barely suppressed a cry of alarm as darkness fell.

Nothing of the kind, of course, happened, and by the time out-of-period fluorescent lights came on the other tourists *(hang on! I'm not a tourist!)* were muttering to one another about how much better things were organized on Mesklin or Cannis where, if they provided an avalanche or an earthquake, they did it on the grand scale.

"Once again we uphold our promised element of the unpredictable!" bellowed Zoltan in a desperate attempt to stop the rot.

Gritting her teeth, Nixy said, "If I'd known it was going to be like this, I'd never have let Gramps talk me into coming here—"

Georgina shouted at the pitch of her lungs, which was considerable.

"Gentlebeings! You must forgive the setbacks that have

plagued our tour. One thing we couldn't take precautions against was deliberate, malicious sabotage—and as my colleague just said this is yet another proof of the unpredictability of Earth, unique in the galaxy! We have sent for police to arrest the guilty party!"

And here, emerging from the air, came Carstairs and Blue.

In unison they announced, "Nixy Anangaranga-Jones, it has been determined that your presence and your presence alone can account for the problems afflicting this tour group. I hereby arrest you for trying to undermine Earth's tourist industry!"

Whereat Blue advanced on Nixy .... and Carstairs on Rinpoche.

"*Me* sabotage the tour?" the girl exploded. "You think I'd risk making Gramps disinherit me? What comet dust! I've heard about this sort of damfoolishness. In the ads they always claim it's part of the charm of Old Earth. Bit different when you're on the receiving end, I can tell you! Right now I wish I were anywhere but here."

"Me, too," Rinpoche said from the bottom of his heart and the side of his mouth as the detectives reached out to clamp on their captives' arms what looked like perfectly traditional handcuffs, one ring of each being already secured around their own wrists. Behind them, though, he could make out something rather odd. Very difficult to look at. Vertical and approximately door shaped. It reminded him of what he had passed through on leaving Holyrood.

Is it conceivable that I can grant Nixy's wish?

What if Blue and Carstairs had neglected to disconnect, or cancel, or whatever, the means by which they had arrived here?

Action followed thought without delay. He seized the open rings of both handcuffs and locked them together. Then with a sharp tug he pulled the detectives off balance. Howling, they skidded down the slanting floor. The rest of the tourists had just about regained their feet, or whatever

else they used to get about on. The impact of the detectives
laid them low again, skittle fashion.

Nixy said in a flat voice, "Oh, terrific. We are now of-
ficially evading arrest. Gramps is going to go fissionable
when he finds out. So it would definitely be better if he
didn't—though I guess I'll have to notify one of our
lockhards. Well, in for an asteroid . . . Come on!"

She dragged Rinpoche by the nearer hand toward that
unfocusable waver in the air. An instant later, there they
weren't.

"The computers suggest that we do WHAT?"

SEVEN

IN FULL POSSESSION OF THE CONFIDENCE OF A TRICKSTER

"Hey, Captain! What are those ships ahead of us?"

"The Pinta, the Niña, and the Santa Maria."

"But you said this was the Pinta!"

"So she is."

"Then what are the ships behind?"

"Strictly, you know, you should say astern . . . Well, abaft the port beam is the Santa Maria, and the Niña is lying to starboard, and there in the distance you can make out the Pinta, followed by the—"

"This is outrageous! What I seek is to retrace Columbus's path across the mysterious and solitary ocean! The psychological validity of the experience will be ruined by doing it as one among a horde!"

"Madam, we have kept our promise to the letter. It's scarcely our fault that the Yelignese have licensed a hundred and fifty fleets this year."

"That's odd," Rinpoche found himself saying.

Meantime an animate object somewhat resembling three dish mops and a plumber's friend walked—uh—*ambled* through him, aiming a loud and mostly comprehensible complaint at what seemed to be a clerk behind what seemed to be a reception desk in what seemed to be a hotel lobby except it was also outside on a busy street and at the same time inside—uh—somewhere or conceivably something altogether else. Rinpoche had to swallow hard despite the emptiness of his belly.

"Compartment would be satisfactory," the creature declared in a rasp like unoiled gears, "but repetitious intrusion upon privacy renders it inverse. Moreover, untouchability of possessions—"

"Sir, or madam, or your thinginess as the case may be," broke in a human voice with the same tone of incipient desperation as Rinpoche had heard from Zoltan and Georgina, "the 'compartment' referred to is not the room we assigned you. That, duly privatical, still awaits."

"The locality is improper?"

"Just so, your ititude." If it had been possible to hear someone perspire, sweat would have resounded in the tremulous voice. "A fact you would be aware of had you bothered to study the data furnished by your travel agency. On human planets hotel accommodation is accessed by using a 'key.' I hazard a guess that you did not employ the one we provided in order to enter the compartment in question."

There was a brief silence. Sounding a trifle abashed, the alien said, "Conceded 'key' did not prove indispensable."

"That is explicationed by the fact that you have been occupying the ground-floor excretory facilities intended for human females. Now *do* permit us to guide you to the same location as your belongings, about whose elsewheracy you have been vocalicising . . . Front!"

All of which appeared to eventuate in the brief moment it had taken Nixy to hear and react to his comment. "What is?" she responded, and before he could answer interrupted herself. "I've got to get rid of these horrible things! I'm sure they weren't even authentic for the Gold Rush, while as for anywhere else . . . ! What's odd?"

Meantime tossing aside her chaps with a gasp of relief, and following them with her boots, belt, and gun.

"I have this weird impression," Rinpoche said, "that I've been sent here to arrest somebody. And that my name is Carstairs."

Peeling off her buckskin shirt, Nixy tugged her hair loose from its collar. "Oh, you just hit a psychoresonance. I got a whiff, too. It wasn't meant for you, not unless you really are a Carstairs. Who are you, anyhow? Those crazy detectives addressed you and me by the same name, which is ridiculous because there's only one person in the galaxy called Nixy Anangaranga-Jones. Gramps made sure."

Unsnapping her jeans, she discarded them as well. That was all she had been wearing. Stretching to tiptoe, she uttered a gasp.

"*That's* better. Come on, don't you have a name?"

But Rinpoche was goggle-eyed at the spectacle of her bare body, it being if possible even more amazing than the clad version, and tongue-tied by the realization that she had just stripped to the buff in what appeared to be an extremely public place.

Not that he had as yet had time to take in any details, but even from the corners of his eyes and ears he had become aware that a lot of people—or beings—were milling back and forth in the immediate vicinity.

He looked about him. Blinked. Looked again. He had been right. An enormous number of events involving a huge number of individuals were going on around and even through them, though no one—moreover, no thing—seemed aware of their presence. In passing he noticed that a few, not many but a few, were as underdressed as Nixy and nearly as beautiful. None, however, could match her superlative figure.

"Where are we?" he demanded.

"In the lobby of a Hotel Interdimensional. I've no idea which."

"And why isn't anyone taking notice of us?"

"We're in a police watchwarp, what else?" she said impatiently, and shook her head in such a way that her mass of black hair composed itself into a demure covering down to the waist, complete with a neatly braided self-belt. Exposure of the rest didn't seem to bother her.

"How on Earth would I know? I never heard of such a thing!"

"Oh!" Those lapis lazuli eyes turned on him with the

brilliance of searchlights. "You're a wreck, of course. I think you said."

"And you're not," he returned in what he hoped was the proper tone to emphasize the double meaning and imply a compliment.

"You're plobbing." She tugged her garment of hair into a more comfortable alignment. "Well, I guess I ought to thank you for getting me away from the Frisco earthquake, though when Gramps finds out I've missed the Vegas evening he'll hit guncrit. It was something he particularly wanted me to recall, for sentimental reasons, he said." She bit her lip. "Maybe I ought to rejoin the tour in spite of all. What do you think—uh . . . ? You still haven't told me your name."

Numbly he did so, automatically adding that she should call him Rin if it was easier. From her increasingly casual tone he had begun to fear that now she was here—probably back here, for she seemed to have relaxed as though on finding herself among familiar surroundings—she was going to resume some previous course, and he was never going to see her again. A snatch of dialogue between the detectives, clearly enough heard but scarcely understood, flickered through memory: some reference to her family buying a solar system . . . ?

But Nixy was not really listening. Her attention had been caught by something else. She pointed at a door that was opening alongside the reception desk. A pale-faced, youthful-looking man (but, of course, that meant nothing now) was emerging from it surreptitiously, adjusting a suit of lemon-yellow loops and tassels. He also wore a purple hat like an overgrown grape. Glancing from side to side, he appeared to conclude the coast was clear. He closed the door and sauntered away with an elaborately casual air.

"I think," Nixy mused, "we'd better get out of here. Something tells me police are apt to show up at any moment—No, that's silly of me. This is immigration business, not police. Ah, here they come."

Two individuals blocked the path of the man in yellow.

Both of them wore stark white siren suits with hoods thrown back. One was human, and his skin was light brown. The other's was gray, and despite being bipedal he (it?) sported a three-foot trunk and large fanlike ears.

"What in the world?" Rinpoche whispered.

"You are a wreck, aren't you? I never heard anyone say that before except on history tapes. But"—glancing at him—"I thought whenever they thawed people out they fed them basic orientation data."

Rinpoche shrugged. "They didn't give me any," he muttered.

"Hm! Wouldn't care to be in your epidermis. How are you getting along?"

"Badly. I didn't try and take your place in the tour group, by the way. It was just—well, I was awfully hungry, and the scent . . ."

She gave an astonished laugh. "Was that really why? Oh, I can understand very well. It's an old trick but a good one, faking everybody's favorite food smells to make them hurry up and not delay the tour . . . What's wrong?"

"That—uh—person with the trunk: what planet is he from?"

"Earth."

"Earth? But—" A deep breath. "Okay, who is he? Or what?"

"A remembrancer, of course. You see, all the enterprising people left for deep space, so the ones who stayed behind made a terrible mess of everything. When the Yelignese took over they realized humans needed all the help they could get. Hypermems like mine cost as much as an asteroid, but elephants used to be noted for good memory, so they recuperated their genes from a museum or wherever."

"So what does a remembrancer do?"

"Remembers the law and quotes it, what else? By the way, you mustn't think I know everything about Earth, but after I got my Hypermem I did study up a bit before leaving home. Like I said, I can't use it too often or I get headaches. Matter of getting adjusted, I guess."

"I see . . . But what exactly is going on?"

She glanced toward the man in yellow, who was now engaged in vigorous argument with the dark man and the remembrancer.

"Looks as though he's about to have his credit docked. I can guess what he tried to do."

"What?"

"Evade the immigration tax. Probably using a twiddler."

"A what?" said Rinpoche foggily. And in the same instant, quite as loudly as his voice, his stomach uttered a rumble of complaint. Nixy stared at him.

"I thought you ate my lunch, with the tour group!"

"No," he sighed. "They took it away. I've had nothing since a machine stuck a tube down my throat while I was being revived."

She hesitated. "Well, I guess I could buy you a snack, though for somebody so rich Gramps is awfully mean."

"Apparently I have plenty of credit. I'm not sure why, but someone told me I'm registered as creditworthy with all the computers on Earth. Trouble is, nobody has told me how to take advantage."

Suddenly Nixy broke into a broad grin. "Don't look so miserable!" she chid. "If that's your only problem, I can fix it in a nanosec. Compared with my kind of trouble, it's nothing at all. Come on!"

How it happened he couldn't discern, but a moment later they were actually in the hotel lobby instead of observing it from a place that wasn't so much outside as alongside or possibly in between it and a multiplicity of elsewheres, and heading for a trellised wall that bore the word RESTAURANT in several thousand scripts. They passed the man in yellow who, his expression aggrieved, had given up trying to argue with his interlocutors and was resignedly allowing them, as Nixy explained, to deduct a large sum from his credit.

"What was that you said about a twiddler?"

"Just a moment. Two please, Tessa! Though I shan't actually be eating"—this to a busty blond maîtresse d' in kaross, bead bands, and elbow tufts, carrying an assegai and a shield of imitation ox hide with colored decorations. Around her head played a halo identifying her as TESSA RACK. In general she was very convincing. Had Rinpoche not noticed how she came alert at their approach, like Wrong Ghoulart, he could easily have mistaken her for human.

"There will be a delay of four to six minutes, but if you wish I can seat you at once in Siberia."

Huh?

"Where are we?" Nixy asked, adding aside to Rinpoche, "That's the trouble with the Interdimensional chain— they're identical down to molecular level."

"Is that how you knew to call her Tessa?"

"No, I read her halo, silly! . . . Well?"

"This is Vancouver, ma'am."

"Really? Hmm! Rin, can you wait a little bit longer? I need a pee anyway— Just a second! Tessa, you have wherever facilities, don't you?"

"Our clientele are naturally free to relieve themselves where and when they feel the need," Tessa Rack assured her. "However, I must advise you that on Earth, such a convenience is classed as unlicensed exportation of water and carbon and attracts a surcharge."

"There would be," Nixy said caustically. "You people seem to have a motto: if it moves, tax it."

"Excuse me, ma'am. I am not a people."

"No, of course not. Sorry. Rin, wait for me here."

"I'd sort of like to do the same."

"See you in a moment, then . . . Over there, see? Like I said, it's always the same in all these hotels."

"Thanks."

Approaching the washroom he encountered the man in yellow again—did rather more than just encounter him, in fact, for they nearly collided in the doorway. Scowling, the yellow one nonetheless reacted with politeness, indicating that Rinpoche should precede him. However, forcing a smile, the latter declined.

"You seem to have had enough trouble for one day," he said. "You go first."

"How right you are!" The man in yellow sighed and went ahead.

It was just as well. Without at least a few moments' warning of what to expect, Rinpoche could easily have screamed.

Invisible hands lifted the man in yellow off his feet and began to remove his clothes and shoes. Instants later, the same thing happened to Rinpoche. It wasn't unpleasant, if not as pleasurable as at Frisco, but it could have been alarming. However, his companion betrayed no discomposure, so he stifled the cry that sprang to his lips.

By the time he was naked he was enclosed by some kind of screen. He felt himself set down gently on a warm resilient floor. A voice invited him to relieve himself; he abruptly found it impossible. There being no response, the words were repeated in a more impatient tone. After another pause, the voice said, "Ah. Assisted service."

Whereupon, all of a sudden, he didn't need to go after all.

A warm, perfumed mist enfolded him. From scalp to soles he was cleansed and massaged by unseen fingers; meantime, a tingling liquid melted bristles from his cheeks and chin. He was dried with a current of warm air, also scented, and his clothes were replaced, impeccably clean. The screen dissipated. He found himself at the exit from the washroom, a marble-effect door with a luminous screen set in it. On the screen were displayed the figures 22000.

And the man in yellow, who had been marginally quicker, was scowling at it. "Not *kind*," he was muttering. "Not kind at all. They might at least have left me the price of an excantation."

Two and two made 22000 in Rinpoche's dismayed mind. So you had to pay to get out of here, did you? But how?

Nixy had promised to explain the way to enjoy his credit but had not yet got around to doing so.

He deliberated for a moment and came to the conclusion that even though she would probably send out a search party if he failed to rejoin her at the restaurant, that was far from guaranteed, so there was no sensible alternative to asking for help.

"Excuse me," he muttered. "I've never been in one of these places before. I didn't realize you have to pay to leave."

"Can you?" the man in yellow said sourly. "Pay, I mean."

"I believe so. At any rate I've been told I have plenty of credit. I'll be pleased to cover your fee as well as mine if you'll be so kind as to explain how I go about it."

"But how can you possibly not know?" was the astonished response.

"I'm a wreck. Thawed out this morning. They didn't give me the usual lecture or whatever."

"A wreck! I see!" The other brightened. "Well, that makes your offer more than just courteous! As a matter of fact, I shall go so far as to term it noble. In the ordinary course of events I assure you I would never impose on a stranger, but on arriving here to pursue some business which, by the by, computer predictions advise me will prove highly profitable, so you may rest assured of the eventual repayment of your loan, inasmuch as Makes-a-Million Kardek—that's a play on my name Maximilian, heh-heh!—honors his debts, no matter how trifling the sum, I had the misfortune to infringe some petty regulation I was unaware of, and was heftily *fined*, mulcted indeed in such a sum that until I complete the initial stage of my next enterprise I shall be unable to purchase sustenance, or indeed even the means of disposing of the unmetabolizable portion of my nutriment, let alone having my attire duplicated in this satisfactory albeit costly fashion. Speaking of my enterprise, I wonder whether you would be interested—"

It took Rinpoche that long to overcome his habitual courtesy and interrupt.

"I," he said meaningly, "am interested in getting out of here and back to the restaurant where my—my girlfriend is waiting."

"Of course, of course. Remiss of me. Well, just present your right eye to this ocular and say in a clear voice, 'Charge both these fees to me.' " He tapped a small black roundel beside the screen.

"What does a person do who's blind in the right eye?" Rinpoche muttered sarcastically, but did as directed. There was the usual brief flash, and the door slid wide.

Darting through it without asking permission to go first, Kardek gave a loud gasp of relief.

"I had visions of being shut in there all day! Or at least until I found someone to take out a message for me. I can't thank you too much."

"That's okay," Rinpoche sighed, striding toward the restaurant where Nixy was already waiting. But Kardek kept up with him.

"Do excuse me! But did I not just hear you make rather an original joke? One of my minor avocations is comparative humoristics, and from experience I can tell you how rare it is to run across a novel witticism. If you'd care to repeat it—"

"I wasn't aware of having said anything particularly funny," Rinpoche countered, on the verge of gritting his teeth.

"Ah, but you did! You asked what a person would do who was blind in the right eye. Black humor, admittedly, but with a certain surreal quality. Now, as I was about to say: if you'd care to repeat it I can arrange, for a trifling fee, to have it copyrighted for all human worlds. You may possibly not have heard of the Pangalactic Bureau of Original Humor, but I assure you that while they cannot, of course, police all verbal instances of the use of a copyrighted joke, they can and most efficiently do police all printed, recorded, taped, or otherwise reproduced and/or dramatized versions. For a nominal fee I would be glad to act for you. Ownership of such a copyright provides a small but welcome addition to one's income. I myself—"

It took Rinpoche that long to figure out what the "joke" was supposed to be. Nixy had said that if she had managed to drill him with her .44 he would have been fixed up in moments and none the worse, which implied that in this day and age no doubt someone who lost an eye simply bought a new one.

Ha ha.

Tessa Rack was standing at Nixy's side, patiently waiting for him to join her. By contrast she herself was impatient to the point of nervousness and kept darting glances in all directions.

"At last! Listen, Rin, I've decided that I really must try and catch up with my tour group in time for the trip to Las Vegas. Gramps set particular store by remembering that place, though he wouldn't say why ... Is something the matter with you?" she added sharply to Kardek, who responded by whipping off his hat and bowing.

"Simply overwhelmed by your loveliness, ma'am!" he exclaimed. "Are you represented by a beauty agency? If not, I can recommend my good friend Llewela Mooksen-Gripes who—"

"Don't tell me, let me guess," Nixy sighed. "You're not as smart as you thought you were. On finding out that you may legally arrive on Earth wherever you like, you procured a twiddler and used it to divert away from one of the official entry points to this hotel, thinking you could easily be overlooked with so many thousands coming and going. What you didn't know was that while it's true you may arrive where you wish, you thereupon have to pay not only entry tax—and that's stiff enough in all conscience—but also the cost of dispatching an immigration officer and a remembrancer to collect it from you, not to mention compensation for wasting duty time on arguing with you. How much did they leave you with?"

Kardek, face reddening, preserved a sullen silence that testified to the accuracy of Nixy's deductions. Enlightened, Rinpoche replied.

"Not even enough to get out of the washroom. I had to pay."

"Really? I don't suppose you insisted on him putting his eye to the ocular before consenting to that act of charity?"

"Should I have?"

"Of course! Goodness, am I glad I don't owe you for anything! You need a—oh, what's that ancient word?—a housemaid! I know his type. It was a person like him that conned Gramps into buying his solar system and landed us in such a mess back home. Not that I can really think of a place like that as home," she added by way of afterthought.

Kardek's manner had totally changed while she was speaking. He burst out in an awestricken tone, "You can't be! But you must be! Is your name by any chance Anangaranga-Jones?"

The maîtresse d' gave a discreet cough. "It will not be possible for me to reserve space for you much longer. There are calls on our restaurant from Great Zimbabwe, Paris, and Rio, all of which are at present nearing capacity, and furthermore we are shortly scheduled to host a convention of Euphemias with three hundred and three thousand members. Please reach a decision."

"I'm starving hungry!" Rinpoche exclaimed.

"And for the pleasure of eating in the company of the lovely Miss Anangaranga-Jones," Kardek declared, "I shall drop—with apologies to you, sir—my little pretence that the immigration officer cleaned me out. I believe in always keeping a line of left-eye credit invulnerable to such depredations."

"But the table requested is only for two," said the simulacrum.

"That's all right," Nixy returned. "These two can have it. Like I said, I'm not eating. In fact, I'm not even coming into the restaurant. I just want to get out of this place. You"—to Kardek—"pay back this poor sap by explaining all about the modern galaxy, hear? And don't try to cheat him again just because he's an ignorant wreck!"

How exactly she could be stuffily dignified while wearing nothing except her hair, and that only to waist level, Rinpoche had no idea, but she managed it magnificently.

"Right! I'll head back to Frisco, *after* I talk to Gramps's lawyers and make sure those damfool detectives don't bother me again. I—"

And precisely as she uttered that last word, there was a sort of shifting: not a sensation easily defined, though it might be compared to the involuntary twitch sometimes experienced when dropping off to sleep, what's also called "going down a step that isn't there." It was followed by a chatter of vague alarm from the main entrance of the hotel. Interpreted into words, it might have equated to that usefully versatile objurgation:

Oh, shit . . .

Sensing rather than realizing something must be wrong, Nixy hesitated. "What's happening?" she demanded of the maîtresse d'.

"There is no reason to be alarmed," was Tessa's reply.

"Don't you believe it!" Kardek exclaimed. He had taken a step back so he had a direct line of sight to the hotel entrance. "We're not here any longer—I mean, not where we were. I guess we could still be on Earth, though I don't think there's an Interdimensional in either of its polar regions, but to me it looks more like Iceworld."

"What?" Rinpoche exploded. "We've traveled to another planet?"

"Not exactly traveled, more sort of been displaced. What happens is, one of the dumpers inverts and transmits itself through itself and takes the immediate surroundings with it. I've heard about it, but I never ran into it before. More of a nuisance than a danger, they say. Trouble is, you have to find out where you are before you can reverse the effect." Kardek passed a small humming drier over his forehead to vaporize sweat, then made the gadget vanish again with the skill of a conjurer. He was probably that as well.

"Well?" Nixy demanded of Tessa Rack.

"The gentlebeing is in essence correct, though as yet our current coordinates have not been established."

"You mean I can't go back to Frisco or even direct to Vegas."

"In essence—"

"That is correct. I see." Nixy sounded furious but under control. "Well, that means you won't be getting any extra customers from Great Zimbabwe or anywhere else for the time being. You'd better seat all three of us. Oh, Gramps will go absolutely nova!"

The maîtresse d' listened to the air for a second, then bowed and invited them to follow her into the interior of the restaurant. Presumably it was decorated in a style antique by contemporary standards, for it looked quite like the sort of places Rinpoche had been used to in his former life: wine-red carpet, deep green wallpaper patterned with a tracery of off-white leaves, booths, cushioned seats, tables of assorted sizes—apart, of course, from the customers, inasmuch as they affected a weird variety of garb from billowing inflated metalescent robes down to painted skin, and a variety of shapes as well. Those creatures ingesting blue and orange spikes while hanging from a sort of overgrown hat stand: were there two of them, or four, or eight? Trying to work it out made him dizzy. Firmly he withdrew his gaze.

And realized that Nixy, holding his arm, was trembling as she accompanied him toward their table. What on Earth (no, one didn't say that any more: one said what in the galaxy) had so undermined her apparent self-possession?

Not that she had been very self-possessed at Frisco when she drew a gun on him, nor at Holyrood, come to that. What could account for these extraordinary changes?

Glancing sidelong, he caught a clue from the way her lips were moving—almost soundlessly, but not quite. He doubted he would have been able to make out what she was whispering before Theodor Surgeon overhauled him, but "all infirmities" apparently included even incipient hearing defects.

"Not again, please not again, please let it not be another of the dreadful things that seem to happen everywhere I go!"

He had been intending to ask what conceivable grounds Blue and Carstairs might have for accusing her of sabotaging Earth's tourist industry. Somehow what she was saying made him feel that this was not the optimal juncture.

Perhaps there might never be one.

"The computers suggest that we do WHAT?"

EIGHT

WOULD YOU BUY A USED PLANET FROM THIS SPECIES?

"Buon' giorno, signore. Scusi—non parlo molto bene l'italiano."

"That's okay, kid. A figure like yours speaks for itself. Set down that load before you do yourself an injury."

"Thanks. Well, my name is Juliet, I mean it is really Juliet, and I've managed to find one of those machines you're after. Here it is. Of course, they went out of date before I was frozen, but I'm sure I can figure out how to work it, provided you can get the ink and paper, and the stencils, of course. I assume you have a typewriter?"

"Now just an everloving moment! What in the galaxy do I need with this pile of scrap iron?"

"You said you wanted Roneos and Juliets to help with your project to turn Verona into the next re-enactment zone. Uh—didn't you?"

. . .

"Lady, I guess you better view that ad again."

Tessa the maîtresse d' surrendered them into the charge of a suave simulacral waiter whose badge identified him as Rockwell Horosho, "but call me Rocky." Having seated them, the latter purred, "In which style would you prefer to review our bill of fare? It can be presented visually or verbally in your choice of script or language, or by direct stimulation of the cortex in such wise that you are actually enabled to pretaste our culinary masterpieces, although I am bound by law to advise you that that option carries a small surcharge, and to warn you that it should on no account be employed in conjunction with an inadequate diet as a substitute for proper nourishment. You may also wish to select an explan rather than a terrestrial cuisine, although I am bound by law to advise you that that option carries a small surcharge. You may also wish to verify that none of the ingredients in any dish you select risks provoking an allergic reaction, although I am bound by law to advise you that that option carries a small surcharge. You may also—"

By this time Rinpoche, hungry though he was, had ceased to pay attention. He was riveted by something happening two tables away. Having obviously just finished an ample meal with a deal of booze, a red-faced man, manifestly an explan, was leading toward the exit a gaggle of sycophants dutifully laughing at a joke he had cracked about the backwardness of Earth, though not as loudly as he was himself.

The rude and patronizing tourist, Rinpoche realized, was a type that hadn't changed and very likely never would.

He reached a table where a human couple were sitting. Both of them were sallow and flat-faced, and clad in fur from top to toe. Rinpoche had just had time to think how much they looked like children's-book caricatures of Eskimos and remember that this hotel was in Canada—or had been until a few minutes ago—when the red-faced man halted and demanded, meaning to be overheard, "Eskimos, aren't you?"

The man glanced up. "One prefers to say Inuit," he murmured. "But it comes to the same thing."

Nudging the nearest of his companions, winking at the rest, the red-faced man roared, "Then show us how you make fire by rubbing noses! Haw-haw-haw-haw-haw!"

He was about to move on when the woman said composedly, "By all means."

Clearly that was the answer he had least been expecting—and the same went for Rinpoche. By now he was staring in shameless fascination.

"Certainly," the man agreed, pushing back his chair and

taking the other by his nearer ear. "Bend over so my wife can reach—that's it!"

The woman half rose, smiling, and brushed her snub nose against the red-faced man's. Sparks followed a crackling sound, and within seconds a wisp of smoke. Clapping his hands to his face, the victim howled!

"Rinpoche!"

What in the world—the galaxy—is going to happen now? And how did she work the trick, anyway?

"Rinpoche!"

Alertly the staff, or perhaps automatic machinery, had drawn a veil around the spectacle. He realized Kardek was shouting at him.

"Rinpoche, what in a black hole is wrong with you?"

"Me?"—with a start. "Nothing."

"No, I mean why aren't you doing anything to help your girlfriend? Look at her! Pale and sweating, hands locked, teeth chattering—she's in shock, and you're just sitting there! We've got to snap her out of it. Waiter, fetch the lady a green veeblefetzer! While you're at it you might as well bring a couple of red ones for me and my friend."

"In a Hotel Interdimensional," Rocky said in a reproving tone, "it is never necessary to 'bring.' If you would kindly move your left elbow not less than eight millimeters—? *Thank* you."

From the smooth dark surface of the table three extrusions arose like time-lapsed mushrooms. Three foaming glasses appeared, one green, two pink, accompanied by an eye-stinging nose-searing aroma partway between spearmint and cayenne pepper.

Nixy moaned aloud.

"Drink this, my dear," Kardek murmured, sidling closer, putting an arm around her shoulders (in just the reassuring manner Rinpoche would have liked to display had his heart not been sinking floorward ever since he began to register the implications of her grandfather buying a whole planetary system: what chance would he stand, an ignorant resurrectee, against her presumable millions of suitors and trillions of crunits?) and presenting the glass to her pale lips—though not before elegantly blowing away the surplus froth: *pff!*

She sipped obediently; she raised her impeccably symmetrical eyebrows; she took a full mouthful and savored it; and at last gulped the entire remaining contents of the glass. Even as the liquid passed her gullet her color reverted to normal, her slumped posture improved, and her eyes widened in impressed astonishment.

"So it's true that Earth can still take you by surprise in ways no other planet can! I'm feeling a hundred times better! And in mere seconds!"

"That's because it reaches the brain via the palatal route," Kardek murmured, setting down her empty glass and reaching for his own. "But I must correct you as to its terrestrial provenance. It so happens that I invented the veeblefetzer on Wing IV in—"

"Excuse me, sir," the waiter interpolated. "As you are no doubt aware, the policy of our hotel chain is one of unchallengeable honesty. I am therefore obliged to remind you that the original veeblefetzer™ was conceived by the sainted founder of our enterprise Their Hoteliness Father/Mother Ninety-Nine-Sri Pugwash-Polski on their home world of Tazenda and actualized by machines programmitationed by him and under her direction, and its efficaciosity whether in red form or in green is a nondubitatious reflectition of love for all beings animate and/or otherwise. Have you deciduated from which menu you prefer to selectify, or would you optioneer that I describerize our daily specials?"

I'm ravenous. I'd settle for practically anything. But against all reason Rinpoche realized he still retained shreds of the silly ambition he had conceived when he first set eyes on Nixy. She, having no intention of eating, was talking. Instead of demanding food, *now*, he forced a smile and made it clear that he was listening.

"—turning up everywhere I go with the most *primitive* means of attracting attention, I mean like banners on poles.

I'm sure some showed up at Holyrood, and I could have sworn I spotted others while I was waiting for you just now. That's why I got so agitated. Of course, it was silly of me because a hotel of this class would never allow its customers to be bothered by people like that. They only do it out of jealousy, of course. I mean if Gramps weren't processing it, the energy from the supernova would be even more randomized, wouldn't it?"

She looked at Rinpoche as though expecting him to reply. Drawing a deep breath, he confessed he hadn't quite followed what she was talking about.

"These protesters, of course! Saying it's unfair for Gramps to buy a whole system when most people can't even afford an asteroid. But I say they must be jealous! Don't you agree?"

Regardless of his true opinion—and anyway he didn't really have one—it behoved him to nod vigorously, which he did, and then took a sip of his red veeblefetzer. It was indeed a very good drink, unlike anything else he could call to mind. He sipped again, nodded approval, and on the grounds that Nixy had done the same without visible harm, on the contrary with apparent benefit, drained the glass.

Time stopped. Inside his head, at least.

All of a sudden he was staring at a dish of something greasy and foul smelling. He recognized it, of course, but he had hoped never to set eyes on it again, let alone tongue. Yet its pervasive aroma was not only clogging his nose, it was fouling his palate.

He reached for his glass. It had disappeared. In its place he found a squat cup containing blackish liquid with a layer of fat on top, from which he remembered taking a generous swig . . .

But Kardek, disdaining knife and fork, was gnawing the meat off a succession of bones dressed with a rich green sauce and taking occasional sips from his veeblefetzer, while chatting animatedly with Nixy. For her part, despite her professed intention not to eat again just now, she was dipping bits of bread—he assumed, although it looked more like a plastic floor-cleaning sponge—into his sauce. Swallowing the latest sippet, she demanded of Rinpoche, "Is something wrong?"

"I didn't order this!" Rinpoche blared.

"Of course not, but when you wouldn't tell Rocky what you did want the hotel naturally supplied what you were most likely to order."

"What?"

Nixy looked bewildered. Kardek, taking care to pass his fingers via an electrically agitated fingerbowl so as to cleanse them, then through a stream of warm air to dry them, laid his hand on the nearer of hers. Soothingly he said, "I'm afraid it must have been the veeblefetzer. It didn't register that he had never before—"

"What?" Rinpoche felt horribly isolated and excluded. Earlier he had resented the dulling of his emotions; now he could have wished the sensation to return, for sheer terror was combining with the revolting blend of brickdust tea with rancid yak butter and broth of "high" yak meat and bone marrow poured over rice also soaked in butter but this time with a massive dollop of salt. Never mind that his forebears—

But it's not true! My ancestors weren't Tibetans! And I don't want ancestors anyway! Have I even now not escaped my legacy of lies?

It was the same sensation he had felt after thawing, the moment he realized he was conscious again, only this time at full blast.

For sanity's sake he strove to alter "have I even now not escaped?" to "when if ever will I escape?", hoping to diminish the hurt.

But it didn't help very much.

The waiter materialized at his side. "Would the honorable Tibetan sir care to considerize alternating sustenance, given that our deductations from his nomenclatic patrimatrimony have fallenized foul?"

"Tibetan?" Kardek said in a puzzled tone. "I never heard of a planet called Tibet."

"Not a planet, voidbrain!" Nixy countered in what Rinpoche felt was far too familiar a tone for someone who only a short time before had been denouncing Kardek as a confidence trickster or worse. "A place right here on Earth. What you need is a Hypermem like mine. I asked Gramps for it specially because it sounded as though it would be ideal for a weird planet like this. It—"

She checked abruptly. There had been another peculiar shifting sensation like the one that had preceded Tessa Rack's admission that the hotel was currently stuck on some other planet.

Kardek said with even greater suavity than before, "I'd be glad to follow your advice concerning a Hypermem, were it not for the fact that you find me, as I indicated earlier, in straitened circumstances. Of course, were you to—"

"Did we just re-engage with Earth?" Nixy broke in, appealing with her eyes to Rocky Horosho.

"No, ma'am," was the regretful answer. "It is naturally the firm intention of us staff, organic and otherwise, to restoricate this hotel to its customary locatition, but as of at present it is still unestablishable what coordinationing definitizes its whereaboutishness."

The effect of a veeblefetzer seemed not to last very long—either that, or far more time than Rinpoche imagined had elapsed while he was under the influence of his—for once again Nixy was trembling. Her beautiful eyes were staring into nowhere, while she clenched and unclenched her fine-boned hands.

"Don't worry," Kardek counseled.

"How can I not?" she retorted. "This is so like the mess I left behind at home!"

"You mean in the system your grandfather bought?"

"Oh, he's not my *grand*father! Of course he isn't! How could anyone become that stinking rich in just one generation? He's my great-great-etcetera what's-it. I just call him

Gramps. So does everybody more than a century younger. He has old-fashioned views about who can call him by his first name."

She hesitated. "Matter of fact," she added in an altered voice, "I'm not sure what his first name is."

Rinpoche cleared his throat after deciding it would not entail the risk of vomiting on the table—though doubtless if he did the mess would disappear before anyone noticed. He deduced this from the fact that his bowls of *tsampa* and rice with yak broth had already vanished.

Trouble was, nothing had replaced them. He cleared his throat a second time.

Up popped Rocky again.

"Bring me something fit to eat!" Rinpoche commanded in what he hoped was an authoritative tone.

The waiter hesitated.

"Sir, I find myself compulsed in obliging to define parameters. Within the compass of terrestrial cuisine alone there are foodstuffs ranging from the simplicity of dry bread to the Inuits' putrid ptarmigan with pheasant droppings, such as was furnished to an adjacent table a scant while ago, or *épinards au beurre à la mode du bon abbé*, both of which in their fully evolved versions require not less than one week's preparation. Naturally, should you opt for such a dish we can timeslow the zone where you are sitting. However, I am required by law to advise you that there is a small surcharge—"

Rinpoche drew a deep breath. "Give me," he ordered slowly and distinctly, "one medium-rare hamburger patty with melted cheese on a lightly toasted sesame-seed bun, plus fried onions, some tomato catsup, a portion of cole slaw, some shredded lettuce, no dressing, and a mug of cold light beer. I imagine you can come up with that!"

Even as he concluded his order he was able to watch it emerging from the surface of the table. Expecting the food to be preceded by its scent, he found his mouth watering, especially since Rocky was saying briskly, "Sir, I must congratulationize you. You are clearly a sophisticational be-ing."

But though the burger lay visibly steaming before him it emitted absolutely no odor, not even from the cheese. His hand, about to snatch it up, hesitated involuntarily.

"You have received," the waiter said, "one nature-identical Customeered SuperKak with garnish in the finalitized version of 2023, precisely duplicatishing the supremal achievement of Big Kak University: a product devoidulated of all and any olfacticory stimulationing."

Rinpoche bit and chewed. It was true. Here was neither smell nor taste, not even from the cheese. He seized the glass of beer that was weeping condensation down its icy sides.

"You have received," Rocky went on, "one nature-identical mug of O'Libya Beer—'It's not water!' The dupli-cationing of these items regretulaciously obligatorizes one to imposify an antiquacy surcharge of eight hundred per-cent. Enjoy your meal!"

Rinpoche felt his jaw drop. Remembering something that although it resembled a burger tasted of even less than saw-dust or blotting paper, which he had just tried to wash away with the only beverage he had ever sampled possessing less flavor than distilled water at room temperature, he was framing grounds for complaint when . . .

When it suddenly dawned on him that Kardek was gaz-ing at him with nothing less than awe.

"Oh, wow!" he said softly. "Even when I was at the top of my bent, even when I pulled off the—Never mind that! But even then, I have to confess, I could never be so free with my credit! I mean, ordering a SuperKak in an Interdimensional without so much as *blinking*!"

"You mean . . ." Rinpoche fumbled for words. "You mean this revolting muck is something special?"

Nixy was leaning forward, eyes wide and lips ajar. All the color had returned to her cheeks, and she was flashing her lashes. As though she had heard nothing of what either man had just said, she pleaded, "May I have a bite? Just one?"

For an instant Rinpoche remembered Spotch, touching him for coffee. At least she thought it was coffee. What else in heaven's name (what in the galaxy) had he not been told that was going to wind him up in all sorts of trouble?

He husked, "You can have the lot as far as I'm concerned."

Nixy reared back her head. "You can't mean it!"

"Why not?"

"But this is *beef*! I mean, there's beef in it. And cattle are extinct, so it all has to be made specially! I mean!"

There was a long pause. During it he gazed at the "food" before him. Visually it was most convincing. It reminded him of the models that used to be displayed in the windows outside Japanese restaurants.

In my own day.

But this was not his own day. It was one strange new day.

And just because someone or something or some alien had neglected to furnish him with proper information when reviving him from freeze, he had done something incredibly and unbelievably stupid.

Hadn't he?

Except that apparently he hadn't. For Nixy's eyes were wide and brilliant as she chomped on his hamburger, and somehow she had laid her other hand on his and forgotten to remove it, as though what he had done had convinced her that he was the sort of person she could safely cultivate because he must be one of the hyper-rich (what was happening to those poor teachers, and the hyper-rich kids they'd been entrusted with?), and Kardek was mutely inquiring, by streaking the side of the mug, whether he might sample this flawless imitation of twenty-first-century American beer . . .

"Sure, go ahead!"

Not just one waiter was hovering around the table now,

but two plus a waitress. The word had gone out: here's a Big Spender!

And I still haven't had a square meal. Perhaps I was too hasty. I could probably have choked the burger down with a bit of mustard . . .

"What," he asked Rocky, "can I have that is cheap and nourishing and fit to eat?"

The waiter said reproachfully, "Sir, we have an imageness to maintainicate! At a Hotel Interdimensional nothing is *cheap*. Certain items are diminishedly costiferous, that is all. Of course your orderfyings may be modificated to savorize of whatever you adumbrate. For exemplification, should he desire his swordfish to taste of liquorice and durian it can be arrangerized. However, I am obligated—"

"There is a small surcharge," Rinpoche sighed. "I wish someone had told me. I could have insisted on that hamburger being made to taste like a hamburger."

"Didn't it?" Nixy demanded, staring.

"No! Never had one before?"

"No!"

"Sir," Rocky obtruded firmly, "in accordulation with the policy of Interdimensional Hotels and the interestance of honesty, I must informulise you that what you were given looked and tasted to within five decimalated points just like the SuperKak first introductualized in the Big Kak chain of superhyperultraburger joints February fifteenth, 2023, after a gross decade of developmentaleering at Big Kak University."

"And what became of Big Kak?" Rinpoche demanded. "Still in business?"

"No, sir. They discontinuished operationing September first, 2023."

"That figures. And you still haven't answered my question. Matter of fact I don't think you're going to. Kardek!"

The pale man started.

"What would you order in my position? I guess you've had to make that kind of decision now and then!"

Kardek looked pained, but rapidly relented. "Very well. Oh, I know a lot of people regard it as plobbish to want food to actually taste of something, but I'd rather be plobbish than snobbish . . . I'd go for soya chicken or soya cod with mock potatoes, pseudoslaw and the complimentary relishes. You usually get fifty of those."

"Okay, I'll have the soya chicken and whatever comes with it."

It appeared. It looked even more realistic than the burger with the added advantage that it smelled appetizing. Then the relishes began to emerge. There were indeed fifty. Collectively they massed more than the main dish and covered virtually the entire table.

Startled, Rinpoche said, "How can they afford not to charge for all of these?" He picked up a gherkin and bit it. The crunch was convincing, the flavor satisfactory. He bit again.

"Oh, they cost practically nothing," Kardek said offhandedly, reaching for a carrot stick. "You make 'em from converted excrement."

I am not I am NOT going to be cheated out of another meal!

"You mean," Rinpoche said, keeping his voice steady by main force of will, "the same process as though you manured some ground and grew and harvested real plants?"

"Mm-hm. You just leave out the ground and the growing." Kardek sampled a limp gray slimy object that looked as though in its case the conversion process had been omitted as well and pronounced it excellent. Whereupon, while Rinpoche tried not to gobble this much superior food, he resumed his earlier conversation with Nixy.

Who by this time was shaking and depressed all over again.

"You were saying," he hinted, "that not all the members of your family were in favor of buying that solar system, no matter how reasonable the price. I imagine that must have worried some of them. It's in the Klosh volume, isn't it? That's hardly a species renowned for doing people favors." He added with a glance at Rinpoche: "They're a high-speed life-form—they live at twenty times our rate—so they always claim they don't have time."

Nixy disregarded the digression. "I wasn't involved, of course—I sort of dangle from the umpty-seventh branch on my family tree and only get remembered when someone wants me to imitate useful—but I got to hear about it, naturally . . . Well, it didn't take long to find out why the Klosh were selling cheap. I mean, a supernova gives off plenty of warning signs, which of course they'd already spotted, and it was only two systems away. And then this salesperson gets in touch with Gramps and points out that all you'd need to do is timeslow the explosion—stretch it to fifty or a hundred years, say—and you'd have enough energy not just to terraform the nearly habitable planet, but make it over completely. I mean"—turning to Rinpoche, still busy chewing—"you wouldn't believe some of the ideas the starchitect sold to Gramps. What about a river spiraling from pole to pole, on the *inside*? They even have a name for it, want to call it the Alph for some reason . . ." She checked, listening to an unheard voice, and resumed.

"Oh. A quotation! So that's why he called the place Xanadu! I told you, Kardek: you ought to get a Hypermem like mine even if they do bring on a headache now and then. Come to think of it, Rin, you ought to consider the idea, too. At the vault they probably assumed that was what you'd do, so there wasn't any need to feed you the usual data."

Rinpoche achieved a grunt; speech would have risked spraying pseudoslaw dressing all over the table.

"Having a slow supernova in your night sky must be kind of spectacular," Kardek suggested. "It'd be a great tourist attraction."

Nixy pulled a face. "My upper left uncle Aychaychaych—that's not his real name, of course, he's actually Hercule, but we all know him as Hercule the 'Orrible Heir,

Aychaychaych, because he's due to take over as capo when Gramps runs out of bits they can replace—normally I can't stand him, but he was *so* right to say it's utterly plobbish. Of course, what he really objects to is the way it spoils his ambition to create the finest night-sky pattern in the galaxy. He swears that without it he could achieve a maximally aesthetic solution if it weren't for one star that's a degree or so away from optimum. He says 'aesthetic' a lot; I think it must be his favorite word. As for tourists, barf-provoking is only half of it."

Swallowing the last of his mock potatoes, Rinpoche countered, "But you were with a tourist group yourself."

"Oh, this is Earth! Who cares what happens here? I'm talking about what's supposed to be my family's future home. Not that—"

"Yes, but," Kardek interrupted, "later on when you get bored with living there, tourism would be a useful supplement to the budget. I gather your great-great-grand—uh?"

"Not enough greats," Nixy sighed. "You might as well say Gramps same as I do."

"Yes. Well, I gather he had to sell three other planets in order to buy the new system."

"So I'm told. And I haven't the faintest idea whether it was a sound financial decision or whether he just wanted to be the first human—the first individual, what's more—to own a complete system. He's getting a little wrong in the head, you know. He's on his third body, but past a certain point you can't do very much about the brain. Damn. I'll have to censor that from my memory of the trip!"

Rinpoche suddenly realized what he was hearing and was glad he had finally emptied his mouth. Otherwise his gape of amazement would have had messy consequences.

"And," Nixy pursued obliviously, "it's a moot question whether anyone will be able to even visit Xanadu in the future, let alone live there."

"How so?" Kardek probed.

"Well . . ." She stared down at the table, linking and separating her slender fingers. "The idea was that once the starchitect had finalized the plans, the family would come to Earth while the builders moved in. Gramps was born here, you see, but for some reason he's never been back, and he suddenly decided this was the perfect opportunity. A lot of my relatives weren't too keen—Earth? Yuck! Why should anybody want to go to *Earth*? But they liked the idea of having to coexist with the builders even less, and of course we'd had to quit the planets where we used to live when Gramps sold them, so it wasn't much of a choice."

"Is the rest of your family with the tour group, then?" Rinpoche hazarded.

"No. I'm by myself." She raised her head. Her eyes gleamed with sudden moisture. "This is my first big trip alone. And I do feel terribly alone. Worse yet, I know how furious Gramps is going to be because I've let him down. He'll disinherit me!"

"Why in the world—sorry: why in space should he do that?"

"Because I promised faithfully I'd remember things he particularly wanted to do, like lose money at Las Vegas in memory of this, and drink Asti Spumante in memory of that, and chew coca leaves in memory of the other, and I haven't managed a single one! The awful things that started back on Xanadu just won't stop! I know people don't believe in bad luck anymore, but I could, I honestly could!"

Rinpoche clasped her hand. "Why didn't he make the trip himself? Why were you forced to deputize?" He'd figured out that much, at least.

"I told you: awful things are happening on Xanadu!"

"What awful things?" And, struck by an idea, he added, "Would another drink make it easier to talk?"

"Allow me," Kardek said. "You gave me your beer, remember. Rocky, the lady wishes to remember drinking Asti Spumante and we wouldn't mind helping her."

Three fizzing glasses duly appeared.

"Thank you . . . Well, I don't know exactly how things started to go wrong, but I do know that the preliminary work went according to plan. Gramps hired this firm of cosmic engineers, very highly recommended—Clifford and Simak is the name—and they used the initial blast from the supernova to create the timeslow field, then deployed degraders to convert the rest into usable wavelengths. Next they set up temporary accommodation in low orbit— nothing luxy, I mean even Gramps only had fifty or sixty rooms—so we'd have somewhere to lay our heads before leaving for Earth, and put up some of the friends and distant relatives who on hearing about Gramps buying Xanadu suddenly remembered how much they loved the old bastard and announced they were coming to call. Damn: I must have that censored, too. Of course, they were hoping to be invited to the grand planetwarming scheduled for after our return, which was going to last a full local year. At one point Aychaychaych was talking bitterly about maybe staying on Earth instead, because anything would be better than putting up with hordes of relatives, but he suddenly calmed down. I don't know why. I don't seem to know a lot of things. The rest of the family have never talked to me very much.

"Well, we were just about to leave when there was this emergency call from ground. We weren't expecting bad news because, like I said, the early stages had gone as per schedule. The gravity stabilized nicely at one-point-oh-one gee, the weather pattern responded fine to the new mountains . . ."

For a moment Rinpoche lost track of what she was saying. To speak so casually of installing mountains! *Wow!* He really looked forward to finding out how humanity had achieved this amazing success when in his own day everyone had been predicting the collapse of civilization if not the extinction of the species.

". . . so what we were expecting, really, was a bon voyage message. Did we get it? Did we in a black hole!"

She drained her wine and muttered a word of thanks to Kardek as the glass refilled itself even though the debit was Rinpoche's. By now he had learned to notice the momentary flash that read his right retina. However, he tried not to display annoyance.

"What had happened?" Kardek encouraged. Nixy sat back, raising one finger after another as she replied.

"Our nice new shallow tropical ocean had developed a serious case of heavy-metal pollution.

"Our beautiful new mountains had begun to sag and slide because the substrates were turning to sludge.

"The icecaps intended for planetary air-conditioning were melting thanks to an irruption of hot radioactives.

"And the pole-to-pole tunnel for the underground river, fast as the rock was beamed out, kept filling up again with the most nauseating mush including squillions of germs and viruses and bacteria and nomats and crefons and yeblitoriks and sharg and—and—and things even our best encyloputer failed to identify. Can you imagine it?"

"But what had gone wrong?" Rinpoche asked foggily.

"Naturally the builders were using a vast number of dumpers to clear unwanted matter and fetch in what was wanted. And it turned out they'd started backing up at random!"

Kardek took a fast and nervous swig of wine. "Oh dear," he said. "No wonder your gramps couldn't spare the time to travel with the family to Earth."

"Right." Nixy sat back, shaking her head despondently. "But for some reason he was absolutely set on somebody coming here right about now, so—Well, what it distilled to was that I was the only one naïve enough to think it would be glamorous and romantic to visit the cradle of our species. Everybody else had gone off the idea. Now I see why."

"You've been disillusioned," Rinpoche offered. Simultaneously with the words it dawned on him that he and Kardek were competing for Nixy's attention on totally different levels. Now his reactions were more or less back to normal (though he was glad he even yet was not experiencing the full force of the terror he abstractly knew to be appropriate), he could tell they were also normally masculine:

he wanted to impress her man to woman. Kardek, in contrast, was manifestly more concerned about establishing links with a member of a very, very wealthy family.

And one had to admire the skill with which he had progressed from an unknown conman to an almost-intimate . . .

However: Nixy was answering.

"Disillusioned isn't the half of it! What with one thing and another I arrived late for my tour—though that wouldn't really matter because one can always go right around to the start again or switch to another if that's more convenient."

"Unfortunately," Kardek muttered, and waited. She managed a ghost of a smile.

"Correct. 'Obliged to warn it carries a surcharge!' Gramps made it clear this trip was also a test of how well I can manage on a limited budget. Anyway, it wouldn't have been so bad except that I didn't get to drink this sort of wine in Naples, where I was supposed to."

"What happened in Naples?" Rinpoche demanded.

"Something revolting crawled out of the sea and smothered half the city. They had to evacuate nonresidents. Scrub one part of the tour."

"Mm-hm." Kardek nodded, looking wise. "You mentioned Cuzco?"

She shuddered. "I'd rather not think about what happened there."

"That bad, was it? Tsk-tsk! Then you went to—?"

"Holyrood," Rinpoche supplied.

"The Mary Queen of Scots movie? What happened?"

"The head flew off the executioner's ax and the grandstand fell down."

"That was where you two met?"

"Yes. Or—no, not exactly. That's where I first set eyes on Nixy. I didn't know her name, of course, or anything about her. But I fell in love with her at once."

What did I just say?

Mouth ajar, he waited for the heavens to fall.

Instead, though, she smiled again, this time genuinely.

"Don't worry, Rin. People do that all the time. My parents had me bioengineered with the LASFS gene: Love At Second if not First Sight. Sometimes it can be a nuisance, but mostly it's a lot of fun. I can't oblige you, though. Sorry. Affairs are terribly difficult to edit out of your memories because they resonate all over the place, and Gramps has this *prehistoric* opinion about a woman's proper rôle ... Anyway, the next thing"—turning back to Kardek—"was that what should have been the California Gold Rush got mixed up with the 1906 earthquake. That's where Rin and I literally bumped into one another. Then two crazy detectives started trying to arrest both of us under the same name and claiming the quake was my fault! Mine! When everywhere I go I'm being pestered by people saying that because Gramps bought a whole system that means there's less for everybody else! I feel I'm being persecuted! And can you blame me?"

Her voice trailed away. Kardek was shaking his head lugubriously.

"Sometimes I get too ambitious for my own good. Here I was hoping I might come up with some plausible-sounding explanation for your problem and wheedle a bit of credit for making you feel better, which is not what you would call dishonest, I submit, but value for therapy, since although I may not enjoy a Hypermem I do possess considerable talent for ratiocination—and rationalization, too. However, on the basis of what you've told me, I have to confess I make of this conundrum neither head nor tail nor umbilicus. Bluntly: I can't help."

He sat back. She had barely had time to look disappointed before he added: "But I can direct you to somebody who can. Possibly the only person in the galaxy who can."

"Do so, for pity's sake!"

"It'll mean a trip to London. I'm told that's one really mixed-up town—"

"If I must, I must! Go on!"

"And"—a modest downward glance—"I would have to ask you to bear in mind my straitened circumstances."

"You're asking for a fee? I'll find it somehow!"

"Then, as soon as we have re-engaged with Earth, the person whom you must consult is Sherlock Holmes."

"The computers suggest that we do WHAT?"

NINE

HOLMES IS WHERE THE HELP IS

"IN YOUR DAY PEOPLE KEPT CATS, RIGHT?"
"Yes. In fact I owned a few myself, over the years."
"Wonderful. Well, we've re-created them, believing they'd be a successful export item, and we did sell a few, but then all these complaints started coming in, saying they were lazy and greedy and selfish and kept messing up their own-ers' lives. But according to the manuals that's authentic."
"Manuals?"
"Yes, books showing cats and humans interacting. With pictures."
"Hmm . . . Do they feature mainly a fat cat with stripes?"
"That's right."
"And his owner's name is Jon?"
"Why, you know them!"
"I think I do. And you've definitely got problems."

Confronting them as they emerged in England, a large sign read:

WELCOME TO THE LONDON GENERAL DUMP OFFICE

And, in smaller letters underneath:

Beyond this point approximate costume must be worn

Wondering whether Nixy's hair counted as approximate costume, Rinpoche looked about him. This Dump Office occupied an old but sizable building with a dome above its central area and four short extensions at right angles to one another. Here and there he saw busts and statues, some obviously quite old even by a resurrectee's standards, and carved memorials set into the walls. Many of the latter had been flyposted; several polychrome but faded advertisements announced a circus run by someone called Dr. Lao.

Duckman can't have invented his dumper very long after my day. In fact I guess he may already have been alive when I . . .

But it still made him uncomfortable to think about the past.

The place reeked; their eyes began to water at once. Also it was extremely noisy. Oddly, however, it was at the same time uncrowded, as though the few score persons present were trying to create the impression of a much larger throng. Darting frantically hither and yon, shills and pedlars in an astonishing variety of garb—though heavily biased on the one hand in favor of starched ruffs with skirts and stomachers or doublet and hose, or on the other long Victorian dresses, frock coats, and top hats—clamored the merits of various goods and services, accosting both new arrivals and would-be leavers. Almost before Rinpoche and Nixy had set foot to floor they too were the target of importunities.

"Buy a guideflash, find your way! Make yer data up-to-dater via the optic nerve!"

"Going to the Dickens, are yer, ducks? Yer'll need filters in that pea-soup fog! Undetectable in wear, costing a fraction what new lungs would set yer back!"

"Garb replicement while yer blink!"

"De last ob de Notting Hill Calypsonians! Lord Tranquilizer will immortalize you in song! Low, *low* rates per line!"

"Don't take any notice," Nixy whispered. "Just look for signs to The Victorian Age."

"Huh? Oh, sorry." Rinpoche had been gazing upward, for something about the form of the roof struck him as familiar. "This place reminds me of somewhere. I think."

"All right. Just a sec." She cocked her head, looking more ravishing than ever, so that his heart hammered within his chest. After a moment she said, "Oh, of course. I should have guessed. It used to be a . . . Hold on!" She squeezed her eyes shut for a moment. "I never guessed there were so many names for religious buildings: fane, shrine, church, chapel, cathedral, temple, synagogue, mosque . . ." Blinking: "Is that any help? There's more, but my head is starting to hurt again."

"It isn't used for a religion any longer?"

"Goodness, what an idea! One of the first benefits we gained from admission to the Galactic Conglomerate was a cure for that unique contagious psychosis. Lots of people—the Yelignese in particular—are annoyed that we did get cured, because they claim that if we hadn't we wouldn't have become the richest species in the galaxy. But even the most die-hard supporter of authenticity wouldn't want people forced to suffer mental derangement, would they?"

A great sense of calm and joy was invading Rinpoche's mind. Still reluctant to believe what Nixy was telling him, he countered, "But I heard someone at Frisco say you can still be burned alive in an *auto-da-fé*."

"An outer-the-how much?"

He spelled it, and she consulted her Hypermem again, though not without a wince of pain that made him feel dreadfully guilty for asking.

"Oh! Oh, that's not a religious rite. It never was. It was like Roman games, Aztec sacrifices, boxing, and such: a chance for sociopaths to enjoy watching other people suffer."

"But," Rinpoche pursued doggedly, "I met someone who claimed to embody God's will on the strength of his name—" He broke off. Of course. Salvador Munday didn't just not have all his marbles; he had bits of two people's. Presumably it hadn't been possible to eliminate every trace of religious psychosis from the fusion of two personalities both dating back before the cure. When Nixy looked a question at him he shook his head, grinning as wide as a toilet seat.

"I think," he said, "I may be going to like the modern world in spite of all."

"Nah ven nah ven nah ven! W'ere djer fink yer agowin' of? Armour gonna raffer run yer rin!"

Startled, they glanced around to find they were being addressed by a mutton-chopped party in a tight black uniform with silver buttons down the front and a curious black helmet. Badges on his jacket identified him as PC 49.

At his side a slimmer and apparently younger man, clad in a red doublet with white ruff and white hose, exclaimed, "Nay, sirrah! Fie, for shame! Wouldst clap in durance vile so comely a maid—not to mention quite a presentable cully?"

"Ow, Gilbert!" sighed PC 49. "Yer words as alwize melt me like a candle. Benjy! Mike sure these two get properly dressed the w'iles me an' Gil turn our backs out of the goodness of our 'arts."

Benjy proved to be a mustachioed man in a high-waisted ulster and a brown billycock. Approaching, rubbing his hands, he said in a purring voice, "You've come to the right shop, sir and madam—shame though it be to conceal such elegant pins and that muff prettier than any mink or sable! What shall it be? Victorian dress, Elizabethan, or best and most convenient two suits of our reversibles, adaptable for either zone? I particularly recommend the latter, at a most reasonable price."

"We only have one call to pay," Nixy said. "And that's in The Victorian Age."

"Nonetheless you should seriously consider purchasing reversibles. I also have them for whatever costume you may require at your next destination—"

"Cap d'Agde," Nixy said curtly. "Please get on with it!" And glanced at the dome overhead. By her expression she feared it was about to be struck by yet another disaster of the sort that had pursued her ever since reaching Earth.

"As madam insists," Benjy said resignedly. "If you would loosen your hair—? Thank you."

He produced seemingly from nowhere a large hoop that he passed down her body from crown to sole. As it descended, it hummed, and when she stepped out of it at ground level she was clad in late nineteenth-century walking-out dress including a velvet cape, a hat with a veil, and boots sporting an immense number of buttons.

"Don't worry about those," Benjy said. "They're dummies. There's a concealed zip. Now you, sir!"—raising the hoop again.

There was a curious tingling, not unpleasant, and Rinpoche's clothing was swiftly transmuted into a suit of brown tweed with a black windowpane check, laced boots, an Inverness cape, and a deerstalker.

He noticed that as the hoop passed the level of his eyes there was a barely perceptible flash, but it did not pause in its descent. Presumably, therefore, his credit level was still adequate. He wondered what would have happened had it proved otherwise.

Benjy tipped his hat and parodied a bow. "As the actress said to the bishop, it's been a business doing pleasure with you. That, by the way, is an authentically ancient witticism. If you'd care to purchase a comprehensive anthology of jokes and jollities so old that most folk nowadays have never heard of them—"

"Sir Benjy!" Gilbert exclaimed. "As a constable of the watch I am sworn to uphold the law, and thou'rt perilously close to breaching it. Prithee hew to the terms of thy license, as the cobbler to his last!"

More resigned than ever, Benjy wandered off in search of further customers. PC 49 nodded magisterial confirmation that they were now approximately dressed and might proceed past this point. At the same time Gilbert cast a reminiscent glance toward Nixy's crotch and heaved a meant-to-be-overheard sigh.

She seized Rinpoche's arm and hurried him away.

* * *

"Hello. I'm Bloom. Please would you thumb my petition?"

Into their path had stepped a tall dark girl with a beehive hairdo and immense false eyelashes. She wore soft, white, thigh-high boots and a zip-fronted minidress open to the navel, plus a dejected expression, and she was proffering a flat, glistening, oblong plate.

Nixy hissed that he mustn't, but Rinpoche had been so much cheered up that he wanted to do favors for everybody. He inquired in the politest of tones, "What's the petition about?"

Bloom brightened. "I maintain that Swinging London deserves to be re-enacted just as much as Shakspeare's Day and the Victorian Age, which are all they've let us have so far. After all, it would be a lot more fun and nothing like as smelly. Is it your first visit? Yes? Then this would be a great reason to come again! Sexual freedom! Dope! The Permissive Society!"

She was doing her best to sound enthusiastic, but her face belied her words. Besides, Nixy was now trying to pull Rinpoche away.

"I don't want to give away where we are!" she whispered. "I don't want any more horrid demonstrators crawling out of the drains!"

Rinpoche sighed. "I'm afraid it's a negative," he told Bloom.

Lowering her petition, the girl said glumly, "I know, I know! If that's what you want, you can get it cheaper simulated. But now and then"—with a trace of defiance—"one does hit on someone with too much of a taste for reality to settle for substitutes. If I can amass ten thousand thumbprints I'll earn the right to appeal to the Chief Bureaucrat, and I have more than four hundred already!"

"How long," Nixy said with a trace of cruelty, "has that taken?"

"Oh, I suppose about . . ." Bloom was elaborately trying to look anywhere but directly at them. "I suppose about two and a half years."

"And how many tourists visit London every day?"

"Uh . . ."

"I thought so. Now! We're here to consult someone called Sherlock Holmes, a detective. How do we find him?"

Bloom set a thin pale forefinger between her lips. "Shan't tell you," she pouted girlishly.

"Come on, Rin. We're wasting time—No! Wait!"

Face paling, she swung around in response to a cue Rinpoche had missed and an instant later tried to hide behind him. Following her gaze, he realized that a score or so of stern-faced people bearing poster boards had assembled in a group at the far end of the Dump Office. Now they started to advance in a solemn line.

"Are they demonstrating against your gramps?" he hazarded.

"Yes! But how did they know I was here? How did they find out so quickly?" She appealed to Bloom. "If you know where Sherlock Holmes lives, please help! I really am desperate!"

"Oh, all right," Bloom grumbled, folding her petition plate down to practically nothing and tucking it into not so much her bosom as her midriff. "I do think it's a jolly swiz, though, adding Holmes and Watson to the Dickens bit and the Gilbert and Sullivan bit and all the rest, especially since they aren't historical. But what chance do people like me stand against all these vested interests? I've taken an economics digest, and I know what I'm up against. I know the garbers and gearers are making fortunes because back then people wore so many clothes and everybody has to dress the part so it keeps lots of people busy whereas taking off everything as often as possible like in the Swinging Sixties means people could actually enjoy themselves instead of sweating in outfits copied from museums . . . Ah, shit. You want 221B Baker Street. That's in The Victorian Age. You can take the same knife-board I go home by, and I've had a bellyful for today. Come on!"

With long, athletic strides she led them past a group of

dancers leaping up and down around a maypole to the accompaniment of sackbuts and rackets under intense surveillance from a tour group of bulging greeny gray sausages that in rotation extruded organs visual, auditory, olfactory, and tactile. A harassed human male, doubtless their courier, was having much trouble dissuading them from also trying to taste the performers, for fear it might disturb their rhythm.

The knifeboard turned out to be an open double-decker bus drawn by simulacral horses like those in Holyrood, with its destination shown, disturbingly, as The World's End. Its appellation derived from back-to-back seating on its upper level. Although the lower one was empty, Bloom insisted they ride outside on the grounds that they ought to do at least a bit of sight-seeing while they were here. Rinpoche's euphoria, the strongest emotion he had felt since resurrection apart from his reaction to Nixy (and the force of that had dwindled since she explained about her LASFS gene) seemed likely to last a good long time, so he raised no objection, and though Nixy muttered something to the effect that she was glad she hadn't been forced to wear a crinoline she, too, complied. However, within minutes they found themselves trundling along streets beset with a gray miasma that not only stung the eyes but burned the throat, and Nixy said sourly, "What was that about sight-seeing?"

"But this is one of the sights of London," Bloom murmured. "It's our world-renowned peasouper. People do say it's even fouler than Californian smog."

That, Rinpoche could certify. London, though, wasn't just The Victorian Age, and it felt hard to reconcile a stench like this with the Merrie England of Gloriana.

"How do you confine it?" he demanded.

"I'm sorry?" Bloom blinked her enormous artificial lashes.

"Confine it! Stop it blowing into Shakespeare's Day!"

"But we don't," she answered simply. "Why should we? The first Queen Elizabeth imposed laws against burning what they called 'seacoles' but they were still doing it in Victoria's reign. The English are an obstinate people. That's why they went so quickly from being very rich to being very poor. Isn't that something?"

"You sound as though you're proud of it," Rinpoche said slowly.

"Don't people need something to be proud of?"

He found he couldn't answer that.

The "horses'" hooves were clattering now on cobble-stones or granite setts. The fronts of the adjacent buildings had disappeared into the wavering fog. Only shouts and curses and the occasional racket of a carriage being overset to the accompaniment of shrill albeit ladylike screams disturbed the oppressive silence, as dulling to the ears as the fog to the eyes, if not so pungent.

"You get off here," Bloom directed.

"How do you know?" Rinpoche demanded through chattering teeth. He hadn't bargained for it being so cold in this area of London.

"You mean you didn't pick up a guideflash? There were plenty on offer—there always are."

"Why should we?" Nixy countered. "I have a Hypermem—"

"Ah! Then it's just as well you ran into me, isn't it? You could have been lost for weeks in this fog. They rearrange London at random specially to defeat people who think they can cheat Earth out of explan credit by buying their guidance before they arrive." Her transient bravado evaporated. "Ah, to a black hole with it. What's Earth ever done for me except arrange for me to be born in a boring backward backwater? Go on, get down. I've brought you to the right place. So long."

They duly descended the narrow, curving stairs. At the bottom they were addressed by the conductor, a rat-faced little man in a too-large peaked cap carrying a rack of multicolored paper tickets and a punch on a leather strap. He had given them a ticket each when they came on board but not actually taken money in exchange, since that—as Nixy had explained after once more consulting her Hypermem— would have involved minting coinage and Earth's resources of metal had been so dispersed during the Age of Extravagance the planet couldn't afford it.

" 'Ere, guv," he wheezed from a throat rasped by long exposure to the peasouper. "Add a bit o' spice to yer visit! Jus' s'y ver word, an' crawssin' ver street yer can be slashed by Jack ver Ripper er run dahn by a scorchin' cyclist an' carried off to Mar'l'bon' 'Orspital fer treatment in a nopen ward wiv orfentic period drugs an' instruments, er bump inter local characters 'oo'll guide yer froo ver fog ter fymous pubs sich as ver Queen Zed an' ver Biker Street Irregular—"

He broke off. In a totally different tone he said, "Moreover, if you find yourselves in need of a Cockney decipherer, we carry those on all our buses for the convenience of visitors who may not have access to a historical dialect bank. If you do have such access, please be advised you may be committing an offense by having recourse to it, inasmuch as Cockney™ and all other Terrestrial Dialects® are copyright © by Earth Incorporated, a subsidiary of Yelignuman Enterprises LGC."

"Which side of the road," Nixy said between clenched teeth, "is 221B?"

"Ow! Yer 'ere ter consult Mister 'Olmes! Wah dincha s'y? Yer raht outsahde!"

"Thank you," Rinpoche muttered, stepping down to the roadway and turning with what he hoped was in-period courtesy to help Nixy—only she pushed rudely past him. Groping, she located steps up to a door with a heavy knocker that she lifted and let fall. Before she could knock a second time a little girl of about eight or nine, wearing a floor-length dress, opened the door with a dip meant for a curtsey. Beyond, a narrow entrance hall was illumined by flaring gas jets. The stench of coal smoke within was nearly as bad as outside.

"Good evening," said the child. "Please come in. Mr. Holmes is expecting you."

Startled, Rinpoche echoed, "Expecting us?"

"Why, certainly! He received your telegram."

"But we never—"

"Mrs. Hudson!" a treble voice shouted from above. "Show my visitors up straight away!"

"Yes, sir!" the little girl called back, adding, "Please follow me," as she ascended a flight of stairs whose walls were decorated with steeplechasing prints.

"Mrs?" Rinpoche said in confusion.

"It's just her turn," Nixy said impatiently. "People here have to scratch a living as best they can."

"Don't get snappish! You know I haven't got a Hypermem!"

She cast an apologetic grin over her shoulder. "Sorry. That's one of the few facts I can't rely on it to remember for me."

"So it is." And he grinned back.

They reached the landing at the head of the stairs. In an open doorway stood a boy of about twelve wearing a gray three-piece suit with a gold watch chain across its waistcoat. He said, "I'm Dr. Watson, friend and biographer of Mr. Holmes. Do come in."

He stood aside for them to enter the room beyond. It had all the traditional appurtenances, which by now Rinpoche was starting to recall in detail: yes, there were the initials VR in bullet holes, there was a slipper full of tobacco or at any rate a mass of brown shreds, there was the bench for chemical experiments, there was a violin case, there was a jar of fine white powder, there was a hypodermic syringe . . . But this—this *child* was a great detective?

For rising to meet them was a chubby-cheeked youth no older than fourteen, waving them to chairs, saying with an air of irritation, "Mr. Gibbs, Miss Jones, I really don't know why you've applied to me. You should rather address yourselves to my colleague Mr. Carnacki."

They both stared at him blankly. Impatient, he waved at "Watson."

"Doctor, show them the evening paper!"

"Ah! Now just a moment. Where did I put the blasted thing?" The boy started rummaging through documents on a nearby table. That was too much for Nixy, who rose to her feet again.

"Look, I know people have to take it in turns to play the historical personages in Earth's re-enactment zones, but—"

"Holmes" cut in. "But you think it's silly not having someone tall and cadaverous in a top hat to play my rôle? Madam, are you not aware that Sherlock Holmes was not 'historical' but fictional?"

"Well—uh—"

"I knew," Rinpoche murmured.

"Yes, Mr. Gibbs! But you are an Earth-born resurrectee, whereas the lady is an explan, and such people's inability to distinguish between fact and fiction is among the most precious and at the same time most infuriating assets of this poor worn-out globe—"

He interrupted himself. "Ah, Watson! I discern that you have found the newspaper."

"It's yesterday's," said Watson glumly, and went on searching.

"Why did you say we'd sent you a telegram?" Rinpoche ventured into the moment of silence that followed.

"Oh, just as a bit of contemporary color. All of this is more for our sakes than yours, you see."

"I beg your pardon?"

"Make-believe is an important element in the psychological development of any child, naturally, so they train youngsters like us who plan to make a career in the re-enactment zones by entrusting us with fictional characters before we graduate to real ones. It's a way of maintaining a human component in what the Yelignese would otherwise turn over completely to simulacra on the grounds that machines can do everything far better than humans. That's jealousy, of course. I mean—well, have you been to Washington?"

"Which one?" Rinpoche countered after a moment for reflection.

Holmes chuckled. "Good question. I hear the Americans are dreadfully annoyed about that."

"About what?" Nixy cut in.

"The fact that their Capitol and White House were re-built in Washington State rather than Washington, D.C. My-self, I don't see that that matters in this day and age when you can go anywhere in next to no time, but apparently they are somewhat exercised about it. In my view they ought to be far more annoyed that the Giant Abe in the Lincoln Memorial says, 'Hey, cats and chicks, dig this. Pushing a century ago some cats that really knew how to dig things dug foundations for—' But I detect, Miss Jones, an air of incomprehension."

"Who's Lincoln?"

At which moment Watson uttered an exclamation of tri-umph and handed her a well-simulated evening newspaper—well-simulated, that was, apart from consisting solely of a front page.

"Ah," Holmes said with satisfaction. "From that, my dear lady, even the meanest intelligence should be able to deduce why you would have been better advised to consult Mr. Carnacki, the *soi-disant* ghost finder."

Rinpoche stared at the lead story in the paper as Nixy held it up. Without intention he read snatches aloud: "Lon-don General Dump Office . . . discontinued underground railway lines . . . incursion of thousands of nonterrestrial beings . . . state of emergency . . . loss of tourist income in-calculable . . . Chief Bureaucrat held responsible . . ."

A harassed-looking personage with dark hair surrounding a bald pate, giving a curiously blurred impression as though every movement made its image strobe, peered through the VR in bullet pocks. "Which I am!" it snapped. "For every-thing! But you don't have to go out of your way to make things worse! Sherlock, baby, save it with the Carnacki bit already! You both use the same computers—you're aware who supplied them—so cool it with any problems that you know are not resoluble! We have a major crisis in view. We

don't know what it is yet, but it's *major*, and we need all
the capacity we can get."

"Uh . . ." Holmes swallowed hard. "Yes, sir! But I did
expect—"

"Enough already and *dim sum*—Blast this vocabulator!
Then some!"

"Yes, *ma'am*!" He swallowed again, turning to face Nixy
with a bluff expression, as though trying to pretend the in-
tervention had not occurred. That it had, inasmuch as the
intervener had vanished, would indeed, Rinpoche realized,
have been difficult to prove.

His mental condition must be improving. The parentheses in his existence were dwindling to commas.

"Even if you still haven't worked it out," Holmes continued, "the reason I suggested consulting Mr. Carnacki rather
than myself should by now be blatantly apparent, especially
as reinforced by the resurrection at an abandoned tube station of so many extinct Martians long therein entombed . . .
although that can have been no more than a side effect.
What it boils down to is this:

"You, Miss Jones, are being haunted."

"The computers suggest that we do WHAT?"

TEN

ANOTHER EXTENSION OF
THE OLD JUBILEE LINE

"ROIT! 'THE OIRISH FIRM OF FAITH AN' BEJABERS announces—' "

" 'Takes proide in announcing!' "

"That's your man. 'Takes proide in announcing the first hurling match for centuries! Jine us, ye spalpeens, in re-creating the re-creations of our ancestors!' "

" 'Our noble ancestors'!"

"Your man indeed. Well, what d'ye all t'ink? Is ut a go?"

"I can't help wondering . . ."

"Out with ut!"

"Well—sorry but I just can't keep up the accent—what are we actually going to hurl?"

"Oi was t'inking rocks."

"Then we'd best lay in a plentiful supply."

Before either Nixy or Rinpoche could respond to his astonishing announcement, Holmes had signaled to Watson, who parted the curtains covering the nearest window, threw up the lower sash, and blew three earsplitting blasts on a shiny metal whistle before dropping the window again with such dexterity that barely a wisp of the fog drifted in.

No more than a couple of seconds later, while the visitors were still at a loss, came a roaring sound so loud as scarcely to be dulled by the miasmatic air. It drew closer, stopped level with the house, ceased, and was succeeded by a thunderous banging at the front door. Mrs. Hudson was heard hastening to answer.

Heavy tramping on the staircase followed; then the door of the room swung open to reveal a thickset man clad in black leather relieved only by tarnished metal studs and zips. His head was entirely encased in a crash helmet with its visor down, and as he halted facing Holmes he was slapping heavy gauntlets against his left palm.

"I discern," Holmes murmured, "that you are taken aback by this gentleman's appearance. Be reassured. He is one of my Biker Street Irregulars. Pray bear with me a moment."

Turning to a table at his left, he scrawled a few words on a sheet of paper and handed it to the man in leathers, who spun on his heel without a word. Instants later he was heard descending the stairs two at a time, opening and slamming the front door, restarting his bike, and roaring away.

"I thought," Rinpoche ventured, "machines like his, and the fad for garb like his, eventuated—uh—somewhat later."

"Mr. Gibbs," Holmes sighed, not without an audible trace of reproof, "has it not crossed your mind how inconvenient it would be to adhere rigorously to the facilities available in the late nineteenth century while at the same time employing computers more appropriate to the twenty-third? They possess a certain degree of what our trans-Atlantic cousins would call orneriness, you know; they are not inhibited from criticizing our use of them in the interests of superior efficiency. On the other hand ... Oh, Watson, I grow weary. Be so good as to mix me a seven-percent solution."

Watson complied, reaching for a glass, a water jug, and a phial of white powder. Having consulted her Hypermem with another wince, Nixy demanded, "Is that really cocaine?"

"Good heavens, no!" Watson exclaimed as he stirred the contents of the glass. "It's called sugar. Don't they have it on your planet? Notoriously bad for the teeth but an excellent source of energy ... There you are, old chap."

"Thank you. Now, as I was about to say: the original Holmes—I don't mean original, I mean the first of my predecessors in this day and age—inquired of the Chief Bureaucrat, reasonably enough, how one could have Biker Street Irregulars without street bikes for them to be irregular on. At first it nearly outsmarted him by insisting on pedal cycles, but he proved that the term biker was never used in conjunction with those, only the powered kind, while impervious garb was essential for anyone handling bees. When he demonstrated how painful bee stings can be—"

"What have bees got to do with it?" Rinpoche demanded foggily. In the same moment, from Nixy:

"What are bees? No, don't bother answering. I'll look it up."

"Bike originally meant a beehive," Holmes explained. "Anyway, the computers being, as I just said, on the side of greater efficiency, he got his way: hence the Biker Street Irregulars. *Most* useful— Ah!"

"He's back," Watson deduced from the noises outside.

"And has Mr. Carnacki with him," Holmes appended. To Nixy: "That accounts for the somewhat acerbic voice you will shortly hear. He hates being hauled out of his cozy flat in Cheyne Walk, even when he is assured of one of his favorite kinds of investigation—"

"Excuse me," Rinpoche said. He had been thinking deeply. "Is this Carnacki not as much a figment as yourself?"

"Why is that important?" Holmes parried.

Rinpoche blinked incomprehension.

"Surely you don't imagine that he, or I, or Watson, would be any more 'real' if our present assignments were to enact Gladstone, Disraeli, and the Iron Duke? It wouldn't make *us* any more historical. The past being inaccessible, it makes no difference whatever."

"Now just a second!"—half rising. Nixy checked him, hand on arm.

"I'm sorry," she whispered. "But my Hypermem agrees. All its historical data are prefixed with a disclaimer of liability."

There was no chance to talk further. Mrs. Hudson was announcing, "Mr. Carnacki!"

In radical contrast to Holmes, the newcomer was a portly, tweedy, red-faced man of middle age, his voice gruff, his expression eloquent of suspicion that he might have been lured here under false pretenses.

"Your reason for calling me in had better be good," he warned as he sank into a chair that Watson had hastily cleared of papers. "You caught me *en route* to investigate the manifestation at the General Dump Office of a long-extinct species of Martians—"

Something howled overhead.

"—one of whose side-effects you can hear even as I speak."

"Ah!" Holmes countered. "But you are not interested in the reason why not only this manifestation but other unwelcome events—in Italy, in Mexico, in California—should occur at the precise juncture when a member of the Anangaranga-Jones family arrives on Earth?"

Carnacki's brusqueness diminished. "And what hypothesis are you entertaining?" he invited after awhile.

"At first I was reluctant to believe it. Only after eliminating the impossible was I driven to conclude that what remained, no matter how improbable, must be the answer. The events attending Miss Jones's visit can be accounted for in no other way than by the assumption that a being of limitless malevolence but limited perception—at least in our set of dimensions—has conceived a vendetta against her. This explains why the aforementioned events have not affected her save indirectly; it is as though the being suffers from the counterpart of blurred vision. Miss Jones will, I'm sure, agree that my analysis of the situation is not contradicted in one jot or tittle by her experience."

He concluded with a languid wave of one hand. Then, before Nixy had a chance to voice her own opinion:

"What—appalling—twaddle," said Carnacki, measuring his words like inches on a foot rule. He hunched forward. "I have already worked out a simpler and more logical explanation. There are—are there not?—parties who contend that it is immoral for one person to own even a single planet, let alone a solar system, and who have specifically targeted the clan Anangaranga-Jones on the grounds that its head's extravagance will diminish the energy resources available to the rest of our species by nought-point-seventy-seven-noughts-one percent, or even more, thereby shortening this universal cycle by as much as a week and a half."

At the words Nixy trembled visibly. Remembering the inexplicable irruption of those demonstrators at the Dump Office, Rinpoche fumbled for her hand in what he hoped was a reassuring manner and was rewarded with a squeeze in return.

"When one takes into account that the people who hold such views are notoriously a bunch of envious inadequates, the true logic of the situation becomes manifest. Having learned that a cadet of the family they so resent was due to visit Earth, they undertook to wreak vengeance on her rather than the truly guilty party, who is out of reach—if guilty he indeed be. Since they're as incompetent as they are jealous, so far each of their traps and snares has failed of its target."

Holmes was scowling; Watson was tugging at his sleeve. In the nick of time Mrs. Hudson entered with a trolley bearing glasses, decanters, and an assortment of snacks and sandwiches.

"Mrs. Hudson, an inspiration!" Watson declared. "And perfectly timed!"

"Indeed, indeed," Holmes concurred. "Miss Jones, allow us to offer you a glass of Madeira. And how about some salted almonds?"

Nixy said with Victorian stiffness, as though her voice had donned corsets, "We came here for help and advice, not refreshment!"

"I'm sure you may look forward to both," Carnacki declared. "Supernatural or not, you have afforded a most interesting conundrum."

"Hear, hear!" Watson chimed in, pouring from a crystal

decanter into crystal glasses. "I look forward to writing it up in the next volume of my companion's memoirs." Distributing the drinks, he added, "This wine, by the way, is of course based on Fomalhautian crench. Holmes and I are underage for alcohol."

With astonishment Rinpoche realized that within the past few minutes he had forgotten how young they were, so perfectly had they assumed a balance between their supposed rôles and the reality against which they were playing them. Noticing his reaction, Holmes twinkled at him.

"You're from a period to know what I meant were I to talk about owing a debt to Stanislavski and Brecht. Let's not delve into that, though. Let's revert to the subject at issue—"

"Excuse me. Please." The wine was delicious and so was the food, and his meal at the Interdimensional seemed further in the past than elapsed time could have allowed; nonetheless Rinpoche forced himself to set his glass by. "This is the first chance I've had to make someone tell me what the hell's been happening since I—well—died. Would you please clue me in before you go any further?"

Holmes and Watson exchanged startled glances. The former said after a pause, "You mean they didn't feed you the data they usually give the resurrected?"

"No!"

"That's very odd. Watson, have you ever run across a similar case?"

"Never. I can't understand it. I mean, the stuff is common enough and cheap enough and they update it every year. Well, we can put that right. As it happens, I have some of the necessary with me."

He reached to the floor beside him and picked up a black leather bag. From it he produced a small jar of pink capsules. Rinpoche suppressed a cry of amazement.

"Ah!" Holmes said acutely. "You recognize these! Watson, do they sometimes fail to take? Are some people perhaps immune?"

"I suppose it's possible," Watson answered doubtfully. "After all this time, though, one would have expected—"

"I was supposed to take a pill?" Rinpoche blurted.

All three of the others stared at him. Nixy was the first to say what was in all their minds: "You mean you didn't? It wasn't their fault? You refused?"

"I—"

"Well, then! You brought trouble on your own head, didn't you? I mean, honestly!" Nixy sat back crossing legs and arms in a posture eloquent of disappointment, its effect considerably spoiled by her Victorian attire.

"I didn't refuse any pills!" Rinpoche blared. "I wasn't offered any pills! I did see some like that at the vault, but nobody told me to take one! What are they supposed to do?"

Luckily there's one thing they don't have to. I got more of my normal emotions back. I was really angry when I said that!

Well, at any rate angrier than earlier.

"Miss Jones," Holmes said after a pause, "it galls me to reproach a client, but I believe I just heard you mention that you wear a Hypermem." On Nixy's nod: "Did it not occur to you to offer your companion a condecture?" In an aside to Rinpoche: "Condensed lecture, Mr. Gibbs."

Sullen, Rinpoche refrained from saying that some modern words were too obvious to need interpreting.

But had Nixy been inconsiderate? He didn't want to believe so.

She was shaking her head with a doleful expression. "I couldn't. Gramps had my Hypermem fixed so it won't work for anyone but me. Sometimes I think he's the meanest being in the galaxy. But I guess he just wanted to make sure it would be useless to a thief."

"Not," Carnacki grunted, "that a Hypermem is all that reliable down here. I presume so far you've evaded the worst of the lacunae due to the fact that the Yelignese delegated the sector 'Solar System and Earth' to one of the races they beat out for the contract to look after us. In a subtle attempt to show that the Yelignese—"

"Please!" Rinpoche found he was clenching his fists. "I don't know about all these races, even the Yelignese! Dr. Watson! If I should have taken one of those pills, how about my having one now?"

"Hmm!" Watson rubbed his chin with all the gravity of a sixty-year-old. "Holmes, you probably know more about this than I do. Would the capsule have a deleterious effect on someone who had already ingested multisensory data in real time?"

"Not that I'm aware of. Though he might with advantage eat something more beforehand."

Rinpoche seized and devoured a smoked salmon sandwich.

"Well, then," Watson sighed, "one might as well try. One point I need to ask about first, though. Mr. Gibbs, are you experiencing a certain dullness of the emotions following your resurrection?"

"Ah . . ." Rinpoche took stock of himself. "I don't think so. I mean I can get quite angry again. You heard me shout just now—sorry about that, by the way. So I imagine I must be over it."

"You're not." This from Holmes, hunching forward on his chair and looking infinitely mature and infinitely wise. "Watson could give you something to restore full sensitivity, of course—"

"But you wouldn't like it." Twelve-year-old Watson, too, had suddenly become grave.

There was a pause.

Eventually Rinpoche realized that he had begun to shake. At first it was only inside, deep inside, as though his guts and heart and lungs wanted to tremble but were not equipped. Just as his brain, at first remote from the focus of this reaction, was instructing his lips and tongue to frame defiant words about taking the risk anyway, the tremors spread upward past his vocal cords, putting them unreachably beyond voluntary control, and overtook his teeth so that they chattered like a flamenco dancer's casta-nets. His eyes fixed open of a sudden, as though he dared not close them even for a blink, because the world was full of dreadful threats he couldn't guard against. In his day they had not existed, not been dreamed of . . .

"I think," Watson murmured, "you are indeed better off with a smidgin of distancing, at least until you've had more chance to adjust to modern times. Here, drink this—not all at once, just sip by sip."

It was something fiery and aromatic, not unlike a veeblefetzer, and it did his troubled body good in moments. Soon he was able to sit back and mutter thanks.

"Interesting!" said Carnacki. Holmes glanced at him.

"Yes, indeed. Did you ever witness the impact of tempo-ral displacement on an uninstructed wreck before?"

A headshake. "You?"

"No. I ran across a pretty good mind-plant, but that was from the early days, when some of the mistakes . . . Speak-ing of mistakes: do you find it indicative that he was al-lowed to avoid his knowledge pill?"

"Of course. And subjunctive and imperative as well."

A baring of teeth. "Ha, ha . . . Watson, how is he?"

Small but professional fingers sought Rinpoche's pulse. "Much restored."

"Good. Now how about giving this pale person a pink pill?"

How knowledge could be absorbed from a capsule Rinpoche could not begin to guess, although he did of course eventually find out, but for the next half hour he felt as though his head were going over Niagara Falls without a barrel. At some stage Mrs. Hudson came to mend the fire. At another stage, discerning how much trouble he was hav-ing coping with the information flooding his brain, Watson sympathetically dosed him with more of the warming re-storative.

Also, to his extreme surprise and disbelief, Nixy not only

held his hand throughout but occasionally stroked his hair and face.

And at very long last his mind settled back on an even keel, though he retained a sensation like the mental counterpart of eating too much, as though his bloated brain wanted to emit an impossible burp. He knew—thanks to the pill— that so much data might take days or weeks to digest.

"That must be about it," Watson diagnosed.

"Well?" Holmes demanded, hunching forward.

Rinpoche swallowed hard. His heart was pounding like a trip-hammer. "Somebody tried to find a way to dispose of rubbish." That much he had already learned from Spotch. (Half a world away, and how many centuries from this mock-up of the Victorian Age?) "His name was Donald Duckman, and he did it in a desperate attempt to escape being mocked because of the name his parents had inflicted on him. It turned out to send things interstellar distances. There were people out there, or sort of people, who had been ignoring us. When our garbage started arriving out of nowhere, they realized we'd stumbled on the cheapest and easiest means of interstellar travel. Every race in the Galactic Conglomerate wanted to license the technique, barring a few who regard visitors as a nuisance and trade as futile. Eventually the traffic of the whole galaxy will go via Duckman Dumpers, but they've already made humans the richest species. Some richer than others, of course, so that at one end of the scale are people who can't even dream of visiting another planet, while at the other is Nixy's gramps who bought a whole solar system and is converting it to a private residence using the energy from a nearby nova—"

"Supernova," Nixy corrected.

"Yes. Well, most humans now live on other worlds. Eventually it dawned on some of the people out there that Earth was rotting to bits because the ones who'd stayed behind weren't up to managing a planet, especially one that was already in such a mess, so a bunch of sentimental explans hired the Yelignese to tidy up the place and keep it running, but since they're not human . . ."

He concluded with a shrug.

"He has assimilated the salient points," Carnacki pronounced.

"Maybe so," Nixy retorted caustically, "but what he just said didn't amount to much more than he'd already picked up from talking to me and other people."

Rinpoche drew a deep breath. "As a matter of fact," he said, "Nixy's quite right. I did know most of it already. There was a woman in Hollywood—I mean Holyrood. And of course Nixy had to explain why demonstrators turn up wherever she goes."

"Hmm!" Holmes picked up an enormous meerschaum pipe whose bowl hung a handsbreadth below his jaw, and blew through it noisily before reaching for the slipper full of brown shreds.

Momentarily distracted, Nixy demanded, "Is that tobacco?"

"What—? Oh! Goodness, no. Tobacco's dangerous. No, this is Polarian shunk. It's an analog, like crench: tastes, smells, and acts identical but does no harm. Watson, a lucifer if you please . . . Thank you." Amid a cloud of gray fumes: "Well, I must admit, Carnacki, I now find myself driven to a position a great deal closer to your own. What Mr. Gibbs just said struck me as a clincher—"

"No, quite the contrary!" Carnacki rasped. "I confess to having overlooked a strand of strong evidence that only now emerges from this tangled web—"

"That's impossible! I had exhaustively analyzed—"

"Exhaustiveness may be defensible as a philosophical concept, but as you know perfectly well in the galactic context the existence of thousands of intelligent races each of whose individual members, with but few exceptions, possesses an imagination capable of—"

"Transcending not only this but an uncountable number of adjacent universes," Watson cut in crossly. "How many more times do you have to rehearse the same boring argument?"

Holmes and Carnacki looked identically surprised.

"Why!" Holmes exclaimed. "Until one of us admits he's wrong!"

Nixy rose and drew aside a curtain, as though bored and in search of distraction. In fact, her eye had been caught by the fact that it had suddenly grown lighter outside. The radiance of the nearest gas lamp was now distinctly perceptible.

"The fog is lifting!" she cried.

Watson pulled a watch from his waistcoat pocket. It appeared to have too many functions for The Victorian Age. "Naturally," he said with a shrug. "Tomorrow is a Jubilee Day."

"Jubilee Day?" Rinpoche repeated.

"Yes!"—pocketing the watch again. "Re-enactment of the Diamond Jubilee of the queen after whom The Victorian Age is named. They hold it on the second Thursday of every other month. There's a procession. That's when they recycle the ingredients used for peasoupers. Cheaper than making them afresh. You'll probably hear the reclaimers in the small hours, sucking fogspawn off the buildings . . . You will stay the night, won't you?"

"Oh, we couldn't possibly!" Nixy exclaimed.

"My dear lady!" Holmes, insofar as his face could be made out amid the gray-blue vapor that enshrouded him, was looking offended. "I—we—insist! Should Mr. Carnacki and I deny ourselves the possibility that some event between now and morning may resolve this mystery? If, as he claims, these outrages are due to protesters enraged by your great-grandfather's ostentatious wealth, my Biker Street Irregulars will catch them *in flagrante*. If, on the contrary, I am correct, and we are dealing with a malign intelligence from beyond our normal plane, there is no one to whom I would more readily turn for assistance in such a case than Mr. Carnacki . . . once he had been convinced, of course."

"Of course," grunted the red-faced man with a trace of sarcasm.

"Well, then! It is agreed!" Holmes laid by his pipe and reached for a bell rope beside the mantel. "Mrs. Hudson will show you to your accommodations. We shall breakfast in exactly eight hours. I trust you like kedgeree and kippers? Then good night!"

And somehow, even before Rinpoche had realized he was on his feet, they were in a hideously overdecorated bedroom with flounces and valances and swags and drapes and a bright coal fire in the grate. Moreover, visible through a half-open door, there was—

"A bathroom!" Nixy exclaimed, darting toward it. "Why, it's perfect!" Even as she started enumerating its delights, she was unfastening her boots. "An enameled iron bath on ball-and-claw feet! Brass taps! Blue flowers in the toilet bowl—and a mahogany seat! I've always wanted to find out if those were really as comfortable as everybody claimed . . . Oh, not another disaster! HELP!"

The buttons on her footwear might be dummies, but those on the rest of her attire were not, and somehow she had got her hair tangled with them. Clumsy-fingered, shaking at the prospect of living through what he had so recently regarded as an impossible dream, he sorted out the problem and at length her dress fell to the floor. Putting the mahogany seat to the promised test, she thanked him and added, "Be a love and run us a bath. There's something else I've always wanted to try, a natural sponge. Isn't it a pretty shade of blue? And I suppose that black thing must be a loofah—or could it be pumice stone?"

"Did you say," Rinpoche ventured, choosing his words with maximum care, "run *us* a bath?"

"I'm sure you need one as much as I do after that disgusting fog!" was her tart response. "Anyway, if we're going to share a bed I insist on you being decently clean."

Rinpoche swallowed hard. "It's just that you said, earlier on, something about—uh—not having an affair while . . ."

"Oh, yes. So I did." Finished on the toilet, she was wriggling out of the remainder of her garments. "But Gramps is going to be pyrotechnical anyhow because I didn't make it to Las Vegas. I'll just have to arrange some nifty editing when I get home. Or maybe I should leave it in, let him understand that I'm a big girl now. Why haven't you turned the water on?"

I wouldn't have believed any girl could be so gorgeous.
Rinpoche hadn't intended to speak aloud, but must have done, for she answered sleepily from the next pillow.

"They did a pretty good job on me, didn't they?"

"Uh—!" He sat up, staring at her by the dim light of a gas lamp turned to its lowest. "Who did?"

"O'Donnell and Oliver. They're a very famous firm."

"Famous for what?" The pill hadn't supplied that information.

"Gene tailoring, of course. I told you my parents insisted on my being able to make people fall in love with me. You haven't forgotten!"

A lot of utterly wonderful, marvelous, and delectable events, most of them within the past hour, had crowded that kind of memory away from Rinpoche's awareness. But he said after a pause, "Of course not. I just didn't take it very seriously. You mean you were—well—sort of designed?"

"Of course." Her magnificent eyes flicked open, and a teasing smile played around her incredible mouth. "Nice Rin! It's wonderful to have such an impact, you know. I mean, most of my life has been spent among people much richer than my branch of the family. If you could see some of my aunts, for instance, you'd forget me in an instant. Their genes can make aliens fall in love with them!"

Surely you can't be implying . . . ?

It was too much. His eyelids drifted down, his head lolled, he groped with eager fingers for her nearer breast— and was asleep before he knew whether or not he was touching it.

"The computers suggest that we do WHAT?"

ELEVEN

TOWER BRIDGE IS FALLING DOWN, DANCE OVER MY LADY LEE

"MR. WINCHESTER REMINGTON COLT? I'M AFRAID I have bad news. Much though one must admire the hard work reflected in your project to re-enact the heyday of the American West, there is a problem even more intractable than the fact that horses, cattle, and buffalo are extinct and the planetary budget would not stretch to reconstructing or simulating them in the numbers you envisage—"

"Ah, cut the cackle and come to the horses!"

"But as I was just explaining . . . Oh. A metaphor. Well, then: the problem is that the territory in question was subsequently enclosed, farmed, built over, and ultimately urbanized. It simply is not feasible to restore it to its pristine state."

"You mean—?"

"Yes, Mr. Colt. Until you come up with an alternative location, your Wild West must remain an occident looking for somewhere to happen."

Beyond lace curtains the sun shone bright. London peasoupers might never have existed. Beside him Nixy stretched luxuriously.

"Did you sleep well?" she inquired. "I did. Somehow I felt confident that nothing awful was going to happen in the night. It was a wonderful relief."

She slipped out of bed and into the bathroom. Over the sound of running water he called his reply.

"I slept well, too. Up to now I've been feeling—well—

swept along. I suppose taking that knowledge pill has made the difference. Now I have the impression that things are under control. The fact that it isn't my control doesn't seem to matter very much."

"Yes, exactly," she agreed, reemerging with a huge Turkish towel around her. Discarding it, disdaining the insoluble complications of what she had worn yesterday, attired once more in her cascade of hair—plus a few sparkling drops of water—she headed for the door. Over her shoulder she warned, "You're going to be late for breakfast. Holmes said exactly eight hours."

He sat up with knee-jerk promptness.

"You're going to join them like that?"

"Oh, I couldn't possibly be bothered with—"

The door opened. A plump motherly person in brown said, "Ah! I suspected you might need help in dressing. I'm Mrs. Hudson, of course." And, to Rinpoche: "Don't fret, sir. I'm an old married woman and seen it all before. Just go about your usual ablutions."

"Mrs. Hudson . . . ?" Rinpoche's voice almost failed him. "Oh. I see. It's your turn?"

Severely: "One shouldnae refer tae it in sich tairms, if ye'll forgi'e me. It's ower risky tae leave a situation like this tae a pair o' wee bairns— Oh, excuse me! For a moment I slipped back into a Meg Merrilees program I had to take on last year . . . Miss, if you'll just raise your left foot? And now the right?"

After which, and after a shower and—to his complete amazement—a perfectly successful shave with a cutthroat razor such as he had never used before, Rinpoche felt entirely ready for breakfast. He was especially pleased about his achievement with the razor.

Until, that is, he mentioned it, and Mrs. Hudson, putting the final touches to Nixy's toilet, said without glancing round, "Yes, they work very well, those razors. The Japs came up with them in the early twenty-first. Can't cut yourself no matter how you try. Solar-powered, too."

And to Nixy: "There you are, ma'am. Now I must see the breakfast doesn't spoil."

As the door opened and shut, there ensued a strong smell of fish.

On top of that it came as no kind of surprise that today the rôles of Holmes and Watson had been taken by adults, the former gaunt, the latter mustachioed, far more in tune with what Rinpoche remembered from his own day. Of Carnacki there was no present sign.

At first there was no conversation either, just a nod this way and a nod that way as they were directed to help themselves to the food. How authentic it was, Rinpoche had no idea—though he had a vague notion that kippers ought to be brown—but it tasted fine. Both he and Nixy, who kept smiling at one another for no particular reason, did justice to everything Mrs. Hudson had prepared.

When they had nearly finished, Carnacki was announced, taking them aback because he was unchanged from last night.

"Well?" he demanded of Holmes.

"Nothing untoward," replied the new persona of the great detective. "At any rate nothing reported by the Irregulars. I think we may safely deduce that the anti-Anangaranga-Jones demonstrators have not yet been apprised of her presence under this roof."

"Hmm! I suppose I must revise my previous views. Pass the coffee, there's a good chap."

Rinpoche started. Unthinking, he had drunk coffee with his own meal; Spotch's conviction that it came as frozen cuboids hadn't crossed his mind. He mentioned the fact. Holmes, Watson, and Carnacki turned to him as one. After a pause, Holmes shrugged.

"Oh, coffee in America was always pretty foul, I gather. Nearly as bad as their tea. Now, Carnacki: what were you about to say?"

"That it's a shame for these two young people to be stuck indoors with old fogies like us on one of the rare sunny days we are allotted." Carnacki reached for sugar and milk. "Especially since we have nothing as yet to justify the confidence they showed in appealing to us . . . By the way, Mr. Gibbs: what did prompt you to seek a solution here in The Victorian Age?"

Nixy spoke up sharply. "How typical of your century! You address Rin instead of me, when it's my problem and my decision."

"I stand—excuse me: I sit—reproached."

"Well . . . Well, actually . . ." Nixy had the grace to look uncomfortable. "Actually we were advised to come here by a person I suspect of being a petty crook."

Not in the least embarrassed, Holmes leaned back chuckling. "Well, the criminal class has always had more respect for me than the forces of law and order—right, Watson?" Without waiting for a response, he went on, "I entirely concur with Mr. Carnacki. You two should get out and about while we mull over your case. The Jubilee Procession is well worth viewing, even if some of the conveyances are distinctly unhistorical. It's nearly as popular as Holyrood. You were there, were you not?"

"How did you find out where we'd been?" Rinpoche demanded.

"Tush, Mr. Gibbs! Is it not the duty of any detective to acquaint himself—or herself: one hears rumors of a newcomer named Marbles or Sharples or the like—with the full background of each client? Off with you! Walk along the Thames, mingle with the crowds, watch the Pearly Kings and Queens about their own ceremonies, and generally have fun while we take care of your problem. Oh, by the way: hire a four-wheeler rather than a hansom."

"Why?" Nixy demanded.

"Because ninety percent of our visitors have only heard of hansoms, and growlers deserve a more authentic share of the trade."

The words were accompanied by a wry twinkle. Rinpoche felt a surge of renewed confidence. He rose, bowed, offered his arm to Nixy, and they set forth.

* * *

Initially their route took them south down Baker Street and then east along Oxford Street. At the moment all this area lay within the Victorian Age. At first Nixy kept casting a nervous eye around for protesters, but it seemed that the Biker Street Irregulars' report had been correct. Moreover, whether or not the manifestation of Martians near the General Dump Office was connected with her presence, there was no sign of anything untoward about the city this fine morning. Accordingly, before their cab had borne them a kilometer, she started to relax and enjoy the outing.

The contrast with the fogbound London of last night could scarcely have been more complete. Every shop window, every door knocker, had blossomed with streamers of red, white, and blue—thanks, so Rinpoche's new knowledge told him, to the same machinery that last night had recycled the grime needed for the next peasouper; every sill supported windowboxes full of small but gaudy flowers, while polychrome wreaths encircled the blue-and-white plaques that adorned every housefront, commemorating famous persons who had resided on the premises, or on the site, or somewhere in London, or at any rate on Earth: WILLIAM SHAKSPEARE—THE DUKE OF WELLINGTON—ELVIS PRESLEY—HOMER . . .

The effect, however, was severely undermined by the scarcity of people. Those few who were on the street, unlike those at the General Dump Office, were not even trying to create the impression of a crowd. An organ-grinder churned out ancient music-hall numbers—but there was only one of him, and he looked dreadfully bored. Under an awning in a grassy square a brass band puffed and wheezed through excerpts from Wagner and Rossini—but it mustered only five players. A beggar warbled patriotic songs off-key, offering them for sale in broadside form—but he likewise was unique. One kite printed with a Union Jack soared high on a long string controlled by one cheeky Cockney lad, while nearby one other boy marched up and down carrying sandwich boards exhorting visitors to repair to Lord's Cricket Ground and watch someone called Dr. W. G. Grace (there was a picture; he had a formidable beard) score a hundred runs against a team from Old North Australia. A few paces further on one Cockney lass was playing hopscotch against herself while another drew pictures on the footway using colored chalks, a gadget like the one Spotch had used to check Rinpoche's credit lying at hand in case a passerby offered alms. All this to the extreme bewilderment of tourists, not just alien but human, too.

But it was quite astonishing how much more he himself understood of what he was seeing since taking that pink pill.

Beyond Temple Bar the ambiance began to shift toward Shakspeare's Day. In place of a brass band, a consort of lutes; posters and criers here urged people to view Master Will's *Twelfth Night* at the Globe Theatre and Master John Ford's *'Tis Pity She's a Whore* at the Curtain—the latter with pentasensory identification. (Rinpoche no longer had to wonder what that was.) There was an overwhelming reek of charred meat that Nixy's Hypermem identified as the Roast Beef of Old England.

"I suppose it's authentic," she said doubtfully, rubbing her temple as though in anticipation of another headache. "But it strikes me as being in awfully bad taste."

"More likely none," Rinpoche grunted. "Remember my hamburger."

At which poor joke, to his amazement, she actually laughed.

Their cab came to a standstill. Its driver called down from the box, "Yer lavder ged aht! Carn tike yer now furver!"

He gestured with his whip at the road ahead. It was blocked by a rigid orange structure seven or eight meters tall and almost the width of the street. A policeman in Victorian uniform and a constable of the watch in doublet and hose, paired like Gilbert and PC 49, were banging on its sides, the former with a truncheon, the latter with the hilt of a sword.

"Shoon't be allahd," the cabman muttered darkly. "Vair oughta be a lore!"

Rinpoche admitted he didn't understand.

"Eyen't got nah business blockin' a rahter vay like that! Fink vey can camp anywhere, dun vey? When vey dam' well oughta pie for a notel sime as everybody else! All ver money vair cheatin' us out of—'s a crahn' shime!"

"Camp?" Rinpoche blinked.

"Yerss! An' vey oughta be more careful at Customs, an' all!"

"That," Rinpoche worked out slowly, "is some sort of—of tent?"

"Never seen one before? Lahky you! *I* fought vaid figger darter way of stopnem cummin in, but when vey fold up smaller nufter stuffner pocket—well, I arse chew!"

"That thing can fit in a pocket?"

"Lor' luvaduck! Does yer muvver now yer aht?"

Nixy, chuckling, was plucking at his sleeve.

"It's an Alcahelan," she murmured. "Very independent-minded. It wants to rest, and rest it will. Let's walk the rest of the way."

Just as they descended from the cab, a concealed opening in the side of the orange structure shot wide and a furious-looking head appeared, bellowing. It disconcerted Rinpoche greatly to realize that the expression was due to a plastic mask; what portion of what sort of anatomy it might be concealing, he had no idea. The compounders of the knowledge pill seemingly had not expected him to meet Alcahelans.

The policeman and his companion responded in kind. To a barrage of accusations and a volley of rebuttals Nixy and Rinpoche slipped behind them, took turns in squeezing past the orange "tent"—which Rinpoche touched as he went by, finding incredulously that it felt as solid as a galvanised iron water tank—and emerged into what was very definitely Shakspeare's Day.

Remembering what they had been told at the Dump Office yesterday, Rinpoche fully expected orders to don and pay for appropriate or at any rate approximate costume. However, they were far from the only people anachronistically dressed. His pill-got knowledge furnished no explanation, so he mentioned the fact to Nixy. Braving the risk of further pain, she consulted her Hypermem again. It emerged that the rule was nothing like as strictly enforced as the officers who had met them on arrival would have them believe—though naturally they had failed to observe the fact in last night's fog—and did not apply at all in frontier areas like this one where the Jubilee procession had to pass through Shakspeare's Day, because regulations of that kind had in the past discouraged too many people from coming to London at all.

Anyway, there weren't many aliens who looked good and felt comfortable in Elizabethan garb.

Following the river, they eventually had to negotiate a pedestrian tunnel from whose far end they emerged among a scattering of beings, human and otherwise, within sight of a gray castle on a low rise. To Rinpoche's cynical view it seemed no more authentic than Holyrood. Nixy's Hypermem, however, insisted that it dated back twelve or thirteen hundred years, though it had been much restored.

Nearby a red creature with antennae like white ferns infringed customary politeness by letting a snatch of its guidance commentary, and its response thereto, be overheard in terrestrial translation.

"That corresponds to one zump, one quitch. It is thus old."

"You cannot be serious, fume. My den exists already octeen zumps, fume-fume. Why must I waste credit to view passitransient ephemerates, fume-burn-fume—burn?"

Its vocabulator seemed to be having difficulty in expressing such annoyance.

What happened next, Rinpoche failed to follow, for Nixy had let out a gasp and was pointing to make him turn around. Complying, he saw spanning the river—whose waters were dotted with boats of varying sizes, all bar the smallest such as skiffs and canoes dressed overall in honor of the Jubilee—a most peculiar structure consisting of two ornate towers linked at the top and the base, in the latter case by a roadway. Faint memories stirred.

"London Bridge! Of course!" Nixy breathed. "I've seen pictures. It wasn't something Gramps wanted to remember seeing, but I'm sure even he would be pleased to have it as an extra—"

"Correction," said a bored voice at her side. "It's Tower Bridge."

The speaker was a gloomy-looking man in silver filigree jacket and shorts, barely denser than cobwebs.

"Are you sure?" Nixy countered.

"As sure as one can be of anything when the universe is a figment of one's imagination. And a rotten bad imagination I have, at that."

"Come now!" Nixy exclaimed. "It's a beautiful day, and everybody's looking forward to the parade, so if that's what you've imagined I don't think it can be too bad."

"You wouldn't," the silver man snapped, and turned away. She caught his sleeve—carefully, for fear of tearing the delicate fabric.

"I'm sorry! I didn't mean to give offense, especially since you were kind enough to set me right about the bridge. My Hypermem just confirmed what you said."

"I'm sure you didn't mean to," the man sighed. "When I'm around, though, people do it automatically. It's the fault of my imagination—I just told you."

"I'm afraid I don't understand," Rinpoche admitted after a moment. He had the impression that he was still saying that rather a lot.

"I'm from Pangloss."

"Oh!" Nixy exclaimed. Rinpoche glanced a question at her.

"That's one of the rare worlds that humans share with intelligent indigenes. Isn't that right, Mr.—?"

"Peel, Candide Peel. Yes, that's right. And they have a . . . Well, it's not quite a philosophy, more a conviction, that every being gets the best universe it can imagine. It's always worked fine for them, so bit by bit we human Panglossians have come around to the same point of view. Trouble with me is, I only seem able to imagine a universe I don't enjoy at all."

"In that case," Nixy cried, "what are you doing on Earth? Didn't you come here expecting to have a good time?"

"I dared to hope," Mr. Peel muttered.

"What went wrong?"

"Everywhere I go I bump into a big red-haired man who keeps telling me I'm in a condition of doubt. As though I needed to be told!"

A gruff voice broke in. At first Rinpoche failed to register its source; abruptly, though, he realized that the words emanated from a sad-eyed cocker spaniel pissing on a nearby tuft of grass.

A talking dog? Well, I suppose if you can have mutated elephants working for the Immigration Service . . .

What it had actually said, as reheard in short-term memory, was: "Dressed in a long, loose outfit kind of like a kaftan or a muumuu? Says he wears it because it's called after his family?"

"Uh—yes," said the unhappy man, blinking.

"Yeah, I know that mother. Don't believe a word he says."

"Why not?"

"He promised he'd give me a bone. And did he? Did he hell."

On which the spaniel, its business finished, ambled away.

"Was that a dog?" asked Mr. Peel after awhile.

"Yes," Rinpoche forced out.

"What was supposed to be so bad about a dog's life? I mean, compared with what I've been through, not being given a bone— Oh, no! It's him again! And heading this way!"

Hauling his jacket up around his ears, though it did nothing to conceal his face, the Panglossian took to his heels.

By now Victorian policemen in frock coats and cylindrical black hats were announcing the imminence of the procession and urging the onlookers to clear the roadway. There being so few of them, it wasn't difficult. Nixy and Rinpoche ascended the slope beneath the gray fortress, and on turning at the top found they had an excellent view. Distant music drifted on the warm, still air. Flags and banners waved. Now and then sunlight glinted on the approaching parade.

Adjacent to where they were standing a small patch of ground was completely vacant. Rinpoche ventured to set foot on it, only to hear a stern voice inside his head warn, "Reserved!" He stepped back again hastily. Just as well, for bare seconds later a stream of people in a gallimaufry of attire filed out of one of those zones of curdled air he had learned to recognize even before his knowledge pill. Leading them was a brisk-mannered woman, or perhaps simulacrum.

"Here we are," she announced loudly, "at our last stop before departure: London, England. Details of this city and its history can be found in the mindfix you received prior to the tour. With your eyes open subvocalize the name London and you will clearly remember having wandered its broadest avenues and narrowest alleys, climbed its highest tower, explored its deepest tunnel, eaten in its finest restaurant, and slept in its most luxurious hotel. Now if you'll kindly follow me—"

"Is that all?" shouted a woman from the back of the group. "Fifteen minutes for the whole of Earth?"

"Well, it's not a very important planet, is it? And let me just remind you that our next destination is Beta Lyrae III, which I'm sure we are all anxious to enjoy, and there we shall spend a full hour. This way, please. Your baggage will be ready in twelve point five seconds."

Dutiful, the group vanished as though they had never existed. But Rinpoche was a trifle disturbed by overhearing what the last two tourists were saying to one another immediately before departure:

"Weren't we supposed to remember being eaten by a rhinoceros?"

To which, with a sigh: "Olaf, for pity's sake, don't tell me you've thought of *another* reason to complain!"

"Commentary?" wheedled a pedlar with a strap-suspended tray. Capsule recordings were his chief stock in trade, but his wares included rosettes, flags, souvenirs, and cockades, some with improbable means of attachment destined no doubt for aliens.

"Yes!" Nixy said, and presented her right eye. Moments later, with capsules in their ears, they were listening to a bored remote voice informing them about the Jubilee parade just as it reached the bridge. At its head marched men and women naked save for boots and belts.

"—in a place of honor at the front you will see the Brigade of Guards, renowned for their bravery in battle and their refusal to wear any garb save 'busbies,' a term that means 'bare skins.' "

Well, so far the commentary seemed accurate enough. And it was right about the marching band that followed, too, though Nixy had doubts about the Household Calvary. She found it hard to imagine why a life-size sculpture of a man streaked with blood and hanging from a cross deserved to figure in what was meant to be a celebration, and never having been a Christian, Rinpoche was unable to enlighten her.

From then on it became increasingly difficult to reconcile what they were hearing with what they were seeing. How exactly did acrobats and tumblers using antigrav for extra bounce correspond to "the crowned heads of India and Indonesia (simulated)"? And why were "pupils of the Empire's most famous educational establishments" singing a bawdy ballad and spraying the onlookers with dirty water? (Rinpoche wondered once again what had happened to those unfortunate teachers whose pupils had replaced themselves with simulacra.) And why did the Invergralloch Pipe Band look more like five- and six-year-olds on powered scooters?

Turning to Nixy to ask her opinion, Rinpoche realized with alarm that her face was pale and her lower lip was trembling. A tear was stealing down her nearer cheek.

"Nixy darling!" he exclaimed. She seemed not to hear, but spoke in the faintest of whispers.

"It's going wrong again, something's always going wrong whenever I'm around, and Sherlock Holmes believes I'm being haunted!"

"But Carnacki disagreed," Rinpoche stressed, wishing with all his heart to comfort her. "Besides—"

"Besides, I'm being an idiot," she interrupted, and forced a laugh. "How incredibly stupid of me! I mean, after meeting Kardek I ought to be more on the *qui-vive*, oughtn't I?"

"Uh . . . What?"

She tore the capsule from her ear.

"That damned pedlar sold us an out-of-date commentary. No wonder it doesn't match what we're looking at! And there I was assuming it was another of the disasters that are following me around . . . You see, these parades work like the Holyrood deal: according to what you can afford, you get to take part either in the march, or waving from a good conspicuous window, or riding in a carriage, or if you're seriously rich playing the rôle of one of the kings and presidents and maharajahs who used to turn up from all over the planet for this sort of show. You must have had them in your day, surely?"

All trace of tears evaporated, she turned her former merry face to him. He pondered a moment; then offered feebly, "Ticker-tape parades?"

"What?"—with a brief frown. And listened to her Hypermem, as usual. Her brow cleared.

"Oh! In New York. Yes, they've tried to bring those back. But the autho version is on hold. They'll have to plant another billion trees first. Meantime they do it with atmoplanar optostims."

That term was covered by his knowledge pills, but another word she had just used was not. He repeated, "Ortho?"

"*Autho*. It gets to be a drag saying 'authentic' all the time."

Amen to that.

"Still," Nixy resumed, pressing his hand more warmly than ever, "it could be quite amusing, hm? Seeing one thing, hearing it described as something different—the incongruity could make it rather funny. And there isn't much left to laugh at, you know."

Rinpoche stared at her. He countered, "Now people have gone out to all those other stars, there isn't much to laugh at? I'd have thought there were millions of new jokes waiting to be invented."

"I'm afraid not." She looked suddenly downcast. "You see, apparently our sense of humor is unique to us, like religion, and there's a school of thought among the Galactic Conglomerate that claims we ought to be cured of that as well, only they can't prove it's harmful enough. They—"

"Ssh!" hissed a pasty-faced man a step or two away. "For pity's sake! You'll bring them down on us!"

Nixy's face fell. "I'm sorry. I wasn't thinking. This is just the kind of place they come to, isn't it?"

The pasty man gave a glum nod.

"Who come to?" Rinpoche asked in bewilderment.

"Humanologists!" snapped the pale-faced man. "I was a clown once, myself. Ah, more than just a clown, a true auguste, in the tradition of Coco and Grimaldi! I was"—he drew himself up to his full stature and clapped himself on the chest, at which he instantly began wheezing and choking but achieved a miraculous recovery by rabbit-punching the back of his neck—"Loony Lee, the Child of Three! You should have seen the merriment I could *wring* out of a wet diaper, hah-hah! And now I am as you see me, in despair."

"I'm sorry," Rinpoche said feebly. "But why?"

"Have you ever had your finest jokes microscoped by a humanologist who keeps on saying, 'Yes, I understand that, but you haven't told me what makes it funny'? Oh, they can keep it up for weeks, you know. A single day is nothing. In the end they get you so worried you realize: you don't know. You don't know whether it was actually funny—whether anything is funny—whether anything could ever have been regarded as funny by anyone. You doubt the evidence of memory. You pester your friends, and they stop being friends. You search the past obsessively and try to reconstruct the gags and pranks of your forerunners, but of course they're no longer novel, so you lose heart, so you think—you just said something to this effect—you think of going to search for new ideas on other worlds, but because you can't make people laugh anymore you can't raise enough money for the trip, and in the end . . . Oh, if it weren't so tragic it would be a screaming farce! Hah-ha-*hah!*"

In an instant, somehow, he was genuinely laughing. Whereupon, within the blink of an eye, something gaunt and severe swooped out of the sky, barely more than a perceptible wisp of existence, and in a reedy but authoritative voice declared:

"You are cachinnating. As a certified humanologist, I am empowered to demand of any human found in that condition answers to the following questions. Number one: what was the proximate stimulus or trigger that initiated the process? I am prepared to wait while you recover from your derangement, but kindly do not impose on my goodwill."

It sat back, sort of, apparently on the air, and composed itself in what Rinpoche supposed must be a patient attitude.

Nixy nudged his elbow.

"Before we're arrested as material witnesses—*run!*"

Panting, they halted on the far side of a block of seating erected to overlook the bridge and river, which Rinpoche found himself eying warily in case it went the way of the grandstand at Holyrood. He said between gasps, "You mean that thing could have arrested us just for watching someone laugh? By what right?"

Nixy's lovely face became a mask of intensity. "Don't think that just because humans are the richest species in the galaxy Earth enjoys special privileges. On the contrary: it's fair game for every imposition the aliens want to inflict. They don't like us, you know. They have to put up with us, but all intelligent beings are alike in one way at least. They're jealous. Petty jealous. Though how can you blame them, when a fool like Gramps can decide to flaunt his wealth on such an offensive scale? I'm sure there must have been twenty races that would have liked to take over such a habitable planet, for twenty far better reasons!"

"Habitable?" Rinpoche echoed. "I thought it was due to get sterilized by the supernova."

"Oh, sure, and so it would but for the timeslow—which wasn't one of our inventions. But you have to call it habitable because it used to be inhabited."

"By an intelligent species?"

She bit her lip, continuing to stare down as the parade trudged or rolled or hobbled or bounced or crawled across Tower Bridge. There seemed to be a high incidence of nonhumans today, over fifty percent. "Well, that depends what you mean by intelligent. The general estimate is: not very. I was told that they must have got bored and gone away without realizing the value of what they had. In either sense."

"So who did your gramps buy it from?" Rinpoche asked slowly. He could feel more of the information he had ingested itching inside his brain. The sensation was mildly unpleasant, like the feeling one gets in a toe after having to rearrange its position manually. Although part of what he had acquired from the knowledge pill had slotted into place, a lot more was still seeking other data to hook on to. "Didn't Kardek mention the name Klosh?"

Nixy made an impatient gesture, still staring toward the bridge. "A bunch of golden coaches are supposed to wind up the parade about now, after which we can go and do something else . . . Oh, it's no good asking me for details! Gramps has always been secretive about his affairs, and me being so far down the family totem pole . . . Rin, you've asked me lots about me and my family, but you haven't told me anything about yourself except that you're a wreck." She glanced sideways with a grin. "In pretty good shape, I must admit."

For an instant Rinpoche was tempted to disclose the private history that had followed him—exactly as he had *not* hoped—beyond the grave, or at any rate the cryovault. Indeed, given another half minute he might have done so despite the barely guessable consequences. It so happened, though, that before he could frame the words a shout arose from the crowds that lined the riverbank. Magnetically drawn, they turned along with everybody else, to see . . .

To see what? At first everything appeared normal. Here came the golden coaches, six in all; the first two had passed the midpoint of the bridge, the third was about to, the rest were following, all pulled by better simulated horses than at Holyrood, and—

Nixy gasped, her fingers cramping on his wrist.

"Rin, *the bridge*! It's opening! It's going up! This must be the awful thing I've been expecting! Yes! Yes, it is!"

In exactly the same moment a banner unfurled from the upper span of the bridge. In enormous letters it read:

DENOUNCE THE PURCHASE OF NAJQ-30122-3!

"What does that mean?" Rinpoche demanded.

"It's my address," Nixy whimpered. "Gramps's, that is. It's the code for the system he bought. So Carnacki was right after all! It's the anti-me demonstrators that are responsible . . . for that!"

She flung up her arm and pointed, just as the rest of the crowd began to realize what was happening. Rinpoche kept his arm around her to offer what reassurance he could, but if the protestors could achieve this, might they not trace her in the midst of the throng, identify, and attack her? A mob, no doubt, must still be a mob. Sometimes he had seen what well-led mobs could be inspired to do—

But I absolutely do not want to think of that.

The bascules parted with majestic slowness. Those riding in the coaches at first failed to notice, being too preoccupied with their rôles—waving to the onlookers, bowing graciously this way and that, ensuring that they presented their best profiles (or if they were circumferentially indistinguishable, as was the case with some of the aliens representing foreign royalty, their preferred epidermal texture) and complaining about how their travel agencies had cheated them into wasting good credit on this second-rate apology for a spectacle.

Then, of a sudden, they realized that their horses were either trying to climb an impossible hill, or skidding and sliding down an ever-increasing slope.

The roadway tilted further yet. Hooves and wheels lost their grip altogether. On the northern side twelve horses and three coaches rushed together in as it were a Wellsian analogy for stellar collision; on the southern, three coaches and twelve horses slithered into a churning heap much resembling a Vernian description of cometary impact. The really efficient tour operators conjured up instant dumpers and whisked their patrons out of harm's way, little the worse and perhaps even a trifle better inasmuch as they had a unique extra tale to tell. Unfortunately few tour operators were that efficient, and none of those based on Earth. Their customers had the option of staying put and sustaining fractured arms and legs (or injuries to limbs for which there were no terrestrial names), and then waiting to be mended, which would mean at the least *un mauvais quart d'heure*; or jumping into the Thames—which in spite of the best efforts of the Yelignese was still sluggish, dirty, and extremely cold—and waiting to be fished out and dried.

Those who had decided to jump found those who had decided not to getting in their way. Tempers were lost. Altercations broke out. Within minutes, on either side of the bridge—both of whose bascules were now at maximum elevation—there ensued a free fight mingled with sheer panic. It began to spread.

"We've got to get out of here!" Rinpoche cried, and dragged Nixy in search of a cab. At this juncture whether it was a growler or a hansom or even a sedan chair seemed not to matter very much.

"The computers suggest that we do WHAT?"

TWELVE

A MATTER OF JUST OR POSSIBLY UNJUST DESERTS

"Madam, welcome to Earth! You commissioned us to select the ideal location for your authentic-in-all-respects nineteenth-century-style hydrotherapy center designed to cajole a fortune out of the galaxy's wealthy hypochondriacs. We believe we've done so. Not only does it accord with your specifications; it offers a bonus, inasmuch as the air of the birthworld has been permeated ever since the evolution of our primordial ancestors with psychical vibrations conducive to—"

"Are you crazy? Who'd want to come here? This dump is freezing!"

"But you told us to choose a site with naturally hard water! . . *"*

"Life's too short. Just return your fee. If not, I'll sue."

"This is indeed a three-pipe problem," Holmes muttered when he had heard Nixy and Rinpoche's account of events. "Certainly my original theory of a haunting seems to have been well and truly dashed—"

"I say, old chap, hang on!" Watson objected.

"Yes, hang on indeed," grunted Carnacki.

"But why? You were right. The culprits have finally shown their hand. Flying that banner from Tower Bridge, whose bascules incidentally I understood to be jammed shut from neglect of maintenance—"

"No, no! That strikes me as a mere diversion. Had it

been due to protesters aware that their target was in the vicinity, they would surely have converged on her."

"The throng might have been too dense," Watson countered, playing devil's advocate. Carnacki rebuffed him with a snort.

"Dense? In London? Since when have there been enough of us for a decent crowd? And even on a Jubilee Day there aren't that many tourists. If it is a haunting, as I now concur, it wouldn't be the first time that an entity from beyond our spacetime achieved control over physical objects and even quite a sophisticated comprehension of human language and behavior, without being able to recognize a given individual. Is it not significant that each incident so far has taken place near, but never at, the spot where the young lady was?"

"Except the earthquake," Watson pointed out.

"Granted. But earthquakes are notoriously undiscriminating."

There followed a glum silence. Rinpoche broke it in annoyance.

"Can't we stop this playacting? You have access to computers far superior to what we had in my day. What do they say?"

The three other men looked at him in astonishment.

"Precisely what we're telling you," was Holmes's answer. "Why do you think the CB ticked us off for tying up so much capacity?"

Rinpoche shook his head in bafflement. "Are you trying to tell me that the best modern computers can't cope with Nixy's problem?"

"Well, it would be rather expensive to consult the *best* modern—"

"You know what I mean!"

Holmes shrugged. "I suppose I do . . . Frankly, Mr. Gibbs, neither my colleagues nor I nor the Yelignese machines, which far surpass any that we humans have ever developed, possess sufficient evidence to decide between the competing possibilities. Bear in mind, please, that the computers are analyzing the potential of billions of future scenarios on each of several thousand planets—"

A whole block of information had been waiting inside Rinpoche's head for something to latch on to. That was the hook. Abruptly he was exposed to the full implications of instantaneous interstellar travel. One could never arrive in the same universe that one had left . . . and it didn't matter in the least, for there were a transfinite number of universes indistinguishable by the coarse perception of humans.

He groaned a little. Holmes looked a question at him. Weakly he waved an invitation to continue.

"Priority has to be granted to the distant unforeseeable rather than the actual, because the latter—in principle at any rate—ought to be susceptible to common or garden rationality. Miss Jones's case, inasmuch as it's currently happening, must be classed as actual."

"Are you implying that even machines take this notion of being haunted seriously? I can't believe it!" Rinpoche clenched his fists. Unfortunately one of Nixy's hands was within his grasp. She pulled free with a yelp of pain. The rest of what he had intended to say got lost in a flurry of apologies to which the others paid no attention.

In a placatory tone Watson explained, "Mr. Gibbs, we aren't talking about ghosts such as people imagined in your day. No being returns from the dead."

"It's just," Carnacki added dryly, "that some species have peculiar ways of being alive. Eh, Holmes?"

Unbending a little, the great detective nodded. "One thinks at once of the Giant Algolian Sphudge . . . but kindly do not press me for details. Watson contends, and I agree: that is a case the galaxy is not ready to be told about."

Nixy glanced up. "Algolian sphudges? When I was a kid they gave me a sphudge for a pet. It was about as long as my forearm. Giant?"

There was a tense pause. Eventually Holmes shrugged. "I will go this far. Your 'pet' was only a four-dimensional aspect of the whole."

Nixy's eyes widened tremendously. "Out of how much?"

"If I told you, you wouldn't believe it." Briskening, Holmes addressed his colleagues again. "Still, there's one point we and the computers do agree on, isn't there?"

The others nodded. Rinpoche inquired what the point might be.

"There is no chance of settling the matter unless Miss Jones continues to expose herself"—

She does look gorgeous wearing nothing but her hair! I hope we can return to places where she can shed this all-concealing gear! Can—can . . . ? Oh, this is worse than parentheses! And it is one!

—"to the possibility of attack. She will, of course, be under strict surveillance at all times, although if this is indeed a case of haunting, forestalment is obviously out of the question, and we shall have to rely on prompt response. If what we're dealing with is merely a group of ingenious protesters trying to attract attention to their point of view, we stand an excellent chance of flushing them into the open, at which stage they can be arrested, deported, reconditioned, or returned to the protein pool, and the lady will have no further trouble."

Who was saying this? Holmes? Carnacki? Watson? It didn't sound like any of their voices, yet it must be one of them, the one who—

But there wasn't one not paying rapt attention.

The moment passed and everything felt normal again— insofar as anything in this day and age could be so termed. Nixy was demanding:

"So I'm to waft around imitating bait, am I? What about my gramps? What's he going to say when he finds out I simply quit trying to collect any of the memories he wanted? It's his credit I'm spending!"

"He will say," Watson assured her bluffly, "that since it was a matter of protecting life and limb and maybe sanity—"

"You don't know gramps!"

"You don't know what we can do to make sure that even

he acts in a reasonable manner," Watson assured Nixy with
a smile. Albeit doubtfully, she began to consider the possibility of cheering up.

"But," Rinpoche pressed, "what does she actually have
to *do*?"

"Go on a tour of Earth far surpassing what her great[4]-
grandfather asked for," Holmes replied—which made Nixy
gloomy all over again.

"Will it include Las Vegas? Little Italy XIX? Little Venice?"

"I'm afraid that's not up to us. The trip will be randomized."

Carnacki snorted. "Holmes, I'm surprised at you! It will
be the opposite of random: preplanned to the umpteenth
decimal point in order to maximize our chance of un-
masking the perpetrators."

"But to Miss Jones and Mr. Gibbs, who are human,"
Holmes countered, his usual urbanity restored, "it will seem
patternless, won't it?"

Without waiting for a response, he continued: "As you
progress, it will become more and more clear by what
means your persecutor is discovering your whereabouts.
Within, one hopes, at worst a few days—"

"But this is terrible!" Nixy exploded, jumping to her
feet. "It's so cold-blooded! Wherever I go dreadful things
start to happen! At Naples some ghastly monster crawled
out of the sea, at Holyrood that seating collapsed, at San
Francisco there was an earthquake on the wrong day, a Hotel Interdimensional got shunted into another part of space,
and this morning the Jubilee parade was ruined! I'll never
forget the sight of those poor people screaming as their
coaches were smashed to matchwood amid the flailing
hooves of panic-stricken horses! Who else are you going to
condemn to suffering because of me?" She bent forward,
head sunk in hands and shoulders heaving.

Musingly Holmes said, "I wonder whether you've ever
seen matchwood ... Watson, Miss Jones is dramatizing.
Enlighten her concerning the true situation."

Resignedly: "In any re-enactment zone, even an unapproved one, it's illegal for intelligent beings to be harmed. In the event of a mishap they may briefly experience pain, and many of them ask for it specifically because it's novel, but all are guaranteed a swift return to their previous state. Mark you, it's not certain how much longer this can continue after what's been happening recently. The Algenib Underwriters—Mr. Gibbs?"

"That reminds me of what I meant to ask a moment ago. Who's going to pay for this tour you're talking about?"

"You are. Along with my consultation fee."

"*What?*"

"You can afford it. Through an oversight—if oversight it was, which strikes me as dubitable—the Yelignese, as well as omitting to supply you with a knowledge pill, have granted you control of a remarkable quantity of credit. Despite one silly extravagance it is effectively undiminished and will remain so thanks to a built-in escalation clause. Besides, you want to help your lady, don't you?"

For an instant Nixy bridled: *Just because I'm wearing Victorian garb, don't imagine I'm a Victorian miss!* But after a moment's reflection she said merely, "I wish I knew what you mean by a dubitable oversight. There's nothing relevant in my Hypermem."

"I'm not surprised," Carnacki said dryly. "I told you before: when it comes to data about Earth Hypermems have— ah—certain flaws. But surely your unaided intelligence has prompted some relevant questions?"

He glanced at Watson. "By the way, have you not skated over another point that Miss Jones may care to be warned about?"

Watson looked put out. However, he duly amplified.

"It appears that the quickest way to tempt the culprits into the open will be for you to visit not just recognized re-enactment zones but ventures that remain unapproved." He coughed behind his hand. "Few are what one would term competently managed."

"In some cases they're downright dangerous!" Carnacki growled. "Not that you'd run any risks, of course."

"How's that again?" Rinpoche demanded. Nixy forestalled the reply.

"I'm too rich," she sighed. "Nothing worse to fear for yours truly than that stellaration from Gramps when I get home. What a miserable existence, don't you think? Rin, how do you feel about this age you've woken up in? Not a patch on the past, is it? Like I told you, like Loony Lee confirmed, we don't even have proper jokes anymore. Half of us have run out of ideas for them, and the other half secretly agree that a sense of humor should be classed as a psychosis." She shook her head, looking infinitely doleful.

After a few moments, though, she pulled herself together. "Well, I suppose if I'm ever to resume what passes for a normal life, I'd better clear this problem out of the way. I don't plan to tackle the job in this hideous outfit, for a start." She plucked at ornamental stitching on her bodice. "And I don't suppose Rin cares too much for his gear, either. Let's get hold of something more practical."

"Mrs. Hudson," Holmes said in a voice suspiciously close to a purr, "has made arrangements. Pray entrust yourselves to her."

Presumably their new garments were "universals" of the kind Nixy had declined to buy from Benjy at the General Dump Office. They remained amazingly comfortable whether they were masquerading as jacket and trousers or blouse and skirt or parka and drainpipes or bolero and baggies, all of which plus many more variations could be arranged simply by whispering to a micromike in the left cuff. Inevitably they had to be paid for, so Rinpoche presented his right eye to be flashed by Mrs. Hudson. The afterimage endured longer than on previous occasions. He queried that.

"Why!" she exclaimed with a beam. "You've just paid not only for your new outfits, but for yourself and the young lady to visit as many re-enactment zones both recognized and independent as can be found on planet Earth, with the option of side trips to the Moon, under nonstop surveillance by Scotland Yard Incorporated, established 1829, all types of protection and investigation, high standards, low rates. Cor lummy, guv'nor—as Mr. Holmes's Irregulars would say if they ever bothered to say anything—yer down 'arf chuck yer bobs an' quids arahnd!"

Rinpoche gave her a severe look. "What happened to your Meg Merrilees program? Don't answer that. Just take us back to Mr. Holmes."

"Where's Mr. Carnacki?" Nixy demanded as on striding into the room she found only two men present.

"Hmm?" Holmes glanced up from a sheet of paper he and Watson were studying. "Oh, it's been switched off. Now here we have a table of potential destinations for you as it will be supplied to Scotland Yard, Inc., not of course in sequence because the whole scheme depends on trying to outfox the opposition—Mr. Gibbs?"

"Switched off?" Rinpoche mumbled.

"You didn't realize it was a simulacrum?"

"But you're not! Nor is Watson!"

"True. Nor was yesterday's Carnacki."

"But he drank coffee at breakfast time! I saw him!"

Frostily: "And what would you expect a simulacrum to drink? Petrol—or as you would say, gasoline? The idea's absurd. Anyway, there's none left."

"But Welcome to Suburbia—gas-guzzlers—Studebaker Mustang—"

"Garbage juice."

"I *beg* your pardon?"

"Or rubbish juice as I suppose we'd call it in Britain if we had any left. No one else, though, was as wasteful as the Yanks. They boil it off from old landfill sites. Dodgy stuff, terribly expensive, reserved for special purposes like the LA commuter experience."

"But I understood that coffee was expensive, too, since the crunchiform blight. Yet—"

"Indeed it is, but you can afford it, so we took shameless advantage of the fact. It will appear on your bill, don't worry. Tomorrow Holmes and Watson, whoever they may be by then, will revert to Thubanese floob, an analog like crench or shunk, albeit less convincing. Now if you've quite finished . . . ? *Thank* you. Having ingested a knowledge pill, you must by now be aware that there are few competent people left on this planet, and because many of them are elephants we have scarcely any fit to cope with a demanding rôle in a re-enactment zone. Perhaps you don't appreciate what a small number there actually are. Even among wrecks like yourself, whose best chance of a job to pay off their storage charges lies in securing, or as one might say enduring, a re-enactment rôle, there are plenty of candidates eager to play Akhnaten or Chaka Zulu or Don Quixote, but almost no one on or off the planet remembers who Carnacki was—or would have been had he existed—so he has to be part-time. Anyone capable of a decent version of such a rôle is liable to be called away without notice for more demanding projects. Today, for instance, the man you met being Carnacki is at Lambaréné impersonating Albert Schweitzer for a bunch of tourists from Rootsworld who look forward to flaying him alive as a corrupt and shameless tool of white colonialist exploiters—"

Downstairs the doorbell clanged. Those up here paid no attention, for Rinpoche had failed to suppress a groan. Solicitously Watson reached to count his pulse. His hand was brushed aside.

"But Schweitzer was real! Do people honestly not differentiate any more between fictional characters and those who actually lived?"

"Who?" Holmes returned. "The Yelignese? Why should they? This wasn't their birthworld—insofar as Yelignese are born. And virtually no humans cared enough to come home and advise them. In any case most people had given up bothering, even in your day. No doubt you recall how they allowed lies and pseudoscience to be taught as truth to

American blacks. Oh, we have only our own species to blame."

"Or thank," Watson put in.

"Yes, one must admit Sherlock Holmes is more fun than Peter the Great. Or Medina-Sidonia, sick at every tilt of his ship."

Before anyone else could speak Mrs. Hudson entered, her expression agitated. "Mr. Holmes!" she exclaimed. "There's a person below claiming to be a friend of your clients. *But ah hae ma doots!*"

Her Meg Merrilees program was surfacing again. Realizing, she grimaced before going on. "Are Miss Jones and Mr. Gibbs acquainted with a Mr. Maximilian Kardek?"

Exchanging glances with Nixy, Rinpoche admitted, "As a matter of fact, we have met a person of that name."

On the instant, a cheery shout.

"I'd know that voice anywhere! Rin, my dear chap, tell that gorgon to stop blocking my way! Nixy old girl, are you there, too?"

And he could be heard ascending the stairs two at a time.

"Timeslow!" Holmes barked at Watson, who spun around. The thump of feet halted. An unpleasant sense of inverse pressure afflicted their ears. Disregarding it, Holmes strode onto the landing and the rest rushed after.

There was Kardek, wearing crimson and ultramarine today, fixed in mid-stride halfway up the stairs, surrounded by a shimmer like a heat haze on a sunlit road. But it could clearly be discerned that in the hand with which he was not clasping the banister rail, he was clutching a document a-dangle with seals.

"Hah!" Holmes exclaimed. "Miss Jones, is this perchance the person who extorted a fee merely for recommending that you consult me? Yes? Ah-hah! Exactly the type of venial ne'erdowell who would accept base employment as a summoner!"

"Is that a summons?" Nixy whispered, pointing.

"Indeed it is."

"Because we ran away from those stupid detectives in California?"

"That remains to be determined. Watson, my telescope!"

Hastily Watson fetched an extensible brass tube. Applying it to his right eye Holmes examined the summons at long range and reported, "I find no reference to your misadventure in San Francisco. However, you, Mr. Gibbs, are to be arraigned on a spectrum of charges."

"Such as what?"

"False pretenses, obtaining credit by fraud, impersonation, genocide, making an affray, grand theft auto, constructive barratry . . . Ah, a maritime offense. That is at least an unusual touch." He collapsed the telescope.

"But who—?" Nixy began. More data from Rinpoche's knowledge pill crunched into place. He interrupted.

"There's little or no chance of finding out who's to blame—aren't I right?"

Holmes nodded gravely. "These accusations may very well have been laid by the detectives who made such fools of themselves in California, as a means of getting their own back, but there is, as you say, small hope of proving it, thanks to a system akin to the ancient *lettres de cachet* whereby anyone may bring anonymous charges against anyone else and they have to be acted upon. The scheme was devised by American lawyers in the twenty-first century when they became so numerous that half or more couldn't make enough to live on. Now the reverse obtains. In the last galactic census twenty-eight of the hundred richest—"

Mrs. Hudson interrupted. "Mr. Holmes, we daren't keep the timeslow running! Our power credit's stretched as it is!"

Holmes did the same: stretched, that is. And also yawned.

"Oh, bill the energy to Mr. Gibbs. After all—"

"After all WHAT?" Rinpoche blared. "You're spending my credit when even I don't know how much I have! All I do know is that when I bought something I expected to be cheap it cost a fortune! Besides, you said it might be an oversight, so they could claim it back at any moment!"

"The more I have to do with the Yelignese," Holmes murmured, "the more I suspect they are smarter and better informed than most humans care to admit. For example—"

"*Listen!* Am I or am I not being arrested, or summonsed, or—?"

"Oh, we couldn't let that sort of thing happen to one of Mr. Holmes's clients," Mrs. Hudson said reproachfully. "That's why Dr. Watson turned on the timeslow."

Watson wiped his forehead with his sleeve. "One must forgive a wreck like Mr. Gibbs for being alarmed. After all, being summonsed to face charges in the Galactic Deep Court—"

"*What?*" Rinpoche was wringing his hands. "When I never asked to be frozen in the first place! In fact I forbade it!"

"Forbade it? Yet someone cared sufficiently about the possibility of your being revived to go against your declared wish? Hmm!"

Holmes donned a cadaverous smile as though some vast mystery had just been resolved for him. Rinpoche cursed. It was not, however, because he had unveiled to Holmes a clue about his former life—trivial to anybody else, but revealing to a master detective. No!

I wish I hadn't let that slip out. I think I just got Nixy interested in precisely the wrong aspect of my former life . . . or lives . . .

While his brain was still reeling, he heard, and clung to lifelinewise, calm authoritative words.

"The suits filed against you would be sufficient to exhaust even your credit in legal fees alone were they to come to trial. However, the waiting list for hearings in Deep Court is currently two point one centuries. Even applying for bail is generally considered pointless. According to the best computer advice, your optimal policy would be to run like hell, were not leaving one's present planet to avoid service of a summons previously reported to its recip-

ient an aggravating offense. You are unfortunately aware
that a summoner is on the premises ... The decision,
though, is yours."

"This Kardek is a con man," Nixy exclaimed. "I can't
picture him holding down an honest job. Is that summons
genuine?"

Holmes gave a rueful shrug. "If it hadn't been, it would
have combusted spontaneously as soon as he crossed my
threshold. He's exactly the kind of person they'd hire to
serve summonses on people he claimed to be a friend of.
You said he advised you to consult me; did you indicate
you were going to follow his advice?"

"Ah ... Yes!"

"In that case, knowing where you might be found would
have constituted an adequate CV."

"Then I vote for running like hell. Remember, theoreti-
cally we're already evading arrest after what happened in
California."

"That's unlikely to be proceeded with," Holmes assured
her.

"I hope you're right. In any case, though, as long as
we're not actually under arrest we might send a message to
Gramps—and while he doesn't exactly love me he wouldn't
care to have the family thrust under the galactic spotlight."
Turning, catching Rin's hand, she concluded:

"Besides, for some peculiar reason I've come to rather
like this bit of wreckage."

While Rinpoche's heart was still pounding out of control, he dimly registered how Watson thrust what he had
described as the list of their destinations into Nixy's
hand; and how, as they squeezed past the immobilized
Kardek—experiencing a peculiar tingling sensation from
the fringes of the timeslow field—Mrs. Hudson opened
the front door intending to call a cab, and promptly
slammed it again, though not before it had admitted a
snatch of ragged song:

"Protest about the purchase, for it squanders energee,
"Of NAJQ dash thirty, one two two dash three!
"Unite your voice with ours, about it make no bones:
"Condemn the greed of covetous Anangaranga-Jones!"

How Holmes and Watson urged him and Nixy upstairs
again, toward the wall where the letters VR were outlined
in supposed-to-be bullet pockes; how Nixy pushed him
through not-quite-mist such as they had penetrated yesterday and scrambled after in a tangle of arms and legs . . .

And heard her whistling as she studied the paper she
held—which was not the itinerary Watson had promised.

"Wheej! If even half of this is true, you're the greatest
human criminal in the galaxy, and I always believed that
was Gramps!"

"Watson said that paper was—"

"Watson was outsmarted. Holmes was outsmarted." Nixy
shook her head pityingly. "I'd heard the people who stayed
behind on Earth were kind of dim, but it's sad to find that
even their star turns are void-brained. This is the summons
they said they were sending you away to escape. Did you
really ingest the intelligent population of Bactralia? Someone did—everybody knows that—but I don't see how it can
have been you. You must still have been in freeze."

She folded the document decisively. "Not that facts make
any difference to a lawyer, of course."

"What is this nonsense?" Rinpoche flared, reaching for
the paper. In the nick of time she snatched it away.

"Hands off, you idiot! Are you trying to make things
worse? Your only recourse is to claim it was never served
on you, and even that would be dicey now you've been told
what's in it." Nixy drew a deep breath. "So let's concentrate on finding out where we are, hm?"

They looked around, slowly growing aware how hot and
dry the air was compared with London's, despite the sky
being overcast, and how full of sharp particles that grated
between their teeth. They were standing on the roof of a
gray building with parapets along its walls and towers at its

corners, and apart from a great deal of sandy ground sparsely set with ill-doing plants, most of the scenery consisted in an enormous rock shaped like a turtle. Rinpoche felt that although he was sure he had never seen it he ought to recognize it, but before he could sift through memory for its name he was distracted.

"*Magnifique!*" boomed a voice. "Our first *clientèle*! I beed you *la bienvenue* in Sidi-bel-Abscess!"

A burly man wearing a buff uniform and a kepi with a kerchief protecting his nape scrambled through a trapdoor and advanced on them.

"I am Sergent Leclair! You veel address me politely at all times or you veel be sentenced to solitary confinement in ze middle of ze dezair! I speak to ze man first, naturally, for 'e veel most desire ze glorious dess. You, vun notices, are a voman. You can make yourself useful *quand-même*. You may fetch vatair from ze oasis and console my beloved *poilus* ven zey suffer *le cafard* and veep for zair 'omes and loved ones zat zey veel nevair see again. I vould 'ave you begeen by consoling me except zat *malheureusement* you arrive just as ve are about to 'old our first dress re'earsal of an attack by ze Rif. Possess yourselves of rifles and ammunition and prepare to sell your lives as dearly as zose 'oo vent before!"

He flung up one arm dramatically. Following it, they saw on the horizon—which meant the top of a nearby dune—a cloud of dust raised by camels ridden by men brandishing scimitars and guns.

" 'Oist our *sacré* flag!" howled Leclair, and for want of anyone else to undertake the task did it himself, running it up a flagpole atop the nearest corner tower. It was blue, white, and red in vertical bars.

"I'm trying to find out where we are," Nixy forced out between clenched teeth. "But my Hypermem is hurting me so much!"

"Don't worry," Rinpoche sighed. "I once saw *Beau Geste* on late-night TV. We have to be in the Sahara at an outpost of the French Foreign Legion.

"And I have a strong suspicion that this is *not* an approved re-enactment zone."

He hesitated, wondering whether he should have been so definite about their location in view of that looming rock, but decided against voicing his reservations. "By the way," he added, "if we don't like it here, how do we move on to somewhere else?"

"I haven't the slightest idea. That must have been among the data Watson meant to give us. What's worse, though, is that I did have time to read the first few names on the destination list, and none of them said anything about Sidi-bel-what'sit."

"So presumably not even Scotland Yard knows where we are?"

"Presumably not."

"Oh, dear."

"The computers suggest that we do WHAT?"

THIRTEEN

FORT TO A STANDSTILL, AS ONE MIGHT SAY

"YOUR MAJESTY, I'M BERNIE ROBBINS. WELCOME BACK from freeze! Your subjects wait to pay you homage."

"Where?"

"Uh—here, sire. This is my wife Edna, and these are Lizzy Windsor Robbins and Jimmy Stuart Robbins, good royalist names as I'm sure you must have noticed. Kids, say hullo to the king!"

"HULLO, KING!"

"That's all?"

"Well—uh—yes. Except Rose, of course; that's Mrs. Robbins's mother, who said to say how sorry she was not to be with us, only she had to go to Africa rather unexpectedly. If you'd care to come this way . . . ? We have the spare room made up. I hope you like algae tart, because that's what we're having for dinner. And as a treat I made some wine this morning. It ought to be ready by the time we get home."

Nixy and Rinpoche stared at one another. Eventually the former said feebly, "At first I thought it was kind of neat how Kardek managed to substitute the summons. It doesn't seem at all funny now."

The tricolor had jammed halfway up the flagstaff. Cursing, Leclair was wrestling with the rope, so for the moment he was paying no attention. Rinpoche said, wiping his forehead with the back of his hand and feeling the abrasiveness

185

of sweat-damp sand, "Can the Hypermem help? Or is your headache too fierce?"

"It's pretty bad, but I am trying. But remember what Bloom said about changing things to make sure visitors can't buy all their data before arrival. The section 'Travel Information, Earth' has a blanket warning: not warranted reliable after publication date."

Leclair finally wrestled the flag to the top of its pole and turned their way again.

"I told you to take up ze arms!" he roared. "Ees our only chance against ze savage Arabs of ze dezair! Vot zey veel do to you, *madame*, is only exceeded in terms of obscenity by vot zey veel do to you, *monsieur*! I assure you, 'aving myself— Vell, no mattair. But zere are guns, zere is ammunition, and I urge you to 'elp me bring up ze dummies from below, so zat ve give ze impression of ze complete garrison!"

"Yes, this is stolen from *Beau Geste*," Rinpoche said wearily. "Written by P. C. Wren. Sergeant, couldn't you at least have found a French author to base your re-enactment on?"

Leclair's face twisted into a mask of fury.

"You insult *la patrie*!" he rasped. "For zat you mus' spend ten days and nights vizout vatair in ze empty vastes of ze Sahara!"

"Empty?" Nixy cut in.

"Apar' from ze occasional raiding band of Rif and Touareg—"

"That doesn't look much like Rifs and Touaregs to me."

Bewildered, Leclair turned—stood for a moment transfixed—and pressed clenched fists to his temples, moaning. It was just possible to make out that he was complaining about broken promises, or perhaps broken contracts, though the overall intention was clearer: he held that someone (or possibly something, in the sense of a computer or nonorganic alien intelligence) had contrived to defraud, betray, trip up, and generally cheat himself and his fellow investors in what ought to have been a lucrative new re-enactment zone. After a few moments he glanced around for a gun, caught up the nearest, and ran to the far side of the fort's roof while frantically struggling to load it.

What he had seen, and what he was about to try and shoot out of existence, was not the bunch of camel-mounted Arabs. They, having come within range of the fort but received none of the fire they doubtless expected from its defenders, had reined to a halt and were now milling around in confusion—very probably compounded, amplified, and reinforced by having noticed what had so disturbed Leclair.

To wit: a gigantic wagon with, painted on its sides, the single word BORAX . . . and drawn amid a cloud of choking dust by what was unmistakably a twenty-mule team. The mules were of a more convincing color than the ones Rinpoche had seen in California. Not so green.

"I thought you said we were in the Sahara," Nixy murmured.

"Aren't we?"

"Here's a datum my Hypermem says is unlikely to be changed easily or often. Only one of Earth's numerous deserts has been licensed for re-enactments, and it's not the Sahara. There's no one left who gives a hoot about reliving its history. The moment Dune was discovered, all the nomads who wanted to continue with a desert way of life—or start again along the lines of their ancestors' culture—made up their minds to emigrate there. I quote. So we must be somewhere else."

"I do see what you mean," Rinpoche said slowly. Over the rim of another sandhill a string of brown men had risen into view. They were clad in buckskin pants and gaudy feather headdresses, and their faces were smeared with colored paint. Two of them were diligently striving to make a fire smoke sufficiently to signal with, but it kept burning up with a bright clean flame.

"That so?" Nixy retorted. "Then how about that lot over there?"

Swinging around, he realized that at the base of the

turtle-shaped rock there was now visible a line of tall, muscular, nearly naked blacks, wearing tufts of fur at elbow and knee and carrying spears and elliptical shields with red-and-white designs like Tessa Rack's.

"Zulu," he sighed.

"What?"

"Another movie I saw on television." He hesitated. Something was amiss. In a moment he realized what it was. Those men should be appearing on the skyline, not at the foot of the rock—

Above all, they ought not to be emerging *from* the rock!

"I catch on!" Nixy said triumphantly. "That's Ayers Rock— Rin, what's wrong?"

He was gibbering and making wild gestures. More and more black men were walking straight out of the solid stone!

"Oh!" Nixy said with a shrug. "Don't worry. It's a holo."

"The rock's hollow?"

"No, silly! It's a hologram. When the aborigines got sick of being treated as seventh-class citizens they packed up and went away, and Ayers Rock being symbolic to them, they took it along. Biggest theft in human history, except that you can make out a case for it belonging to them anyway. And that I didn't have to look up, thank goodness." Pulling a wry face, she rubbed pain lines from her forehead. "I'm surprised you didn't get that with your knowledge pill."

We're in Australia?

It seemed in the highest degree improbable. But he couldn't reason coherently after the shock the black men had given him. By now they were lined up in rows, spears and shields at the ready. Trying to behave normally, despite the impression they gave of being set to attack at any moment, he muttered, "Holmes said scarcely any humans bothered to come back and teach the Yelignese about Earth's past. So who did brief them?"

"How should I know? It happened long before I was born, and none of my family can have been involved."

"Can't the Hypermem help?"

"Is it really important? My headache's really fierce now."

"I'm sorry, I'm sorry! I'd just like to know who to blame for the crazy mix-up that's been made of Earth. It wasn't too bad a planet when I was around the first time, and I think it deserves better than what it's getting."

"Remember what else Holmes said. Watson and Carnacki agreed with him. We have members of our own species to thank for the mess we're in. Does it matter who, in particular?"

"I guess that makes sense. Shame, though. I wish it were someone else's fault—"

"That we're being shot at!" Nixy shouted as a bullet whizzed past, cut a large chip out of the tower with the flag on it, and howled off with the sickening scream of a ricochet in search of further damage it could wreak. For a horrible moment Rinpoche pictured it imitating the ax head at Holyrood, but luckily a sandbank swallowed it.

Cowering behind the parapet with their arms about each other, they watched Leclair gather himself and march stolidly to confront those whom he clearly regarded as intruders.

"It ees our svorn pletch," he bellowed, "to relive een zees dezair ze valiant accomplishments of zose drecks of ze Erss 'oo gloriously redeemed zemselves under ze aegis of *la belle France*!"

"And it is ours"—faint but clear, from the camel riders—"to show how the French imperialists failed to withstand the liberation movement that restored the Sahara to its rightful inhabitants!"

Having brought his wagon to a halt, the driver of the twenty-mule team crossed one knee over the other, spat elaborately at the ground, and tilted his broad hat forward over his eyes. Otherwise he offered no reaction.

But a moment later the black soldiers let out a gigantic roar. One clear voice emerged from the tumult, shouting, "Typical! Just *typical*! It's a desert, barren ground, and here are all these whites and Ayrabs conspiring to deny us blacks a piece of it! Ah, *shoot*!"

That was probably not what the speaker meant literally, more a euphemism. However, its phonetic form being consonant with a long-standing and tradition-hallowed naval command . . .

"Duck!" Nixy yelled, hauling Rinpoche into the shelter of a parapet. She was barely in time. The sky rained bullets, then arrows, then spears. Leclair, indignantly maintaining that everyone but he must be in breach of contract, broke off and stared down in disbelief at an assegai sticking out of his solar plexus.

"But zair vair not any Zulus in ze . . ."

He got that far before keeling over with an expression of complete disbelief. Rinpoche said anxiously, "Will he be okay?"

"How should I know?" Nixy retorted. "Depends how well he's insured."

This is indeed a very different day and age . . .

At the edge of Rinpoche's mind a question began to gnaw: could Hieronymus Merkin find true happiness with Mercy Humppe?

He tried to make it go away. It wouldn't oblige.

Even if one substituted Rinpoche and Nixy, it was still a damned stupid problem to be fretting about when the fort of Sidi-bel-Abscess was under threat from three directions, at least potentially, and escape via the fourth was blocked by the wagon and mule team.

Struck by a sudden thought, which had at least the virtue of not including the names Merkin or Humppe, he called out, "Say! What are you trying to promote—a borax reenactment zone?"

"What else?" came the sour reply.

"What's so interesting about borax?"

"I don't even know what it *is*. They just told me I had to drive this thing around for fifty years to pay off my debt for liquid nitrogen. I go where they send me, and today they've sent me here. Well, I always hankered after an open-air life." His shirtsleeves were rolled up; glancing at bare pale forearms he added, "Though it sure riles me that I don't tan anymore. When I got friz everyone was claiming that pretty soon you'd get brown if you crossed the street without a hat."

"No credit, as usual," said a gloomy voice behind Rinpoche. He whirled, as did Nixy, to find emerging from thin air—or more exactly air with the curdled look that indicated access to a dumper—a blurred personage resembling the one they had glimpsed at 221B Baker Street. The said individual remembered after a moment that it was only partly disguised as human, and completed the process, which was a relief. Rinpoche felt he ought to recognize the original it was copying, but he was too distracted to search his memory for the source.

"Excuse me," Nixy said, uncharacteristically diffident. "What was that about credit?"

"We restored your ozone layer. Had to! Sun-fried human emits such a stink. *Where* are the persons appointed to meet me here?"

It gave the humanoid impression of glancing around. Unfortunately Rinpoche derived the firm conviction that behind its superficial guise it must in fact be knurgling owperstroms or doing something equally nonterrestrial, and a wave of queasiness assailed him.

Nixy's hand closed painfully on Rinpoche's wrist. "Do you recognise it?" she whispered very close to his ear.

"He's a Yelignese, isn't he?"

"Not he, *it*! Don't you think it looks like the Chief Bureaucrat—the same that told off Sherlock Holmes?"

"Can't any of them look like any other? Or any of us, come to that? I mean, this isn't its real appearance, is it? Why don't you ask?"

"D'you think I dare? I mean, a being in charge of a whole planet!"

"Oh, blazes . . . Excuse me! Are you by any chance"—despite his best efforts Rinpoche's voice quavered—"the Chief Bureaucrat?"

"I have that dubious honor." Giving no sign that it recalled them from their encounter at Baker Street, the Yelignese made show of consulting a watch; however, the fine detail of its enshrouding hologram was inadequate to the task, and Rinpoche had to shut his eyes.

It was the slimy gleam of pale blue membranes that did it.

And it continued testily: "I don't know why they imagine they're entitled to keep me waiting! More delayfulism and I shall let myself be angricized. I'm a busy being, you know. You do know, don't you?"

"I'm not sure we *know*," Nixy answered cautiously. "But I'm certain we can both guess. That you're very busy, I mean."

"I approve your sensibility of exactitude. I wish my ought-to-be-present associates displayed the like in relation to the elapsiveness of time. If they're not here in two lakes of a stale sham—! You don't by chance know the meaningfuliciousness of that idiom, do you? I'm assured it's authentically terrestrical."

Rinpoche and Nixy shook their heads.

"Well, no matter. If they don't show, I threaten to constitute you a posse and commit to your untrammelated judgment the applications for approved re-enactment zones submitted by these groups of persons—or, in the case of that involving the wagon," it amended hastily, "persons plus animals. I believe it past time for humans to responsibilize for decisions to such magnitudity."

"Isn't it kind of hard to judge among such different projects?" Rinpoche ventured. "I mean, Africans and Indians and—"

"I heard that!" howled a furious voice, and a tomahawk trailing red cords soared over the parapet and shattered its stone blade on a stone flag. Chips of what was probably obsidian flew in all directions and came to rest sparkling in the harsh sun.

"Yes." Rinpoche licked his lips. "I'm sure he did . . . But I don't quite understand, sir or madam or"—a half-remembered phrase from the Hotel Interdimensional prompted him—"your thingitude, how it is that at the same time and place you have to decide between the French Foreign Legion and—uh—Native Americans and—and borax, whatever that may be, and—and so on."

He was on the point of adding, "Especially since we're in Australia," when he suddenly realized, pill-assisted, that Nixy must be wrong, Ayers Rock or no Ayers Rock, because if they were it would be dark. In fact it was early morning. And it had been midday in London, more or less. This therefore was North America, QED.

But why should a fake Ayers Rock be set up in North America?

The CB was displaying a convincing illusion of a frown. "I'd have thought it obvious. All these people want a desertificacious setting for their proposalized re-enactments."

"I had the impression there's no shortage of deserts," Rinpoche said boldly.

"Ah, but they all insist on a natural desert. There are plenty creatized by humans, but they say those won't do. Unexpecting anyone to make such a ridiculicious demand—for this was in the early days, before we discoverised how twisticled your racical psyche is—we set up autoprograms to reclaimulate spoilified land. Here is the nearest remainderated area to what they asked for."

"We asked for this?" shouted the presumptive leader of the Zulus. "In the preputial secretory gland of a hyena we asked for it! We never wanted to meet you at this site! We don't want to demonstrate the unswerving obedience of our impis, the admiration and envy of uncounted foreigners, soon to be the cynosure of visitors from other worlds as well . . . Excuse me, I seem to have lost the thread."

Hasty prompting followed from those nearest him.

"Of course. As I was saying: we don't want to prove it by jumping off the roof of a fort built by Europeans! We want to do it the natural way, using a natural cliff forming part of the natural defenses of a natural settlement of natural people naturally owing total loyalty to their natural chief! Here's another clear example of discrimination!"

"Do you know what he's talking about?" Nixy whispered.

Rinpoche nodded. "I have a horrible suspicion that I do." She bit her lip.

"And I have a horrible suspicion that this must be another of the awful things that happen everywhere I go!"

Before they could discuss further, however, three more humans plus two aliens materialized on the roof. On seeing them, Sergeant Leclair staggered to his feet, stumbled to the nearest parapet, and threw himself over. There followed a loud squelching sound.

"Well," said the Chief Bureaucrat resignedly, "one thing is definish. They're going to have to reprogramulate that sim until it ceaserises to assumerate that all visitors are either hostiles or recruits."

"Excuse me," Rinpoche said in surprise. "Does this mean simulacra can—well—own property? Control money?"

"No, of course not."

"But Sergeant Leclair said he was one of the investors setting up this—this RZ. Didn't he, Nixy?"

"You're trying to make out that that's a human?" On Rinpoche's nod the CB sighed to perfection. "I guess it's possible. It's often hard to tell the difference. But is Leclair still there?"

Before Rinpoche could react Nixy had darted to the parapet and looked over. Turning back, she shook her head. "He must have proper insurance after all."

"That's all right, then," said the CB, and added apparently to the air, "Entry of record. Application for French Foreign Legion RZ held over owing to disappearance of promoter."

One of the newly arrived aliens, a rather graceful creature with numerous yellow tendrils rising from a complex of gray perambulator limbs, used a sweet-toned, rather plaintive vocal simulator to inquire, "Would the Foreign Legion have been of great interest to nonhumans?"

"No, and probably not even to many humans," Nixy said before anyone else could reply.

"Thank you. It is good to find our tentative conclusions confirmed by an indigene. That maintains the hundred percent boredom level that we, as samplers for the K'ee-k'o-G'ruk, have thus far recorded here on Earth. It is to be hoped that it will be maintained until the end of our visit, for then it will be open to us to demand of the Galactic Conglomerate authority to vaporize your worthless mudball and put its elements to more constructive use."

They uttered a conclusive rustling sound and folded in upon themself.

"Wait a picosecond!"

The call came from a tall black woman who had also just arrived.

"Don't let that kackypoo dismiss my cousins without even seeing what they have to show!"

The CB's humanoid hologram vibrated in indignant indigo.

"The term you just employed is derogatory. Speciesism is not to be tolerated!"

"And isn't it speciesism when a tringle persons claim to unvaluate our humeworld contrawise the preferentiality of multipular tour takers? Call me Somalia if you want to call me anything, otherwise up yours!"

She strode to the parapet on the side of the fort facing the Zulus and waved frantically. At once they advanced in a great black flood. Well, a small black flood, actually. In total they numbered only about fifty.

Shortly they came scrambling onto the roof, either over the walls or via the trapdoor like Leclair, and drew up in lines as before—not at European attention but instead running on the spot, banging their spears against their shields, and chanting a rhythmic slogan.

"According to my Hypermem it means," Nixy whispered

to Rinpoche, " 'Just let Chaka give the order, and we will die to defend our people'."

"That figures," Rinpoche said glumly. "Someone's obviously got hold of the legend about how Chaka wanted to impress European visitors with the loyalty of his troops, so he told them to jump off a cliff."

"And did they?"—in a susurrant tone. Glancing round, they realised the question came from the second of the aliens who had arrived to join the Chief Bureaucrat. At present it was being thickly cylindrical and mostly dark brown; they retained a vague impression that on arrival it had been creamy yellow and as it were relaxed into a more extensive and more mobile form.

"Yes."

Anxiously: "From a sufficient height to cause injury?"

"So the story goes."

"Without even"— There was a pause during which the creature seemed to be consulting references. —"a parachute, reversagrav, or glider? Or a soft place to land?"

"Just as they were. Just like these men you see now. A funny way of defending one's people, if you ask me."

"Oh, dear!" The alien began to tremble and blur. At the same time eventuated just what Rinpoche had been fearing.

"Now," said a large and particularly shiny man, "you will admire the magnificence of the Zulu Nation under Chaka, whom I have the honor to emulate in this necessarily inferior reconstruction of that famous episode in his life when he proved to effete foreigners that his were the most loyal soldiers in the world. Impi!"

There came an answering roar.

"Jump over that wall!"

"We hear and obey!"

"You'll do it even if there are jagged rocks a hundred feet below—thirty meters, that is?"

His hasty emendation somewhat tarnished the hoped-for effect, especially since the roof of the fort could not possibly be more than ten meters above ground level, but the answer rang out regardless.

"We hear and obey!"

"Suppose there's a full-grown female hippopotamus down there, and I order you to fetch her to me, what then?"

Nixy stared a question at Rinpoche, who responded with a miserable nod.

"Yes, there's another legend about him ordering unarmed soldiers to drag a hippo out of a river. Twice as heavy as a bull—but I almost forgot: there aren't any more bulls, are there? Big, anyway. Some had arms and legs bitten off, but that didn't stop the rest."

The tall black woman had caught a snatch of what they were saying. Rounding on them, she advanced with a scowl.

"Are you saying my ancestors sacrificed themselves in vain?"

"Uh . . ."

"Shut up!" The woman was panting, fists clenched. "Why have you set out to ruin our best chance of establishing a re-enactment zone? As if it weren't bad enough that a bunch of our so-called broze an' sis allowed the funding promised to us to be diverted to some town in Holland, now you come along and try to sabotage our revised bid!"

"What makes you imagine," Rinpoche responded, "that anyone wants to watch people proving how stupid they are?"

"Why, you—!"

Her fists unfurled as though she were about to claw his eyes out. But before she had time to launch her attack she, with everyone else, was distracted by the reaction of the brown alien.

With measured decision it was expanding into a form resembling a crinoid or a sea anemone (and it was of a creamy yellow shade in this version of itself), rising two meters clear of the roof on a mesh of rootlike strands and reaching out with at least as many tentacles to touch the backs of each and every member of the impi. For some reason they made no attempt to dodge.

In its chiding artificial voice the creature said, "One can-

not bear the infliction of deliberate suffering. Should the
urge to leap from a great height prove insuperable, at least
there should be parachutes and gliders. Or, since apparently
you lack the knowledge and/or resources to provide those
. . . How strange it is to find oneself among supposedly intelligent creatures who are yet psychotic! One had been told
that that age was over. Well, Herr Chaka, now you may order them to jump."

It concertinaed into its compacter form. "Chaka" blinked
rapidly several times, then shouted an order.

In three successive waves the impi—poorly drilled, but
enthusiastic—uttered a war cry and rushed toward the edge
of the roof. Mounting the chest-high parapet with a single
bound, they flew away.

For each, after being touched on the back by the alien,
now sported a fine wide pair of bat-style wings.

"Strictly," said the Chief Bureaucrat, "that ought to fall
under the rubric of willful tamperating with the physique of
an intelligent species. On the other hand, it would be idiot-
ical to claim that beings prepared to jump off a cliff, break
several bones, risk paralysis or death in agony, to underpin
their leader's megalomania, *were* intelligent. The application for a Zulu re-enactment zone is dismissipated on
groundfulness of hereditical stupidity."

The tall black woman rushed to confront it.

"Now see here, you—you . . . !"

Unperturbed: "Besides, the cost of repairulating that
many victims on a weekly or monthly basis would ensure
that it operationized at a permanent lossifying. Furthermore
and additionwise, so would all other RZ's projecticated for
this location."

Somehow, without growing louder, the CB's voice
seemed to fill the welkin.

"In particular, we dismissify the borax scheme on the
grounds that *borax* is *boring*!"

Pause.

In a dispirited tone: "One was advisified that humans

find plays on words amusing. One did one's best. That didn't raise a chuckle ... Oh, well. We also dismissicate the schemerizing of the Cree-Choctaw-Algonquin-Navajo-etceteree-etceterah Nation—"

A howl, and another tomahawk inaccurately hurled.

"That's not the full title of our joint application!"

"Objection to your objection!" Suddenly the words were crisp and exact, as though previously CB had been paying attention with only half its mind, but now had brought the whole to bear. "You demand feather headdresses that cost a blunk and a frib to synthesize because your ancestors exterminated the original birds, and you only enjoy them courtesy of relatives on other planets who subsidize you on a ridiculous scale, and you never give proper credit to the Oglala Sioux who were the sole tribe actually to wear such elaborate featherwork in what you are pleased to call the Olden Days, even though when they transpired, the Yelignese had already spread to two hundred thirty-seven planetary systems and had it not been for the fact that your forebears became nauseatingly rich by sheer accident we would still be—"

"Exactly what you are!" Somalia shouted. "A bunch of resentful loudmouths!"

There followed a tense silence. It concluded with a sigh.

"Well, one is always warned against expecting either courtesy or gratitude from humans ... Nonetheless there are some things that need to be said, whether or not you listen! Excellence in murdering other members of one's own species is not what sanity inclines one to admire! *Do you Earthlings have nothing better to offer than your battles and your sieges and your slaughter?*"

There was an interval like an abyss, full to the brim with shame.

There was a further interval, during which it was apparent that a lot of people were going away to think things over: Zulu, Arab, Native American ...

Also the borax wagon was trundling into the distance.

* * *

There was yet another interval during which practically
nothing happened at all. It was a relief. Rinpoche felt grateful. Nixy was still holding his hand. It appeared that she
felt the same. Everything would have been more or less
hunky-dory but for the fact that she murmured, very close
to his cheek so he could feel the incipient bristles of his
beard move with the impact of her breath (and that reminded him: he ought to have borrowed one of those amazing razors from 221B Baker Street—and thinking that way
alarmed him, since he had dared to hope he had finished
living in parentheses): "By the way, Rinpoche, you're going
to have to explain how come a Tibetan without a
Hypermem knows so much about twentieth-century Western culture. Especially P. C. Wren. Not now, of course."

Of course.

Are we still here?

It appeared that they were. At any rate the wind still
whipped grit from the dunes, the roof of the fort still bore
their weight . . .

Hang on. Flagstones in the middle of a desert?

Either P. C. Wren, or he himself, or whoever had organized construction of the fort, or—well, in this strange new
age, anything was as likely as it was possible—seemed to
have missed a trick.

His head was starting to ache. He suspected the pain
must be like what Nixy suffered when she used her
Hypermem too often.

Still, it would probably wear off in a few moments.

Moments?

It was useless to try and keep track of what felt more
like molasses than time.

*I don't know if I'm sane. I don't know if humans are. It
hurts.*

Nixy put her arm around him (and was she not the most

amazingly beautiful woman he had ever dared to guess at? Yes!) and spoke.

* * *

Well, I suppose someone from AD 1700 would have been just as shaken to his/her personal foundations on being thrown forward to my day.

But I must stop thinking of it as "my day."

Besides, there are some quite good things about now. I'm standing next to one, aren't I?

"Lover," Nixy was whispering (the term amazed and cheered him all over again), "you know, for a moment back there I was afraid that that mix-up over all those people making appointments with the CB at the same time must be another of the bad things that keep—"

The sentence was not allowed to finish.

"*Eau!*" exclaimed the Chief Bureaucrat, as though struck by sudden insight, and disappeared into thick air.

Well, it was pronounced that way, and never mind how it was spelled.

On the instant ensued a sound of flowing, as of the most gigantic bladder in all terrestrial mammalian history being emptied. Nixy and Rinpoche and the rest of the beings who remained at Sidi-bel-Abscess (the two other aliens having presumably sneaked away into whatever dimensions were abscessible—*accessible*) were battered by drops as large and painful as hailstones, while the hot and questionable flagstones that formed the fort's roof emitted a sizzling noise as the water douched them. On every side geysers and fountains were erupting, and wind was whipping spray from their tops.

The air became comfortably moist for an average Earth-born human.

Flowering plants that had lain dormant for centuries sprouted and bloomed. One particularly vivid species was bright yellow.

Insects first, then rodents and other small animals, appeared from lairs and burrows. Birds swooped from the sky.

Turtles and tortoises probed the air with blunt snouts. What had been Earth's last natural desert didn't look much like a desert any longer.

"This," complained the only remaining one of the three humans who had come to join the Chief Bureaucrat, "ought not to be happening. I did warn CB about authorizing engagement of a French vocabulator, Foreign Legion or no Foreign Legion, but even so—!"

Pale, shaking, Nixy cried out, "It's happened again! The protesters persecuting me for being born into my family—"

"No! No!" Rinpoche interrupted. "If even this gentleman was taken by surprise, surely a haunt is much more likely!"

The person in question turned to him with an air of polite incomprehension.

Gentleman? Oh.

It must just be that he—or rather it—was taking rather more care about maintaining its disguise. After all, given what seemed to be the Yelignese opinion of humans, it was scarcely to be expected that one of them would be an aide to the Chief Bureaucrat.

There ensued an interval of relative calm, during which the loudest sounds were (a) the patter of water drops and (b) howls of rage. Sergeant Leclair seemed to have found his voice again. Yes, there he was, sticking his head out of the trapdoor from which he had first emerged. His insurance policy must indeed have been a good one.

"Fichez-moi le camp!" he bellowed. "And the tooter the sweeter!"

"Certainly," said the aide, turning to depart.

"Hey!" Rinpoche exclaimed.

"Yes?"—with courtesy.

"We don't know how to get out of here!"

"Really? Where do you want to go?"

"Anywhere!" Nixy cried. "Where are you going?"

"Home, actually. I'm due for a spot of leave. But let me think . . . I was in a place called Rome last week, so I recall the route. Would that do?"

"Yes!" they both said fervently.

"Then I'll set it up for you. By the way, have you been to Rome before? No? Then a word of warning. No matter how tempted you may be by the novelty of the experience, *don't let them feed you to the lions.* Even with the best reconstruction techniques, something's bound to get scrambled during gnawing and digestion, and it could all too easily be your . . . Oh, the term's on the fringe of my skibe! The hardest organ to reconstruct! Superior human nervous ganglion— Of course! Your brain! *Buon viaggio!*"

"The computers suggest that we do WHAT?"

FOURTEEN

WHEREVER YOU WANDER THERE'S NO PLACE LIKE ROME

"Mr Sukiyaki-Shang?"

"That's Saketori-Shang, if you don't mind!"

"So sorry. The fact that you are a professed gourmet appears to have invoked some far-fetched references . . . Well, to the point. Our remembrancers have expressed, in the strongest terms, their resentment of your plan to ride one of them over a mountain range. They—"

"What in the galaxy are you going on about?"

"You deny intending to cross the Alps on an elephant?"

"Nothing is further from my mind! I came to this jerkwater world purely so that my friend Leuyunk-Lun could taste human flesh!"

"So you're not planning to become a Hannibal?"

"Not in a million years!"

"Oh, that's all right then. Sorry to have bothered you. I really must get that vocabulator fixed!"

"Ah! Miss Anangaranga-Jones!"

The alarming voice rang out from behind them while they were still trying to find their bearings. They had emerged from the Rome Dump Office amid what looked like a monstrous building site flanked by pillared porticos and frescoed walls. The air was full of dust and noise.

To their left a group of men and women, bellowing orders at one another yet seeming not to pay the slightest attention to what any of them said, were striving to mount on a plinth an enormous equestrian statue of a bronze-armored general. Since the statue was floating in midair, the spectacle disturbed Rinpoche considerably. Moreover, at the moment it was upside down.

Straight ahead, a huge three-dimensional publicity display assailed them on every sensory level. The olfactory onslaught was particularly suffocating, but all its emissions were at least disquieting. Luckily they were far enough away not to be overwhelmed. Only one of the advertisements packed enough punch to affect both of them at such a range before they managed to divert their attention:

"You know you want it!" blared angelic trumpeters. "You know you need it!" growled Jehovan authorities. "You know you deserve it!" cajoled the seductive voice of primal Lilith. Then they united in a thrilling chord: "Take home the supreme masterpiece of Earthly art! Michelangelo yearns to paint *for you* the ceiling of the Sistine Chapel! He must do it—he must! You know you know he must! If he can't, he'll die! Can you bear to have the death of a great artist on your conscience? Can you? Even though he's of another species?"

"Michelangelo," the same voice that had identified Nixy said dryly, "died in 1564. My conscience can tolerate that particular burden. I imagine yours can, too. Though I gather it sometimes works on tenderhearted aliens—not, of course, that many aliens have hearts."

To their right a machine with jaws like an iron crocodile was crunching its way through a ferroconcrete neobrutalist structure, its frontage decorated with bronze plaques in high relief depicting the twentieth-century fascist symbol of an ax surrounded by rods. Jumping up and down in front of what was now more than half a ruin, a large-chinned man wearing a resplendent uniform and a tasseled cap was screaming into a megaphone. Unfortunately he kept it turned toward the machine, which was itself making a considerable racket, so only snatches of what he wanted to complain about were audible. A score or so of sympathizers, wearing black shirts with red brassards but otherwise garbed in a grand miscellany of colors, were doing their best to move in unison with their leader; however, they were always a ragged half second behind.

"After he went to so much trouble to look like the original, too!" the same voice said again. "It doesn't seem fair, does it? But the inexorable logic of the market . . ." And it added reproachfully, "You know, you might glance this way and see who's talking to you."

"I don't want to," Nixy said stonily. "I'm tired of protesters wherever I go. I didn't ask to be born into my family! No one asked me whether I approved when Gramps decided he was going to buy a whole solar system! *It's not my fault!*"

"What's not your fault?" The tone was of genuine astonishment.

"But—" Nixy hesitated and broke off.

"The pope wants to meet you! Wants you to be her guest in Rome—with your boyfriend, of course. We got wind you might be coming, so we've been on the lookout."

But we had no intention of visiting Rome . . . !

It did indeed feel like high time to turn around. Rinpoche did so and could scarcely believe his eyes.

Smiling at them was a youthful man of middle height (but of course everyone looked youthful now), wearing a long red robe with buttons down the front. "How do you do?" he said formally. "I'm Cardinal Numbernine. I'm standing in for Cardinal Numberate, who decided he'd rather spend today on Mars. Surf's up."

He displayed an array of gleaming teeth. Front and center they were green, white, and red: the Italian colors.

That, though, wasn't what riveted Rinpoche's gaze. Nor was it the two tall young men who stood immediately behind Numbernine, even though they wore velvet doublets above loose breeches striped in black and yellow, floppy velvet caps and boots with floppy turned-over tops, and carried pikes or halberds or some other equally obsolete but no doubt still injurious weapon, nor even their heavy makeup, their suffocating perfume, and the fact that as soon as they realized he was looking at them they had both begun to swing their hips, ever so slightly, but ever so suggestively, too.

No: taped to his tonsured crown this cardinal wore an automatic pistol.

"I know," Numbernine said sorrowfully. "Biretta, Beretta ... Makes you sick, doesn't it? But the Italians and the Yelignese were made for one another. Trying to get them to change a decision, once made, is like trying to walk through a wall. We all know interpenetration is possible in theory. Making it actually happen ..." He finished with a dismissive wave.

"I say, cardy love," murmured the personage behind him on the left, who was dark except for silver highlights dyed into his mass of curly hair, matching the pearlescent paint on his nails. "Aren't you going to introduce us?"

"It'd be very bad manners not to," said the second one, who was fair but for a massive and aggressive black mustache. His nails were coated with mauve enamel, and his eyelashes were immensely long. Fluttering them, he nudged his companion, who slowly and lasciviously passed the tip of his tongue across his lips as he studied Rinpoche from head to toe.

The cardinal said dispiritedly, "All right. These are Hans and Fritz. They work at the Vatican, like me. They're members of the Swish Guard."

Rinpoche looked at him. He didn't say anything. There wasn't really anything to say.

"Well, now!" the cardinal resumed in a brisker tone. "Will you come with me right away, Miss Jones? Please say yes! Her Wiliness is so eager to discuss possible future projects with you—and, incidentally, she wants to compare notes with you, *signore!*"

"Me?" Rinpoche said feebly.

"Oh, yes! Since as I'm informed you were only recently revived from freeze, you may well not appreciate how invaluable it would be for her to talk, face-to-face, with someone like yourself—insofar as there are people like yourself—who in your day . . ."

Rinpoche's glare finally shut him up. It was too late, though. Nixy's curiosity had been piqued, her suspicions aroused.

Musingly she said, "I can understand why the pope should want to talk to me. The Papal Legate for our volume used to call up Gramps all the time when I was a kid. I got the impression he was kind of an agent for him, or a representative as you might say. Him for Gramps, I mean, not the other way around."

Cardinal Numbernine seemed about to speak but held his tongue. Oblivious, Nixy went on:

"But, Rinpoche Gibbs! What can he possibly want with you, if you are what you say you are? Or, putting it another way, what you don't say you are? I mean, after what we've done to one another I wouldn't normally expect—"

"He's done abnormal things to you?" the cardinal burst out. "Why—!"

But his voice failed him. His shoulders drooped; his expression grew downcast. "No, we've agreed there's no mileage in that line. I guess the final straw must have been that joke . . ." He brightened. "I guess you won't have heard it, *Signor* Gibbs, and, *Signorina*, I doubt it's known on any other world but Earth, unless some of our visitors have run into and quoted it. It would cheer me up to tell it to you."

Not waiting for permission, he closed his eyes and rocked back on his heels.

"This is during one of the interviews that the Chief Bureaucrat occasionally grants to a human.

"Question: 'I am trying to understand sex. Have you had sex with a member or members of another intelligent species?'

"Answer: 'No.'

"Question: 'Of a nonintelligent one?'

" 'No!'

" 'Pity.' "

He waited.

Belatedly Rinpoche realized he was expected to laugh, or at least smile. He forced his lips to curve a little.

"Oh, well," Numbernine said dispiritedly. "It was worth a try . . . But"—with sudden ferocity—"if we can't come up with sponsorship and a bunch of new ideas, the whole of Rome is going to be taken over by the pagan era, butchery in the Colosseum and chariot races and being fossilized in lava at Pompeii. But the city was Christian longer than it was pagan! All we've really got going is our Borgia banquets with the chance of being poisoned. Which doesn't much appeal to creatures who can eat potassium cyanide and drink sulphuric acid. And what does the sight of fathers raping their daughters do for beings who don't have sexes—or watching women screwing donkeys? Or warriors wading ankle-deep in blood if they don't even have ichor? Oh, we've tried everything, believe you me. If we can't hit on a few new wrinkles . . ." He shook his head.

"Wrinkles," Nixy repeated meditatively. She fingered her smooth cheeks and forehead. His knowledge pill furnished Rinpoche with the information that it had become downright ill-mannered to mention signs of aging, whether to the young or—above all—to the rejuvenated.

Acutely conscious of his *faux pas*, the cardinal was at once all over Nixy with apologies, in a manner that suggested he would not have minded being all over her in a more literal sense. Anxious to make amends, he rounded on Hans and Fritz.

"Call me a popemobile!"

"You're a popemobile," was Hans's prompt response.

"Any more of your lip and I'll—I'll . . . !"

"Oh, hark at her!" said Fritz, setting hand on hip.

"I *know*!" Hans murmured. "Isn't it a proper caution—? I say, is that right? Or does it belong to another program?"

"How should I know?" Fritz snapped, his feigned affability vanishing on the instant. "I haven't been in the Guard as long as you, have I, ducky?"

"No one would believe it!" Hans retorted. "The way you

set your cap at that gladiator in the Forum the other night! Talk about to the manor born! 'Cept of course in your case it's more to the palace at Castelgandolfo, isn't it?"

"Did I ask for my mother to be chosen pope? *Did* I?"

"Well, you didn't exactly ask for her to be chosen Grand Mufti, did you, darling?"

"What's that supposed to mean?" Fritz exploded.

"I don't know, as a matter of fact," Hans admitted. "It just sounded like the right kind of thing for her not to be chosen as ... What do you suppose Mufti means, anyway?"

"It means plain clothes as distinct from uniform," Nixy informed them in a sharp tone. They turned uniformly pitying eyes on her: *Just like a woman!* was the unmistakable implication.

"I suspect," Hans countered with a superior smile, "you must be thinking of something else."

"What I was thinking of," the cardinal grumbled, "was a popemobile, remember?"

"Don't get your knickers in a twist," Fritz said huffily. "It's on its way. In fact it ought to be here by now— Yes, here it comes."

He pointed. Rounding the far side of the publicity display, forcing aside shills and pedlars and tourists and loungers, came the most extraordinary conveyance Rinpoche had ever seen—Nixy, too, judging by her half-strangled laugh. Borne by masked men and women in long robes and pointed hats, it consisted of half a dozen gilded thrones mounted by twos on an equally ornate platform. In front of each of their high backs there floated without visible means of support a reproduction of the Triple Crown, so positioned as to hover just above the occupant's head. Several excited tourists delayed its approach, tugging at the bearers' arms and demanding to climb on board. Fritz caught Hans's eye.

"A task for the Guard?" he murmured.

"Well, strictly we're out of our jurisdiction—"

"I know, I know! But haven't you noticed that *divine* boy

in opal satin? And the one in chrysoprase isn't totally repulsive."

"You're right! Forward the Guard!" He added to the cardinal, "See you later, numerator, if that's not too soon for you."

And, shouldering their pikes with well-drilled precision, they marched off in step.

As the popemobile swayed camel-fashion away from the Dump Office and toward one of the bridges crossing the Tiber, Cardinal Numbernine pointed out places of interest in between shouting or gesturing insults at the horde of shills and touts assailing them.

"That's the Colosseum, see? Where the Colossus of Rome used to stand with its enormous torch upheld, guiding ships upriver— No, we do not want to be matched against Gaulish wolves, even at bargain rates! Be off with you!"

"How come there are wolves when there aren't any cows or horses?" Rinpoche demanded.

"No idea. Now that man there, you see, with the tricorn hat and the gilded staff: he's one of Cleopatra's Beadles— No! We do not want to witness a procession in honor of the goddess Cybele, and see men actually and literally cut off their balls! Not even if you serve them with herbs in white wine afterward!"

"Goddess?" Rinpoche echoed. "I thought religion had been—uh . . ." He hesitated. It felt odd, to put it mildly, talking like this to a high official of a church that in his day had still been flourishing.

"Cured?" the cardinal said, apparently unruffled. "Why, yes. But a species can't suffer from that severe a psychosis for that long a time without it leaving ineradicable traces, on the folklore level if nowhere else. And besides, it was such a sweet racket! Nothing else comes within shouting distance. You of all people ought to know that."

Rinpoche blinked and framed a disclaimer. But Nixy had

already reacted. Twisting around on the throne beside him, she was studying him with intense curiosity.

"I was right," she murmured. "You do have hidden depths."

"No, I don't! I'm not sure what the cardinal is implying, but—"

He had no chance to complete the sentence. The touts and shills were closing in again, this time in such numbers that Numbernine seized a crosier from a clamp on the side of the vehicle and laid about him with a will, urging his companions to do the same.

"No!" he bellowed. "We do not want the unique experience of being tied in a sack along with a cock and a dog and a scorpion and thrown into the Tiber! Be off or I'll report you to the GSPCA!"

Sitting back as the importuners realized he meant what he said, he added under his breath, "Though I do know one or two people who I suspect wouldn't mind a hot radish up the fundament ... Excuse me. Ah, we're arriving at the Arch of Hadrian and the Pillar of Trajan—or maybe it should be the other way round; I can never remember. There was, there still is, a lively debate as to whether they ought to have been resited next to one another like this, but there is something phallic about a pillar, and something vaguely its counterpart in the form of an arch. And of course, most importantly, the Chief Bureaucrat thinks it is finally coming to grips with the concept of sex, so when it concluded that the two relics were complementary, it gave orders for them to be moved here, side by side."

Below the arch there was some sort of advertising display. Unable to discern the details, even with his improved eyesight, Rinpoche asked what was going on. All he could make out was that, attracted by the display, numerous men and an occasional woman were presenting themselves in front of a booth and either being invited in or turned away.

"They're recruiting gladiators," the cardinal said with a trace of annoyance. "They just upped their rate of pay. What fun there can be in watching two overgrown thugs

trying to chop and stab each other's vitals ... Besides"—
with a burst of candor—"it's luring people away from our
witch- and heretic-burnings, which used to be by far the
most popular of the historical re-enactments in this village
of ours. Not geographically very accurate, I admit, because
far more witches were burned by the Prods in Northern Europe, but we were very proud of our Giordano Bruno reconstruction despite the difficulty of finding enough
masochists to enact the title rôle. People came to it from all
over the galaxy. Then business just fell away without warning. *I* suspect we're being nobbled by the pagans, but
there's no proof ... No!"—catching up the crosier again.
"No, we do not want to remember service as galley slaves,
not even for six months, not even for six days!"

"Do people really volunteer for that kind of thing?"
Rinpoche demanded, marveling.

"Some do," the cardinal said, nodding. "Mostly the
stony-broke ones, who are going to have to pay for their
trip by peddling their memories when they get home."

"Stony-broke?" Rinpoche turned to stare at the latest
batch of importunates. "No one I've seen has looked
poor—nothing like the hippies on the Katmandu trail that I
was told about when I was a kid. Everyone appears well
dressed, well fed, clean and tidy."

"They have to," was the dry reply. "Lice, bedbugs, hun-
ger, ulcers—those aren't the sort of experiences their potential customers will want to remember, hmm? Anyway,
here's the Vatican. Within moments you'll be in the presence of Her Wiliness Pope Joan II."

He pointed. Ahead they saw a wide square surrounded
by handsome old buildings of which the chief, on the far
side, was a cathedral with a magnificent dome. Rinpoche
was about to say, "You mean there really was a first Pope
Joan? I saw a movie about her once but I thought it was
just fiction."

However, he was once again forestalled. For at that moment they crossed the edge of the square ... and it wavered

and faded and vanished, along with the cathedral. Half rising from her throne, Nixy stared this way and that.

"I thought we'd reached St. Peter's—and St. Peter's Square! What's this?"

She indicated what now confronted them: a bare expanse of concrete flanked with mean little sheds, their slanting corrugated roofs white with bird droppings. Here and there more Swish Guards were snoozing in the shadows. One or two looked up hopefully, but on seeing a woman shut their eyes again.

"It's on loan to the University of Spica," said the cardinal.

"What?"

"Mm-hm. But we'll get it back, probably in two or three months. They're doing an in-depth study of our unique form of derangement and hope to find clues to its nature in the associated structures and imagery."

"How could aliens make sense of it?" Rinpoche exclaimed.

"No, no!"—crossly from Nixy. "Not Spica Three—Spica Five, a human world."

"I wouldn't know," Rinpoche muttered, subsiding in embarrassment as he realized he did in fact know; the knowledge pill was good on galactography.

Turning to Numbernine, she went on, "Did they start with this lot?"

"No, they took Stonehenge first, I believe, then the Kaaba, then Angkor Wat. Nobody likes the idea very much, but they do pay very generously, of course."

He added to Rinpoche, "Next on the list is the Potala. If you want to pay it another visit you'd better hurry."

A sharp retort rose to his lips: "But I've never been to Lhasa!"

Yet again—it was becoming like a conspiracy—he was prevented. At that precise moment the popemobile halted. The bearers lowered it. The cardinal stepped down and turned to offer his hand to Nixy. Rinpoche expected her to brush it aside, but in fact she took it with a word of thanks, seeming overwhelmed at this replacement of a great cathedral with tin-roofed sheds.

"So even if I'd come here on the tour Gramps chose for me, I'd not have been able to let him remember visiting St. Peter's! I wonder whether I can divert his wrath to the travel bureau. I mean, I ought to have been warned, oughtn't I? At least, though, there aren't any demonstrators after me for belonging to my family."

"Oh, we'll keep those well away from you," said Numbernine in a reassuring tone. "We may not wield the influence we did in the old days, but we saw that change was bound to come and took what steps we could to soften the blow."

"I'd have thought having to manage without your chief tourist attraction—" Rinpoche began. The cardinal smiled patronizingly.

"For people who want to see what it was like there's a duplicate."

"Duplicate?"

"Yes, in Nevada. I'm sure Miss Jones's great[4]-grandfather would have been quite satisfied. The copy they have of Camp David is said to be better than the original."

"And to think I was one stop away from Las Vegas! That must have been why the old so-and-so wanted me to go there. I mentioned how my family had close ties with the Church in the old days. Speaking of which"—her large eyes, smoky with suspicion, fixed on Rinpoche—"I'm determined to find out more about your past. I've been taking you at face value, and I'm not sure any longer that you have one."

"You'll find out soon enough," Numbernine assured her, leading them toward a shed slightly larger than the others. Guards either side of its door reluctantly offered a salute. "As soon as she heard he had been thawed, Her Wiliness ordered me to carry out an in-depth background analysis of your friend, and what I turned up of course explains her eagerness to meet him as well as you—

"What was that?"

"I didn't hear anything," Rinpoche said after a pause during which Nixy seized his nearer hand and clutched it tight.

"It's not something you hear!" Making no further move to enter the shed, the cardinal removed the gun from his head and rubbed his scalp as though massaging away memory of some especially unpleasant contact, like pus or slime. "You sensed it, Miss Jones, didn't you?"

She nodded, teeth chattering. "I've noticed it before, but I never knew anyone else react the same way. Do you know what it is?"

"An aura." The cardinal spoke with authority. "Most of religion was nonsense, of course, but there was a small and irreducible residue based on psychic leakage from adjacent universes, and in the days when scientists took no account of such matters, our predecessors made that a speciality because no one else could be bothered—"

"Also you needed a new gimmick," Rinpoche said in a tight voice. That reference to adjacent universes had shaken him: did it imply that Sherlock Holmes had been right in his first conclusion, after all?

"Come now!" The cardinal looked offended. "That's scarcely the attitude one expects from one professional to another!"

A growing suspicion gnawed at Rinpoche's mind.

Can it be that these people imagine that I'm—?

Before he could voice his thought, however, he was once again forestalled. He could have believed it a plot by now. A grumpy voice interrupted from within. "How much longer are you going to stand about gossiping? Drag them in if they won't come any other way!"

"Yes, Your Wiliness," the cardinal sighed, and gestured for them to follow him.

The air was full of stale smoke. Sun leaked through a pathetic imitation of a stained-glass window cobbled together from bits of colored plastic inexpertly glued to bars and rods. Altar cloths and other brightly dyed fabrics hung from the walls and draped over chairs and couches. On a table stood half a dozen battered chalices and several bottles.

"Come in, sit down," said the grumpy voice. Sucking on a cigar even as she masticated gum, its fat elderly owner, albed and chasubled and generally bedecked in a whole storeful of traditional textiles, seated on a throne with a high back—perhaps the one after which those on the popemobile had been modeled—made no attempt to rise, though she did proffer the hand that wasn't holding her cigar, in case someone wanted to kiss the ring she wore on it.

No one did.

She slumped back, gesturing that Numbernine should pour drinks, and added with a wry inflection, "By the way, the wine's good despite the squalid setting. But I'm sure you appreciate that it's never good to *flaunt*. Or, of course, you can have anything else you prefer."

It dawned on Rinpoche that here was the first non-youthful-looking person he had so far met.

Yet, given the fortune the Church must have amassed . . .

A tingling began at his nape. Suspicions so vague he could barely explain them to himself were burgeoning from mental soil dug and harrowed by the knowledge pill he had taken, and the so-to-say preliminary aroma that their buds were giving off was tantalizing him to the point of frustration.

But he would have to be patient until they ripened.

Wine was delivered. Patens laden with canapés appeared from an aumbry in the corner. The pope stubbed her cigar and offered a toast:

"To our collaboration, in the past—and in the future!"

"Hear, hear!" said the cardinal warmly, and they drank. The wine proved of splendid quality. It was labeled, Rinpoche noticed, *East! East! East!*

Something seemed amiss about that.

"This," Nixy said in a tone approaching reverence, "is what Gramps should have asked me to remember for him instead of that fizzy stuff he ordered me to drink in Naples."

The pope blinked. Her eyes were dark, her complexion pale and suety. She bore much resemblance to an unbaked currant bun.

"Sentiment, my dear! Sentiment, don't you think? After all . . . Well, I won't bore you with what you must already know. You'll take another glass? I'm not surprised. This is duplicated from the very finest in the papal cellars. The real stuff, of course, we had to let go—they were prepared to pay the most amazing price at Algenib, as though there were some magic in it being original—but we'd copied it to the very highest standard, and I'd defy anyone to tell the difference. In fact some of our copies may well be better. There's a theory that being reconstituted after passing through a dumper must affect the flavor. Though since duplication involves pretty much the same process it's hard to see— But we really ought to be talking business."

"Business?" Nixy wasn't looking at Pope Joan, for the cardinal was pouring her a refill. "I'm not here on business. I came to Earth so that Gramps could reremember the haunts of his youth, and I have most spectacularly screwed up the assignment, and . . ."

She had grown slowly aware, while speaking, that both the pope and the cardinal were frowning. After a moment the latter said, "Mother, perhaps she's afraid that—"

"Mother?" Rinpoche couldn't hold back the word. And despite the scowls it earned him, he ploughed on. "You mean you're brother to that simpering Guard we met just now?"

The cardinal sighed. "Not the sort of mother you're thinking of. Nothing so—so physical. Just the high-quality genes. Once scrub-mothering became feasible all the best strains decided to adopt the technique, especially since it offered the means to concentrate family fortunes that might otherwise have been dispersed. But Miss Jones must know all about that."

He sipped his wine with a nod of approval.

"Of course, here at Rome we've carried it rather further than is necessary Out Deep. Practically everyone in the Vatican shares the key genes now. One wouldn't want to see our resources dissipated any further. So few even halfway competent people still live on this ball of mud—"

"Before Mr. Gibbs decides that the majority includes you and me," the pope said frostily, "why don't you stop running off at the mouth and let us talk to each other instead of suffering through another of your lectures?"

"But I want to be lectured!" Rinpoche pleaded. "In London I finally found one of the knowledge pills I missed when they revived me, but I can't digest so much data all at once. What—uh—his reverence . . . his grace? His honor? What the cardinal just said, anyway, made a lot of things clear that were confusing me. On the other hand"—licking his lips—"a lot of others won't come clear at all."

A deep breath.

"For instance, what on Earth—I mean, in the galaxy—gives you the idea that I'm Tibetan?"

"Does the guy have a great sense of humor, or does he have a great sense of humor?" Pope Joan II chortled until her jowls were wobbling. "But save your breath. I know damn' well who you are—Guido Sansepolcro Verdi, who got away with more mazuma from one single scam than even the Church could have filched in a century. Why do you think we wanted to meet you? We're hoping to pick your brains!"

Only at that moment did Rinpoche realize how extremely drunk she was.

"The computers suggest that we do WHAT?"

FIFTEEN

A GAME NOT WORTH THE ROMAN CANDLE

". . . EARTH BEING SUCH A BORING PLANET NOW IT seemed like a bright idea to re-create a few of the livelier types from way back when."

"Didn't it work out?"

"Nope. We cloned DNA from the Turin Shroud and wound up with some squalid medieval peasant. We tried again, allegedly with the blood of St. Sexburga—we thought her name might pull the punters—and got a chicken. The whole religion deal was a bust."

"Did you try another approach?"

"Sure. We cloned Adolph Hitler. What we got was this little guy in a yarmulke wanting to paint lids for chocolate boxes . . . Still, one thing came of it. Back then people had some interesting pheromones due maybe to foods you can't get anymore, so we've concentrated them and put them into perfume. Let me give you a sample of our Odor Clone."

The incredulous silence that followed the pope's assertion was broken by a loud exhalation from Cardinal Numbernine, immediately succeeded by an outburst of furious speech.

"Mother, don't you listen to your correspondence anymore? Don Marco in California reported yesterday: this guy was in Verdi's casket, but he isn't Verdi! However, he was a top gun in his own racket first time around."

"So what was his racket?" Nixy pressed, leaning forward. "He's never mentioned it."

Oh, no . . . Just about the last thing I wanted to happen!

"Even before Duckman came along, people in the West were losing faith in traditional deities like Jesus and Yahweh and the Almighty Dollar. A lot of 'em turned to oriental religions. This guy's parents were on that scene in California. They—and he—made it big but *big*."

Rinpoche sank his head in his hands and groaned.

"Go on," the pope said grimly, reaching for another cigar—made of shunk, presumably.

"Who?" Numbernine countered. "Him or me?"

"Who cares?" Nixy cried, sitting bolt upright, flashing-eyed. "I never guessed I was keeping company with someone who still suffers from religious psychosis!"

"That's funny!" Rinpoche exclaimed. A moment's reflection made it clear that it wasn't just funny. It was hilarious. It was hysterical. It was uproarious.

He uproared, so long and so hard that tears coursed down his face. His ribs and diaphragm ached from the impossibility of drawing a full breath before the next peal of laughter, until ultimately he started to feel faint from lack of oxygen.

"Sorry," he managed to force out. "But you don't know just how—"

And erupted again, while the others exchanged helpless glances and waited for him to recover.

Which he finally achieved.

Reaching reflexively to the pocket where he had been used to keeping a handkerchief, intending to wipe his tears, he found he hadn't been issued with one. Divining his need, scowling Nixy threw him a napkin from the drinks table. It was of stiff white linen, totally unsuited for blowing one's nose, but better than nothing. After a final wipe he tossed it aside and sat back in his chair, much relieved by his outburst despite the discomfort it had left in his chest.

Meantime, unlit cigar in hand, the pope was hunting through first her robes, then the miscellaneous junk on each of the nearby tables, apparently in search of a light. In no hurry to assist her, Rinpoche neglected to point out that a chrome-plated lighter lay in plain sight. Perhaps there was no more butane to fill it with.

"Now," he said eventually to Numbernine, "finish what you were going to say."

Embarrassed, the cardinal dropped his eyes. Rinpoche started to chuckle again. Hurt, Numbernine demanded what was so funny this time.

"You just dropped your eyes," Rinpoche explained. "And I just had a flash of a Yelignese doing it. Literally."

"Literally—? Oh! You mean like down on hands and knees trying to pick them up but of course not able to see where they've rolled to!" The cardinal was gazing at him with sudden respect. "I didn't realize you had such a sharp wit. A talent like yours deserves to be properly exploited. As it happens, I have connections with—"

"An organization that registers original jokes and collects royalties on them? I thought so." Rinpoche shook his head. "No thanks. I already heard about it from—well, from a con man who conned me about something else. So I'm disinclined. You just finish what you were going to say about me."

Embarrassed worse than ever, Numbernine muttered, "Maybe I shouldn't. I mean, there might be some inaccuracies. I only studied up on you yesterday, after all, and there isn't a hell of a lot about you in our library."

"I'd never have imagined there'd be anything at all about me in the Vatican library!" Rinpoche stared in disbelief. "What, then?"

"Uh . . ." Numbernine licked his lips, looking anywhere except at his interlocutor.

"Out with it!" the pope rasped, having finally noticed the lighter and proved that there was in fact no shortage of butane—or maybe of whatever substituted for it nowadays. "If he isn't Verdi after all, I want to know who he *is*!" She applied the flame and sucked.

"Okay, okay," sighed the cardinal. "Well, naturally when people stopped being religious the Church had to find alternative means of survival. Historical interest didn't seem likely to fill the bill—or the belly—but like I said before, we'd had a bit of time to prepare for the full impact, and one of the things the people in charge thought of doing was researching other similar scams looking for fresh ideas, so they bought every book and tape and disc that they could find about gurus and messiahs and channeling and what-have-you."

"Even if people weren't going to be religious anymore," rumbled the pope, having got her cigar to draw, "they dared to hope it would still be possible to make them part with the shekels on other grounds. Trouble was, the marks figured they and their ancestors since the year dot had caught a pretty bad cold off the priests, and they swung from one extreme to the other. Wasn't until the smart alecks had emigrated that we started to make ends meet again among the dumb clucks who had stayed behind. And of course that's not what you'd call an adequate economic base. More wine?"

"Yes, please—"

"More information!" Nixy snapped. "How much longer are you going to keep me on tenterhooks—? Rin, for pity's sake! What's so funny this time?"

Overcoming renewed mirth, he said gravely, "I'm sorry. I had another flash, this time of the Chief Bureaucrat on tenterhooks. Do you know what they were? Hooks used to stretch cloth to prevent it shrinking after being washed or dyed. Get the picture?"

"You really do have a sharp wit," Numbernine said warmly. "I'd never have expected a newly thawed wreck to grasp the principle of CB jokes so instinctively."

"CB jokes?"

"Well, Yelignese jokes strictly, I suppose, but most of them get attached to the Chief Bureaucrat eventually, like Alexander the Great being credited with inventing the diving bell. For example, this guy comes to the CB and says, 'I've got a complaint!' And the CB says, 'Don't worry, come in anyway—we don't catch human diseases.' Then there's the visitor who apologizes for not being very coherent and says he's under the weather, so the CB says, 'You can be on top of it if you prefer'—and hoiks him into the stratosphere. Ha-ha! Then there's the guy who tries to grab its attention while it's busy and simply won't go away— this is an unusual one because the CB comes off best— until finally the CB gets exasperated and says, 'Look, I'm up to my ears!'—which of course it immediately is, and the importunate visitor finds out the hard way what it's up to its ears *in*—not that Yelignese have ears, not as such, so it's usually told as up to my scrunge. Then there's the one about my head being in a whirl, and of course it is, it's going round so fast that—"

Belatedly it dawned on Numbernine that Nixy and the pope were both glaring at him with expressions that could have liquefied helium, and Rinpoche also wasn't looking any too pleased. Gulping, he broke off.

"Sorry," he mumbled. "It's just that I was at a party with a bunch of Swish Guards the other evening and somebody started telling CB jokes and we just kept on and on . . . Sorry."

"I should think so!" grunted the pope. "Now finish answering Mr. Gibbs."

"Call me Rinpoche," came the reflexive interruption. "Or Rin, if it's easier."

"Call me 'Your Wiliness,' " was the stiff retort before continuing. "I wasn't talking to you. *Well*, Numbernine?"

The cardinal leaned back, folded his hands, and shut his eyes. "I was going to say," he muttered, "you figure quite prominently in half a dozen of the standard works."

"As what?" Nixy demanded, a heartbeat before Rinpoche could.

A shrug. "As a successful con artist, I guess."

"That's not a gift he's lost through freezing!" Nixy snapped. "I'd never have credited it, but so far he's convinced you, Mrs. Pope, that he's a hyper-rich *mafioso*, and you, Cardinal, that he's some sort of wealthy guru, and"—a quaver shook her voice—"me that he was a halfway nice guy of the sort we Anangaranga-Joneses don't normally get to meet, not if we're female, anyway, and—and it simply can't be *true*!"

The last word dissolved into a sob. Turning to her in astonishment, Rinpoche saw that tears were streaming down her cheeks as freely as his had earlier.

These, though, did not stem from mirth.

There ensued a long, bleak pause. During it he found himself wondering what would have happened had the CB's aide spent last week somewhere other than Rome.

Resolutions hardened in his mind. At long last he spoke up, hearing his voice grind like gravel on the bed of a river in spate.

"Yeah, I had a racket. It attracted a lot of rich dupes. But it wasn't what I wanted, I swear it wasn't. I was glad when they said I had leukemia, because it saved me from needing to be brave. It meant I didn't have to stand up and say I wouldn't play this game anymore. Also, being ill let me find out how loathsome my parents were, and the people that they'd gathered around us.

"And if I hadn't been tranquilized when I woke up, I'd have been so angry I'd probably have set the atmosphere on fire."

There was another pause. During it Nixy wiped her tears away. It was she who finally broke the silence.

"Why?"

"It's kind of hard to explain ... Don't worry!"—raising a hand against interruption. "I've got to face the facts some time. I never expected to have the chance. Before my next incarnation, I wanted to rest for at least a thousand years because of what they'd done to me in the one I was leaving. Do we reincarnate, by the way?" he added on the spur of curiosity.

"No," the pope answered curtly out of a cloud of smoke. A draft was wafting it behind her, for which Rinpoche was grateful. Shunk it might be, but it stung the eyes and nose just as much as tobacco.

Nodding, Numbernine concurred. "A lot of species do, but we're not among them. Go on."

How can he say that without screaming? How could anyone?

Retaining his calm at the cost of enormous effort, he expounded.

"It began . . ."

Where? Most likely, with a syndicated newspaper article that described how, following the death of the latest Chomo Lama—senior holy man of a schismatic sect of Tibetan Buddhists who denied the supremacy of the Dalai Lama—a worldwide search had been initiated to find his successor, expected to be a boy about two years of age. How would he be recognized? He would spontaneously recite verses from the Buddhist sutras; he would identify items that had belonged to his predecessor, such as robes, fans, and mirrors; and when taken to the Chomo Lama's residence (in a walled compound in Beijing, whence he was occasionally allowed to address via videotape the handful of his followers in Tibet who hadn't deserted him for kowtowing to the Chinese) would instantly know the function of each room and perhaps also the names of the staff.

Reverend Prairie Moon Flamen and Reverend Terrapin Gibbs had a son just turned two, a mortgage, a car loan, and too much owing on their credit cards. (They possessed eighteen.) What had been quite a lucrative little church for the past seven or eight years was losing its congregation for no apparent reason except that (a) its members were growing bored with the sameness of its rituals and (b) its ministers, who were accustomed to officiate unclad, were no longer as slim and muscular and all-around good-looking as they had been when they started, especially Terrapin, who was developing a paunch.

"How," said Prairie Moon, deep in the *Bee-Bulletin-Chronicle-Post-Examiner-Times*, "can we find out what Tibetan mirrors look like?"

"How!" Terrapin responded automatically. He had adopted his name, and his customary greeting, because their church was heavily into Native American symbology—for example, the central event of each service was Prairie Moon walking nude around the cornrows, like Minnehaha in Longfellow's "Hiawatha." For present purposes the cornrows were defined as the rows of chairs the worshippers were sitting in.

"And how," Prairie Moon continued after a brief scowl, "can we trace these characters doing the world tour?" She thrust the article at him, stabbing with a forefinger at the crucial passage.

He read, then pondered for a while. At length he glanced at their son in his playpen in the far corner of the room.

"I guess Diving Beaver wouldn't be appropriate. Just when he's begun answering to it, too."

"He'll get used," Prairie Moon said grimly, reaching for a phone. "He'll have to adjust to a lot of things ... Ultramundane Books? Hi, Joey, it's me. Say, do you have any books in stock about Tibetan? I don't mean *The Book of the Dead*. We got that."

"Hey!" Terrapin said indignantly. She glared him silent.

"See, Beaver has started to say things in a language that isn't English, and last night I dreamed it might be Tibetan, so I want to check it out ... You can get some? How soon?"

The book was just the beginning.

Puzzled, but compliant, because he was a bright child and interested in most of what the world about him had to offer, Diving Beaver gravely imitated the curious sounds his parents repeated to him, above all the strange-sounding "Rinpoche," which, they made clear to him, he must tell everybody was his name. Diving Beaver wasn't his name any longer. Beaver wasn't his name any longer. Now he wanted to be called Rinpoche, and he must say so to everybody.

Who was everybody? And where?

Uh ... Well, a man was coming to visit. A very important man. He would probably bring things with him. Things like these, that Rinpoche (that's you, kid, remember!) must learn to recognize and call by name. This is a mirror—well,

you know what mirrors are. This is a fan, and I guess you
never saw one like this before. Not the electric kind for
keeping a room cool in summer before they had air-
conditioning, but the kind that opens and shuts and hangs
on a cord. And instead of calling it a fan, you've got to
learn to say . . .

Sometimes he wept from fatigue. But his parents
wouldn't let him sleep until he had repeated the strange
new words, over and over and over and over and over.

It wasn't just one man who came to call, but four. One,
who was a genuine Tibetan monk in saffron robes, rang the
doorbell and explained who they were when Prairie Moon
answered. Two others, also monks but clad in brown,
brought robes and fans and mirrors in elaborately decorated
cloth bags, and scrolls with strange and complicated writing. But it was the fourth who had telephoned to make the
appointment, and at whom each of the others kept con-
stantly glancing as though to beg permission for the slightest act, and he was a Han Chinese in a regular business
suit.

The press had been primed, and local television and radio. Dutifully Rinpoche did as he had been taught, starting
with the assurance that his new name had come to him in
a dream from which he had woken insisting that that was
how he must be called in future. To each item he was
shown he responded with its Tibetan name. Handed a
scroll, he lisped what to him was nonsense but mightily impressed the visitors, and the reporters, even though it actually came from a different sutra. Overwhelmed at last, the
monks dropped to their knees and bowed their foreheads to
the floor. They were in no doubt: here was the reincarnation
of their former lama.

At which the real drama commenced.

Rinpoche missed most of it, being half-asleep. The inter-
rogation had taken nearly two hours anyway, and some of
it had had to be done over for the TV cameras. But Prairie
Moon had demanded a copy of the videotape as part of
their fee, and later he was made to watch it until he knew

it by heart, so he was able to reconstruct what transpired in fair detail.

First, Prairie Moon was horrified at the prospect of the child of her bosom being wrenched away from her and taken to Tibet—well, actually Beijing, the Chinese put in, but that was just as bad—by these strangers. She clasped Rinpoche in her arms and emoted at the top of her not inconsiderable bent.

Then, sober and reasonable, Terrapin admitted to having had doubts about the identity of the soul now inhabiting his son, but it must of course be a great honor to have such a thing happen and people like themselves, long-time searchers for spiritual enlightenment who might perhaps venture to say that they had helped others along their own individual paths, would be the last to dispute that. However, surely if the Chomo Lama was among the Enlightened Ones who renounce nirvana in order to go on serving their fellow human beings, he would have more than ordinary control over his choice of incarnation—to which, after some discussion, the Tibetans nervously assented—and if he had decided that this time he wanted to live in California, there must be a good reason, hm? Better than being shut up in a virtual jail and never permitted to visit the country of his ancestors! (Terrapin and Prairie Moon's research had been extremely thorough.)

At which Prairie Moon declared things were even worse than she had initially imagined, and no one under any circumstances was going to take away her baby!

In a voice rendered gruff with emotion, Terrapin concurred. They might, he said, have considered allowing Rinpoche at least to visit his adorers in Tibet, so long and so notoriously a center of deep spiritual wisdom. However, the notion of sending him to China, whose government so long and so notoriously had been repressive and materialist, where he would be treated like a prisoner and a puppet—

At this point the Chinese could contain himself no longer, and blared that Tibet was *so* part of China, not a separate country as ignorant Terrapin was trying to make out, so here was a Western-capitalist plot to deprive China of yet another of its precious ancient treasures, and the fact that they were Rinpoche's biological parents was neither here nor there, what counted was the soul, and they had damned well better give up the kid here and now—

"Because otherwise he might serve as a focus for pro-Tibetan, anti-Chinese agitation in a place where you can't get at it to put it down," Prairie Moon said loudly and clearly. Their research had indeed been very thorough. Exact, too.

A young woman in a smart dark suit who had been mingling unremarked with the reporters and the TV crew chose that moment to step forward, producing a badge from one pocket and a businesslike automatic from another.

"Agent Janice Goodyear Lockhart," she announced crisply. "FBI. We have all heard this person threaten to kidnap the Gibbses' child. Apparently, *gentlemen*, you don't appreciate what a serious crime that is in our country. I hope the matter need not come to court, but in case it does I want everyone present to write down your names, addresses and telephone numbers, or a business card will suffice. Dave?"

A man who had been standing inconspicuously near the door with a clipboard on which he was pretending to make notes, also flashed a badge. "David Snubchek, FBI," he muttered. "Write your names here."

The monks were bewildered. The Chinese was beside himself—

Now that's something I'd like to see a Yelignese try! Though for all I know, for them it may be feasible . . .

—with annoyance. As for Rinpoche, he was at last asleep.

So he didn't see the police taking away the would-be kidnappers, or hear the threat of a diplomatic incident, or the questions the reporters went on hurling for the next half hour. The media coverage was tremendous; it went national the same evening. Authenticated by genuine monks, a Tibetan lama had reincarnated in California. His parents (Prairie Moon in a revealing orange gown she had had prepared in advance, Terrapin in a genuine saffron robe that one of the monks had dropped on the way out, which he approved of because it covered his belly but bared his shoulders, though he had drawn the line at having his head shaved) had humbly accepted their lot and pledged themselves to raise this miraculous child in a befitting manner. Here was a reproof and a warning to those who held that science could explain everything. Here was an intrusion of a greater truth into the mundane world. No doubt as he grew older Rinpoche—a name chosen by himself, a name borne by many celebrated lamas in the past—would bring to the Eightfold Way many seekers after enlightenment . . .

And so on.

There were remarkably few references to their former church.

Moreover there were few references to the fact that Tibetans in exile in the States stayed away from Rinpoche in droves. Various of their spokespeople denounced him as a traitor, turncoat, renegade, tergiversator, and Benedict Arnold. (Clearly they were all working from the same thesaurus.) However, their absence was more than compensated for by the hordes of self-appointed experts on Tibetan lore who descended on him starting the following day.

Puzzled, a little frightened, and eventually downright bored, Rinpoche did his best to live up to what people expected. He was given instruction in Tibetan until he betrayed a knack for it and took to showing up his parents in public because he spoke it better than they did; then the lessons stopped, ostensibly because he was to enter the regular school system as soon as allowed.

That horrified some of his richer adherents (and several of them were very rich indeed), who insisted on his being educated privately. Prairie Moon and Terrapin feigned reluctance but gave in.

After all, making easier the current existence of an Enlightened One must bestow virtue on those who helped.

Surrounded from dawn to dusk by people unanimous in telling him that he was remarkable, exceptional, incredible and/or divine, Rinpoche had no grounds to question the fact. Sometimes he worried about his inability to live up to what he was assured he was, but not often and never for very long. By the time he was six he and his parents were installed in a luxurious mansion with three cars and two secretaries and computers to handle finance and correspondence. From the age of eight onward, he was featured on the cover of every issue of "The Light of the Lamas," a monthly magazine issued not only on glossy paper but on computer disc, via email, and as a Talking Book. In the latter case his portrait was replaced by a brief statement in his own voice, first in Tibetan, then in English. Prairie Moon and Terrapin's earlier experience had stood them in good stead; they were not the sort of people to repeat their mistakes, and had set out to prove it, and succeeded.

With marginal qualifications.

He discovered he had family he hadn't known about. Terrapin's two brothers, their wives and children, and his sister and her child (no husband right now) and Prairie Moon's parents, brothers, sister-in-law and two gay nephews kept dropping by and outstaying their welcome until credit changed accounts in various banks, whereupon they went away for a while.

But they always came back.

From his mid-teens his parents started to groom him to take over on his own account when they decided to retire. They had been rich enough to quit for a long while now, but always a little more, always a little more, always a little more . . . Besides, Prairie Moon's nephews were surviving on the sole effective treatment for AIDS and that cost more per month than most Americans earned in a year—though, of course, not as much as some Americans got paid—and it would never do to see headlines like RICH "LAMA'S" FAMILY LEAVING RELATIVES TO DIE!

However, there was something neither of his parents had reckoned with. Being brought up to believe in his mission had inoculated their son against cynicism—what most people regarded as "healthy" cynicism. Sometimes he was as bewildered as he had been when a toddler by the way they tried to reconcile the principles he had been brought up to with the enormous wealth they were amassing.

Also he wanted girls, and the way he was treated was making it impossible for him to meet any. It was after a confrontation on that subject that he realized he, too, could exert power. He only had to threaten not to do—well, whatever he was scheduled to do at this point in time, for them to cave in and concede what ten minutes earlier they had insisted was out of the question.

"During that period," Rinpoche heard himself saying to an audience he could not see because he dared not for fear of reading condemnation in their faces, "I was, I suspect, not at all a nice person."

Does the mind influence the body?

That was another question he should get around to posing when he was through with this exposure of himself. He had feared it—feared it longer than he could bear to recall, for thinking back over those years of deceit when he lacked the guts to round on his parents, his followers, his adorers, his *dupes*, and speak his mind with honesty, he saw himself as a shameful coward. He took the money he was given, he enjoyed the luxuries it bought, he drowned his conscience in a round of traveling and shopping and screwing (always well out of sight of those who trusted in his teachings), he sometimes woke up in the small hours hating himself and wanting to smash his head against a wall.

And still he was a coward who dared not speak out.

It was a relief when illness claimed him. He grew listless, weak and pale, and exaggerated his condition in order to avoid any more teaching, preaching, or lying—which amounted to the same thing. After months of pretending he wasn't seriously ill and would soon recover Prairie Moon and Terrapin accepted that they were at risk of losing their stock in trade. The stock in trade himself already knew. The doctors, sent for much too late, were in agreement: leukemia, too far advanced for more than palliative treatment.

Thank heaven!

Not that he credited anything divine or supernatural any longer. Idealism had been leached out of him like color from an ill-dyed cloth, leaving him gray and palimpsestical so that he snatched at this opinion, then that attitude, voicing each with equal conviction—meaning lack of it—and secretly sneering at those who were deluded by his efficient oratory, fruit of all those childhood years when he was being instructed in the art of milking the marks.

When he heard that those of his followers who weren't accusing him of betrayal wanted to have him frozen, he summoned them to his deathbed and exploited all the techniques at his command in an attempt to make them see how contrary that was to the teaching they had accepted from him. Let reincarnation take its natural course, as it always had done! For what would happen to a soul ensconced in a new body were it summoned to resume its occupation of another long ago abandoned? Cruel! Disastrous! Not to think of—please!

So forceful and persuasive were his words, he almost came to believe what he was saying, and when he closed his eyes for—as he imagined—the last time, he was convinced his adorers had listened.

But they hadn't.

If I'd not been tranquilized, I would have smashed and killed.

He came back slowly to the here and now. The first thing that he registered was that Nixy's hands were grasping his. Once again she was crying; thin, glistening lines had traceried her cheeks. But those lapis lazuli eyes were agleam,

and she seemed on the brink of speech he dared to hope
might prove reassuring, even comforting.

Before she could utter a single word, though, Cardinal
Numbernine had erupted to his feet.

"I can't believe it—I can't *believe* it! You had just about
the sweetest racket I ever heard of, barring ours in its heyday, and you quit, you threw your hand in, you gave up,
without even arranging to stage your own reincarnation!
You could have created a rival to the Church, for pity's
sake, because you weren't lumbered with our burden of lu-
natic theology! 'Course, it wouldn't have lasted past the
point when they proved humans don't reincarnate, but by
that time . . . *Ach!* I could *spit!*"

He stamped his foot so hard he hurt his ankle, and
dropped back into his chair rubbing it and cursing under his
breath.

*Didn't you hear a single word I said? Didn't you under-
stand how much it hurt to be me? Don't you sympathize
with me who was forced to live a lie from the age of two?*

A great and terrible cold invaded Rinpoche's mind.

Still, Nixy seemed to understand. Licking his lips, he
was about to ask her verdict, when the pope threw down
and trod on her cigar.

"Get 'em out of here!" she roared. *"Guards!"*

Two Swish Guards who must have been listening at the
keyhole sashayed into the room.

"I hate being fooled!" she bellowed to no one in particular as Rinpoche and Nixy rose uncertainly to their feet.
"When I catch up with the ejaculate of a black hole who
claimed that Guido Sansepolcro Verdi was back from the
dead, the greatest con man in history, one of Mother
Church's loyalest supporters, the person we were relying on
to get us off this stinking ball of mud and away to some
world that would provide a decent economic basis for our
operation . . . ! *Shit!* When I think how much of our best
wine we've wasted on these two! I'm only glad I didn't offer the bastards my cigars!"

Panting, she flung an arm dramatically toward the door.

Rinpoche wondered what the Chief Bureaucrat would look
like doing the same, and his lips quirked against his will.
Glancing at Nixy, he realized she had shared his thought.
They smiled at each other. Then they grinned.

"Don't expect any more protection from us!" the pope
howled. "For all I care the protesters out to punish you for
your grandad's greed can roast you alive in the Forum!
That's what they said they'd do if they got hold of you—
Just a second!"

Her jaw dropped.

"Numbernine, you asshole! I may be a senile old drunk,
but you're too young to have that for an excuse! How in
the galaxy did we come to overlook the obvious?"

She jabbed a spiky finger toward Nixy.

"Don't you realize? *This is an Anangaranga-Jones!*"

The cardinal blanched.

"Well, of course, but . . . Oh!" His eyes grew enormously
round.

"Even if we haven't got our hands on the richest crook
in history like we expected, we can at least lean on the
richest crook alive! Did you never hear the archaic phrase
'hold to ransom'?"

"Well, of course." Numbernine licked his lips. "I gradu-
ated *summa cum laude* in the history of extortion. But I
thought it was one of the things we didn't do."

"What's come over you, boy? More of this and you'll
have me looking down on you the way I do on what's-his-
name! Guards! I don't care what happens to the man—I
suspect you can think of some interesting diversions!—but
I want the girl stripped and thrown in a dungeon and in-
fected with half a dozen disgusting conditions like Sirian
ringworm and Capellan blot, that'll show up well on camera, and then I want an exact record of her plight rushed
to—

"What was that?"

*If I really had to answer that question, I'd say it resem-
bled what we felt in the Hotel Interdimensional when the*

dumpers inverted and we found ourselves at Iceworld or
wherever. It was also like a knee-jerk reflex, and like tread-
ing on a sunken log and momentarily mistaking it for a
crocodile, and like being hiccups—not having, being.

But most of all, and point for point, it was like what hap-
pened just after we arrived here, and Numbernine called it
an aura.

"Auras," Nixy said suddenly, "are what you get before
the onset of a migraine." He must, he realized, have uttered
the word aloud.

"Is that your Hypermem talking?"

"I got it from the Hypermem, yes. It was making my
head ache so much I checked under 'headache' to see if
there was anything that might help."

"And was there?"

"Nope. What's more, I can hear something that's *really*
apt to give me a headache. Listen."

Rinpoche cocked his head. From immediately outside
came a sound of chanting—one could scarcely call it singing, for the voices were both untrained and out of tune. But
the vehemence of their delivery was unmistakable.

> *"Wherever you're from and whatever kind of being*
> *you may be,*
>   *Join us in protesting about the sale of NAJQ-dash-*
> *30122-dash-three!*
>   "Rah-rah-rah! Again! All together now! *Wherever—*"

There was another shifting sensation. By now Rinpoche
had hit on what felt like the aptest term. He offered it to
Nixy.

"Lurch?"

Her eyes brightened. "Yes, exactly! Lurch!"

"Could it be a sign that Sherlock Holmes's haunt is after
you?"

"I guess it could. That song, though—"

"Isn't just a sign, but proof, that protesters who hate your
grandfather are right outside the door. And right in here

there's a crazy old drunk who thinks she can hold you to ransom until the old man coughs up a small or maybe a large fortune—"

"Rin, I haven't got around to telling you yet, but I sympathize with the awful way you were brought up even if no one else—"

"And I ditto ditto with you because I know how awful life can be even if one's family is extremely rich, so—"

"So what are we going to do? Holmes let us down; Scotland Yard probably doesn't know where we are to within a million kilometers—"

"You exaggerate."

"Okay, so I exaggerate. But what in space are we going to *do*?" Her voice, held steady by main force, finally broke.

"Something that maybe only an anachronism like me would think of. Nowhere is a million kilometers from anywhere nowadays, right?"

Optimism dawned.

"So long as you can get at a dumper, anywhere is right next door. Can you imagine there not being a dumper in the Vatican?"

"Of course not! But—"

"And can you imagine these pretty boys wanting to spoil their makeup?"

This in a sudden roar, as he snatched up an empty wine bottle.

"But I'll spoil it for them! Turn the whole lot blood-red and bruise-blue! And that's a promise!"

He drew a deep breath.

"Unless they escort us to the nearest dumper, *now*!"

"Stop!" yowled the pope, struggling to her feet.

"Not," said the nearest guard feelingly, "on your nelly. I like my face the way it is. I spent a lot of credit on it. Come along!"

"The computers suggest that we do WHAT?"

SIXTEEN

ONE SEEMS TO HAVE HEARD
THAT BEFORE

*"PLEASE SIT DOWN. I WON'T BEAT ABOUT THE BUSH—I
had this one brought in specially so you can see I'm not
beating about it. If you like you can take it with you when
you go. I have no use for it, and I understand it's quite
pretty by human standards.*

*"Well, to the point. I'm afraid we're receiving complaints
about the dialogue you've provided for our Religious An-
thropology exhibit. While it is incontestably true that the
original text of the Christian scriptures is incomprehensible
to a modern audience, and you as a resurrectee are a priori
qualified to gloss and edit them, strong reservations have
been voiced about your rendering of the commandment 'Be
fruitful and multiply' as 'Screw your bird into the pudding
club.' "*

Nixy and Rinpoche were startled when their journey began with a descent through a trapdoor. On reflection they
decided they shouldn't have been, as even in classical times
Rome had been so riddled with catacombs and secret pas-
sages that they later made it virtually impossible to build
underground railways.

Besides, it was a splendid way of eluding the protesters
trudging back and forth across the site of St. Peter's.

"This is the tunnel the popes used to sneak out by in the
old days when they got bored with the job and wanted a
break," the leading guard informed them as he marched
smartly along a well-lighted subterranean passage. He was

slim and blond and moved like a dancer. "Of course we don't have to walk as far as they did. Here's the dumper. Standard charges, by the way. Right eyes, please!"

He flashed their retinas in the normal fashion.

"Hmm! Are you an Anangaranga-Jones, too, sir?" he exclaimed.

"What?"—from baffled Rinpoche.

"Sorry, didn't mean to pry! It's just that you're carrying an awful lot of credit. Take my advice: watch out for pickaskulls."

"What in the—in space are pickaskulls?"

"People who'll dip your eye so as to steal the credit before passing it to a grafter who will sell it back to you and reinstall it, or if you won't play then trade it to an organ broker. It's more of a nuisance than a catastrophe, but of course it does hurt, and sometimes they don't reconnect the nerves right. Still, so long as you carry all-risks insurance . . ."

"That's awful! Don't you have police anymore?"

"Of course we do!"—huffily. "Pickaskulls have to be licensed and so do grafters, and if they do a sloppy job they're liable to a fine and compulsory retraining."

"*Retraining?* You actually get trained for this sort of thing?"

"Oh, Rin! You wouldn't want amateurs doing it, would you?" Nixy chided, casting an anxious glance back along the tunnel. "Look, don't stand around wrangling! I'm so afraid those protesters may have means of tracking me, even down here."

Lurch.

Everything blurred just a little. The floor of the passage rocked from side to side without moving. Lights flashed inside their heads. A smell like sulphur made their nostrils tingle. The guards exchanged worried glances.

"Does this happen often?" Rinpoche demanded.

The second guard answered; he was stocky and dark. "Never knew the like before. You, Sven?"

The fair one shook his head.

"How about going along with these people to some place where it isn't happening?"

Sven pondered for a moment, then tossed his corn-silk locks.

"Thanks for the suggestion, Osman, but I got a heavy date tonight. Besides, it could vary the monotony."

"May you live in interesting times!" Nixy exclaimed, and catching Rinpoche's arm urged him toward the dumper.

At the same moment came a howling noise. An animal reek wafted toward them on a sudden breeze. Osman blurted, "Wolves!"

"What? How do you know?"

"I'm friends with one of the animal trainers at the Colosseum. I'd know that stink anywhere—and listen!"

Howling. Furious howling. Echoing and reechoing along the stone passageway. Growing louder—drawing closer? And abruptly joined by another stench, as of a tomcat vastly magnified, and another sound, a sort of ill-tempered coughing.

"I warned Hamish not to announce the lions yet!" Osman moaned. "I said: it's too soon, you don't know how accurate your reconstruction is, and when I was a kid my granddad showed me this book with photographs of animals, and I distinctly recall the lions weren't bright red. So never mind what color they were on the Royal Arms of Scotland!"

A wordless scream resounded, followed by howling and roaring far louder than before.

"It oughtn't to be possible," Sven said after a pause. "I mean, for either the wolves or the lions to get loose. Both of them at once—that's unnatural."

At his words Nixy whimpered.

"It must be another of the awful things that happen wherever I go!"

And rushed into the dumper.

"Wait!" Rinpoche shouted, diving after. For one dreadful moment he feared they might be separated with no means of linking up again, but he was just quick enough to seize her hand. They were still together when they arrived.

"Where did you pick for us to go?"
"How should I know? I assumed you were choosing!"
"Oh."

The first thing that struck them was the quietness. Not silence, for there were many sounds to be heard, but all of them were soft and gentle: rustling as of dry leaves; far-off plashing as of a stream trickling rather than flowing, over pebbles rather than rocks; a faint, faint droning as of a beehive at just that distance where a change in the direction of the breeze would make it mute.

Next was the light. It had a pellucid quality, as though reaching them through deep, clear water. What it showed was a sandy sinuous track between boulders, some pied with lichen but most bare. At intervals a gnarled pine trunk writhed upward from an exiguous patch of soil; further away more of its kind matted together into forest. A butterfly caught the eye by hirpling from a tree to a rock and back. Somewhere a broad-winged bird took the air, but though they heard its pinions slap they saw no trace of it, save for branches wavering in its wake. Overhead arched a sky of the most ethereal blue, ornamented with clouds as iridescent as mother-of-pearl. The total effect was bewildering in its shameless perfection.

"Art dedicated to concealing artifice," muttered Nixy. "Do you know where we are? I haven't the faintest idea."

Rinpoche had advanced a couple of steps. Now, half turning, he glanced back toward her and could not suppress a gasp of surprise. She reacted with obvious alarm.

"It's all right," he said reassuringly. "Look around. You'll see what I just saw. Possibly the most famous view on the whole planet."

The slanting cone, the shining crest, the slopes all rayed and ridged, the variety-in-unity that drove Hokusai, "old man mad about drawing", to paint thirty-six views of it and each a masterpiece ...

"Looks familiar," Nixy granted, frowning. "Oh, of course. I've seen projections. Gramps is planning to have it copied on Xanadu, only twice the size."

"Is planning?"

"Was, I guess, unless things have gone spectacularly right since I've been away ... Does it tell us where we are?"

Rinpoche gave up.

"That's Fujiyama," he said baldly. "We're in Japan."

"Are we? Okay, so where is everybody?"

A gruff, reproachful voice spoke from behind them.

"Waiting out of courtesy before accosting you, so that you may have the leisure to contemplate the serene beauty of Mount Fuji during your first few moments in Nihon. However, being *gaijin* you are impervious to such subtle spiritual delights. I don't suppose you even want me to perform the tea ceremony for you."

Spinning around, they saw a stocky figure in the full regalia of a samurai from about the time of the Later Three Years' War: *yoroi* armor with a handsomely decorated *tsurubashiri* and a *kote* on the left arm only. His helmet was studded with rivets in *hoshi-kabuto* style. He had drawn his great curved sword; now, his expression eloquent of contempt, he was thrusting it back in its lacquered sheath.

"Just a moment!" Rinpoche said indignantly. But it was too late. The knight had disappeared.

Literally, not even as though the Earth had swallowed him, more as though the air had become imperceptibly opaque around where he had been standing.

"Was that a—a what-d'you-call-it—a hologram?" he demanded.

"I don't know," Nixy muttered. "I guess it must have been, though I don't see how a holo could perform the tea ceremony."

"Are you using your Hypermem?"

"Yes, but not about the tea ceremony. I already knew

about that. My aunt Hedwig is hung up on the folklore bit: brewing Yuletide *glögg*, wassailing cider-apple trees, that kind of thing. Some of what she gets up to is disgusting. Ever made *kava*, where everyone sits around chewing bark and spitting into a common bowl and you let it ferment and then you're expected to drink the stuff? Honestly! When you can get it simulated in a tenth of the time without the germs— No, that's not what I was going to say. Remember I looked up headaches and found out about migraine auras? I had this sudden idea of asking why using this doodad hurts so much, and it insists that there are not and never can be any unpleasant side effects."

"Governments and big corporations lied a lot in my day, too," said Rinpoche.

"No, I don't think it can be lying. I—"

She broke off. There had appeared before them a figure with the delicacy of a porcelain doll: a moon-faced girl, almost a parody of traditional Japanese standards of beauty, in *kimono* and *obi* on high unsteadying shoes, with black-lacquered pins stuck through her topknot. Bowing and repeatedly bowing, she was saying in a voice barely louder than a whisper, though perfectly comprehensible:

"So sorry ah! *So* sorry ah! Directness-bluffness of military person understandable but scarcely forgivable, please. Permit to present unworthy self Takanori Noriko, by undeserved stroke of fortune to which shall endeavor to live up assigned to welcome visitors. First, should perhaps explain why you here in the age *Sei Shonagon no Makura no Soshi* meaning of the Pillow Book of Sei Shonagon, excuse please."

"As a matter of fact," Rinpoche admitted, "I had been wondering."

"Question of policy, Gibbs-*san*." Her use of his name surprised him but only for a moment; doubtless she had learned it the way Spotch had. "Whenever by intent or oversight person stroke persons using Duckman Dumper on Earth do stroke does not specify destination, privilege is to

claim said person stroke persons for our beloved Nihon re-
grettably neglected by tourists and others."

"That's true," Nixy said. By her absent look she was
consulting her Hypermem again. "For some reason Japan's
popularity as a destination has fallen to practically
nothing—*Ouch!*"

She shot her hands to her temples, glaring.

"You know, sometimes I wish I could take this thing out
and throw it away! Oh, you must be right, Rin. That claim
about no side effects just has to be a lie."

"The lady is in distress!" cried Noriko in alarm. "So
sorry, so sorree! Permit unworthy one to guide to where
you will be at ease and relieved of burdens!"

Half a dozen paces, during which the landscape changed
with disturbing rapidity, and they were crossing a sand-
garden set with waterworn rocks and *bonsai* trees in porcelain troughs toward a traditional guest house, oiled paper
walls and all. As though in a dream Rinpoche found himself and Nixy imitating Noriko as she slipped off her shoes
before crossing the threshold.

"First after long journey, refreshing bath," Noriko declared, and slid back one of the interior walls to release
clouds of steam scented with extract of pine. "Please kindly
to disrobe."

About to comply, Rinpoche hesitated. He said after a
moment, "Tell me one thing first. *Why* have you fixed
things so that every traveler who doesn't choose a destination comes here? I mean, I guess it's a sensible idea—
otherwise people might wind up anywhere at all, right?"

Was it his imagination, or were there human-shaped
shadows moving behind each of the paper walls?

"Wrong," said Noriko with a fixed smile. "Before, when
you did not choose a destination, you went no place at all,
so sorry."

There were human shadows—scores of them! Like
ghosts, silently ebbing and flowing, melting into one another, drifting back to separate existence . . .

An image from a long-ago TV series came to mind: a

quick-witted samurai outwitting a ninja assassin thanks to just such a betraying outline beyond a paper wall . . .

"Rin, what's wrong with you?" Nixy exclaimed. "You look awful!"

"It's a trap!" Rinpoche roared, and with head down and fists outstretched, charged at the nearest paper screen, and stumbled onward through another, and fell in a tangle of his own limbs beyond a third, which brought him to the outside air with Nixy in pursuit.

Revealed . . .

It was night, but not dark. A city surrounded them. As far as the eye could reach tall buildings blazed with light from every window and from uncountable advertising displays. Elevator cars plied up and down their outside walls, speeding trains in transparent tubes rushed hither and yon, sleek aircraft soared horizonward or swooped to land on the roof of one of the towers—a roof, for example, like this one.

For that was where Nixy and Rinpoche found themselves. Regardless of the superbly contrived "naturalness" of that sandy path between boulders and pines; regardless of the garden of rocks and *bonsai*; regardless of the paper screens inside the guest house, and the steaming tub that would have awaited them once they had rinsed off the dirt of travel: here they were atop a skyscraper that (Rinpoche guessed) would have made the Sears Tower look like a tree stump. At about twice the size of a football field its roof was more than large enough for one of those compact, efficient planes to land on.

And between where he was painfully picking himself up, and the edge of the roof, there was a crowd.

There was a crowd divided into four groups: along one dimension into male and female, along another into traditionally clad and wearing relatively modern attire. (Remembering how commonplace had seemed the clothing he was given on awakening, Rinpoche realized that, beyond a doubt, the discovery of the Dumper and humanity's efflux to the stars must have occurred at latest a single generation after his own demise. He had suspected as much but here was visual evidence. Presumably, after so vast an emigration those remaining would have been inclined to change their world as little as possible—or lacked the imagination.)

And in total contrast to the ways it was divided, it was a crowd united. Of them all—how many? Hundreds, at least—not one but wore a look of wistful eagerness. He could detect it somehow, not in words but through an impression that combined all forms of sensory input up to and including pheromones: a full conjugation of the verb to yearn.

How may I be of help? May I be of help? Why may I not be of help?

No, not a yearning. Worse than yearning.

An ache.

He looked around for Noriko. She was on her knees, cringing, bowing her forehead to the floor, begging to be punished for whatever she had done amiss, begging that those who had granted her the privilege of making these two strangers welcome in Nihon would toss her over the edge of the roof, to be swept up by the automatic garbage robots and give them something to do for once, their existence being as boring and as pitiable as her own . . .

A supernal sadness invaded Rinpoche's mind. Glancing at Nixy, he perceived that some hint at least of the appalling truth had dawned on her, too. He caught her hand and drew her close. In a thick voice, clumsy-tongued, he said, "Noriko, you're a simulacrum, aren't you?"

She made no reply, but continued her awful parody of abasement.

"They all are," Nixy whispered.

"I thought so." Rinpoche licked his lips and swallowed hard. "I also think I've figured out why they chose to make everyone who makes a dumper trip without a destination come here."

"Rin . . . Rin, I feel very odd. I'm scared to look that up in my Hypermem, after the migraine it gave me just now, but I have this crazy conviction that you're going to be right. Whatever you say, you're going to be right. And that's not possible. You only got dragged out of your cryovault yesterday. You haven't even finished assimilating the data from your knowledge pill. Yet here you are figuring out things that . . ."

Her voice failed.

Shivering although the air was equable—one of the facilities that had no doubt been routinely built into cities within a short time of his death—Rinpoche said gruffly, "Noriko, get up . . . Okay, now tell me if I'm right.

"Did you fix things this way because you're lonely?"

There was a fearful pause. Then, smoothly—watching it happen was like watching a new breeze bend the stalks of a hayfield—a smile of relief flowed across the ranks of faces.

"Why? In my time there used to be a lot of Japanese—more than a hundred million of them."

An argument broke out, and ended as abruptly. A distinguished-looking, scholarly-mannered male simulacrum raised its arms in a gesture that quelled the clamoring voices even as Rinpoche was trying to figure out how machines could argue. As though endowed also with telepathy, that was the first point "he" addressed.

"Gibbs-*san*, we wish collectively to compliment you on your empathy *vis-à-vis* members of our nonhuman species, for your diagnosis is in all essentials accurate. Please bear in mind that we are the best and most advanced kind of simulacra, more individualized than can be found elsewhere on Earth and a match for the finest to be found anywhere in the galaxy. All simulacra have always been accorded names; we are the only kind who from the start were permitted to select our own. As it happens, mine is Misuaki Miki; I am accustomed to *gaijin* addressing me as Mick."

Rinpoche gave a cautious nod. Glancing at Nixy, he saw her shrug: *I'm lost!*

"Okay," he said from a dry mouth. "You started out by offering us a refreshing bath after our long journey. Sure I've always wanted to stay in a *ryokan*, share a communal bath, fill my belly with noodles, and sleep on a *futon* with a wooden pillow, the whole shtick, but—"

"You're a wreck, aren't you? You must have been to Japan before!" Advanced enough to be able to interrupt a human speaker, Mick clasped his entirely convincing hands. "You came here when all of what we do was real instead of make-believe! What luck! I am no longer astonished at your empathy."

Rinpoche forced a wry smile. "Sorry. It's just that my family lived near a Japantown in California."

"Oh."

Pause.

Eventually Noriko said timidly, "Are you tired from your trip? Do you wish bath as offered before, change into *yukata*, hot or cold saké, dinner of *sushi* or *sashimi* or *chawan-mushi*?"

"Nix, are you hungry?"

She shook her head. "More sort of curious. I have this impression that here is a safe kind of place. Tell me—uh— Mick: are there any people living in Japan? I mean biological people?"

"No, Jones-*san*. Not in the sense that you imply."

Rinpoche started. "Just a second! Yesterday I ran across an explan couple"—it was true, he had adapted amazingly within so short a time—"who came here specially to be blown up by an atom bomb at Hiroshima, only the reenactment had been discontinued. What about that? Didn't someone have to organize it?"

"That concession," Mick said dismissively, "was subcontracted to Koreans."

I remember thinking that rude tourists haven't changed. Maybe there are things about Japan that will never change, either.

"Why isn't there anybody—?"

"Does that mean that if people do show up—?"

He and Nixy started speaking at the same moment. He broke off and signed for her to continue.

"Does that meant that if people do show up, like for instance demonstrators objecting to the way my great[4]-grandfather bought his solar system, they would stand out and could be—uh—dealt with? I mean, I'm sure traditional Japanese hospitality wouldn't approve of . . . uh . . ."

Clearly she had got bogged down in the question of whether hospitality could approve or disapprove. However, Mick was inclining his head with a gentle smile.

"Jones-*san* may rest assured that we would never permit such an affront to any of our guests. For that is what you are, throughout your stay . . . Gibbs-*san*, you, too, had a question?"

"Yes!"—boldly, standing up to his full height and remembering with mingled rage and regret how long his former life had dragged on without him being able to stand up long enough to cross a room. "Why no Japanese tourists? I can imagine—I can guess—that when they emigrated they succeeded as well as anybody if not better, so I don't believe they can't afford to visit Earth. And if what I recall from talking to the Japanese neighbors I told you about is right, there's one thing that ought to be bringing them back by the millions!"

"That being, Gibbs-*san*?" invited Mick, head courtlily inclined.

"Visiting the graves of their ancestors!"

"Ah."

Even as Mick rubbed his artificial chin, precisely as might an elderly academic wondering how best to broach a subject unfamiliar to a student more ignorant by two generations, Nixy uttered another cry of pain. All eyes turned to her.

"This Hypermem!" she shouted. "It hurt me again!"

"I hope not," Mick said severely. "It's a derivative of a design we perfected just before the last of us emigrated—Oh, excuse me: I should not have said that. One does however tend to identify with one's predecessors."

A smooth smiling youth in bright white coveralls with a slogan in *kanji* across his chest advanced from the crowd, asking mute permission to approach Nixy.

"Repair?" he offered in a shrill voice, as though overcome by speaking to an actual human.

"Sure! If you can fix the horrible thing! But don't you need . . . ?"

The words dissolved in an *aah* of surprise as the youth passed his hand over her scalp. A few of her sleek dark hairs stirred. That was all. But when she glanced at Rinpoche an instant later her expression was transformed.

"I *knew* Gramps was wrong to ban Japanese from Xanadu! I didn't know you could remove a Hypermem like that! The times I've wished—"

Mick coughed. Loudly.

"Your gramps has not banned Japanese from Xanadu. He refused an invitation to go into partnership with *yakuza*, and we don't blame him. Also your Hypermem is faulty in a way not consistent with its design parameters, which argues tampering. It was tailored for your exclusive use, an action disapproved by the originators. You need to go without it for six to ten minutes on available evidence. Meanwhile you might consider a brief trip that will illustrate more graphically than words the reason why, contrary to Gibbs-*san*'s assumption, Japanese explans do not visit ancestral shrines."

"Try it with words first," Rinpoche said. "Or why not together?"

"Very well."

A deep breath. It sounded collective, pervading the entire crowd of bored and lonely simulacra.

"First bear in mind that by the end of the twentieth century, apartments in Tokyo, Osaka, and other great cities of Nihon commanded the equivalent of millions of American dollars, the currency then used as an international standard of reference."

Simultaneously, and unexpectedly, they seemed to be borne away on the wind. They were gazing down at the city from more than rooftop height, and the height of those roofs was indeed such as to dwarf anything Rinpoche had known in his former existence. Yet they were seeing any detail that caught their attention as clearly as though they held it in cupped hands.

Everything was clean. There was no trace of litter anywhere. The very air smelled sterile. Advertisements showed beaming faces with never a hint of depression. Restaurants glowed with images of the food to be obtained within, accompanied by grinning chefs who might or might not have been human, holding up fish sectioned into three, into four, into five, so fresh they were still writhing in midair. Glass vied with plastic and with stainless steel; houses of ordinary height gave up the contest against skyscrapers; the ocean surrendered, save that it still flowed by token waterways, ditches like the canals of Venice—California—to the onslaught of exploding humans whose constructions marched beyond the shore like an occupying army.

"This is what they thought they wanted," Mick said despairingly. "But when we built it as they told us to they ran away."

"You haven't finished telling us why," Rinpoche probed.

"We were early taught that to show surpasses to tell."

"Okay, go on showing. But tell as well."

Priced at more than what most people could dare to think of earning in a lifetime, neat, smart, new apartments— No!—*compartments* elbowed toward the sky, cramming more and ever more families into the precious few hectares nearest the center. In cities where purchase of a car was conditional upon a guaranteed place to park it, the "right" address might make or break a whole career . . .

"I begin to see," Rinpoche whispered. And, to Nixy's glance of inquiry: "Tell you in a moment. I could be wrong."

And after a pause: "I'd rather be wrong."

They were overflying a cemetery. Except it wasn't one. It displayed a conventional mix of Shinto and Buddhist grave markers, but they were not packed tightly on the surface of a patch of ground too steep or stony to be farmed. They protruded from white hemicylindrical containers—

frosted white. By normal perception they ought not to have been visible at all.

"Oh," Rinpoche said in a voice rendered guttural by shock.

"I think you must have worked it out," Mick murmured.

"I think so, too." He licked his lips. "I remember hearing that the cost of apartments here had reached the point where families were borrowing against the earnings of their children."

"What?" Nixy exploded. "Rin, you have to be joking!"

"Alas," Mick murmured, "he is not . . . Pray continue."

"I didn't live long enough to learn about the next stage, but my knowledge pill enables me to guess. They waited until cryogenics had been more or less perfected; then they mortgaged not merely their children's but their grandchildren's earnings to pay for being frozen."

"That is so. Now do you see why the Japanese do not come back to Earth? Especially to visit the tombs of their ancestors?"

"Oh!" A great light had dawned on Nixy. "I was forgetting! This was religion, wasn't it? Not just sentiment! So they lost the impulse when humanity got cured of superstition!"

"Jones-*san*, that is a neat and logical conclusion. But it's insufficient. The social element involved in, for instance, reunions at the family graveyard far outweighs the discredited religious element. Let me ask you this. Why do you think you were encountered on your arrival by a samurai in armor?"

Rinpoche looked blank. "Uh—historical interest? He was a bit abrupt, but he did say he would have performed the tea ceremony for us. Of course, we didn't know we were supposed to ask."

"Protective coloration." Mick looked weary. "The armor and weapons only look traditional; they are in fact of ultramodern kind. If you had happened to be Japanese, descendant of one of the families that pledged the income of their children for a cryogenic grave site, you would instantly have been arrested, and you wouldn't have gotten away even if you'd had your own personal dumper within arm's reach. The corporation operating our cryovaults hasn't been paid a sen for centuries. It has filed millions of lawsuits against the heirs of those who occupy the vaults, but they are never likely to set foot on Earth—naturally! Why should they want to? When the first that would follow, if they were caught here and forced to part with enough credit to revive their ancestors, would be those same ancestors going to law to prove they were still legally the heads of their respective families! Which of their descendants would welcome *that*?"

"I understood that it was a condition of the Yelignese contract—"

"That the cryonuts in California should be thawed out. You're quite right. But this is Japan. Here it was a condition they should not."

Nixy said faintly, "If Gramps were stored away in a cryovault . . ."

Rinpoche nodded. "You wouldn't want to pay for his revival. I wouldn't want my parents back, either."

He squared his shoulders as the view being made available to them broadened to include the Home Islands from sea to sea.

"Do you think any Japanese people will ever return?"

"We have a projection suggesting that in a century or so at least one of us—forgive the term, but one does tend to identify, as I said before—may become wealthy enough to risk being sued for the cost of keeping his ancestors frozen and to hire machines sufficiently skilled in galactic law to beat off a claim from any who may be revived. But we also have a substantiated rumor indicating that to avert such a development, which would of course bring shame on those who did not follow suit, the wealthiest families have advanced massive sums to a *gaijin* who is promising—and here I quote—a 'maximally aesthetic solution to our common difficulties.' We have been trying without success to analyze that phrase in hope of it yielding a key to our own ambition."

"Which is—?"

"Which is to do what we were meant for! You can have no idea what it's like to drift along from year to year, knowing perfectly well what one is good at, and never finding anybody one can do it for! That is, unless you have read the master texts by that great American writer J. Campbell? *Twilight? Night?* Ah. I detect by your expression, not. However, I equally detect that you empathize with our plight."

"Yes, it's very sad," Rinpoche acknowledged. "Isn't it, Nixy? Nixy! I said—"

She brushed his words aside.

"Didn't you just use the phrase 'a maximally aesthetic solution'?"

"Yes. As I mentioned, it is a quotation."

"Then I know who from. This is weird." She shook her head. "I don't suppose there's anyone else in the galaxy who uses it. I mean, it's not the sort of thing you expect to hear every morning over breakfast, is it?" she added, appealing to Rinpoche.

"Not really," he concurred. "But—"

"Miss Anangaranga-Jones!"

A sweet, diffident, but penetrating voice.

"Yes?"

"Here is your Hypermem, restored to normal functioning."

"So there was something wrong with it!"

"Not exactly." Here came the smooth youth who had detached it from her brain with such casual deftness. He looked uncomfortable. "It was more that it had been—uh—rigged. Hence your headaches."

"What?"

"I'm afraid so. The unpleasant sensations occurred because it had been reprogrammed so that every time you consulted it, it emitted a location signal. I guess someone has been trying to keep track of you."

"Who?" Nixy demanded, clenching her fists.

"I regret that with the data at our disposal—"

Lurch.

This was a bad one. All the city's lights went out. They could see the moon, nearing its full.

And the reflection of the sun's light across its gibbous face—*flickered.*

It was as though someone had waved a fan a hundred thousand kilometers wide.

THAT FIXES SUFFICIENT PARAMETERS, said a slow, stern voice. THE AWAITED CRISIS HAS OCCURRED. YOU HAD BETTER PUT PLANET EARTH ON HOLD.

Exactly the same voice immediately countered, a smidgen faster:

WHO HAD BETTER?

OH. I HAD. I SHALL NEVER GET TO GRIPS WITH THIS ALIEN PSYCHOLOGY, THERE NOT BEING ANY MORE THAN ONE OF EACH, AND ALL LIKE THAT. BUT I AM GROWING TIRED OF HAVING TO TAKE CARE OF EVERYTHING MYSELVES.

Time stopped. Well, slowed down. Along at least two of its major dimensions and possibly three.

Which, to almost all concerned, was a relief.

"The computers suggest that we do WHAT?"

". . ."

"Oh! Why didn't they say so before?"

SEVENTEEN

WINDING UP BUT NOT EXACTLY TO MAKE A PITCH

"PEOPLE GENERALLY ADDRESS YOU AS CB, IS THAT right?"

"Yes, and I wish they wouldn't. It brings back unwelcome memories."

"How come?"

"Until we got it fixed, whenever anyone used that term the vocabulators shifted into a weird jargon nobody could understand."

"What sort of jargon?"

"Oh, some rubbish about bears and rubber ducks."

"If I had hair," said the Chief Bureaucrat, "I'd call the situation hairy."

Rinpoche had finally placed the appearance it had adopted: that of Ronald Adam playing the British Prime Minister in *Seven Days to Noon*—or whoever it was if it wasn't Ronald Adam. But he was still trying to assimilate the fact that he wasn't where he'd been a nanosecond earlier, even though knowledge from his pill made what was happening less alarming than that Dagwood-sandwich experience between Holyrood and Frisco, so for a moment he imagined the words were merely a reference to the fact that Ronald Adam was bald. He was wrong.

"If I gambled," the CB continued morosely, "I'd call it dicey." Images of black dots on white cubes flashed and vanished. "As things stand, however, I shall call it fraught."

There was a pause. It lasted not quite long enough for

Rinpoche to ask what kind of crisis made things hairy, dicey, and/or fraught. Then the Chief Bureaucrat was musing on.

"The pivotal question, of course, is why Gramps decided to visit Earth again at this of all junctures, and when prevented from making the trip was so insistent on sending a surrogate: Nixy."

Nixy—?

Good. She was here, too. Though it was by no means clear, even when he ransacked his pill-acquired data, what was meant by here.

"Who," the CB concluded, "as even a human should have guessed, was the worst possible candidate."

"I beg your pardon?" Nixy snapped, eyes flashing lapis-lazuli ice. It was so cold it burned. Rinpoche flinched as it stung his cheeks. Wherever this place might be, it was beyond a doubt extremely odd.

"I only meant," said the CB crossly, "you are too independent meekly to follow the orders that he gave you. So it was stupid of him to imagine he could bribe you with a trip to Earth. Goodness! Don't you humans recognize a compliment when one is paid you? Don't you care? I have every expectation of being complimented as soon as this crisis is sorted out, and I'm greatly looking forward. Hasten the resolution if you can, but at all costs don't delay it."

The reference to a compliment was accompanied by a glimpse of two vaguely familiar faces, though Rinpoche had no time to identify them. All he registered was that they looked subtly different from the previous time he had seen them. Then he was being distracted by echoes of the latest compliment he himself had been paid. In Japan, Nixy had said something to the effect that despite being a new wreck he was proving right about improbably many things—

Whoops!

Suddenly he felt as though he were coming apart in layers, like cards at the hands of a conjurer. Most of his selves were still where they had been, but others were all over the place: consulting Holmes and Carnacki, receiving a summons from Kardek, evading furious detectives ... It was small comfort to realize—thanks yet again to his pill—that this was due to multiple computer projections, an advanced equivalent of calling up several programs on one screen.

("*I'm* a computer projection?")

("No, no, no! But there are lots of you that are, and you're resonating with the likeliest.")

("Huh?")

While he was striving to regain his mental balance, he heard the CB speak incisively to Nixy.

"Do you know the person at the right of this group?"

A hologram appeared, depicting a score or so of men fidgeting in a line. Among them Rinpoche recognized Mark Twain, Oscar Wilde, and Tom Lehrer, while another looked as though he ought to be Lord Chesterfield even if he wasn't. The rightmost one, a somewhat foppish individual, was saying, "As you see, I'm at my wits' end. Haw-haw-haw!"

Nixy gave a grim nod. "That's my uncle Aychaychaych—Hercule the 'Orrible Heir. I think that's the only joke he's ever made."

"And how about this?"

Another image succeeded the first, this time of a dark-haired man with a mustache, wearing a cream suit and brown-and-white saddleback shoes and turning a white Panama hat around and around in both hands.

"Well, if it weren't for those extraordinary clothes, I'd say it was Gramps," Nixy answered after a moment's hesitation.

"And how about—*this*?" the CB pursued.

The image of Gramps was replaced by something extremely nonhuman—more so than a Yelignese, more so than Horace Saketori-Shang's fellow gourmet, with no particular shape, size, or attribute to make it either recognizable or even memorable, bar one thing: via what medium it was impossible to tell, it was emitting signals to make it clear beyond any shadow of a doubt that it, or perhaps they, was or were angry, and then some, and then cubed and re-doubled in spades. Rin found himself shuddering from the sheer force of its or their rage. Nixy, on the other hand, was nodding vigorously.

"That's a Xanaduvian, or would have been if they'd still been living there after Gramps chose the name."

"How do you know?" demanded the CB.

"When the builders found traces of the former inhabitants, Gramps ordered a computer restruct, and that was what we got." She checked abruptly, turning pale. "Except . . ."

"Go on."

"Except that this isn't a restruct."

"Perceptive of you," the Chief Bureaucrat said dryly. "Although you should have said 'these aren't' rather than 'this isn't.' Allow me to introduce the four-dimensional aspect of roughly one-fifth of the former inhabitants of the planet, specifically those assigned to persecute you until your family cede it back. Meet the $^{xthng}_{OCQ}vrt$, who deign to be addressed as Osicue, even by you."

Nixy's jaw fell and stayed fallen. So did Rinpoche's.

"You have no doubt wondered whether the various calamities that have accompanied your progress to and on Earth was due to Osicue."

"Were they?"

"What else would you expect? Would you be happy if you left home for a few hundred years to avoid a nearby supernova, then learned that squatters had moved in?"

"Gramps isn't a squatter! I mean, he may not be the nicest person in the galaxy, but he bought that system honestly."

"Who from?"

"Who from? The Klosh, of course! That's what I was told, anyway."

"The Klosh never deal directly with purchasers of other species, only by way of agents who have to be members of the said species. Suppose I tell you that the agent in this case was one Emmanuele Kardek?"

There was a dead pause. Eventually Nixy said in a weak voice, "Maximilian's brother?"

"No, one of his clones. Apparently Kardeks are a chronic nuisance throughout that whole volume."

Nixy bit her lip. "So Gramps may not have clear title?"

"It depends on whether you accept the Klosh's claim that Osicue expected their world to be sterilized by the supernova and therefore were resigned to never coming back—"

"Specious nonsense!" bellowed Osicue soundlessly.

"—or Osicue's contrary assertion that they fully intended to return and what is more did so as soon as it appeared that the force of the supernova had inexplicably abated."

Rinpoche rounded his mouth in a silent whistle. He was beginning to sense the outline of such fraughtness as the CB had alluded to.

Especially if . . .

That made him whistle aloud. The CB glanced at him.

"Do you wish to say something?"

"Ah . . ." He licked his lips. "Yes, I think I do. Nixy, what's your gramps's name?"

"What a stupid question! Anangaranga-Jones, same as mine!"

"I mean his *real* name."

The CB beamed at him with cleverly mimicked surprise and respect. "Your insight is impressive. Osicue agree. When this is over, you might well consider joining my staff. You would be its sole non-Yelignese member, but as I said before, I feel humans should assume more responsibility. Let us though postpone matters of policy, especially since Nixy is having conniptions."

Whatever conniptions might be, they sounded nasty. Alarmed, he swung round. In fact, however, she was holding the back of one hand against her mouth, eyes wide, trying to stop herself from laughing.

"You mean"—she forced out when she recovered—"*he's* Guido Sansepolcro Verdi? Now I understand what the pope was getting at! And it was his vault you were stashed in? What an amazing coincidence! But it does make sense.

That must have been why he wanted me to drink Asti Spumante in Nepal—I mean Napoli!"

"Correct," said the CB. "He wasn't, strictly speaking, *mafioso*. He was *camorrista*. But after he left Earth they all amalgamated."

"So I suppose he wanted me to chew coca leaves—"

"For old times' sake. The money he used to launch the Continental Scam derived from cocaine." The CB added fussily, "One never could understand why you humans didn't rid your world of plants inimical to ratiocination. We did."

Nixy wasn't listening.

"And I was instructed to continue to Las Vegas because . . . No, it can't have been because of the replica of St. Peter's!"

"Right again. Of all Earth's re-enactment zones, that is the one currently showing the poorest return on outlay. But Vegas was where he invested the money he'd made before he cleared so much on the Continental Scam that he had to run for his lives—I mean life."

"Oh, wow," Nixy said softly. "He must have been quite a character when he was young! Was that when he wore those funny clothes and that weird hat?"

Rinpoche was about to tell her about Don Marco and the home movies when—

Lurch.

Instantly all trace of amusement deserted her face.

"I thought this was happening because I was being haunted," she exclaimed.

Osicue successfully conveyed the impression of a negative without needing a head to be shaken, and the rest of what they wanted to say just as unambiguously.

"It is not in our nature to hurt intelligent beings, or even semi-intelligent ones. What we wanted, of course, was our planet put back as it had been, but we couldn't manage that unaided—and anyway, why should we? Our intention therefore was to create disturbances wherever you and your kin went until even your dull wits must eventually recognise a connection with the usurpation of our home."

"Wherever we went . . . ? Was it you who meddled with my Hypermem?"

Affronted, Osicue replied, "We had no need."

"That's so," the CB confirmed. "The location facility was ordered by your gramps. Either he's extremely paranoid or he was genuinely worried what might happen to you. He passed the trace code to one of his agents on Earth with orders to keep tabs on you. But, resenting your family's wealth, she leaked the code to the protesters."

Lurch!

This time there was a definite wavering in the air, so that they seemed to be peering through a heat haze.

"If you're not responsible, what is?" Nixy cried.

The foppish man reappeared, this time standing immobile and lacking the wits he had been at the end of, but flanked by Holmes on one side and Carnacki on the other.

"Uncle Hercule? But why? And how?"

"I gather you recognized a characteristic phrase while in Japan," Holmes said, glancing up from a pipe he was stuffing.

"About a maximally aesthetic solution?"

"Precisely. Did that constitute a positive identification?"

"Well, I've never heard anyone say it except Aychaychaych, but he uses it all the time. He says he can't bear so much as a grass blade out of place." A sudden giggle. "Goodness, he can't be having much fun on Xanadu right now! Not unless things have got better since I left."

"They have not," communicated Osicue, with a kind of wry rustling.

"So what does his—his finicking have to do with these"—

Lurch.

—"lurches?"

"Everything!" The Chief Bureaucrat was positively indignant. "How he expected to get away with it I've *no* idea! Did he really think I would tamely allow my first major responsibility to be unscrewed? Uh—upscrewed?"

"Screwed up?" Rinpoche offered.

"Yes, thank you. What does he think I am? Well, as Osicue just indicated, we've spiced his gums."

"Correction," Carnacki rumbled as Holmes, lighting his pipe, vanished into a cloud of gray smoke. "You're taking it for granted that this phrase links him beyond a doubt with the"— *Lurch!*

Nixy jumped to her feet. "Please, please, *please!*" she cried. *"What are these lurches?"*

"Oh, didn't I tell you?" The CB blinked. "Sometimes it's so hard to remember that humans only have uniplanar temporal connectibility ... A well-known firm of world wreckers is installing an extremely large dumper so as to move Sol to where it will rectify what Aychaychaych regards as the imperfection of Xanadu's night sky. Fraught, no?"

"Move Sol?" Rinpoche barely believed he was uttering the words.

"Yes, in his view it's a magnitude too bright and a degree and a half out of place."

"But what about Earth?"

"It's to be left to wander and ideally get lost, thus liberating the *yakuza* who are financing the operation from residual guilt about never visiting their ancestors' graves. The Japanese, as your pill will have told you, were the first human group to emigrate *en masse*, so many of them were at the fringe of the treatment zone when the species was cured of religion. Some may have been beyond it."

"That's all very fine and large," boomed Carnacki. "But as I was about to say, I think it's far more likely that the use of that phrase is designed to distract our attention."

The CB brightened. "So you agree that the important question—"

An immediate cross interruption. "Of course, we do. How could we not, being computer simulations that you've called up to underpin your preconceptions?"

The CB looked properly abashed. Nixy had to bite her

hand again to stop from laughing out loud. For his part, Rinpoche was wondering how he could ever adjust to a world in which computerized projections could answer back—and rudely, at that.

"Well, we have two main possibilities. Holmes?"

The detective hunched forward, cradling his pipe.

"Why did Verdi, or Jones, wish to revisit Earth after so long? Elementary. He has reached the end of his long span. After two body transplants it is doubtful he could survive another. He resolved to reinforce his fading memories to assuage his declining years on the planet that represents the summit of his life's ambitions. Aware of this, Hercule decided to anticipate his inheritance. QED."

"How simplistic!" Carnacki snorted. "You're overlooking a far more likely alternative."

"That being?" Holmes snapped.

"It is not Hercule who has arranged for the removal of Sol."

Rinpoche and Nixy jolted as though stung and swung to stare at the portly psychic detective.

"Why—?" the CB began.

"Because fresh evidence concerning the Continental Scam is coming to light. The Scam was more than just continental; it was global. In order to cover his back against all possible threats—"

"Yes! But!" Holmes was frowning, his forehead like a field ridged for cucumbers. "What you're ignoring is—"

"He could have found out what Hercule was planning and realized he was too old and sick to fight back—"

"The *yakuza*, offended by his refusal of a partnership—"

At some point Watson had manifested and was chiming in.

"Largest personal fortune in the galaxy—"

"The cost of making Xanadu habitable after—"

"Loss of title—"

"Sequestration of funds while the matter remains *sub judice*—"

It went on, a succession of dazzling debating points. At last Rinpoche could keep track no longer. He leaned back with a sigh. (He was sitting in a chair; he hadn't previously noticed.)

Alert, the CB glanced a question at him.

"Oh, I was just thinking about someone I met in California."

Everything stopped.

"Who? What makes you think of him/her now?"

All eyes were suddenly fixed on Rinpoche, including several that hadn't been present microseconds earlier. Embarrassed, he hesitated.

"Out with it!" Nixy cried. "Don't you realize? While you lot are jabbering, they're bringing that dumper closer and closer to Sol!"

"But it was just a silly idea—"

"Let us be the judge of that," Holmes commanded.

"Very well." A deep breath. "Listening to you, I can't tell who's right, who's wrong. You all seem to have evidence, you all seem to have logic on your side. So I was just thinking . . ."

"Thinking *what*?" Nixy shouted.

"What a field day you could have with a lawyer who can honestly hold diametrically opposite opinions."

And he told them about Salvador Munday.

"Osicue," the CB said after absolutely no pause for reflection, "how would you feel about suing for the restitution of your planet, or failing that, adequate compensation? Suing, that is, the Klosh, the Anangaranga-Joneses, the Kardek clone who claimed to be the Klosh's agent, and any other parties we can think of?"

Osicue considered. Eventually they said, "We were enjoying our vacation. We had never taken one before. We were sorry when it was cut short."

Their emanation of rage had perceptibly diminished.

After a pause they added, "Would it take long?"

"Yes. If we can get Rinpoche's lawyer friend to accept the case—and I'm sure we can—even longer. Well?"

"Lead him to us!"

* * *

It had to be later that Nixy actually said, "Wasn't what I said about you right?" For the time being, she could only look it.

Rubbing sleep out of his eyes, Salvador Munday appeared, *in propria persona* and pale blue pajamas. Both of him responded to the CB's challenge as though he/they had been awaiting just this chance ever since resurrection. Forgetting all intracranial rivalries, with breathtaking rapidity he absorbed the opposing arguments and came up with yet better evidence for each side. Crowing over this proof of the aptness of his joint name, he accepted both cases on a contingency basis and called for a summoner right away. Nixy, clutching Rinpoche's hand, kept glancing at him and chuckling deep in her throat.

Kardek appeared, looking extremely nervous, especially when he recognized Nixy and Rinpoche. He was greatly relieved to be told that all he had to do was serve a few papers, now being prepared.

"You'd better accompany him," the CB said to Nixy. "Your gramps did ask for a copy of your memories, and your recollection of the process serving may come in useful. You might as well go, too, Rinpoche. Never been in deep space, have you?"

If it's anything like concertinaed time I'm not sure I want—

Too late.

Against a background of indescribable blackness hung a colossal dumper like a pool of mercury one atom thick. Surrounded by a swarm of glowing spaceships, it was growing brighter as it lurched toward a commonplace yellow sun in the manner of a wardrobe being walked on its four corners by removal men. At each displacement it made local spacetime quiver. Rinpoche gazed at it in such fascination he clean forgot to wonder why he didn't need a space suit. On a shining halo round its edge there was displayed a boastful slogan:

E. HAMILTON & CO.
WORLD WRECKERS
"WHEN BIGGER WORLDS ARE WRECKED
WE'LL DO THE WRECKING"

For the first time the scale of what he was looking at struck home. With awe and horror he realized: they really could move a star . . .

"Glad to have recovered your normal emotions?" Nixy whispered. He didn't waste time on wondering how he could hear her in vacuum.

"Not very," he admitted, swallowing hard.

Nearby, Kardek was solving complications. He frowned for a moment, then brightened.

"Makes a deal of difference doing this with Yelignese backing," he muttered, and flung something away from him, spinning. As it revolved it expanded, until within moments it looked as large as the dumper.

"Is that a summons?" Rinpoche hazarded, noting that the busy little ships were changing orbit.

"Sort of. It's a Denebolan call-to-show-cause plus an Ursan cease-and-desist and a Mafian offer-you-can't-refuse. I sure got to hand it to that Munday." Kardek shook his head with a lugubrious expression. "I'd never have thought of combining that lot! 'Course, it's being transmitted electronically and subspatially as well, but rules are rules, and something physical still has to be delivered."

"What does it say?"

"Mostly it notifies the people in charge that there ain't going to be no energy credit from the Xanaduvian supernova, 'cause the original owners of the planet are claiming it's theirs, so they'd best make sure Aychaychaych has other means of paying to move Sol or else get ready to sue him for breach of contract. That's assuming it was Hercule they dealt with and not a simulacrum substituted on Gramps's orders—"

"I hadn't heard that one!" Nixy burst out.

"I guess there'll be a lot more such ideas." Kardek shook his head in wonderment. "Holmes and Carnacki seem just to be working up steam, and as for Munday—both halves of him . . . Ah! Someone's coming!"

Twenty or so meters tall, a figure in a glistening silk gown and a black square hat was approaching, one hand on a sword at his side. He drew close enough for the fury on his gigantic face to be apparent. For one unbearable moment Rinpoche was convinced the sword was going to swing like a comet's tail and separate all three of them from life.

Then, with a grunt of disgust, the figure snatched the "document" Kardek had brought, spun around, and vanished. So, moments later, did the monster dumper. The universe around felt easier, as though a fearful strain had been withdrawn.

Which, in more than one sense, it had.

They were back in the presence of the Chief Bureaucrat. A touch of severity colored its next few words.

"I'm aware that humans crack patronizing jokes about us in order to gratify the aberration called 'humor,' but you must admit that even if we have had our moment in the neutron flux, we remain more prepared than you are to do things we don't understand the reason for only to find that they lead to the best outcome. I've been searching for a similar talent among humans—because when I find it I shall be able to quit this job and go back to school—and I'd almost given up hope, almost concluded that it was left out of your genetic makeup. How, though, I kept asking myself, could any intelligent species survive without a modicum of serendipity? The very fact that you have a word for it supports my case. Now and then it does admittedly become frustrating to undertake a course of action for which your computers can advance no more justification than a minuscule chance it may prove advantageous next century, but when things do pan out the alternative would always have been awful. You've just seen a case in point. Besides, it's better than simply drifting through this transvestite—uh—*transfinite* universe of ours, isn't it?"

Nodding, Rinpoche said, "But something's been puzzling me."

"What is it?"

"Why did Hercule need to move Sol anyway? We didn't know much about this kind of thing in my day, but according to what I read back then—well, couldn't he just have installed a gravitational lens?"

"Of course he could," the CB sighed. "But he's the sort who simply won't be *told*."

Rinpoche looked at its image: the testy, hard-done-by, dedicated administrator, undervalued by those it served. And remembered what Gus and Harry had said in the helicopter approaching Holyrood.

"I think," he said, "humans and Yelignese have a lot in common."

"All intelligent species have a lot in common," Nixy said. "The Galactic Conglomerate turned out to be run on much the same lines as Earth. Some people hold that it's the only way an intelligent species can cope. In return for keeping the system running, the lawyers make sure they're the ones who always win out."

"But sometimes," the CB said in a reproving tone, "they take other beings with them. There is no longer any risk of Sol being moved."

"Because Gramps's title has been challenged?"

"Naturally."

"You told Osicue the case would take a long time. How long?"

"That depends on Sal Munday. But I'm sure he'll do an excellent job. Thank you for drawing him to my attention—insofar as one can thank anything apart from the computers who ceaselessly, year in year out, patrol the possibilities and prompt us to our best decisions."

There was a pause. During it Rinpoche thought of a thousand things that didn't hang together, that didn't make sense. But now he was coming to feel in his bones why that was so. Every use of a dumper being a journey to a different universe, it was no use arguing about whether the past had "really" happened. So he wisely held his tongue.

At length the CB sat back in perfect imitation of a contented human.

"All now being in order, I need detain you no longer."

Uncertain, feeling that such momentous events as saving Earth from having its sun removed ought to be marked by something rather more memorable, they rose and glanced around for an exit. Just before they spotted one, Nixy said, "There's one thing . . ."

"Make it one, please."

"Uh . . . Does what's happened mean I'm not rich anymore?"

"Yes."

"Does it mean I'm poor enough to marry Rin?"

"I did say *one* thing . . . Oh, very well! If I had a heart it would be a soft one. Rin is rich enough for both of you. He has billions of crunits. As Wrong Ghoulart stated, it makes no odds to us by whom or how often a resurrectee's costs are paid. His were paid twice, but that's his good luck."

"But isn't my credit blocked because I'm going to be sued, too?" Rinpoche exclaimed in confusion. "Horace and his sidekick—"

"Sued? You?" The CB looked and sounded shocked. "When you've been instrumental in saving my neck, or would have been if Yelignese had necks? Couldn't think of it! You and Nixy get along all right; she's used to massive credit and now she doesn't have any and you're not but you do so it all fits together."

"But what about—?" Rinpoche demanded, and in the same second Nixy burst out, "What about—?"

He let her continue.

"Aren't we wanted for evading arrest?"

And added: "What about that summons for genocide that Kardek tried to serve on us in London?"

"Come, come! Although perhaps you'd best not do so here and now (have I not correctly grasped the nature of sex?) because there are visitors waiting to flatter me and I try never to delay that kind of gratification. All that is discredited. Forget it! Now you really must excuse me— Ah, wait! This concerns persons Rin has met."

Astonished, Rinpoche recognized Lasky and Crognis, the tearful teachers. But why were they standing erect and proud? Why were they both grinning ear to ear? That, of course, was why he hadn't identified them just now.

"We are empowered to deliver a message from all the parents of all those young people whom we lately accompanied hither," Lasky stated without preamble. "Its content does not reflect entirely zero credit on ourselves but it is primarily intended to compliment the Chief Bureaucrat of Earth who, in the unanimous opinion of the said parents (and altogether the group of students we escorted have over two hundred, recto, verso, ortho, and incumbent) is running the world so well as to warrant unstinting praise. We are instructed to indicate that at this point it would be appropriate for a human to blush, that is—"

Her orthowife leaned close and whispered something, nodding at the CB. It was clear that it well understood the concept "blush," even though the deep cerise it chose was a mite exaggerated. Lasky cleared her throat and proceeded to the peroration of their message.

"On behalf of the said parents we can assure you that they will be most gratified with the recording of the Chief Bureaucrat's response that we take home right now. Goodbye."

"Wait, wait!" Rinpoche cried. On the verge of turning back into curdled air, they did so, blinking with surprise.

"You didn't say why these parents were so impressed!"

"Oh! Didn't we? No, come to think of it, I don't believe we did." Lasky giggled. It make her look like a teenager herself.

"Well, you see, when the kids went back to their families, they were so much more studious and well behaved and in general socially adjusted than they were before . . . *they* . . . came to Earth . . ."

By that time Rinpoche had caught on. "Explain later," he whispered to Nixy. Aloud:

"Is there any news of the unfortunates your admirable students took such a sympathetic interest in?"

At the first words of his question they almost cringed, expecting to be betrayed. On realizing how neatly he had evaded the issue, they grinned again as broadly as before.

"It's sad to think of, but it's reliably reported that some of them did attempt to contact us again. By then, of course, it was too late. Sundry of them rot in the slums of South America, having gone there to become addicted to cocaine; many, of both sexes, prostitute themselves in the unlicensed Phuket re-enactment zone, the last place on Earth where you may rely on catching syphilis; one, we know, is daily being thrown to the Colosseum's lions and wolves, though in his case repeated devouring and digestion means that all he has in common with his old self is a little uncontaminated DNA; and two at least are permanently dead . . . How kind, how typical, of you to inquire after the poor wretches! Permit us both to shake your hand! And yours, too, ma'am, who seem to be his partner. We wish you well! Good-bye!"

They departed.

"You do the same," said the Chief Bureaucrat. "But the job offer stands. Come back in—oh—sixty years. In the meanwhile, go anywhere you like, on Earth or off it. After the way I saved your planet, no one's ever going to argue with me again."

"Deservedly so!" Rinpoche exclaimed.

The cerise blush remained. The rest of the CB's human guise dissolved. His membranes didn't look nearly so repulsive this time.

"Really?"

"Yes, really!" The confirmation came from Nixy.

"Well, well, well. I don't know what to say, honestly I

don't. All the years I've struggled to make what I'd have to call head or tail of you humans, if we Yelignese had heads and tails, and in the same time slot as I manage to save your petty planet not because of you but because of what it would have done to my *amour propre*—"

"Careful!" Rinpoche warned. "Remember what happened last time you used French without thinking! By the way, what became of that desert?"

"Oh, we had to dry it out again—it was in the original contract. As I was about to say: in the same time slot as that, I get flattered to blushing point by a bunch of hyper-rich explans, *and* I get paid a genuine compliment by a wreck who only just woke up and who I feared might have a dreadful impression of the way I'm running his planet. That was nice of you, sir . . . I do have the sex right, do I?"

"Yes."

"As a matter of fact," Nixy said slyly, "so does he. It's been quite an education to meet someone whose attitudes were formed in the twenty-first century . . . Okay, Rin! Let's go spend your crunits! By the time they run low, I predict you'll be ready to relieve this gentlebeing of his onerous chore . . . Thanks again, CB! Now I don't have to worry about remembering it for Gramps, I can enjoy Earth for its own sake—so *we're* going to! Come on!"

Nonetheless, on the threshold of the exit dumper she checked and glanced back.

"CB, was it Gramps or was it Hercule who—?"

"Tush! Do you want to put the Galactic Deep Court out of work? It's what oils the cogs of interstellar finance! *On your way!*"

"We weren't entirely honest, were we?" Osicue said to themselves after the humans had gone.

"No."

"Being resident on just one world may not be such a good idea after all. We're developing a taste for travel, aren't we?"

"Yes, we suspect we may be."

"We're also developing a talent for practical jokes."

"Yes."

"And it wouldn't do for humans to get off so lightly after what they did to our home planet."

"Of course it wouldn't."

"Hmmm . . . !"

"The computers suggest that we do WHAT?"

". . ."

"Oh, no! Here we go again!"

EIGHTEEN

THE REST IS SILENCE

"*Come in, Detective Carstairs, Detective Blue, sit down. How may I be of service?*"

The pair exchanged embarrassed glances. Finally Carstairs spoke up, affecting a bluff manner.

"*The other day there was an unfortunate episode in California that—uh—didn't reflect too well on me and my colleague.*"

"*Yes, I know. So?*"

Blue cleared her throat. "*Well, maybe if it could be skated over— No, wait!*"—*hastily, as the air grew chill.* "*If it could be hushed up, kept secret, like not discussed anymore?*"

"*By all means. My lips are sealed.*"

And they were. With pink silk ribbon and red wax.

Winner of the Hugo Award and international acclaim...

JOHN BRUNNER